A BATTLE
WON

a novel •━━━━━◆

S. THOMAS RUSSELL

BESTSELLING AUTHOR OF *UNDER ENEMY COLORS*

ALSO BY S. THOMAS RUSSELL

Under Enemy Colors

A BATTLE WON

S. Thomas Russell

B

BERKLEY BOOKS

New York

THE BERKLEY PUBLISHING GROUP
Published by the Penguin Group
Penguin Group (USA) Inc.
375 Hudson Street, New York, New York 10014, USA
Penguin Group (Canada), 90 Eglinton Avenue East, Suite 700, Toronto, Ontario M4P 2Y3, Canada
(a division of Pearson Penguin Canada Inc.)
Penguin Books Ltd., 80 Strand, London WC2R 0RL, England
Penguin Group Ireland, 25 St. Stephen's Green, Dublin 2, Ireland (a division of Penguin Books Ltd.)
Penguin Group (Australia), 250 Camberwell Road, Camberwell, Victoria 3124, Australia
(a division of Pearson Australia Group Pty. Ltd.)
Penguin Books India Pvt. Ltd., 11 Community Centre, Panchsheel Park, New Delhi—110 017, India
Penguin Group (NZ), 67 Apollo Drive, Rosedale, Auckland 0632, New Zealand
(a division of Pearson New Zealand Ltd.)
Penguin Books (South Africa) (Pty.) Ltd., 24 Sturdee Avenue, Rosebank, Johannesburg 2196,
South Africa

Penguin Books Ltd., Registered Offices: 80 Strand, London WC2R 0RL, England

This is a work of fiction. Names, characters, places, and incidents either are the product of the author's imagination or are used fictitiously, and any resemblance to actual persons, living or dead, business establishments, events, or locales is entirely coincidental. The publisher does not have any control over and does not assume responsibility for author or third-party websites or their content.

PRINTING HISTORY
G. P. Putnam's Sons hardcover edition / August 2010
Berkley trade paperback edition / August 2011

Berkley trade paperback ISBN: 978-0-425-24132-5

The Library of Congress has catalogued the G. P. Putnam's Sons hardcover edition of this book as follows:

Russell, Sean.
A battle won / S. Thomas Russell.
p.   cm.
ISBN 978-0-399-15689-2
1. Ship captains—Fiction. 2. *Themis* (Ship)—Fiction. 3. Great Britain—History, Naval— 18th century—Fiction. 4. France—History, Naval—18th century—Fiction. 5. Naval battles— History—18th century—Fiction.   I. Title.
PR9199.3.R84B37   2010   2010015253
813'.54—dc22

PRINTED IN THE UNITED STATES OF AMERICA

10 9 8 7 6 5 4 3 2

This book is dedicated to the memory of three friends,

all of whom departed far too young.

Jean Kotcher, Jan Daley, and Art Meck.

Deeply mourned and terribly missed.

Nothing, except a battle lost,

can be half so melancholy as a battle won.

—Arthur Wellesley,
  Duke of Wellington

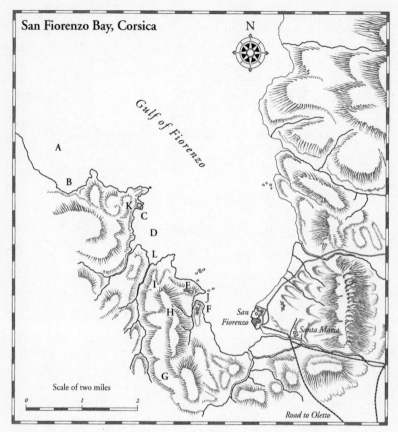

San Fiorenzo Bay, Corsica

N

Gulf of Fiorenzo

A

B

K
C

D

L

I

E

J
F

H

San
Fiorenzo

Santa Maria

G

Scale of two miles

0   1   2

Road to Oletto

KEY

A Bay where the squadron first anchored and remained from 7 to 18 February

B Landing place of the troops on 7 February

C Tower on Mortella Point taken 10 February (2 eighteen-pounders and 1 six-pounder mounted)

D Mortella Bay

E Convention Redoubt taken by storm the night of 17 February

F Tower of Fornali with the different batteries dependent on it, taken the night of 17 February

G Lieutenant Colonel Moore's encampment, with the 51st Regiment, from 8 to 20 February

H Upper battery of 2 eighteen-pounders and 1 eight-inch howitzer against Convention Redoubt, at 800 yards distance and elevated 650 feet above the sea

I Lower battery of 2 eighteen-pounders and 1 ten-inch howitzer against Convention Redoubt, at 1,000 yards distance and elevated 450 feet above the sea

J Fornali Bay, where the French frigates *Fortunée* and *Minerve* were anchored beneath the batteries

K Battery of 1 eighteen-pounder, 2 nine-pounders, and 1 eighteen-pound carronade against tower on Mortella Point

L Landing place of the guns. Distance to the upper battery about 2,000 yards

One

It was a desperate progress. In the stern-sheets of a cutter, among his honour guard of marines, squatted a doughy paymaster, an iron-bound box cradled in his ample lap. Trailing in his wake, a fleet of tawdry bum-boats, the hungry faces of the merchants eyeing the paymaster as though he were a scrap of food. And astern of these, a motley squadron of fishing craft and lighters of all descriptions, their rouged passengers clinging anxiously to the gunnels—non-swimmers, the lot.

"Cleopatra's barge carried no one as comely as you, darling," a grinning, pockmarked sailor called from the deck of a ship to one of the girls, only to find a bosun's rattan smacking down around his ears.

Hayden gazed at the poor women who followed the paymaster, expecting to ply their trade among the briefly moneyed seamen. An hour earlier he had been in the company of Henrietta Carthew, and these fallen creatures who were being ferried out to slake the thirst of sailors seemed of a different species altogether. It occurred to him that if not for the luck of birth his own Henrietta . . . No, it was unthinkable. His spirits lowered ineffably, and Hayden looked away, gazing around Plymouth Harbour. A drab, windless day, November chilled, sea leaden and heaving in a slow, ponderous rhythm. His boat passed into the Hamoaze and the midshipman in nominal charge tore his gaze away from the whores' fleet, suddenly remembered Hayden, and smiled embarrassedly.

"A sad metaphor of our English way of life, I fear," Hayden offered, nodding toward the paymaster's progress, which disappeared at that moment behind the point, but the young gentleman did not seem to grasp the jest.

The powder hoy passed at that moment, and the midshipman turned his back to it, hunching his shoulders visibly, as though prepared to receive a blow. Hayden noticed the coxswain, an old seaman, suppressing a smile, and Hayden did the same. If the powder hoy were to explode so near, turning one's back would not offer protection.

Hayden gazed down the river where every kind of craft imaginable either lay to a mooring or made their way through the still water. War had shaken the dockyards and surrounding waters out of everyday dullness into a sudden fever of excitement and motion. The towns of Plymouth and Dock swarmed with sailors, with the massive drays of enriched victuallers, with marines, red-coated and red-faced. Herds of moaning bullocks blocked up the lanes, stalling wagons from the ordnance board. And all about and underfoot campaigned delighted boys, waving wooden swords and firing imaginary muskets as the frenetic commerce of war spilled out of the offices of the Navy Board and into the noisome streets.

"There she is, sir, the admiral's flagship," the midshipman offered, with no trace of irony.

Hayden turned to gain a view of the Hamoaze and the eighty-gun guardship, *Cambridge*, from which the port admiral executed the duties of his office. It seemed a strange affectation that a port admiral must have a ship and not an office in a building ashore—certainly he had a rather elegant residence supplied by the admiralty. The affectation was not carried so far as to cause him actual discomfort.

Hayden had, for some time, been contemplating the meaning of

his summons but tried to put this worrisome activity to rest. All
would be revealed in the fulness of time, and worry would change
nothing.

The cutter was laid expertly alongside the ship, and Hayden went
nimbly up the ladder. He ignored the lowering of his mood and the
anxiety that told him his ill-fated career was about to receive another
blow. The First Secretary of the Navy had given him his commission,
and the little ship-sloop, *Kent*; certainly no port admiral could take
these away.

The bosun piped him aboard, and a line of marines presented arms
sharply, a ritual they must have performed fifty times a day given the
constant traffic in captains and even admirals visiting the ship. Lowly
masters and commanders, such as Hayden, were likely seen with less
frequency.

Several turns about the deck were necessary while Hayden awaited
his audience. He was not the only officer present, but the captains
and flag officers were all strangers to him and they did no more than
bob heads in his direction, hardly interrupting their hushed conversations. Hayden felt more an outsider than usual, and that was saying
a great deal.

A guardship was not quite a vessel in "ordinary" but a ship with
spars standing and crewed to partial muster. Guardships were maintained in this state to provide the admiralty with a reserve of vessels that could be readied for sea in mere days if there were a sudden
need. The *Cambridge*, however, was not about to go to sea anytime in
the near future, for she neared the end of her days. "Receiving hulk"
would constitute the next stage of her natural life and then the ship
breaker. His Majesty's ships were rather like phoenixes, Hayden knew,
rising from the ashes, for though the admiralty might discard a ship
they almost never abandoned a name—there would certainly be another *Cambridge* within a few years of this particular ship's demise.

"Captain Hayden?"

Hayden turned to find a pink-cheeked marine corporal touching his hat.

"Yes."

"The admiral sends his respects and requests the honour of your company."

A moment later Hayden was let into the admiral's outer cabin by the marine sentry and met by a guarded secretary. No words were offered in greeting, only a quick leg, the man constantly glancing back toward the door which led to the admiral's day-cabin. From beyond the door, the muffled thump of heavy footsteps sounded, paused, and then immediately resumed, traversing larboard to starboard.

The secretary beckoned Hayden, then hastened almost silently toward the inner door, hesitated, knocked, and when no answer was forthcoming, steeled himself visibly and applied knuckle to wood with greater force.

"Come in, dammit! Have I gone deaf, now, as well?"

The secretary opened the door to let Hayden in and then, exposing only his arm to the glaring admiral within, pulled the door quickly but silently closed. Moments such as these Hayden found most difficult. He was not about to appear intimidated, yet to defy such an officer's mood would do nothing to further his cause, as he well knew. But Hayden was simply not given to servility.

Admiral Rowland Cotton stood glowering after his secretary a moment and then turned his pinched and darkened countenance upon Hayden, who attempted to appear utterly neutral.

"You do realise that my predecessor died of apoplexy?" the admiral stated.

Hayden nodded. It was well known that Sir Richard Bickerton had died in a fit of frustrated rage the year previous, though in fact he was not Cotton's precise predecessor—Admiral Colby, very briefly, claimed that honour.

"Your ship—what is it named?" the admiral began, without any further attempt at pleasantries.

"The *Kent*, sir."

"It has not arrived. . . ."

"No, sir. Two days of sou'west gales and now a calm—"

But Cotton was not interested in meteorology, nor had he been making an enquiry. "You were Hart's lieutenant, yes?"

"I was, sir," Hayden answered guardedly. The mention of Hart's name filled him with trepidation. He harboured a fear that he would always be associated with that officer and the infamous events aboard his ship, and it seemed his fear was being borne out.

"Then the *Themis* is familiar to you?"

"That is correct, Admiral—"

Cotton began his pacing again. "No doubt you are cognisant of the fact that she was given to Captain Davies? Yes? But it seems the good captain has been seized by an attack of . . . some mysterious ailment, after a lifetime of unblemished health. The truth is, and I do not care who knows it, the man is busy making interest among his friends in London and in the admiralty because he is too proud to take her. It appears that the *Themis*, a new-built frigate of excellent moulding and character, is beneath the captains of the fleet because to be given a ship so . . . *notorious* would be a sure sign that they were not held in high regard in Whitehall Street!" The man shook his head, his face hardening with anger. "But you are in perfect health, yes? Not about to contract a sudden case of dyspepsia . . . ? Good. I have been complaining daily to the admiralty that the *Themis* swings to her mooring awaiting a competent officer, and after a number of missives they have finally condescended to allow me to assign a man to convey her to Admiral Lord Hood in the Mediterranean. Finding her a captain will then be Hood's problem, not mine." He stopped and glanced at Hayden. "I don't need to spell it out for you, I suppose?"

"You wish me to deliver the *Themis* to Lord Hood, sir."

The man leaned forward. "I do not wish it, Captain Hayden, I order it."

"But what will become of me then? What of the *Kent*?"

The admiral waved a hand dismissively. "Hood will have a use for you, I am sure. Or he will send you back to Mr Stephens." The admiral spun on his heel and resumed his pacing, clearly done with Hayden, who made no move to leave, even so.

Seeing Hayden still fixed to his place, the admiral asked, "Is a frigate not better than a sloop, Hayden?"

"It is better to have command of one's own vessel. To be a job-captain is—"

The admiral rounded on him. "Too many officers think first of their careers and secondly of the service. They forget there is a war to be fought and sacrifices to be made."

Yes, but *I'm* the one being sacrificed, Hayden almost said.

But the interview was over and Hayden was quickly ushered out by the fussy secretary, who placed in his reluctant hand both orders and commission, which clearly had been made out in advance of his arrival.

Hayden was on the deck in a moment, the gathered captains glancing his way with chilling disinterest, then back to their quiet conversations. Over the side Hayden went and down into the waiting boat, where he sagged onto a plank in the stern-sheets.

The midshipman ordered the boat away and then, when Hayden said nothing, enquired softly, "Plymouth quay, sir?"

"Do you know where the *Themis* is anchored?"

"The mutineers' ship?"

"The very one."

"You haven't been sent into her, I hope."

Hayden fixed the boy with a cold glare.

"Cawsand Bay, sir. We'll have you there quicker than you can say—"

"Twice cursed?" Hayden ventured, completing the sentence, but the middy thought better of offering a reply.

A whispering rain spattered the harbour as they left the protection of the river, dimpling the surface and sending dull silvered rings expanding all around. The oarsmen bent to their sweeps, breathing hard from the effort, and soon Cawsand Bay appeared, crowded with ships as it almost always was.

The black hull of the *Themis* could soon be seen among the vessels, all streaming to the tidal current—the runt among a fleet of larger ships of war. The midshipman ordered the coxswain to lay his boat alongside, where Hayden was asked, by the marine sentry, to wait, as he sent for the officer of the watch. Word quickly came back that Hayden should be allowed to board, and as he ascended the ladder, a memory of first climbing the side of the ship came to him— she had been slovenly then, her crew drunk and officers barely in control; the legacy of the tyrannical Hart. It seemed such a long time ago—not mere weeks. There were no sounds of revelry this day, but only the quiet pounding of a carpenter's hammer somewhere inside, the tolling of the ship's bell, and calls of *"All's well,"* though Hayden could not bring himself to agree. As he climbed over the rail, a familiar face emerged from below.

"Mr Archer," Hayden greeted him, pleased to find aboard anyone he knew. When Hayden had quit the ship, all the officers and warrant officers were to have been sent ashore—no doubt at the insistence of the new captain, who had not wanted to serve with men who were in any way connected to a mutiny. "I am surprised to see you here."

"And I am just as surprised to see you, Mr Hayden. I should have thought you would never want to set foot aboard this ship again. We are awaiting our new captain, but it seems he has an aversion to our company."

"Hmm. Let us repair below, out of this rain. Are you well, Mr Archer?"

"Oh, quite well, sir." Archer smiled. He habitually looked as though he had just come, somewhat befuddled, from slumbering in his cot, and this day was no different. As they walked the deck he attempted, stealthily, to straighten his waistcoat, which had been fastened one button out of place so that it made an awkward angle across his chest.

"Have your numbers been brought up?" Hayden asked, by way of relieving the embarrassment. He pretended not to notice Archer in combat with his uniform.

"Near enough, sir. We've been waiting on the press to bring us a few men, but I believe they have done with us."

After the mutiny, the *Themis'* crew had been reduced to a mere 80 men—at least 120 men shy of her complement.

As they reached the companionway ladder, Archer spoke down to a man below. "Look who has come to call, Mr Barthe—a newly minted master and commander, it seems." And then to Hayden: "I have neglected to offer my congratulations on your promotion, sir."

At the foot of the ladder Hayden and the corpulent sailing master grasped hands. Mr Barthe was red-faced and puffing, as though he had run up stairs. "I thought it might be our new captain," Barthe laughed, clearly pleased to see Hayden, "and came at a run so as not to appear lax. Come down to the gunroom, Mr Hayden, it is warmer there." Barthe stepped aside and let Hayden precede him down the ladder. "Will you not accompany us, Mr Archer?"

"Just measuring the wind, Mr Barthe."

"Straightening his waistcoat," Hayden whispered to the sailing master, who answered with a knowing grin.

The master muffled his laughter, then cleared his throat. "The rumour is you have a ship, Mr Hayden. The *Kent*. Is that correct?"

"As of an hour ago, that was my situation, Mr Barthe, but the port admiral had other ideas."

Archer came rushing to catch them up.

"Bloody-minded Cotton?" Barthe wondered, lumbering down the steps after Hayden.

"You've met him, I see."

"Thank God, no. But he has a reputation."

Hayden opened the door into the gunroom and found Dr Griffiths sitting at the table, bent over an open book. The man removed his spectacles, a smile overspreading his narrow face. Quickly, he rose and cracked his skull cruelly against a beam.

"Damn and blast!" he cried, reaching up to clasp his scalp. He winced and laughed at the same time. "You would think I had never been below decks before. Mr Hayden . . . what a pleasure it is to find you entering our gunroom once again."

"A pleasure no greater than my own at finding you in your usual place. I thought you had all been sent ashore?"

"The new captain wanted to be shut of us," Barthe answered, "but by all accounts he has gone up to London to lobby the admiralty for a different ship. So we were all ordered back aboard, if you can believe it, our services not wanted elsewhere—such is the bad name we have acquired who served Captain Hart. I think the ship will swing here and rot for want of a captain."

"Rotting is not in her immediate future, Mr Barthe." Hayden reached inside his coat and removed the letters given him by the port admiral's stealthy secretary. "My orders and commission. I am to take command and convey you all to the Mediterranean to join Lord Hood . . . at Toulon. We might gather all hands on the gun-deck at the change of watch and I will read my commission." Hayden broke the seal on his orders and read. "Well, here is a little detail the admiral failed to convey. . . . We are to act as convoy escort as far as Gibraltar."

"Is this not late in the season for a convoy?" Archer wondered, incredulous.

"I have heard there is a convoy delayed in Tor Bay these six weeks past, due first to weather, then to one damned thing or another." Barthe shook his head as though this were clearly the result of some admiralty incompetence.

"That is the one," Hayden responded, referring to his orders. "Pool has command of it."

"Richard Pool? I know him, Mr Hayden," Barthe said, his mouth turning down. "There is not a more ambitious man in the fleet, I would venture, though I will confess he is a passable seaman."

"His vaunting ambition has landed him on convoy duty, it would seem. We are to carry a pair of passengers with us—parsons, if you can believe it—sent out to minister to Hood's heathen hordes, apparently."

Archer laughed. "A pair of parsons for Hood's heathen hordes. Very good, Mr Hayden."

"Mr Hayden is only in temporary command, Archer," Griffiths said. "No need to patronise him."

Archer laughed and blushed.

"Is there a man aboard we might send to reliably collect my belongings and carry them aboard?"

"Childers, sir."

"He will do nicely. We are for Tor Bay on the morning tide, Mr Barthe. How are we for stores and water?"

"A sufficiency to see us all the way to Gibraltar and beyond, sir. We have shot and powder aplenty, our copper is clean, and sails and rig are in near perfect order. We are a few hands short, sir, but that is a small matter." Barthe smiled. "We have almost all the men who sailed with us to France, Mr Hayden, for no other ship wanted them, not thinking that the mutineers had all gone to the hangman and the men remaining all seamen of the first water. The press has brought us some very good men—fishermen and merchant sailors. Oh, we've a passel of landsmen and boys, but Mr Franks has been teaching them their ropes and they will soon pass for seamen."

"How fares Mr Franks?"

"Hobbled, sir, and he goes aloft but slowly. There is nothing wrong with his arm, though; he can still wield a rattan with the best of them. He'll manage."

"Are you first lieutenant, Mr Archer?"

Archer, who had appeared to be contemplating other matters, shook himself like a schoolboy caught daydreaming. "No, sir. Saint-Denis is first; he is ashore at the moment. I am second and we have, as yet, no third. Without a captain we have not a single middy, though I am sure Hart's former charges would all sign on with you in a moment, were there but time to alert them."

"We must find some reefers. Perhaps they might join us in Tor Bay." Hayden took out his watch and thumbed it open—not quite noon. "Will you have all the bills of lading, manifests, accounts, crew lists, et cetera, put into my cabin, Mr Archer. And I will require a boat to carry me ashore for a dinner engagement. Can we find Lieutenant Saint-Denis? There is much to do before we sail."

"I will send someone with Childers to track him down, Captain."

Hayden took Barthe and Franks with him and went over the *Themis* from keel to truck, surveying all her gear, stores, armament, the crew's quarters, sick-berth—in short, every aspect of the ship that pertained to her coming voyage, which was nearly everything. To Franks' embarrassment, Hayden had the bosun renew a few ropes aloft, and guessed from the man's reaction that neither his mates nor the crew were being quite honest with him about what work was needed high up in the rigging—taking advantage of the bosun's difficulties with climbing.

When this task was complete, and it required several hours, Hayden repaired to the captain's cabin, only to find it already occupied, or at least containing another's belongings.

"It seems, Mr Archer, that someone inhabits my cabin."

"Saint-Denis, sir. I shall have his servant remove his belongings, immediately. My apologies, Mr Hayden."

"*Mister* Hayden should be addressed as 'Captain' now, Mr Archer," Barthe reminded him slyly.

"Of course," Archer said quickly. "I shall not make the mistake again."

"Not to worry, Mr Archer." Hayden laughed. "I have not grown used to it myself."

Servants were sent for and the first lieutenant's belongings carried away, leaving Hayden walking about an empty cabin. Perseverance Gilhooly, Hayden's former writer, appeared at that moment, leading two seamen who bore a small writing-table.

"Gilhooly!" Hayden greeted the boy, known as "Perse" to most. "Are you ready for a promotion to captain's clerk? Or perhaps we should make that job-captain's clerk."

"I am quite prepared to be a job-clerk, if that is my title, sir, and very pleased I am to see you back aboard."

"Thank you. There is a mass of paperwork to be got through and I intend to start at once. Are there chairs . . . ? Ah, there they are." Two seamen bearing chairs entered at that moment.

Barthe's mate hurried in, pushing through the door past the exiting seamen. He placed a leather-bound book in the sailing master's hand.

Barthe held it up for Hayden to see. "Harbour log, if you please, Captain." He placed the book on Hayden's desk.

"Let us keep an eye on this one, Mr Barthe. I shouldn't want it going astray."

"I don't think we have any thieves aboard at the moment. It was never explained to me how my log suddenly reappeared at the court-martial. . . ."

"Nor was it explained to me," Hayden said. Hayden turned the cover of Mr Barthe's log so as not to meet the man's eye. He was responsible for retrieving the stolen journal, but did not want it known. His hand stopped as he flipped a page, and he glanced up at the sailing master, who appeared more careworn than usual.

"You were aboard for the hangings, Mr Barthe? This is your hand?"

Barthe glanced down at his neat, four-square writing, his eyes closing for a second, the round face falling slack. "I was, sir. The new captain was too ill to attend. Mr Franks and . . . and I made the nooses. Saint-Denis oversaw the executions—and rather coolly, too—earning him the distrust of the crew. At least we were able to use men new to the ship to haul the ropes, sir, so they were strangers to the condemned. A small comfort."

"I am sorry you had to take part in that, Mr Barthe. It was a nasty business."

"A few men I did not mind seeing go up, sir. They abused us terribly after they took the ship, even to the point of killing men, but others were less guilty, if that is possible. The sight of them being hauled aloft will haunt me all my days, I fear."

"The price for having a conscience and a sense of duty."

The two seamen stood awkwardly a moment, and then Barthe, unaided by Hayden's homilies, performed a quick bow. "I must leave you to your work, Captain." He retreated, his habitual rolling gait suddenly mechanical and stiff.

Hayden gave his coat to a marine who had been assigned as his servant, forced himself down into a chair, and drew the first paper off the pile—the ship's muster. There were many names he recognised: Chettle, the carpenter; Childers, who had been Hart's coxswain and would temporarily serve Hayden in the same capacity, or at least so Hayden assumed. Among the familiar, though, he found many names he did not know. A few of these were so evocative in their own right that he could almost put faces to them. Herald Huggins would certainly be a solid, no-nonsense seaman, Hayden was sure. Makepeace Bracegirdle was no doubt a God-fearing belt-and-braces type.

Manifests, bills of lading, sick and hurt lists, watch and station bill, the harbour log. A veritable tidal wave of paper sent to overwhelm him, Hayden thought, but stuck with it until the pile had, one wretched sheet at a time, passed across the desk to the "signed and read" side.

Hayden sat back in his chair, lifted his forgotten coffee cup, and drained the cold remains. A glance at his watch confirmed what his stomach suggested—dinner was in the offing. He looked around Hart's cabin, which was his temporarily and not for the first time. It seemed a post captain's rank, and the ship that he hoped would come with it remained very distant. Damn and blast Cotton for taking away the *Kent*—a position he felt was less than his due. And now he was a job-captain again. A bloody *job-captain*!

A knock at the door.

"Enter," Hayden called, trying not to let his anger and frustration boil over onto the innocents.

The sentry stuck his head in. "Lieutenant Saint-Denis, if you please, sir."

"Send him in."

Saint-Denis swept in, hat tucked beneath his arm, a forced, not unpleasing smile, manner too familiar. Above a high forehead, lank yellow hair, thinning. A beautifully tailored uniform could not hide the narrow chest, angular shoulders, or broad hips. Although only just Hayden's senior, the lieutenant appeared to be rushing toward middle years, his handsome youth already behind him.

"Mr Hayden, I cannot begin to tell you what pleasure it gives me to meet you." He waved a hand toward the empty chair. "May I?" Then sat before Hayden could answer. "I fear I shall not be with you long, and for that I apologise, but Captain Davies will no doubt send for me. I am very confident that the admiralty will honour him with a ship of the line—perhaps a flagship—and he has vowed to take me with him; believes he cannot do without me, really. But I am sure you will find an adequate officer to take my place. Archer has not my years of experience nor, if I may say, aptitude, but might do . . . if you cannot find another."

"Yes," Hayden answered. "I dare say he might, but until such time as the admiralty has instructed me otherwise you are still first lieutenant of the *Themis* and there is a great deal of preparation to complete before we can sail, which we shall do, weather and tide permitting, on the morrow."

Saint-Denis glanced away, turning a little in his chair so that he hung an elbow over the back, and then crossed one thigh over the other. "Certainly, Hayden, I shall give you every assistance within my power until my summons arrives. I am cognisant of your situation—lacking middies and without a full complement of officers." He raised a finger and wiggled it at the deck-head. "Perhaps I might find you some midshipmen among my acquaintance, though most of the families in my circle might think a career in the Navy beneath their progeny—unlike our own families, eh?" He laughed. Hayden did not.

"I shall choose my own midshipmen, Lieutenant, thank you. Would you find the purser and locate these stores?" Hayden took up a list from the writing-table and held it out. "I have a suspicion that some of our victuals have gone astray."

For a moment Saint-Denis made no move to take the list, but then rose and reluctantly retrieved the paper from Hayden. "As soon as I have changed my uniform." He made the slightest nod. "Mr Hayden." And retreated stiffly.

As Saint-Denis passed out, Dr Griffiths leaned in. "Have you a moment, Captain?"

"By all means."

Griffiths glanced over his shoulder at the retreating back of Saint-Denis and, when the door was closed, enquired quietly, a smile only half suppressed, "How went your interview with Saint-Denis?"

"He is, I am informed, to be recalled by Captain Davies and shall grace us with his presence but a few hours." Hayden did not add that, clearly, searching for mislaid stores was beneath so gifted an officer.

"I should not count upon his leaving," Griffiths said, almost a whisper. "I have heard a rumour, yet to be substantiated, that Davies wished to be shut of the man. None of the captain's other chosen officers were sent aboard—only Saint-Denis, who has been directing daily missives to Davies, and to his father, with increasing desperation. No replies have been forthcoming."

A blast of wind produced an extended, wailing moan and rain pelted down on the deck overhead.

"You mean to say I might not rid myself of the man?"

"I fear it is so. I gather you cannot simply allow him to go off to London to join his patron?"

"No. I'm afraid I cannot. Who is he, pray? He appears to believe himself a person of some consequence."

"So he does, and it would appear to be true, but there is something amiss in the world of Caspian Saint-Denis. Time, I suspect, will see the story come out." Griffiths glanced at the pile of papers on Hayden's little desk. "I have been sent to invite you to dine in the gunroom this evening, but I am informed by Childers that you have a previous engagement?"

"I fear it is true, Doctor. Another night, I hope?"

"The first you are not spoken for. I have one other small problem that I hate to bring to your attention when I know you are so busy. . . ."

"It is my lot, I fear, to hear the problems of others. What is it, pray?"

"My assistant has been away these six days attending to a private matter, but he is now a day overdue. I fear we might sail without him."

"Ariss?"

"The very man."

"There is little we might do, Doctor. I am to sail for Tor Bay the moment weather permits. Any not aboard will have some small chance of finding us there, but I believe the convoy is to depart the moment this sou'east gale abates. You might send a letter apprising Ariss of this, but beyond that there is little either of us can do."

"I shall sit down and write immediately. Have a pleasant evening ashore, Captain."

"Thank you, Doctor, but I do not look forward to bearing news of my impending absence—likely for several months—to a certain lady."

Two

Has your ship come in, Captain?" Henrietta asked as she entered the room. She smiled and flushed with pleasure, then even more so realizing how transparent this must be.

"In a manner of speaking." Hayden felt a deep sense of embarrassment, almost humiliation, over what the port admiral had done to him that morning.

"There is a mysterious answer," Elizabeth said, her face suddenly solemn, lovely head tilted to one side. "Pray, what do you mean, Captain Hayden?"

Elizabeth and Henrietta continued to take singular pleasure from addressing him as "Captain," though each and every time Hayden was reminded that he was only master and commander. And now he did not even have a ship of his own, information that it pained him to reveal.

Hayden worked a little moisture into his mouth. "The *Kent* is still at sea and the port admiral has, with the blessing of the admiralty, placed me in temporary command of the *Themis*. I am to escort a convoy to Gibraltar and then deliver the ship to Lord Hood, who will find her a captain from among his own officers."

Robert stifled a curse and turned away in anger and frustration.

Henrietta looked confused by the reaction of Robert and Elizabeth, whose countenance had undergone a drastic change.

"But is a frigate not more desirable than a sloop?" she asked. "Is it not a post ship?"

"It is, Miss Henrietta, but unfortunately I am only a job-captain . . . yet again, and my own ship will be given to some other." Hayden felt his face flush warm. "Once I have delivered the *Themis* to Hood, I shall be without a ship, cooling my heels in Gibraltar, perhaps, until a vessel can be found to bear me home."

"Oh . . ." Henrietta said softly. "Then you could be away for some . . . weeks?"

"Months . . . I fear," Hayden almost whispered, as though he might soften the blow.

Henrietta's eyes glistened and she turned her head away.

"Come, Robert," Elizabeth said, beckoning to her husband, "I have something to show you . . . in the dining room. Please, excuse us."

Hayden and Henrietta stood by the fire. A gale of wind finding its way down the chimney sent a little puff of greyish smoke spinning out and ceilingward. A graceless silence prevailed for a moment, and then they both moved forward and their lips met, almost shyly. They had been stealing kisses for the past two days, as though already engaged.

"Your disappointment is very great, I can see, but it will all come out right in the end," Henrietta whispered, overcoming her distress.

"Yes, I should not let temporary setbacks affect my mood so." He took her hand.

"Some months, you say?" she said softly.

Hayden nodded, trying to read the look in her eyes.

"Well . . ." she said, glancing away from his questioning gaze.

Neither knew what to say, but then, as was often the case, Henrietta rescued them from this troublesome silence.

"I suppose it is a banality to say, 'I will wait for you'?" Henrietta offered, trying to smile.

It touched Hayden to his very core that she would try to cheer him at that moment, when she must feel the pending separation as greatly as he.

"Or that 'I will think of you every day.'" Hayden attempted to rise to the occasion.

"Not 'every minute'?" she chided.

"If you would prefer it."

She considered this, her mouth turning down a little. "Every second does seem a bit much. There must be a limit to devotion." She did meet his eyes, and he saw distress that her smile and manner could not hide. "Don't think of me when your attention is required to keep you safe. I shouldn't want you distracted by thoughts of my inestimable beauty at the wrong moment."

"I shall only contemplate upon your inestimable beauty when alone in my cabin."

"Perhaps just once a day—as you fall asleep and into dream." She closed her eyes suddenly, a hand springing up to shade her face from view. "This will not do! I am tormented and wretched at your leaving. Every moment I shall worry until I see you safe again." She took his hand in both of hers so tightly that her nails dug into the skin. "Come back to me unharmed—you must promise me."

"It is a difficult promise to keep—"

"I care not. You must keep it. Promise me," she demanded.

So he did.

She leaned against him, her breath warm and sweet. Beyond the door, footsteps were heard; faltered and then resumed. The two separated quickly, Henrietta wiping ineffectually at her eyes.

Lady Hertle entered, appearing stooped and tired. Hayden thought her recent illness had aged her some years, at least temporarily.

"There you are," she said, smiling at the two of them, pleased by the budding affection that could not be hidden. But the smile was erased by concern. "My dear Henrietta, are you not yet recovered? Your eyes are all rimmed red and your complexion is high. I fear you are fevered, yet."

"Not in the least, Aunt. I have naught but a wretched cough—and that descends upon me only by night. I am otherwise perfectly hale."

Lady Hertle did not look convinced, and her gaze lingered on her niece a moment before turning to Hayden.

"Captain Hayden," she said. "It is a pleasure."

"I hope it is not a pleasure you are experiencing too often, Lady Hertle. It is not my intention to impose upon your hospitality."

"You could visit me every day of the year and I would not grow weary of it. There is nothing I fear so much as to be left each day with only my own company to keep. I would be driven to utter distraction within a few months. No, visit as often as you wish. Robert frequently says you are like a brother to him, and therefore you are like a nephew to me. Where are Robert and Elizabeth? They are very poor chaperones, I must say," she teased. She beckoned them to walk with her into the dining room. "Sailors are very prone to taking liberties, you know," Lady Hertle instructed her niece. "Why, Admiral Hertle, when he was a young man, would kiss me every chance he got. Of course, we were engaged to be married, but even so, he was highly undisciplined when it came to kisses." A smile hovered about her lips at the memory—only a little sad.

"I am completely scandalised," Henrietta said, "to learn that you would allow *any* young man kiss you, even one to whom you were engaged."

Lady Hertle made a dismissive noise. "I rather like kisses and miss them more than you know."

"Why, Aunt, I kiss you every day," Henrietta responded.

"Indeed you do, but it is not quite the same thing. Ah, Elizabeth," she said, finding her niece and Robert by the window in the dining room, apparently interrupted in the very act of affection presently under discussion, "you have been shirking your duties as chaperone."

"Not at all, Aunt. I have been performing them admirably. I leave Charles and Henrietta to keep their own company just enough to foster their affection for one another . . . and no more. I should say I am the perfect chaperone."

"Well, all of this courting going on beneath my roof makes me feel terribly lonely for the admiral, I am not ashamed to admit it. Terribly lonely." She stopped by her chair. "Do you know what we called it when we were young—kissing, that is? *Osculation.* We thought no one could possibly know of what we spoke, but everyone did. I think that awful Dr Johnson had gone and put it in his dictionary. We went about thinking we were terribly clever, but everyone knew all along. I near died of embarrassment when I learned it." A faint rosy blush coloured her cheeks. "Now, I understand you are off to the theater?"

"Are you certain you do not wish to accompany us, Aunt Hertle?"

"Another time. I am feeling a little tired this evening. What is it you see?"

"Shakespeare, Aunt. *Romeo and Juliet.*"

The theater was filled to capacity that evening, but Robert had arranged a snug little box, large enough for their party and no more, just before the stage. At Elizabeth's insistence, the chaperones took the seats nearest the rail, allowing the courting couple to sit behind in a sliver of shadow.

"Can you see the stage, Henrietta?" Robert asked, twisting about in his chair.

"Perfectly, Robert. Do not be the least concerned."

Hayden could feel a palpable air of anticipation in the theater box. When she spoke, Henrietta's voice seemed squeezed just a bit, and she drew breath with every few words. This anticipation was not for the play, however, unless it was for the distraction it would provide so that the two lovers could touch, perhaps steal a few kisses.

The floor below seethed with an unruly mob, many sailors and soldiers whose boasting and posturing escalated with each drink. Boxes were filled with officers, some of very high rank, from both services. The hubbub and calling out and quizzing of the ladies made for a lively scene. Just below the height of the ceiling, a smoky haze began to form like a squall on the horizon. As the night progressed it would thicken and descend until it hung like a storm over the audience on the floor.

The first play began with a crash of cymbals and beating of drums, certain signs of an approaching tempest. A short farce ensued that appealed greatly to the common sailors, who left off threatening the soldiers and turned their attention to the stage, shouting out sallies and bits of wit, even giving direction to the players.

With all attention elsewhere, Henrietta's soft hand stole into Hayden's and they shifted but a little in their chairs so that their arms touched. Hayden reached across his body with his right hand and caressed the delicate skin inside Henrietta's wrist, making a small circle with a single finger. Her eyes closed and a long, sighing breath was released, almost silently. Without a word they turned toward each other and kissed.

Too soon the play came to an end. And then the famous phrases floated up from the stage:

"Two houses, both alike in dignity, In fair Verona, where we lay our scene. From ancient grudge break to new mutiny, Where civil blood makes civil hands unclean. From forth the fatal loins of these two foes, A pair of star-cross'd lovers take their life . . ."

Even the sailors grew quiet a moment to hear this.

Sampson and Gregory took their cues and engaged in the type of wordplay the sailors approved of, the jest on maidenheads receiving a squall of laughter. Soon enough the more important players appeared, and then young Romeo, whose secret sadness Benvolio had promised to discover.

A rather aged Benvolio spoke his lines to Montague: "See where he comes: so please, you step aside: I'll know his grievance or be much denied."

Montague: "I would thou wert so happy by thy stay, To hear true shrift. Come, madame, let's away." Montague and his lady slipped off the stage in a scuffling patter of feet.

A rather dapper Romeo appeared, so full of his own importance that there were titters in the audience. An extravagantly feathered hat perched, almost pregnant, upon his head. His costume deferred not at all to his headgear, the sleeves of his doublet hanging like silky jowls, his breeches so tight one could not help but wonder how he managed to walk. Betwixt hat and doublet suspended the face of a simpleton, innocent and debauched at once, right eye larger than the left.

"If ever a man wore motley," Hayden whispered to Robert, "this would be he."

Benvolio made a deferential bow. "Good morrow, Cousin."

Romeo seemed rather too surprised by this to be considered reasonable, looking about as though suddenly noticing the sunlight. "Is the day so young?"

Benvolio: "But new struck nine."

Romeo laid the back of a wrist against his brow. "Ay me! sad hours seem long. Was that my father that went hence so fast?"

"My, has this company a player ill to use such a ham?" Elizabeth whispered to her husband. This drew Hayden's attention from his love to the stage.

Benvolio: "It was. What sadness lengthens Romeo's hours?"

Romeo threw his hands up in an awkward gesture, walking away a few paces in apparent agitation. "What sadness lengthens Romeo, one might ask. Am I not handsome, well known a dandy, Ben?"

Henrietta was almost startled from her seat. "What in this world . . . ? *That* is not Shakespeare!"

"Nor is it Romeo." Hayden laughed. "Or not the Romeo we came to see. That is Fowler 'Romeo' Moat, I am quite certain."

"Who?" whispered Henrietta.

"A planter's son—by no means poor," Hayden explained. "He fancies himself an actor and pays theater managers to let him perform in their productions. Romeo is his preferred part. He thought to rewrite the lines to better suit him—Romeo is now quite a dandy."

"And we paid for this?" Robert complained, outraged.

They returned their attention to the play in time to hear Romeo say, "Why such is love's transgression, griefs of mine own lie heav—" Whether Moat had forgotten his lines or his look of utter confusion was feigned, no one could tell. "Grief!" he cried, not so much in pain but as though he called an oddly named dog, "were it only brief! But grief bears me a grievance. She who is passing fair, and fairly passing, virginal in her chastity, has sworn that if no man is found worthy she shall perish without passion, before marrying a man . . . who has no eye for fashion."

"This is blasphemy!" cried Henrietta, offended but amused in spite of herself. "The man should not be encouraged. . . . He should be stoned!"

And so the play went, the blameless actors confounded at every turn by the prancing, posing Romeo, whose lines had been reworked without reference to their own. The crowd, however, could hardly have been more delighted, calling out to Romeo, applauding his every appearance, his every utterance. For his part, Moat took all this acclaim as though it were his due, thinking it all sincere, convinced that his skills as player and playwright were of a superior nature.

The play progressed, and even the officers and quality convulsed with horrified laughter.

As Romeo stood beneath Juliet's balcony, Henrietta hid her face. "I cannot bear it," she moaned, but soon took her hands away.

Juliet slipped gracefully out into the moonlight.

"But soft!" Romeo cried. "What light through yonder window breaks? It is the east and Juliet is the sun! But what thing is it she wears upon her breast? Is it a rag, cast off by scullery maids? A gown it cannot be—"

But Juliet was apparently determined to save the scene, and to cut Moat's foolishness short. "Ay, me!" came her anguished lament, causing such laughter that she coloured through her makeup.

Romeo pointed at his love, his dangling sleeves wafting about like limp folds of skin. "She speaks! O! speak again, bright angel; for thou art—"

But again Moat was interrupted. "O Romeo, Romeo! wherefore art thou, Romeo!" Juliet cried in desperate passion, causing more laughter, for what woman in her reason could pine for such a dolt. "Deny thy father, and refuse thy name; or, if thou wilt not, be but sworn my love, And I'll no longer be a Capulet. 'Tis but a name that is my enemy; Thou art thyself, though not a Montague. What's a Montague? It is nor hand, nor foot, nor arm, nor face, nor any other part—"

"How little she knows of a man's parts!" Romeo chortled.

An unsettled Juliet tried to soldier on. ". . . B-belonging to a man. O! be some other name: What's in a name? that which we call a rose by any other name would smell as sweet—"

But this, too, was interrupted, not by another aside, but by Romeo inhaling an immoderate pinch of snuff. The laughter stopped Juliet mid-soliloquy. Before she could take up her speech again, Romeo climbed up a step and offered her his open snuff box. The response from the audience to this act of inane chivalry thwarted Juliet from proceeding for several minutes.

Hayden and his companions could not help but join in.

"Poor Juliet," Henrietta said, her eyes brimming with tears. "This is a far greater tragedy than Shakespeare ever intended."

"There has never been anything to equal it!" Robert pronounced, turning to his companions as the scene drew to a close.

The play began again, taking their now rapt attention, for no one wanted to miss what Moat might do next. Another scene, as farcical as the ones that went before, was followed by yet another until, at last, the final scenes played out. Romeo entered Juliet's tomb to find his love lying silent, still, beautiful.

"She's died of embarrassment," Henrietta whispered.

"Ah! dear Juliet," Romeo said. "Why art thou yet so fair? Is it this gown I gave thee? Night-slip for thy endless sleep? The green that made thine eye so bright, now makes bright mine doublet red. At last we lie together this long night, dark shades of jade and crimson velvet. Who will not say we are a pretty sight?" Moat took his draft of poison. "O true apothecary! Thy drugs are quick!"

But apparently not quick enough. Moat pulled a handkerchief from his pocket and with it swept clean an area of the stage. After laying his hat for a pillow, he died the most prolonged and embellished death in the history of that famous tragedy until, as he knelt by poor Juliet, he cried, "O Death! how longst hast thou been dying? Thus with a kiss I join my deadly bride." He swooned down, his head landing softly on his ridiculous hat, its vast plume waving back and forth like some banner raised in theatrical surrender.

The applause was beyond anything Hayden had ever known, and then cries of *"Encore! Encore!"* were taken up by the entire crowd.

Not one to refuse his audience, a delighted Romeo hopped up and died a second time . . . and then, by popular acclaim, a third, each death more lingering than the last. Poor Juliet's demise could not summon a single tear after that; in truth, her death caused almost as much hilarity as Moat's, the poor actress' heartfelt declarations made ridiculous by contrast.

"Never has a Juliet looked so relieved to finally make an end of it," Henrietta pronounced.

"Moat thought he played Lazarus, not Romeo, at the end," Robert said.

"Yes," Hayden agreed. "Gravity, apparently, could not keep him to his tomb."

To which Henrietta gave him a playful tap on the arm with her fan.

The audience departed, many in little strolling companies declaiming Moat's rewritten lines in more or less accurate imitation. On the street before the theater, a company of sailors performed the death scene . . . repeatedly. Hayden and his companions were carried along by this noisy crowd, but a few blocks put them on a quieter way.

They were all still giddy from the performance, which had been unlike anything they had seen. "Where have you met a Shakespeare to compare with that?" Robert asked. "'With a kiss I join my deadly bride'!"

"'Virginal in her chastity'?" Elizabeth quoted. "Can you imagine?"

"I should pay triple to see him play Hamlet," Robert declared.

Hayden laughed at the thought. "To starch or not to starch, that would be the question."

"I was only surprised that Juliet did not stab herself in the first act," Henrietta said.

"That would never have stopped Romeo. He would not be denied his two hours in the public's eye. What strange character that he would make a spectacle of himself for so brief a fame."

Hayden and Henrietta slowed their pace a little so that they might converse in private. Taking his arm, Henrietta asked, "Hast thou mistaken me for the sun of late?"

"The sun is too common by far," Hayden declaimed, though quietly, "rising daily like a drudge, to trudge across the earthly sky."

Henrietta laughed. "I am uncertain of 'drudge' and 'trudge.'"

"I am sure even Shakespeare reworked his verse a little."

"As I am sure Moat did not!" Henrietta said, but then grew more serious. "I do not like these tales of lovers dying. Even our simpleton-Romeo could not take the sting from that."

Hayden nodded.

Giving his arm a little tug, Henrietta said, "Let us not be star-crossed. Such things never turn out well."

"As long as our families do not fall to murdering one another, like Capulets and Montagues, I think we shall be safe from such a fate."

At the door of Lady Hertle's home they stopped. Robert and Elizabeth had preceded them inside. A moment they hesitated, allowing a father and son to pass. And then a soft kiss followed by a sweet embrace.

"You will sail tomorrow?" Henrietta asked so quietly he could barely hear.

"Wind and tide permitting . . . yes."

Henrietta burrowed a little further into his embrace. "I find no sweetness in my sorrow," she whispered.

"Nor I."

For as long as they dared tarry, they remained thus, and separated with such terrible reluctance. Henrietta would not release his hand even as she put her own upon the door's handle. "Robert claims that you have no fear," she said hurriedly, "but Charles . . . do not be too brave."

"I shall be no braver than required."

A quick embrace, then Henrietta ducked inside.

Leaving Hayden on the dark and empty street. A moment he stood, and then very softly whispered, "And I shall say adieu until the morrow." Feeling only a little foolish, he tore himself away from the shadow of Lady Hertle's home. His shoes echoed down the faintly moonlit street, the touch of Henrietta's lips on his a fresh memory.

Let us not be star-crossed, Henrietta had said.

"Yes," Hayden muttered, "let us be anything but that."

Three

Is it not just like the channel?" Barthe complained, waving a pudgy hand toward the waters beyond Plymouth Sound. "When we do have a fair wind there is too much of it by half. This bloody gale shows no signs of abating, Captain. It will blow another day yet, I am certain." He crossed Hayden's cabin to the gallery windows and gazed intently out through panes that ran with rain. "I am certain we can make Tor Bay, sir, if we've a need to."

"I am certain you are right, Mr Barthe, at some cost to our gear and danger to our people. No, Pool's convoy is not going anywhere in this. We shall wait."

Early morning, oily sky, rain-streaked. A metronomic *pop-plop, pop-plop* in the quarter gallery as water dripped into the tin sink through a leak above. Hayden was already able to estimate how hard it rained by the cadence.

"What was that bloody row on deck at eight bells?"

"Some bum-boat men, sir. It appears Saint-Denis has considerable debt among them, and moneys expected from his family are now long overdue."

"Pass the word to the marines that I do not want such a scene again—not upon my ship. Where is Mr Hawthorne, anyway?"

"Due back today, Captain. I believe there was yet a heart in Bath he had not broken but will return as soon as that matter has been settled."

"Inform the ladies of Bath that they shall have to release him, for I require his presence aboard. His corporal is not quite up to a lieutenant's duties yet."

"I agree, sir."

A knock on the door. "Lieutenant Saint-Denis, Captain."

"Yes, show him in."

Saint-Denis strode in, several sheets of paper in one hand, hat under the opposite arm. "I cannot account for it, Mr Hayden, but it appears your suspicions have been borne out. Stores have gone missing." He raised the paper and glanced at the figures scribbled there. "Particularly, three barrels of beef, a keg of tallow, and sundry bosun's stores." He lowered the papers so that they slapped against his thigh. "I suspect it is the purser, Mr Hayden. Perhaps even the bosun."

"I am quite certain it is not Franks, Lieutenant." He turned to the sailing master. "How long have you served with Taylor, Mr Barthe?"

"Some years, sir. He is the most private man upon God's earth, but there has never been even a suggestion that he is dishonest. And Franks . . . though not the most careful keeper of records, is honesty personified. I believe we shall have to look elsewhere for our thieves."

"I agree with Mr Barthe. Franks I trust utterly, and Taylor has a long record of reliability. I suspect we will find our thieves among the new men, Lieutenant. I trust you will ferret them out quickly enough. Anything more?"

"No, sir. Oh, there is a Jew asking for you."

"Does this man have a name?"

"He did say his name. . . ." The lieutenant's brow furrowed. "It might have been Gold, sir."

"Ah, Mr Gold. Please have him shown in."

Barthe and Saint-Denis retreated from the cabin, and a moment later one of the local merchants who served the needs of sailors and officers in port was let in. He stood, hat in hand, just inside the door. Hayden had known Gold for at least a decade, an honest, highly reserved man who navigated the sometimes hostile waters of Plymouth Sound and His Majesty's fleets with such skill that Hayden had long since come to believe him a kind of social genius.

"Mr Gold. I hope your labours go well?"

"They do, Captain Hayden. And may I congratulate you on your promotion, sir."

"Very kind of you. I believe you have come to enquire about moneys outstanding on my account?"

Gold attempted to appear surprised at this question. "Not at all, Captain Hayden. I heard of your prizes, sir, and knowing how slow the Prize Courts and agents can be, I thought you might wish to increase your credit, as you now have a table to keep and other expenses as senior officer of a frigate."

Hayden was very short of money, and was indeed worried about keeping up the social requirements of his new post.

"You shall see a good sum from the frigate and the transport, I think, sir, and I should advance you moneys at the most reasonable rate. In truth, Captain Hayden, I have come to ask a favour and in return shall advance you any amount you require at no interest at all."

"You know, Mr Gold, that I would never take a bribe. . . ."

"Of course not, sir! And I never meant to suggest you would."

"Then I shall pay you to advance me money, which offer I will accept. What is this favour, which I might do out of friendship?"

"I am flattered that you would consider me so, Captain. I understand you are in need of midshipmen, and would like to, respectfully, put forward the name of my son, Benjamin. He is a very clever boy, sir, and as eager to please and do well as any you will find."

Hayden was more surprised than he could say. "I remember him well, Mr Gold, and he is everything you say and more. There is, however, a very ancient act of legislation called the Test Act. . . ."

Gold nodded quickly. "I am aware of it, sir, but you might know my wife is a Christian and my son is willing to swear the same."

"But is he willing to publicly take the sacrament, for he could be so required if the Navy wished?"

"I believe he would be willing, sir."

"You believe or he would be?"

"He would be, Captain Hayden. I am quite sure of it. You must know you have Jews among your own crew." The briefly distant look indicated he was gathering evidence to prosecute his case. "And the Schombergs are a Jewish family . . . though the sons have converted to the Church of England. I have oft had the honour of fulfilling some small service for Captain Isaac Schomberg myself, sir."

"Yes, Mr Gold, all that is undeniable, but the truth remains that the officers' corps is a bastion of Anglicanism. My father was a post captain, which for most men would almost make their career, but my mother is French and Catholic and I have been the object of bigotry all my years in the Navy. For your son, success will be very hard won if he succeeds at all. I highly recommend you reconsider." Hayden could see the disappointment in Gold's face. "Why would you want to subject your son to this life, Mr Gold? It is dangerous, uncomfortable, all-consuming."

A sad smile flickered over Gold's face. "It is his heart's desire, sir, to be an officer in the King's Navy, instead of a bum-boat man . . . like his father."

"We all play our part, Mr Gold."

"Some parts are more respectable than others, sir." The man was kneading his hat brim with both hands. "Will you not take him?" he asked softly.

Hayden felt a strange helplessness descend upon him, almost a weakness of limb. To his very core he understood what a difficult life the boy would face—an outsider in an insider's world. He also retained a perfectly vivid memory of how blindly determined he had been to enter this profession, and how devastating he would have found a refusal. "I cannot keep him out of danger, Mr Gold—you must comprehend that."

"I do, sir." Gold made a quick bow in Hayden's direction. "And thank you, sir. I shall have him aboard as soon as you like, sir. I'll kit him out this very morning."

"There is yet one thing more, Mr Gold. I am but a job-captain: when a post captain is appointed to the *Themis*, any middies sailing with me will certainly be cast free. Their future will be as uncertain as my own."

But this did not seem to dampen Gold's excitement in the least. In truth, Hayden had never seen the man so happy.

"I believe you will have a great future, Mr Hayden. I am quite certain of it. My Benjamin could not be in better hands. I know that full well."

The moment Gold had departed, Hayden regretted his decision. "No good will come of this," he muttered to himself in the mirror.

Some three hours later, Hayden was making the best arrangement of his few effects in the great cabin, which seemed palatially large compared to the eight foot square he was used to, when the sentry knocked on the door and announced Mr Archer.

"There is a midshipman making application to you, Captain," Archer said upon entering. "He bears a letter from his father, I believe."

"So soon? Well, send him down, Mr Archer, and then I will have you settle him in the midshipmen's berth."

"Aye, sir."

A moment later the door opened again and Hayden looked up from his labours to find Arthur Wickham standing just inside the cabin and grinning somewhat foolishly.

"Wickham!"

"Captain Hayden," the boy said, making a rather exaggerated bow. He held out a letter. "My father has asked me give you this. It is a request that you might find a place for me in the midshipmen's berth, for once I had learned you had a ship, I was determined to have him ask such a favour of you." He gestured around the cabin. "But I was not expecting this, sir. I heard you had command of a sloop, not a post ship."

"Nor am I a post captain, Wickham. Only a job-captain, and once I have delivered the *Themis* to Lord Hood, I shall likely be without a ship again and my midshipmen without positions."

"Not for a moment do I believe such an event possible. You will have a ship, I am quite certain."

"Your faith is heartening, Wickham. Truly it is." Hayden received the letter and broke the seal. A rather ill-formed hand very graciously requested that he take on Lord Arthur as midshipman, a request Hayden was delighted to grant.

"And who is this letter from?" Hayden asked. "The Marquis of Sanstable is unknown to me."

"My father came into the title only recently," Wickham admitted.

"Well, Lord Sanstable has made such kind application on your behalf that I cannot help but grant his request. You will have a great deal to learn, I expect, young and green as you are."

"I shall apply myself with a will, Captain Hayden. You will not regret taking me on." Wickham laughed with pleasure. "I understand that you are in need of middies, sir?"

"I have only one other, and he truly is green—utterly new to the life. I hope you will give him the benefit of your experience and be kind to him."

"That I shall, sir. I have taken the liberty of alerting two other young gentlemen in my position—having recently been released from their ship. I can vouch for them, sir, most highly."

"And might their names be Hobson and . . . Stock?"

"Madison, sir. Hobson and Madison. I don't think Tristram Stock will go to sea again. He was much affected by the loss of his friend Williams. It will be some time before he recovers, I fear."

"I am sorry to hear it. But Madison and Hobson I should be happy to sail with again. Are you certain of them?"

"I left London before I received answers to my letters, but I would be very much surprised if they did not make straight for Plymouth the moment they received word."

Hayden could hardly have been more pleased with this turn of events. "They will need all speed, for we make sail the moment the weather allows. Are you well, Lord Arthur?"

Wickham looked suddenly serious—his habitual pose when asked a question. "I am, sir, and better now that I am to sail with my old shipmates. I understand from Archer that we have much of the *Themis* crew intact?"

Hayden shook his head at this. "Yes. Is it not passing strange? No other captain would take them—a terrible mistake, but much to our benefit, for only the most loyal men were left after the mutiny, and there are some very good seamen among them, too."

"I will miss Aldrich," Wickham said.

"As will we all. Poor fellow, rest his soul. He was never found, so I suppose he did drown, after all."

Wickham shrugged. "I almost forgot! My father has sent you a gift as well, for advancing me so far in understanding my trade, sir."

"My part in the advancement of your understanding was very small. You have a natural gift, I believe, and few men are so born."

Wickham actually coloured a little. "Why, thank you, sir. I count it a great compliment, Captain Hayden. But my father has sent you a rather handsome table—all the finest mahogany and fit for a cabin such as this. Perhaps he had a bit of foresight, Captain. It will seat a dozen or can be reduced to accommodate as few as four. The chairs are terribly cleverly made, sir, and fold up completely flat. You shall not have the least trouble storing them away when we clear for action, which I hope we shall be doing soon enough."

"That is a very handsome gift! Too generous by a great deal, I fear. How shall I ever repay him?"

"It is Lord Sanstable who is repaying you, sir, for furthering my education. And perhaps for the prize money that will be coming my way."

"When we finally see it. I shall sit down this evening and write the marquis a letter expressing my gratitude."

Wickham eyed Hayden's writing-table, with its impressive pile of papers. "If I may, sir, I should go down and pay my respects to Mr Barthe and the doctor, and leave you to your work."

"Indeed you should. They will be very pleased to see you."

Another quick leg, and Wickham was nimbly out.

Having had his fill of paperwork, Hayden left his cabin intending to visit the sick-berth and then see to some particular racks he had ordered Chettle build in the bosun's storeroom—an attempt to bring order to Mr Franks' realm and allow him to keep a better tally of his stores.

As he left his cabin, he was met at the foot of the companionway ladder by three men in the most disastrous state owing to the near-torrential rains. The smallest and youngest was a mere lad of perhaps fourteen years, who stripped off oilskins, revealing an almost gleaming new midshipman's uniform beneath. Every motion the boy made seemed a self-conscious parody of a human movement, and he smiled awkwardly all the while. The tallest, and eldest, was a spare, cheerless-appearing man who gazed about with a look of poorly hidden distaste upon his narrow face. The last of the three was his apparent opposite, round-faced and rather vacantly satisfied-looking. A little twist of a smile hovered upon chubby lips, and Hayden thought him the kind of gentleman who would stand, perfectly pleased with the world, in horse droppings without ever noticing or the smile being displaced.

Archer hovered just to one side.

"Here is our captain," he said to the small gathering. "The Reverend Dr Worthing." The austere gentleman nodded. "The Reverend Mr Smosh." The smaller of the two made a leg. "And our new midshipman, Mr Gould."

"Gould?" Hayden echoed.

"My father arranged my place with you most recently, Captain Hayden."

"Ah. Gould. Pleased to have you all aboard." He turned to his second lieutenant. "See these gentlemen to the cabins arranged for them, if you please, Mr Archer, and introduce young Gould to Mr Wickham, who will see him settled." Hayden turned to the chaplains. "I hope you will be free to dine with me this evening? Ship's fare, I am afraid, but one is forced to it eventually."

That being arranged, Hayden left the men of various faiths to Archer. A package had been given to him by Benjamin Gould—from the boy's father. The package contained some moneys, which Hayden would hold for the boy and release as needed—quite traditional—as well as the moneys Gold had advanced to Hayden.

Hayden's newly appointed steward passed by at that moment. "Mr Castle. What is on the menu this evening?"

"It is pork day, sir."

"So I feared. I shall be having a dinner in my cabin for a number of people and we shall be serving the lamb sent aboard for me this afternoon. Along with the most reverend gentlemen, I shall have Wickham, the new middy—Gould—and . . . I shall make you a list."

They were ten at table: Mr Barthe, Lieutenants Saint-Denis and Archer, Midshipmen Lord Arthur Wickham and Benjamin Gould, Dr Griffiths, the Reverends Worthing and Smosh, the recently returned Hawthorne, and, of course, Hayden. The table itself was an object of much admiration, for it was a magnificent affair, far finer than anything Hayden could ever have purchased for himself. It had very conveniently arrived with exquisite linen, which was on display, putting all of Hayden's modest china, flatware, and plain serving bowls and chafing dishes to shame. The fare, however, was first-rate—lamb sent aboard by Mr Gold, whose son's patronymic had evolved into *Gould*, it seemed.

"I am surprised to find a physician serving in a frigate, Dr Griffiths," Reverend Dr Worthing offered into a lull in the conversation. "I *assume* you are a physician, as you are habitually addressed as 'Doctor'." Worthing had a rather ponderous, haughty manner of speaking, as though his slightest observation was of undeniable import.

"I am a mere surgeon, Dr Worthing."

Worthing's laden fork stopped on the journey to his sour mouth and returned to the plate. "Is it not presumptuous to style yourself 'Doctor,' in that case? My own brother was a surgeon and never claimed any title other than 'Mister.'"

Hayden thought it proper to intercede here, on Griffiths' behalf. "It is the habit of sailors to refer to medical officers, indeed to address them, as 'Doctor.' Of the ships I have served aboard, it has been so upon all but one."

"Why, I think it is a strange custom. Do seamen not appreciate the great disparity in learning between a surgeon and a physician?"

"Upon the land such a disparity in knowledge may exist, Dr Worthing," Barthe said gently, "but upon a ship the surgeon is also apothecary and physician. You will find that Dr Griffiths has educated himself, at great effort, far beyond the understanding of most Navy surgeons."

"Well, I hope you will not be offended if I do not participate in this custom, Mr Griffiths, for I must tell you, I think it . . . undue."

"I shall take no offence at all, Dr Worthing," Griffiths answered easily. "'Mister' me all you wish."

Despite his claim to wish no discourtesy, Hayden thought that Worthing could not quite hide his disappointment that his censure had been accepted with so little sign of offence.

"What of this other doctor I heard mentioned?" Worthing went on. "Is he a surgeon, as well? I must say, I am surprised that a frigate should require two."

"Which doctor is this?" Hayden asked.

"Dr Jefferies, I believe the man's name was."

Grins were suppressed all around the table, and at least one smirk obscured behind a wineglass quickly raised.

"Jefferies is the ship's cook, Dr Worthing. It is a jest in the Navy to refer to the cook as 'Doctor.'"

"It is an odd conception of a jest." The man seemed a bit offended that anyone might find humour in this. "Address within the service does seem peculiar. Am I given to understand, Captain Hayden, that you are no captain at all but hold the rank of master and commander?"

"That is exactly correct, sir," Hayden replied.

"Even an admiral would address Captain Hayden as 'Captain,' Dr Worthing," Wickham interjected. "He has command of a ship and is therefore 'Captain.' You will soon find that Captain Hayden is very deserving of such address, for he is as fine a sea-officer as any man who has earned his post."

"Then I do not doubt it," Worthing responded.

When Wickham spoke, Hayden noticed, the reverend was all attention and amiability. After all, the progeny of a man who might have a living to bestow was worthy of cultivation.

Thwarted from offering offence in this particular channel, the chaplain retreated into silence.

"Mr Gould," Hawthorne offered into this moment, "you must be something of an authority on the matter of physicians. Am I informed correctly that you have two brothers in medicine?"

"Yes, sir, Mr Hawthorne," Gould answered eagerly, pleased to be noticed. "My eldest brother has opened a practise in London, and the next eldest, Peter, is studying to do the same."

"And why is it you didn't follow their example, Mr Gould?" Barthe asked. "Lord knows it is a more sensible and gainful profession than the sea."

"I contemplated it most seriously for some time, Mr Barthe. I even read many of my brother's texts, helping him with his studies. Med-

icine is an absorbing subject, I will grant you, but in the end, being
shut up in rooms all day in London . . ." A visible shudder passed
through him. "Two doctors are more than enough in any family, I
am convinced." He turned to the elder clergyman. "Are you a physician, then, Dr Worthing?"

"My doctorate is of divinity," Worthing replied, clearly wondering what sort of blockhead did not know that.

Griffiths glanced Hayden's way, much unsaid.

"Did I see golf clubs among the baggage being carried aboard?"
Saint-Denis enquired.

"They were mine," Worthing responded.

"I have been thought quite a golfer in my time," Saint-Denis informed them. "I only regret that I cannot indulge my skills oftener.
It is a capital game."

"It has been spoiled somewhat by this foolish notion to reduce it
from the proper twenty-two holes to an unholy eighteen. But I trust
such a wrongheaded idea will shortly fail. Do you not agree, Lieutenant?"

Saint-Denis smiled winningly. "Twenty-two is the proper number. I could not agree more."

"I have played but once," Wickham offered, "and only managed
nineteen. I was wholly fagged after that."

"But that was only your first attempt," Saint-Denis replied. "After
a few more matches you would soon see that twenty-two is the proper
number. Why, perhaps we shall have the opportunity to indulge in
a match someday, Wickham, and I will give you proper instruction.
It is an endeavour in which every kind of nonsense is promoted as
wisdom. When to use a track iron. Whether ash or hickory should
be employed for shafts. I will set you straight, you needn't worry on
that account."

Wickham did not look terribly grateful for this offer, but Saint-
Denis seemed rather pleased with his own generosity in the matter
of golf instruction.

"I am not sure that you will find a proper course upon which to play in the Mediterranean," Barthe offered innocently.

"I only hope to find a suitable bit of pasture, now and again, in which to practise," Worthing said. "Accomplishments are very easily lost if they are not kept up by repetition."

"That is why we have the men holy-stone the deck every morning," Saint-Denis said, laughing at his own wit.

"Why do you call it a holy-stone, pray?" Smosh asked.

Saint-Denis looked suddenly embarrassed, glancing around the table as though hoping someone might offer rescue, but no life-rings were thrown. "I do not know the answer to that, Mr Smosh," the lieutenant lied.

"Why, is it not because the stones used are the size and shape of the Christian Bible?" Gould asked.

Smosh laughed, earning him a withering look from Worthing, who was clearly offended by this insult to the holy book. The silent criticism did not affect Smosh in any way. He continued to take full enjoyment from the remark, his face turning crimson.

After a moment his laughter dwindled and he applied himself to his supper once again. "If I had known the fare aboard His Majesty's ships was of this quality, Captain Hayden, I would have considered a career in the Navy. I believe I would."

"It would appear you *do* have a career in the Navy, Mr Smosh," Griffiths pointed out.

Smosh was not the least offended, but only chuckled. "So I do, Dr Griffiths. So I do, and pleased I am about it, too. To have such fine companions and a chance to see some part of the larger world, not to mention the prize money . . . The Navy never came into my mind, and so I fell into the church for want of a better situation."

This admission caused a great reaction from Worthing. "You mean to say, sir, that you admit to entering the clergy for want of any true vocation?"

Smosh wiped his wine-moistened mouth with Hayden's new linen. "I do, most freely, but I must point out that the church does not much care by what means a man comes to it. The church has long been gaining souls, not through love of God, but out of fear of eternal damnation. Though I think it passing strange, the church does not consider the man who fears the fires—a coward by any definition— any less a Christian than the man who comes to the church out of true religious feeling. Therefore, I conclude that they do not much care how they get their ministers and consider the man who loves God no better than the one who comes for want of some better situation. It is all the same to Mother Church."

"This is not only an affront to the church," Worthing responded, so completely offended that he stumbled for words, "but it is an affront to . . . to God!"

"I don't know why you would feel so," Smosh replied mildly. "I know several men ashore in possession of not one but *two* livings who leave curates do all their duties but the occasional Sunday sermon. Their valuable time is spent in shooting and similar pursuits. You'd be as like to see these gentlemen at a ball as visiting the sick or even in their own churches. No, I am merely honest about my reasons for entering the church, and there is no merchandise in so little demand as honesty."

There was no saving the dinner after that, though thankfully it was soon over. After the guests had departed, Hawthorne and Griffiths sat with Hayden and took a glass of port.

"I dare say the gunroom shall not lack for amusement for a few weeks," Hawthorne observed. He appeared to be still so pleased by his exploits ashore that he was aglow, the trace of a self-satisfied little smile fixed continuously upon his face.

"Worthing was rather determined that he would be the only man aboard addressed as 'Doctor,' was he not?" Griffiths smiled.

"I thought the good doctor of divinity might have an apoplexy when Smosh began to philosophise on his reasons for joining the church." Hawthorne laughed. "And Smosh seemed hardly aware that he had offended the man to his core. Such innocence."

"It was not in the least innocent," Griffiths assured him. "It was carefully calculated and delivered so dryly as to appear without intent. Do not be taken in by Smosh's manner, Mr Hawthorne; it is utterly contrived, I am sure. Beneath the amiable half-wit offered up for public consumption lies a very shrewd mind. Much is hidden there, and for what reason I know not."

"Oh, Doctor, I am certain you are wrong. An empty head upon a rather replete body, that is the Reverend Mr Smosh. I dare say, he has a weakness for food, drink, and the fairer sex, if one may judge his appetites by this one night. Did you not hear him asking after the women we might meet upon our voyage? He was near to salivating."

"That weakness he may share with the rest of us, but weakness of mind is not at issue with him. You will see." Griffiths stood. "I should look in upon my charges, if you will excuse me."

Griffiths slipped quietly out, his footsteps retreating quickly to silence as he descended the stair.

"Have you ever noticed that each man has a footstep that is as characteristic as his voice?" Hawthorne asked. "Although the secret of man's character is said to be contained in the fairness or unfairness of his hand, or in the shape of his skull, I have come to believe it is in his footstep."

"Perhaps you should write a pamphlet on the subject," Hayden suggested, smiling.

"Perhaps I should. But think on it. . . . Have you never noticed that our doctor—or perhaps I should say 'surgeon'—has the lightest possible footfall? I think it is more than just chance or even some physical cause that dictates this. I believe it is a desire on his part to discommode no one. Not even the sound of his footfall should cause vexation to another. And this is not mere shrinking on his part. No, in the proper situation, Griffiths will offer his opinions or even con-tradict another. But he is, above all things, considerate."

"And what of Barthe? I can, from my cabin when the skylight is closed, hear the man walking on the forecastle . . . in a gale. Does this mean he has consideration for no one?"

Hawthorne laughed. "I don't believe the opposite holds true in all cases. Mr Barthe is stomping about because he is always fuming over something—the world is nothing but a constant affront to our sailing master's belief in the order of things. His stomping is much like his cursing—a manner of protest against the injustices of the Navy and life in general."

"You have been contemplating this for some time, I see."

"Only a few days. But I have begun to listen to the sound of men walking."

"I hate to think what you might comprehend from my manner of getting about."

"Oh, your footfall is easily understood, Captain. You know where you are going. It is a very decided footstep, yours. I know it the mo-ment you pass overhead. No deck can hide you from me."

"I know we are going to the Mediterranean, Mr Hawthorne. Beyond that all is hidden. Perhaps you will hear me stumbling about the deck in a few weeks, this way and that, one moment running, the next in a stagger."

"No. Never you, sir. Always firm and decided." He took a sip of his port, his expounding on the matter of footsteps exhausted, ap-parently.

"Well, here we are all together again, Mr Hawthorne."

The marine raised his glass as though in toast. "It is the greatest good fortune that we take such pleasure from each other's company, for no one else will have us," Hawthorne observed.

"It *is* good fortune. Your affairs in Bath were brought to a success-ful conclusion?"

"To my greatest satisfaction, Captain Hayden—kind of you to enquire." Hawthorne sat forward and spoke very softly. "By utter chance, I learned something of our doctor while in Bath. Did you know he joined the Navy to escape a situation? He was very attached to a young woman in Portsmouth and his hopes were terribly disappointed; her family, you see, did not approve of him."

"So it was not his family he came to sea to escape? I am sorry to hear of his ill fortune, though I should have known—he has hinted at it more than once, I now realise."

"There is more. When I learned of this I was determined to meet the lady, as her family were staying in Bath. I managed to discover her at a ball and insinuated my way into her company through the agency of an acquaintance. When first I saw her I thought that all made sense, for she was quite a striking beauty, but when I was near enough to hear her speak, I discovered that she was of the sort who has never been silent more than a moment altogether in her entire existence—I swear this woman must prattle on in her sleep—all while saying nothing of any interest or value. I know that love makes fools of the most practical, levelheaded individuals, but even so, I was astonished. For a moment I was struck with the idea that I would attach her feelings and then dash her hopes cruelly, repayment for all the pain she had caused our friend, but I soon came to my senses on that account. But then, some time later, I was talking to a handsome lady of great charm and learning, when I discovered that she was not only the elder sister of the woman I believed had so injured Griffiths, but in fact I had been misinformed. *She* was the lady who had occasioned the disappointment. In a way, this made much more sense—I could easily imagine the doctor falling under her spell. Here is how I learned it. When some few details of our cruise came out in the natural course of conversation, she asked me if I were not much more inclined to make a life ashore, now that I had witnessed all the dangers. I answered that we sailed with such a fine surgeon that we never worried— Griffiths would patch us up. 'Obediah Griffiths?' the younger sister

enquired. I had to laugh, partly from embarrassment and partly because I realised I had never known Griffiths' Christian name—and
now knew why. We quickly sorted out that, indeed, Obediah was the
very surgeon of whom I spoke. I saw her glance her elder sister's way,
and the poor woman, all of her animation of spirit dissolved. Someone in the circle made a polite enquiry about Griffiths' well-being—
on her behalf, I expect—and that was that."

"Poor Griffiths. He has joined a larger corps than the Navy in
that—the legion of disappointed hopes. Two years it has been since
he took ship. Has this lady married?"

"She has not, and much surprised you would be if you met her,
for she is of a perfectly good family—not rich, but with some prop-
erties and excellent history—and is herself amiable and thoughtful
and good-hearted. Just the sort of woman who would make Griffiths
a most satisfactory wife, though his family are certainly beneath her
own."

"Perhaps she has come to regret giving him up, if she felt as you
perceived when his name was mentioned. But there is little anyone
can do about it now. We are off tomorrow for points south. Griffiths
will have to find himself a new love." Hayden rose and cupped a
hand to a pane in the stern gallery, shading out reflections, and pressed
his face close to the damp glass so that he might peer into the darkness. "The wind, I swear, has been making all day, but the gale finally shows signs of blowing itself out."

"Perhaps we will finally get to sea, and the French will offer up
a ship to us so that we might add to our prize money."

Hayden turned away from the windows. "Our purpose on this
voyage will be to see that no British ships are offered up to the French."

Four

Pool was a terse, impatient man who appeared much offended to find himself put in charge of a convoy on his way to join Admiral Lord Hood. The massive cabin of his seventy-four-gun ship was crowded with the masters of the transports and the escort captains.

"I expect everyone to make enough sail to keep their place," Pool said loudly. "I will hear no excuses or tolerate the least independence in this matter. My signals are to be obeyed and repeated to the ships down the line. We must cross Biscay in this season, and I do not plan to heave-to until spring. Is that understood? Weather will not be with us, and we must make the best of any wind we can." He looked around at the gathered captains and masters, almost daring some poor fool to ask a question. "Even so late in the year, the French will be on the lookout for us. They cannot have failed to learn of our convoy forming, and will snatch any who lag behind. Hayden will bring up the rear in the *Themis*, but he cannot abandon that position to rescue your ship if you fall out of line." He held up a small book. "Everyone has their copy of the signal book and my instructions? Good. If any among you has a question, ask it now."

But no one did . . . or perhaps dared. The masters went out, muttering, leaving the escort captains behind.

Pool gathered them round a table, where a chart had been unrolled, his sailing master dumbly at hand. "I will not hide it from you:

I am much out of humour with this convoy duty. I have reason to be in the Mediterranean where Toulon is endangered, and my presence will serve some real purpose. These masters will do everything within their power to hamper us, but I have learned that the loss of but one ship to French privateers will add a little urgency to all their evolutions and speed their indolent crews. Let us hope some enterprising Frenchman gathers up a laggard sooner rather than later so the lesson is quickly learned."

Hayden dearly hoped that Pool said this in jest, but there was nothing in his manner or face to suggest that it was not utterly in earnest.

Pool put his finger on the chart. "We must give Ushant a much wider berth than I should like, and keep all these unweatherly vessels away from the French coast, for gales from the south-west are too common in this season. We all know it is a bloody foolish notion to send a convoy to sea so late in the year, but we must make the best of it. I expect you all to do your part in hurrying these ships along and to bring the majority of them safely to Gibraltar. Captain Stewart shall be the whipper-in and try to keep transports in their places and carrying sail." He glanced up at Hayden. "You have not made your post, Hayden, but I expect you to play your part, even so. If a French squadron appears, you must be prepared to meet them until such time as we can send you aid and, if aid is not possible, to forestall them as long as you can that the convoy might get clear. Is that understood? Your crew is up to it?"

"Completely up to it, sir."

The other captains glanced slyly one to the other. Faint Hart's crew, it seemed, had a reputation that its recent endeavours had not yet erased.

Thirty-one transports made up the convoy along with Pool's seventy-four, Bradley's *Syren*, a twenty-six-gun frigate, and four other vessels—two schooners, an armed brig, and, to Hayden's dismay, the *Kent*. Her captain, a lieutenant recently promoted to master and commander, stood across the table from Hayden. He could have been a schoolmate of Wickham's, he displayed such a youthful appearance. A little smile of happiness would spread over his face at times, to be chased away by mock seriousness.

He is utterly thrilled to be here, among his elders, Hayden realised, but they are men of experience—he is playing at war.

"I understand your little schooner is a flyer, McIntosh?"

"She is that, sor," McIntosh answered, unable to hide his pride.

"Then you will carry my signals throughout the convoy when the weather is too close for them to be clearly seen."

"I will, sor." McIntosh, whom Hayden knew slightly, had been even more recently made master and commander, despite being a few years older than Hayden and most of his life at sea. It was always surprising to realise there were officers in His Majesty's Navy with less interest even than he.

Pool gazed down at the chart of Biscay, as though the hidden positions of privateers and French cruisers could be made out if one but stared long enough. His right hand rose automatically and massaged his temple in a gentle, circular motion.

"I will station the *Kent* to the west—likely to windward. Do not be alarmed, Jones: although French cruisers would almost certainly attack from windward, I expect to meet only small privateers, and they will be on the lookout for stragglers and position themselves to leeward and aft of the convoy. Captain Bradley shall take the leeward position in *Syren*." He glanced up at the others. "In truth, gales shall be our greatest enemy. If the fleet is driven to leeward and any appreciable number of ships separated from it, they will be in real danger of becoming prizes." He straightened and looked quickly around the gathered captains, his eye meeting that of each man in turn. "I have made myself clear, I hope?"

Nods and sounds of agreement.

"Hayden, if you would stay a moment, I wish to speak with you." He nodded to the others. "Keep a sharp watch for my signals, obey them without hesitation, and, God willing, we shall raise Gibraltar in a fortnight."

Shoes clattered on the wooden deck as the captains made their way out, each more gracious than the other, insisting this officer or that go first. Pool watched them leave, his gaze thoughtful. He could stand beneath the greater deck beams, making him five feet and perhaps nine inches. (Hayden, by contrast, could stand only between the beams.) Women, Hayden guessed, would find him a handsome man, dark-haired and -eyed, face well formed, though slightly marked by the smallpox—less than many. An athletic manner of moving and build gave him great presence in a room. A man not to be trifled with, that was certain.

"I will be perfectly candid, Hayden, and tell you that I would rather have a post captain in command of your frigate. I know you were Hart's first lieutenant, but I expect you to take your place in the convoy and not to shrink from enemy ships, no matter their rate or weight of broadside. Is that understood?"

Hayden felt his ears and neck suddenly flush with heat. "Perfectly, sir. And let me say that I was Hart's lieutenant for a few weeks, only. Before that I was Captain Bourne's senior lieutenant, and he would be the first to tell you that I am neither fearful to meet the enemy nor lacking competence in the management of my ship."

The look on Pool's face, barely controlled outrage, told Hayden that he had spoken out of turn.

"Did I ask you for a history of your service, Hayden?"

"You did not, sir."

"No, I did not. But I will ask you why Bourne, a captain very senior to me on the list, has command of a frigate, only. Why has he never been put into a seventy-four or a flagship?"

"He has turned them down, sir," Hayden responded, jumping to his friend's defense. "The first lord knows that he was made to be a frigate commander. The day Captain Bourne is given his pennant will be a great loss to the service—though he will make a very fine admiral, I am sure."

"He will never fly his flag, Hayden, believe me." Pool's voice and manner altered but a little, the edge of outrage replaced by something else—firm conviction and a touch of concern. "The day Bourne leaves frigates will be his last day of active duty. Men like Bourne do not understand the workings of the Navy. He has condemned himself, foolishly, to a brief career, for he has never once proven himself capable of more." Pool shook his head in something like frustration. "I will grant Bourne his well-advertised bravery, and I hope this example has been well and truly learned by you."

"I will not disappoint you, Captain."

"Then be off to your ship," Pool responded, not unkindly. "We make sail immediately."

On deck Hayden found Jones lingering by the rail, and when he saw Hayden he crossed to him immediately. "It seems, Captain Hayden," Jones began, "that I have been given a ship meant for you. I was much concerned for any wound this might have caused, but see you have been put into a frigate. My congratulations!"

"I am conveying her to Lord Hood, who will find her a post captain. But do not concern yourself. I hold no grudge against you for the actions of admirals and higher officials."

"Very decent of you." Jones paused. "Have you been on convoy before?"

"Oftener than I would like. Yourself?"

"One or two, in the North Sea. Rather boring business, commonly. I expect this will be the same . . . but for the weather, perhaps."

"I am sure that boredom, in this case, is a wish common to us all."

"Oh, not at all, Captain Hayden," Jones informed him. "Captain Pool and Bradley are hoping they might have the opportunity to take a prize!"

Hayden smiled. "I am quite certain they were jesting."

The man looked slightly offended. "Not in the least were they jesting. They have both taken a number of prizes this year—small ones, admittedly—but they are hoping for greater things. I'm quite certain they meant every word."

Hayden went down into his cutter wondering what kind of people he had fallen in with; the commodore thought him a coward for no reason other than his service with Hart, and it seemed Pool and Bradley believed themselves on a cruise.

"He has mistaken you for Landry," Hawthorne responded when Hayden related his meeting with Pool.

"Perhaps, but I fear too many within the service have heard only Hart's tale of our cruise and not got it from some more reliable source."

A knock on the door of the great cabin and then Archer thrust his head in at Hayden's bidding.

"We are ready to weigh, sir."

"I shall be on deck directly," Hayden replied. He retrieved a hat from his lovely table and went out and up the stairs, stopping only for an instant on the gun-deck to be sure that all the men were in their places.

"It is a relief to see men both ready and willing to perform their duties," Hawthorne said as they ascended the ladder to the deck.

"I was thinking the same." Hayden could not help but remember the day in Plymouth when half the crew had all but refused to sail. How many lives might that have preserved had they been successful? And why were they not? Because Hayden had intervened and convinced the men to sail, preserving Hart's command and leading to all that followed. Performing one's duty should not be so fraught with ambiguity.

Hayden quickly surveyed the gathered convoy, a collection of ships of every size and shape. They anchored in no particular order, all streaming to a faint nor'east breeze, like so many horses straining at their tethers. Signals fluttered aloft on the flagship, visible against a dull sky.

"We have permission to weigh and make sail." Hayden turned to Saint-Denis. "Take her out, Lieutenant, if you please."

Saint-Denis touched his hat, his most charming smile in place—a smile that Hayden was already coming to detest. "This is an excellent opportunity for Archer to perform this duty, Captain. But I shall watch over his shoulder and be certain that everything is done handsomely. You needn't be concerned for a moment about Archer's inexperience."

Before Hayden could respond, Saint-Denis had gone off calling for Archer.

Hawthorne, who had been standing but a few feet away, glanced over at Hayden, his eyebrows rising only a little. A slow fuse of anger had been lit in Hayden's breast.

At that moment a cutter under sail drew near. *"Ahoy, Themis!"* her coxswain called. *"Post."*

Sitting in the stern-sheets by the coxswain was Griffiths' assistant, Ariss, a number of packages balanced in his lap. The post came over the rail with the surgeon's mate.

"Will you open it, Mr Hawthorne?" Hayden asked. "Saint-Denis' summons might be within."

"God willing," the marine lieutenant muttered. Hawthorne opened the bag and began quickly sorting through letters and packages. "Here is a letter for him . . . and another."

The first lieutenant had paused on the gangway and was looking back toward the quarterdeck, his attention captured by the call of mail. Hayden motioned to him and Saint-Denis jogged quickly back.

"Letters for you, Lieutenant."

Saint-Denis took them from Hawthorne with barely a nod and, walking away a few feet, tore open the first. He read, squinting at the creamy square, then turned his back before opening the second. There was no mistaking the fall of his shoulders, his long arms dropping away, the letters shivering loosely in the muted breeze. Hastily he shoved them into his coat, a long-fingered hand massaging his brow absently, then he walked silently back down the gangway to observe the anchor being catted, his buckled shoes making no sound.

"Apparently he has not been recalled to glory," Hawthorne whispered.

"No. Davies has very deftly avoided command of the *Themis* and shed his first lieutenant in the same stroke."

"His cunning is almost admirable," Hawthorne said.

"Isn't it, though?"

Hayden walked forward a little, watching his crew work. The new men were fitting in well, and Franks was unable to find a soul to start, but limped about flexing his rattan and scowling threateningly. Forward, Wickham was explaining the evolutions to the new midshipman, pointing here and there, Gould attentive to his every word and gesture. Archer quietly gave orders to Mr Barthe and Franks that were passed along sharply to the men. The somnolent lieutenant appeared surprisingly confident, even cheerful.

To avoid thirty ships all weighing at once, Pool had ordered the most leeward ten to make sail, to be followed immediately by the next decade, and then the last eleven. Tor Bay was crowded and they would more easily make their sailing formation—the transports in a rough square surrounded by their escorts—out in the Channel.

Mr Barthe came and stood by him, speaking trumpet under his arm.

"My compliments to you and Mr Franks." Hayden nodded to the sailing master. "The hands appear to know their business very well."

"They will take a fair amount of working up, sir," Barthe allowed, "but we will make a crew of them, yet. Like many who have not served in His Majesty's Navy, they show a marked increase in enthusiasm when we exercise the guns, but they have yet to fire a single shot."

"I think they will make a crack crew, Mr Barthe. In fact, I have no doubt of it. We are short a lieutenant and a middy or two, but we will make do. I believe I shall promote Wickham to acting third lieutenant. Do you think he can manage it?"

"He is already more competent than several lieutenants I have sailed with." Barthe did not glance toward Saint-Denis, though he did not need to. "But he is barely sixteen—three years shy of the age such responsibilities would normally be given."

"If I had a midshipman of eighteen or nineteen years I would give the position to him, but we are deficient in several ways—a mere master and commander for a captain, one lieutenant short, fewer middies than I would like, a ship no captain will take, and a crew no one will have. What am I to do?"

Barthe laughed. "When you state it so, Captain, I cannot argue. It is Mr Wickham for third lieutenant."

"I am pleased you agree."

Sail was made with an alacrity that pleased Hayden even more, and the frigate gathered way and set out into the Channel. Much of a fair wind was wasted forming up the transports, but finally the convoy shaped its course downchannel and for the distant ocean. Sail was soon reduced to allow them to keep pace with the slowest transport—the vessel that would set the speed for their passage, which, despite Pool's constant signals to make all sail, was going to be very slow indeed.

Leaving Archer as officer of the watch, Hayden went below to his cabin. Passing by the scuttle over the gunroom, he heard laughter and conversation within and imagined Hawthorne pouring wine for all and sundry. His cabin seemed both empty and damply cool when he entered, despite the lamps his servant had lit. For a moment he stood in the centre of this vast space—many times the size of his cabin off the gunroom—and felt a strange sense of separation.

"You aspired to it," he muttered aloud, then peeled off his coat and hung it on the back of a chair. The ship heeled but little to the small wind, bobbing over the short sea kicked up by flooding tide and outbound wind.

The marine sentry let his servant in and Hayden asked for coffee. The sentry made a knuckle and cleared his throat as the servant passed. "One of the men asked me give you this," he said, holding out a sodden square of paper. "He found it on the deck, sir."

Hayden took the sheet of paper and held it up to the light. The ink had blotted and run over most of what was apparently a letter and was only barely legible here and there.

. . . *ese debts, accrued against my express wishes, will not be honour* . . .

And then, near the bottom: . . . *make your own way in th* . . .

Hayden attempted no more, but sent for Saint-Denis. The lieutenant arrived a moment later, his colour high—from drink, no doubt.

"You wished to see me, sir?"

Hayden proffered the sodden letter. "This was found on the deck. I wondered if it might belong to you?"

Saint-Denis took the letter, glanced at it, folded it quickly, and hid hands and letter behind his back. "Does everyone aboard know what it says, then?"

Hayden shook his head. "The man brought it to me because he could not read, and it is all but blotted, anyway."

Neither knew what to say.

Saint-Denis looked like a man who had been told his wife had died. "No flagship, it seems," he said, attempting a little self-mockery.

Hayden shrugged, unsure how to respond.

Saint-Denis nodded—at the ship, Hayden guessed. "Only this."

"It is possible to work one's way up through the service without interest."

"As you have done?"

Hayden tried to muzzle his offence at this remark. "It is not the quickest route, I admit, but still possible . . . for a competent officer who distinguishes himself."

"Good to learn it is not hopeless. Will there be anything more, Captain?"

"Yes. One thing." Hayden paused to choose his words. "When I give you an order, I do not expect you to pass the duty on to Archer. You will perform it. Do you understand?"

Saint-Denis gazed back at him with ill-concealed resentment. "I am the first officer. Am I expected to scamper aloft and take in sail?"

Hayden's not-inconsiderable temper flooded up. "You know precisely to what I refer. If you do not feel equal to the duties of first lieutenant, please tell me so. I am quite certain Archer can perform them competently."

The man shook his head, glancing away. "That will not be necessary."

"As we are short a lieutenant, I will have to ask you to stand watch. Wickham will be acting third until a new officer is sent aboard. That will be all."

Saint-Denis went stiffly out, the sound of his footsteps echoing back through the door as the soles of his shoes bumped slowly down the stairs, stopped, and then continued.

Coffee arrived and the acting captain poured himself a cup with a hand trembling from anger.

"Send word for Mr Wickham, if you please," he said to his servant. At least he would have good news for someone.

The coffee, steaming and strong, had the effect of an elixir. It turned his mood and changed his view of the world. Wickham arrived and Hayden offered the youngster coffee.

"Thank you, sir." The boy sat expectantly, waiting to learn the cause of his summons. There was such a contrast between Wickham's will to please and to excel in his duties and the character of Saint-Denis—a dilettante if Hayden had ever met one. Wickham would make his way in the service if his father were a tradesman. His connexions were helpful but not necessary.

"Can I assume, Mr Wickham, that if I offered to make you acting lieutenant you would not refuse?"

"No, sir, I would not! Thank you, sir! It is a great honour."

"It is a great necessity. You are yet sixteen and should not be thrust into such a position for several years, but we have need of a lieutenant and I believe you will fulfil the position admirably."

"I will do everything within my power not to disappoint you, Mr Hayden. I mean, Captain."

"I have no doubt. I regret you cannot have a cabin in the gunroom, but the clergy have taken two. I'm sure you will be very welcome in the mess, however."

"Thank you, sir."

"How is our new middy adapting to life afloat? Not seasick, I hope."

"Not in the least, sir. No, he has a great store of knowledge about ships and the Navy, Captain. Far more than I could claim when first I came aboard. But then, he has been around ships most of his life." Wickham paused. "His father is a bum-boat man."

Hayden was surprised. "He told you."

"No, sir. I recognised him. On occasion he would aid his father . . . when not in school. I am sure I am not the only one who will remember him, Captain."

"Do you anticipate a problem?"

Wickham raised his cup and, gazing down into it, swirled the liquid. "Well, sir, his faith means nothing to me, but the admiralty might feel differently."

"He is prepared to take the sacrament, if required."

"So he's become Christian, then? There is no impediment to his service?"

"You heard what Mr Smosh said at dinner—the church does not much care how people come to it. Like the good reverend, perhaps,

Gould had more need of a career than a new faith, but I shall not sit in judgement."

"He is very bright and capable; I hope the men accept him."

"Yes, let us hope they do. Enquire of Saint-Denis what watch he would have you stand."

"Aye, sir. And thank you again, Captain."

Hayden waved a hand in dismissal. "You might as well join the play—acting captain, acting lieutenant. We are all actors here, it seems, and all the sea's our stage." Thoughts of "Romeo" Moat made Hayden smile.

Outside the door, Wickham's dignified retreat turned into a joyous gallop, the sound of his shoes clattering down the stairs—a colt released into a spring field.

Having accepted a dinner invitation from the gunroom for the evening next, Hayden supped alone in his cabin, constantly listening to the sound of the wind and measuring the sea state by the motion of the ship. The northerly was holding and bearing them out toward the Atlantic, but it was a cold wind and Hayden was pleased to see his supper arrive steaming.

When lids were removed from chafing dishes, Hayden was surprised to find a meal in the French style, with exquisite sauces and cooked to a nicety.

"Good God," he said finally to his steward, "did Jefferies produce this meal? It is exquisite!"

The steward was suppressing a self-satisfied grin. "Not quite, sir. Childers and Dryden learned you didn't have no cook, sir, so they found you one. I hope you don't mind, sir."

"Mind? They are to be commended. I shall thank them myself. Who is this man—the cook, I mean?"

"Rosseau, Captain."

"He's French. . . ." Hayden felt a sudden apprehension. "An *émigré*?"

"I don't rightly know, Captain, but I should think so."

"Well, I am happy such a man would agree to come to sea. I shall

have to meet him. Would you bring him when I am finished? And
Childers and Dryden too, if Saint-Denis can spare them."

"Aye, sir."

When Hayden had finished overeating, Childers and Dryden
came trooping in, followed by a third: an oddly shaped, almost misshapen, face crowned by coarse coal-dust hair. His eyes were aston-
ishingly dark, large and fevered-looking. Skin pale and glossy, chin
small, cheekbones high and overly large. Hayden hoped the man was
not ill, for certainly, he looked it.

Hayden rose from his chair. "This is the man who prepared the
exquisite meal?"

"Yes, sir," Childers answered. "He don't speak much English, but
you'll find his French is crackin'."

"And speaking of finding, wherever *did* you find such a man?"

Childers and Dryden glanced at each other, oddly uncomfortable.
"In Plymouth, sir."

"So he *is* an *émigré*." Hayden turned to the cook. *"Vous êtes un
émigré, n'est-ce pas?"*

The man looked confused. *"Non, monsieur . . . le ponton."*

Hayden's smile melted. "A hulk . . ."

The Frenchman nodded. *"Oui,* the 'ulk."

Hayden turned on Dryden and Childers. "Not a prison hulk . . ."

Dryden threw his hands up and looked at Childers, alarmed. "We
thought he was wandering around Plymouth looking for a position,
sir. That's what we were told."

"And who told you this?"

Both Childers and Dryden looked flummoxed, now. "Well, sir,
this fellow, uh . . . I don't rightly know his proper name."

"Monsieur . . . Worth," Rosseau said, his comprehension of English
clearly better than had been represented. *"Monsieur Worth,"* he said
again, nodding hopefully.

"Worth . . ." Hayden could not quite believe what he was hearing.
"Our Worth? Speak up!"

"Aye, Captain," Childers admitted.

Hayden turned to Rosseau. *"How did you come to England?"* he asked in French.

"I was the captain's chef, monsieur, aboard the Dragoon.*"*

"The Dragoon*!"*

The man nodded, a curious bobbing of his small head.

Hayden turned back to his coxswain and master's mate, both of whom stood ramrod straight, eyes fixed forward. "And Worth got him out of a hulk? Bloody hell, was no one thinking? The authorities will be looking for him."

"They'll give it up after a few days . . . won't they?" Dryden responded softly.

"We thought you might like to have a French cook, sir, as we know you're fond of their victuals," Childers spluttered.

"Indeed I would, Childers," Hayden said, *"if he were not a prisoner of war!"* Hayden paced across the cabin. Worth would be involved in this—the man who had risked prison, at Hayden's request, to steal back Barthe's logbook. He was greatly in Worth's debt . . . and now look what the man had done! "Well, there isn't anything for it now. He can't swim back to Plymouth, and we will all be in some difficulties if we turn him in." Hayden stopped to stare at the two crewmen. No one returned his gaze. "We shall have to keep him, for the present."

"Shall he continue cooking for you? He's on the books, sir."

"What else would he do? Fight the French?"

"I don't imagine he's much of a fighter, sir," Dryden offered meekly.

Hayden almost laughed at the absurdity of the situation. "No, I don't imagine he is. Back to your duties."

Dryden turned as he was about to pass through the doorway. "Is Worth in trouble, sir?"

"You are all in trouble, Mr Dryden. I just don't know exactly what kind or how to mete out punishment to men who intended me

such a kindness. No more such gestures, Mr Dryden. Do you hear?
And tell Worth the same."

"Aye, sir."

Hayden nodded to the chef, who looked confused by these strange
Englishmen. "Excellent meal, Monsieur Rosseau. *Très bon. Merci.*"

Five

Winds, varied in strength and point of origin, carried the convoy fitfully across Biscay. Ushant was left, unseen, to larboard, as Pool hoped to slip out of the Channel and into the Atlantic without privateers being alerted to their presence. But the chops of the Channel was one of the busiest shipping areas on earth, and sails were seen. Hayden had no doubt that news of their convoy was speeding faster than they were. They would not outrun it.

Unable to sleep and suffering mild dyspepsia, Hayden took the deck at dawn of their third day. He found Wickham and Barthe on the quarterdeck, huddled in muted conversation. The night was very close, the decks wet from an earlier rain, but there was little weight in the wind—north-west by west. Before them he could see a few fitful lights of the convoy vessels, winking in and out of being.

Hayden addressed the helmsmen loudly, to alert his officers to his presence. Many a captain had come on deck to hear himself being discussed, not always in the most flattering terms, and Hayden wanted to avoid that.

"Captain," Barthe said, touching his hat.

Hayden greeted them in return. "All is well, I hope?" Their manner, serious, almost anxious, made him wonder if this was true.

"We believe so, sir," Barthe replied, "but Mr Wickham thinks he saw a light about an hour ago, off our starboard quarter some two miles distant. And then again more abeam just a few moments ago."

"It was just for an instant, sir, when the rain let up."

"Have we a straggler?" Hayden turned and looked out to sea in the direction the light had been seen. Wickham could discern more in the dark than any man aboard, so Hayden was inclined to take this seriously.

"I hope not, Captain," Barthe said, "but it would not surprise me. Even so, we have had no signal if a ship has fallen behind."

"It will be light soon, and then we shall know." Hayden made a tour of the deck, speaking with the sentries and some of the hands. He was trying to learn the names of the new men and make judgements as to their characters. A number had been sailors in the merchant fleet and were fitting in well, but among the landsmen, most of whom had been impressed, there was, if not discontent, despondency and confusion. Hayden had seen this before: men taken from their familiar world and thrown into a situation they neither aspired to nor understood. A hostile sea all around, enemy ships seeking them. It was enough to undermine the stoutest character. A little prize money would set them to rights, Hayden thought. But there would be little chance of that on convoy duty.

By the time Hayden had completed his circuit of the deck, the eastern sky had paled to tarnished silver and the dull waters stretched, restive, to a near horizon. Stepping back onto the quarterdeck, Hayden found Barthe and Wickham standing at the rail, the corpulent sailing master beside the slender youth. Wickham was pointing to the west and they were both staring with some intensity.

"There! Did you see?" Wickham clapped the master on the arm.

"No. But I cannot think that one of our transports has climbed so far to windward. Ah, Captain," Barthe said as Hayden approached, "Wickham has found sails out in the murk. One ship on our beam and maybe a schooner hurrying away to the north-east. Shall we signal Pool?"

Hayden leaned his hands on the wet rail and felt the chill bite into him. "Have the flags readied, but let us wait a moment. Perhaps we can discover what manner of ship this is."

Light penetrated the clouds slowly, revealing the myriad shades of grey. For a moment it appeared to grow darker, but finally the brightening sky, and a momentary break in the distant murk, revealed sails and a dark, unmistakable hull.

"Not one of our transports," Hayden pronounced, and felt his breath suddenly grow short. He raised his hands, but instead of slamming fists down on wood, he slapped them down gently.

"I could not make her out," Barthe said, still squinting into the distance. "What manner of ship?"

"A frigate, Mr Barthe," Wickham informed him. "Shall I make the signal, Captain?"

"Yes. Pool has likely seen her himself, but let us not count on that. Call all hands, Mr Barthe. We shall beat to quarters."

A moment later the remaining middies tumbled out on the deck, the officers in their wake. Hawthorne, pulling on his pipe-clayed straps, crossed to Hayden.

"Privateers?" he wondered, finding Hayden with a glass held to his eye.

"It is a frigate, Mr Hawthorne," Hayden replied, not lowering the glass. "Very likely French, though she has not the courtesy to show her colours."

He passed the glass to the marine lieutenant, who steadied it against a shroud.

"We were not expecting that," Hawthorne said. "She is raising her colours, Captain. Do you see?"

"On deck! A hoist of flags going aloft," the lookout called from above.

A train of massive flags, twelve feet broad, became barely visible between the sails.

"She's signalling," Hawthorne said, confused. "To whom?"

"Well, Mr Hawthorne," Hayden ventured. "We have differing possibilities; she has confederates just over the horizon whom we cannot discern, or she is signalling to no one at all but hoping we will believe she is not alone."

"But which is it?" Hawthorne asked.

"If I knew that, Mr Hawthorne, I should be a seer, not a sailor." Hayden nodded to Saint-Denis, who came up at that moment. "We have a consort ship, it seems, Lieutenant, feeling a bit lonely on the great ocean."

Saint-Denis raised his glass, his mouth drawn in a thin line, skin pallid. "How many others are there, I wonder."

"We will know by and by," Barthe said, appearing beside them. "If there is a squadron, the ships will soon show themselves."

"Signals, Captain!" Wickham called out, pointing to the convoy ships that ranged out before them. Wickham clambered up onto the rail, took hold of the shrouds, and leaned out to gain a better view. His shadow, midshipman Gould, stood on the deck, gazing forward.

"I believe Captain Pool wishes us to exchange places with the *Kent*," Gould said to Wickham. "Or have I got it wrong?"

Wickham swung around and smiled at his protégé. "It is right in every way—and without a signal book to hand. Well done, Gould!" He turned to Hayden. "Did you hear, Captain? We are to exchange our place with the *Kent*."

"Yes. Mr Barthe, make sail. If the wind shifts into the sou'west, which I believe it will this day, we shall have a nasty turn to windward to catch the *Kent*." Hayden turned and found the bosun a dozen yards away in the midst of men releasing the quarterdeck carronades. "Make all speed, Mr Franks. Let us show Pool that we know our business."

Archer and Wickham knew their jobs well and sped the men in their work. In the midst of the ship being cleared for action, sail was made, yards braced, sail trimmed, and the helm put over. They began to overtake the convoy, sailing out toward the western edge of the ragged formation toward the ship that was once to have been Hayden's.

A long ground-swell from the south-west reached them, and the sound of the *Themis* rising and parting each low sea would have gladdened Hayden's heart if the ground-swell had not been a harbinger of bad weather—and from an unfavourable point of the compass, too.

Hayden fixed the French frigate in his glass and watched her put a little sea room between them, perhaps thinking the *Themis* was being sent out to challenge her.

"She is keeping her distance, Captain," Hawthorne observed. "I would say her people are a bit shy of us, though they boast thirty-six guns to our thirty-two."

"Her captain is merely being prudent, Mr Hawthorne, fearing Pool's seventy-four might be brought into any action." Hayden called for Wickham.

"Sir?" Wickham replied, hurrying onto the quarterdeck and touching his hat.

"How certain were you of this sail going north?" Hayden asked the boy.

Wickham peered off north, as though he might yet catch a second glimpse of this phantom. "Quite certain, sir. A schooner, I think, shaping her course for Brest."

Hayden nodded. "I will send a message to Captain Pool. It is not news that will improve his humour, but if there will soon be a French squadron hunting us, he should be apprised of it. I will write Pool a note. Signal McIntosh that I have a letter for Captain Pool."

Before Hayden could go below to his desk, the clergymen appeared on deck, Worthing red-faced and in obvious ill humour. He glared about, spotted Hayden, and stomped across the deck to him.

"Mr Hayden, not only have I been insulted by your surgeon, but I am being prevented from exercising the duties of my office! I demand you discipline this man immediately."

Smosh followed meekly behind, though Hayden thought he saw just a hint of pleasure flicker across the pudgy face.

"Whatever do you mean, Dr Worthing?" Hayden asked. "What duties of your office?"

"Mr Griffiths will not allow me to visit in his sick-berth, to which place I had gone to bring comfort to the sick and hurt."

"Ah," Hayden said. "Did Dr Griffiths not explain that the seamen believe that a clergymen visiting in the sick-berth is a sure sign that one of them will die?"

"Are we to run our ship on superstition!" Worthing thundered. "It is no wonder that you are not a proper captain."

A sudden urge to throw this pompous ass into the sea came over Hayden, and he stepped back, clasping his hands behind his back lest they failed to resist this temptation.

"I do not give way to superstition when it comes to the running of my ship, Doctor, but in this one matter there is no choice. The men will not go to the doctor if a clergyman is allowed to visit them, and then all manner of illness can spread before Dr Griffiths is even aware of it. So, I am sorry, but I must insist that you—both of you—not enter the sick-berth."

But Worthing was not about to concede this point and if anything became angrier. "What kind of heathens are these men that they will turn their backs on the God of the Christians when they are ill?"

Hayden's temper got the better of him, but he managed to speak evenly. "No offence, Doctor, but I do not believe you are the God of the Christians."

Smosh turned away, his shoulders shaking silently.

Worthing drew himself up. "I did not for a moment suggest that I was. You are aware, Mr Hayden, that my presence was requested in the Mediterranean fleet by the Lord Admiral himself."

"A very impressive credential, I am sure, but I can tell you with authority that the parson aboard the *Victory* does not visit in the sick-berth; Lord Hood would not allow it."

"That cannot be true."

"It is, if I may say it, God's truth. Ask any officer aboard. It is a tradition of the Royal Navy, Dr Worthing, and I must ask that you respect it."

"Well, it is a foolish, apostatical tradition, and I am not pleased by it. I have half a mind to bring this before Commodore Pool—if he is a commodore and not some crossbreed of a master and a lieutenant whom Navy tradition demands I address as 'Lord High Admiral.'"

"I can assure you that such an action will not endear you to Captain Pool, nor will it improve your situation aboard this ship. I am to convey you to the Mediterranean, Doctor, but you have no official capacity aboard the *Themis*. You are a guest, and I expect you to conduct yourself accordingly. Now, I am in the middle of clearing this ship for action and must ask that you remove yourself from harm's way for the time being. Excuse me." And Hayden turned away. He would never have spoken thus to Worthing if the man had not insulted him so—and upon his own quarterdeck! Had the man no common sense at all?

Hayden soon caught the *Kent*, and the little ship dropped back into position in the convoy's wake and then exchanged places with Bradley's frigate so that the *Kent* was on the opposite side of the convoy to the enemy ship.

The day wore on, wind varying a point or two this way or that, making a little, then taking off. Rain, icy cold and hard as hail, stuttered down upon the deck like beads of glass. A confused northwesterly sea overlaid a long ground-swell from the south-west, rolling the *Themis* in a strange, unnatural manner. Seamen easily adjusted themselves to a ship's rhythm, but this day it had none, rolling and rising in ways no one could predict.

Hawthorne and Barthe stood by the taffrail, eyes fixed upon the ominous frigate that maintained its distant vigil. Twice since the morning she had moved out nearer the western horizon and made signals to invisible ships, but then she would resume her place, two-thirds of a league distant, her course parallel to their own.

"I have never known a ground-swell to last so long without bad weather following," Hawthorne observed to the sailing master.

Barthe shifted uneasily. "No, and when it does happen it is commonly a sign of hard weather coming. Ah, Captain," he said as Hayden approached. "Do you think we are in for a harsh gale?"

"This ground-swell is making me fearful, that is certain."

Hawthorne, who suffered a little illness in bad weather, did not look happy. "Well, we have come through many a gale," he said stoically. "I expect we shall do so again."

"No doubt, Mr Hawthorne."

The schooner *Phalarope* appeared among the sails of the convoy, her course clearly set for the *Themis*. In a few moments she had rounded the *Themis* and ranged up alongside, a ship-length to leeward.

"Captain Hayden!" McIntosh called. The man stood at the rail, back to a sudden rain squall, his head drawn down beneath his sou'wester. "The commodore requests that you come aboard *Majestic*."

"Pass the word for Saint-Denis," Hayden ordered.

"Aye, sir."

Hayden reluctantly passed command of his ship to Saint-Denis and climbed down into the *Phalarope*'s boat. As the boat pushed off from the *Themis*, Hayden was hailed from aloft and looked up to see Wickham in the tops, hand cupped to his mouth, calling down over the sound of wind and sea.

"Captain Hayden, sir! I believe I saw a sail on the horizon. Beyond the frigate."

"Are you certain, Mr Wickham?" Hayden called back.

The midshipman hesitated a moment. "No, sir. 'Tis thick as mud out there, sir, but even so, it appeared to be a sail."

"Can you see it now?"

Wickham looped an arm around a stay, then raised his glass, sweeping it slowly across an obscure horizon. "No, sir, I cannot."

"Keep looking. If you perceive a sail, have Saint-Denis send word to Pool immediately."

"Aye, Captain."

The oarsmen dug in, and a moment later Hayden was aboard the schooner and making his way among the ships of the convoy. Hayden was made uncomfortable by Wickham's report and borrowed McIntosh's glass to examine the horizon himself.

"Do you think he really saw a ship, Hayden?" McIntosh asked.

"Many a time he has spotted vessels before any man aboard. It is not impossible."

McIntosh gazed thoughtfully out toward the western mists. "If there were French ships over the horizon, why would they hide themselves away?"

"I don't know, but I fear we will soon learn."

Phalarope made the rounds of the escorting vessels and carried all the captains up to *Majestic,* where they went quickly aboard. Oilskins were shed and taken by servants before the gathered officers were let into the captain's cabin.

Pool appeared as impatient as always, pacing across the cabin as they entered. He stopped as the officers filed in, and waved them to chairs gathered round his table.

"We have no time for pleasantries," he began, taking his place, standing, at the head of the table. He leaned forward and put his hands on the back of his chair. "As you no doubt all know by now, one of Hayden's middies saw a schooner hurrying north at first light. I have decided not to wait until it returns with a squadron. I propose to engage and take the lone frigate just before sunrise. Thus, if a squadron does overtake us, there will be one ship fewer for us to fight."

Hayden could feel the excitement and anticipation among the gathered officers. He felt it himself, and hated to be the one to ruin this mood.

"If I may speak, Captain Pool, the same midshipman thought he saw a sail on the western horizon just moments ago. Certainly the French frigate has been signalling as though to ships in that direction."

"Did you see this sail, Hayden?" Pool demanded.

"I did not, sir, but he was in the tops and I had just climbed down into McIntosh's cutter."

"Was he certain?" Bradley enquired.

"No. I questioned him and he was not, but he has better eyes than any man I know, so I think it is something that should be carefully weighed in any discussion."

"There is no discussion, Hayden," Pool stated firmly. "But you needn't worry—Bradley and I will go after the frigate and you will stay with the convoy, so there will be no danger to you."

Hayden almost rose to his feet, his anger was so immediate and immoderate. "Sir, I should gladly put myself in harm's way if it is required, and no one has any reason to believe otherwise."

"Be at peace, Hayden," Pool said soothingly, but not without a little sarcastic smile. "Perhaps you shall yet have a chance to prove your courage. But not this day, nor tomorrow." He turned his attention back to the others. "Bradley and I will douse our lights and, just before first light, slip out to where the frigate has been holding position. If the Frenchman flies, Bradley will give chase and bring her to or harass her so that I may bring my guns to bear. We shall have a prize and all of you shall partake of the profit. I assume no one will complain of that?"

Hayden looked around the table. He thought he detected some doubt in more than one face, but no one spoke. "I believe we shall have a gale from the south-east," Hayden said, forcing confidence into both his voice and his manner, "and what if there is a French squadron just out of sight?"

Pool sighed theatrically, almost throwing his hands up. "Captain Hayden, if there is a gale and we cannot open our gunports, then clearly we will not attempt to take this frigate. We are not fools. And if there is a French squadron, why do they hide over the horizon? There could be no reason for it. This French captain is signalling to no one, hoping to confuse us—hoping to keep us from doing exactly what we are about to do—sailing out to take him." He turned away from Hayden. "No one need move from their place in the convoy. Bradley and I shall take this Frenchman by surprise."

A toast was drunk to the success of the action, and the gathered officers left, climbing quickly up to the deck. Hayden went down into the boat and then across to the *Phalarope*. None of the other captains spoke, as would be usual before an action, excitement and anticipation high. There was instead an awkward silence, most difficult to read.

Bradley was brought first to *Syren*, and once the boat was beyond hearing, Jones turned to Hayden. "Do you truly believe there is a squadron out there, Hayden?"

Hayden felt both oppressed and sullenly angry. "I only know what my midshipman said—a most reliable and enterprising young man. Certainly it was my duty to relate this to Pool."

"But why would they remain there, out of sight?" Stewart asked.

"Why, indeed. I cannot give an answer to that. I only felt that, as we are on convoy escort and not a cruise, this information might be taken under consideration—which it was not." Hayden knew that he had said too much, but anger and resentment were like an oil that loosened a man's tongue—his tongue, anyway.

He was back aboard the *Themis* but two hours after he had left her. In the interval Saint-Denis had created conflict with Barthe over the sail being carried, and Worthing, Hayden learned, had applied to Saint-Denis to visit the hands confined to the sick-berth. Saint-Denis had prudence enough not to accede to this request—a surprise to Hayden, as the lieutenant appeared to have little common sense when it came to anything else.

Night was quickly upon them and the wind veered to the west, making noticeably until a high chorus sang in the rigging, slurring up and down a minor scale. Lights from the other ships winked in and out as the ships rolled and squalls of wintry rain soaked the canvas. An ancient mizzen topsail split from the mere weight of water.

Hayden invited Griffiths to dine with him, and the two made

company in the great cabin, which had been reconstructed after being cleared entirely away when they had beat to quarters. The rolling of the ship was such that only a little more and tables and chairs would need to be moved and secured, dinner eaten in some awkward arrangement that resembled a merry-andrew juggling.

"Thank you for sparing me another speech from the good parson on what a favourite of Lord Hood's he happens to be." Griffiths smiled and shook his head. "The man cannot secure a living ashore, and yet, expects us to believe a personage the eminence of Lord Hood has taken special notice of him. With such an amiable character and interest upon high, it is a wonder he is not a bishop. Good Lord!"

Hayden laughed. The ship rolled heavily to leeward and Hayden preserved the wine bottle and a saltshaker, Griffiths the gravy boat. A fork slid away and clattered across the floor.

"We are carrying too much sail," Hayden observed, and began to rise, but at that moment he heard hands being called. "Ah, Barthe must have taken the deck." He returned to his chair.

Griffiths took a sip of his claret. "I understand our Frenchman is a royalist?"

"To which Frenchman are we referring?"

"The cook. Or should I say *chef*?"

"Rosseau. He's hardly going to claim himself a Jacobin aboard our ship, is he?"

"No, but Wickham informed me the man only just learned that the queen had been guillotined—if you can believe it. Wickham claims the Frenchman wept like a baby. Rosseau apparently told Wickham that he once served a noble family and cooked a meal attended by Louis and his queen."

"I suppose it is possible. A man of such talents would hardly have been cook for a shoemaker."

"From what the French claim of English culinary skills, you would think the cook of a French shoemaker would be fit for the king of England."

"Actually, Doctor, according to the French, a French *shoemaker* would be fit to cook for an English king."

Griffiths laughed. "I'm sure he would have some excellent sole recipes. Ha ha!"

Ever since Hawthorne had told him that Griffiths had had his hopes disappointed, Hayden had thought the doctor rather more melancholy than usual. His laughter seemed forced, his pleasantries mere formalities, with even less sincerity than was common. But then he had not known the doctor before his misfortune; perhaps he had always been thus. Or perhaps Hayden was merely reading more into Griffiths' manner than was reasonable. It had been two years since his suit had been rebuffed; perhaps he had put the past out of mind and looked only forward.

"I hope we survive having this man aboard," Griffiths said, his manner suddenly grave. "Worthing, I mean."

"He is froward, there is no doubt, but I hardly think he is a danger to the ship's company. No one likes him."

"That is true, but I wouldn't underestimate the trouble such a man could cause. His kind have great capacity for creating conflict. I have seen it before. He cannot be happy unless he is stirring the pot of others' emotions, setting one man against another, and taking insult where none is intended or could be perceived by a man of more moderate character. No, he will cause us trouble, you will see. Already he has tried to undermine your authority by going to Saint-Denis when you refused him entry to the sick-berth. He and your first lieutenant can make common cause, as Worthing is . . . *reverential* of his social betters and both feel they have been valued beneath their worth. But I will say no more and hope to be proven wrong."

"In this particular matter, Dr Griffiths, I will hope the same."

"I am told we are going after a prize at first light."

"No. We are to observe this action, and perhaps admire it, but in no way are we to be involved, though, of course, we will stand by ready to offer assistance should it be required."

Griffiths considered his wineglass a moment, the stem caught between two fingers, palm flat on the table. A small circle of the hand swirled the wine up the sides. "You know I claim no particular knowledge on such matters, but is this prudent?"

Hayden drew a long breath. "Perfectly so, if the French ship is alone."

"But if it is not?"

"Then it is not."

Six

Hayden rose before first light, ate a meagre breakfast, and then ordered his cabin cleared, the guns moved back into position. Chettle and his assistants appeared, quickly taking down the bulkhead panels, his few possessions whisked away by servants.

"Take care with that table," he ordered the hands.

Hayden climbed up a dimly lit ladder to the quarterdeck; a fresh wind, harsh and dense with spray, almost took his hat. Hawthorne and Wickham stood at the starboard rail, gazing out into the darkness. They ducked behind the bulwark and turned their backs as spray dashed over the rail, then up again.

"Mr Wickham," Hayden said, "do you never sleep?"

"Apologies, Captain, we didn't see you," the youth replied.

"No need. Can you make out Bradley and Pool?"

Wickham shook his head, his youthful face pale with worry. "It is too close, sir. But we should have some light, by and by, and then, mayhap, I will know what goes on."

Archer came up, then, and touched his hat. "We are cleared, Captain Hayden. I have the men at their stations and no drum was beat, sir, as you ordered."

"Well done, Mr Archer. I think this Frenchman will lower his flag after firing a single broadside," Hayden observed, forcing confidence into his voice, "especially when he sees both a frigate and seventy-four appearing out of the darkness."

"It appears our gale is finally going to arrive, though." Archer peered into the darkness. "The weather-glass is falling, and the wind continues to veer. I fear our transports will not be able to lay their course if the wind goes even a little farther south."

"You are right—they will not. We'll wait for Pool's signals, but I expect we will heave-to on the larboard tack. He will not like it much, but there will be little choice."

Hayden took a turn of the deck, both to stretch his legs and to be sure his ship was ready for any eventuality. Ducking his head, he went down to the gun-deck, stopping to speak with the gun crews, making certain there was shot and powder enough. Many of the landsmen had never heard the great guns fire but had participated only in exercises without shot and powder. Still, they knew the drill well enough, even if they were utterly innocent of the result. There was, about the men, an air of anticipation and anxiety, all of them sober-faced in the poor light.

"Do you think we'll be in an action, Captain?" Hobson asked.

"I do not, Mr Hobson, but we must be ready in case our assistance is required. I believe a frigate and a seventy-four gunship can manage a French thirty-six quite well. We need only watch and cheer."

He could see the men relax a little as they heard this. They were also a little disappointed, Hayden sensed.

On deck the sky seemed as dark as ever, and time dragged by as though dawn would not come that day.

Rain began to fall, swept against the topside planking and the decks, clattering like a dropped box of lead balls. The gun captains covered the locks of the carronades with lead covers, and powder cartridges were hurried below. It was all but impossible to look to windward, and Hayden gave up, hoping the squall would pass.

Forty minutes the deluge lasted, then it began to abate. Light seemed to follow, the sky growing brighter by the instant.

"On deck," the lookout called. *"Sail two points aft on the starboard beam."*

"There she is, sir, *Majestic*." Wickham pointed.

A two-decker appeared, gunports open, her course parallel to their own. And then a frigate, only two ship's lengths before.

"Is that Bradley or the Frenchman?" Barthe demanded. "I cannot tell."

"Nor can I, Mr Barthe," Wickham answered.

"You're a lieutenant now; we expect you to see things when they need to be seen," Barthe observed.

"My apologies, Mr Barthe, I shall endeavour to see better." Wickham's hand shot up. "There is a second frigate, I think."

"Where?"

"Beyond *Majestic*, Mr Barthe."

For a moment no one spoke, but all gazed anxiously into the gloom, grey wisps of fog, obscuring rain, and dark, rolling seas.

"Well, this will be a surprise for the Frenchman," Hawthorne observed with satisfaction.

"That ship seems very large for a frigate," Hayden said, trying to make out the vessel beyond Pool's seventy-four. "That can't be Bradley. . . ."

"Damn my eyes," Wickham declared, straightening. "She is a two-decker as well."

Before anyone could frame a reply, the more distant ship unleashed a broadside on the one nearer, several balls passing over the decks and holing the waves nearer the *Themis*.

"Is it a Frenchman?" Barthe demanded. "Jesus! Can you not see, Wickham?"

"*One* of them is a Frenchman," the boy replied, even his keen eyes unsure in this murk.

The nearer ship fired her broadside and then the frigate fired into the gloom, to be answered by a phantom. And then all the ships

began firing, an incessant, random booming echoing across the rolling seas. A British flag was hoisted on the nearer ship.

"That is Pool," Hawthorne announced unnecessarily.

"Yes, caught by surprise!" Barthe called over the noise. "Where
did that fucking French seventy-four come from?"

Another ship ranged out of the fog and, to cries of dismay from the
crew of the *Themis*, ranged across *Majestic*'s stern, raked her once, and
then bore up alongside.

"A heavy frigate," someone declared, and cursed.

She was, indeed, a French thirty-six, her boats streaming aft like
ducklings.

"Mr Barthe! Make sail. We shall tack immediately."

"It is heavy wind to tack, sir," Barthe called out over the sound of
cannon. "I fear we shall carry something away."

"We shall tack, Mr Barthe, and then give us the mainsail. Handsomely, now. Mr Franks! Call all hands. We shall tack, then return
to the guns." Hayden hurried to the helm and took it from the surprised sergeant-at-arms. "The yards must be braced around with all
speed."

The moment the hands were at their stations, Hayden brought
the ship through the wind, everyone aboard staring up apprehen-
sively to see if spars would carry away. The fingernails-on-slate
screech of stretching cordage rose above the wind, lingered too long,
but then the ship came through the wind with all spars standing.

The mainsail rippled down, filled in an instant, and the ship heeled,
picked up her skirts, and surged forward, seas breaking against the
larboard bow.

"I'm not sure our gunports will be dry, Captain!" Barthe shouted.
The master grabbed the rail and clapped his hat down to his eyebrows.

"There's nothing for it, Mr Barthe. We will keep them closed until
the last moment." Hayden turned to find Saint-Denis. The lieutenant

stood by the capstan, appearing undecided in his actions. Hayden gave the helm back to the sergeant-at-arms, crossed the few yards of deck, and put his hand on the lieutenant's arm, leaning close to speak over the crash of the guns. "Man the larboard guns, Lieutenant. Do not open the gunports until you have an order from me. Then we will run the guns out with all speed, rake the near frigate, pass by Pool's stern, rake the French two-decker, wear ship, and give them our starboard battery. Have three of the gun captains—Tull, Brown, and Windfield—aim for the seventy-four's rudder. Is that understood?"

Saint-Denis nodded. Hayden watched him make his way to the companionway, but the man lost his balance and almost fell before reaching it, then went awkwardly below. Hayden had come to believe the man's character so false that he worried he would lose his nerve at the crucial moment. It was impossible to know. One could never judge a man's courage before it had been tested.

Hayden stayed near the helmsman as they beat toward the firing ships, wanting to be certain they passed neither too close nor too far. All of his shot would have to tally if he wanted to preserve Pool from his present situation. Too far off and his carronades would be ineffective; too near and the *Themis* could pass the frigate on the wrong side of a sea and be unable to fire.

Smoke from the great guns blew down on them, sweeping, dark and ghostly, across their decks. A topmast tumbled on the *Majestic*, hung for an instant in the rigging, then toppled down into the sea.

As they drew nearer, rocking over the gathering waves, the pale faces of the officers came into focus. Hayden stood by the weather rail, grasping a mizzen shroud with his left hand, the cordage slippery wet and hard with tar. The distance between the *Themis* and her enemies seemed impossible to overcome, labour as she might. Hayden made his way forward onto the gangway, pausing by the hammock netting. Gould had been assigned as his runner, and the boy stood by, staring fixedly toward the battling ships, his face creased and ashen as though he aged before Hayden's eyes.

Leaning near to the boy, Hayden said, "Run forward and tell Madison to fire his carronades into the frigate when he sees fit." Hayden patted the boy firmly on the shoulder. He well remembered his first action at sea and knew a little of what the boy was feeling. It was a sobering moment to realise one's life could end within the hour.

"Aye, sir," Gould replied, his voice thinned by apprehension.

Hayden watched the boy hurry forward, frightened but overcoming his fears—a good sign.

Hawthorne ranged up alongside.

"Mr Hawthorne . . . here we are again."

"Yes, and I thought convoy duty would be a bore. I should have known, with you in command, we would soon be in action."

"I am not sure how I should take that, sir," Hayden responded.

"As a compliment, to be sure," Hawthorne assured him. "You seem to need to fight the French every other day, which I approve most heartily. It is Tuesday, and here are the French right on cue."

Hayden could not help but smile.

Hawthorne went on. "Tuesdays, Thursdays, and Saturdays we fight the French. Sunday, rest and prayer. Mondays, make and mend, and then Tuesdays it is the French again. Predictability is a virtue." Hawthorne was pensively silent a moment. "I must see to my men. Good luck to you, Captain."

"And you, Mr Hawthorne."

The French frigate was near, now. Hayden stood a moment more, judging their speed to a nicety, stepped quickly across the gangway, descended two steps, and stood watching the approaching frigate. Bending low, he looked down onto the gun-deck. The men all stared back in awful silence.

To his first lieutenant Hayden called, "Open larboard gunports, if you please, Mr Saint-Denis."

Hayden stood again, stepping up one tread so that he could more clearly perceive what transpired. The ship rolled to larboard, and Hayden ducked and called out, "Cast free your guns!"

The ship rolled slowly back to starboard.

"Run out your guns!"

Hayden stood again, watching the frigate's stern draw near. The Frenchman fired a stern-chaser at the *Themis*, but Hayden did not take his eye away to see what damage it might have done. A second gun spoke.

A dull thud on the starboard side could only be the Frenchman's trailing boats colliding with the *Themis*.

Forward, a carronade spat fire and smoke, and Hayden squinted as a cloud enveloped him, hiding everything for an instant. The brisk wind carried the smoke away just as another forecastle gun fired, and then another.

Hayden ducked his head below. "Fire as she bears. Rake her, lads."

Hayden went up onto the deck then and watched the effect of his guns. One by one they fired, like the chiming of a massive clock. *Boom! . . . Boom!* He felt the power of them through the deck and the echo in his chest. The wind swirled smoke about the sails, and through it he would catch glimpses of the enemy frigate's stern, the shuttered gallery shattered, splinters flying up from the rail. He could hear men crying out. The orders of officers carried to him on the wind—his mother's tongue. Voices called upon God to aid them or to damn the English.

The wave of gunfire reached him, the gun beneath his feet shaking the deck, and Hayden turned his back for a moment, holding his breath and pressing his eyes closed, waiting for the wind to carry off the smoke. The next gun aft spoke, then the next. They were past.

Hayden had only a glimpse of the ruin they left behind as the stern of *Majestic* hid the French frigate. Above the crashing of guns he heard orders called to reload.

Majestic's stern towered over the *Themis*, and Hayden looked up to see a hatless lieutenant, his face bleeding, gesturing wildly and calling out words that could not be understood above the din. Hayden did not even make an attempt to reply, but sailed by, his course of action not about to be changed by some lieutenant who likely understood the situation less well than he. Pool had made a terrible error. That was the undeniable truth. Where the French ships had come from, Hayden did not know. Perhaps they *had* been waiting over the horizon.

Hayden climbed down a stair and crouched, looking into the dim gun-deck. Men were past their apprehension now, caught up in the drill of loading and firing.

"The second ship is about to come abreast, Mr Saint-Denis. Fire as she bears. We made a ruin of that Frenchman and now we shall attempt to do the same to the seventy-four. Do not waste a shot."

Saint-Denis' ashen face was powder stained, but his manner, though still awkward and stiff, did not lack resolve, which Hayden realised disappointed him; it would be easier to dislike Saint-Denis if he were shy as well.

He stood and climbed a step, seeing the stern of the French ship not far off the larboard bow. The *Themis* plunged into the growing sea, the wind making by the moment. High above, on the stern of the French ship, Hayden could see men bearing muskets gathering at the taffrail. Climbing quickly out onto the gangway, Hayden called for Hawthorne, but the marine lieutenant had not missed the meaning of this and was already scrambling aloft with a company of red-coated marines, muskets slung over their backs.

Hayden hurried forward, finding Mr Barthe and Wickham on the forecastle. The crack of musket fire sounded and lead balls rang off the guns and buried themselves in the deck. With the motion of the two ships it was almost impossible to stand without holding on, so hitting any target would be a matter of luck, but the gun captain of the forward carronade collapsed to the deck and was borne away by two sailors.

To Hayden's surprise, Wickham ordered Gould into the man's

place, and the boy stepped up smartly and took the offered firing lanyard. Barthe was barking orders to Franks and to his mates, trying to repair the small damage done by the French frigate's stern-chasers.

One of the French musketeers plunged over the rail and down into the sea, brought down by Hawthorne's marines. And then a horrible muted thud on the deck ten feet off, and a marine lay in a shattered heap, killed by the fall from aloft if not by enemy fire.

A perfect accident of the sea occurred then: The *Themis* was thrown up on a freak wave as the French ship plunged into a deep trough. Hayden found himself staring along the enemy ship's upper deck, the surprised musket men not thirty feet away at eye level. Gould yanked the firing lanyard before Hayden could speak, and the party of French gunners were torn from the rail, bodies rent and strewn over the quarterdeck as though they had been cut down by a scythe. The gun had been loaded with grape.

The *Themis* plunged into the trough. The next gun did not fire as it should, for the men all stood, gaping in horror. Hayden forced himself to the next carronade, took·hold of the lanyard, and yanked it as the ship rolled up. He made his way quickly aft, down the stair onto the gun-deck, where cold water washed around his ankles.

Archer looked over to him, grim and worried. "I'm not sure we can keep the gunports open, Mr Hayden."

"Fire this broadside and then close them all. We will call hands to wear ship and chase the frigate again."

Guns fired, one after the other, and the ports slammed shut as they did so, muzzles neatly elevated and lashed in place. The ship rolled again, and green water spilled over the port sills and ran across the deck. It was a dangerous, dangerous thing they did, but Hayden felt he had no choice. Ships had run under doing just this, and every sailor aboard knew it. If a gun broke loose with so many men at hand, there would be injuries, even deaths.

The last carronade fired on the quarterdeck and Hayden hurried aft, watching the ships bear away south, guns still firing. Barthe came down the starboard gangway and met him on the quarterdeck.

"Shall I port my helm, sir?" the helmsman asked.

"Not yet," Hayden answered. "I want to rake the seventy-four once more, and we shall need room to make our way to windward. Hold your course."

Hands were called to wear ship, and Hayden asked for his glass. Gould appeared at his side then, his face fish-belly white.

"How fare you, Mr Gould?"

"Did you see what I . . . what I did, Captain?" The boy's voice was raw with awe and horror. "A dozen men torn limb from limb. It was like a slaughterhouse, sir, a slaughter—"

The boy slumped a little and Hayden caught him beneath the arm, Mr Barthe grasping the other. They stepped a little behind Gould to bear him up and shield him from the eyes of others. The men at the near carronades looked away.

"You'll be right in a moment," Barthe said, his voice kindly. "Breathe. Lean over the rail if you must be ill."

The boy nodded, gasping for air. Hayden felt him take a little weight on his legs, then a little more. His hands, limp a moment before, reached out and grasped the rail.

"I am recovered, sir," Gould said faintly.

"We will hold you a moment more," Hayden replied.

But then he felt the boy take his own weight and he released him, turning away and crossing to the helm.

"We will wear ship, Mr Barthe."

"All hands to wear ship!" Barthe called into his speaking trumpet.

The rising wind was brought across the stern, the yards braced quickly around; for a moment the ship wallowed, then steadied, heeled, and began to make way. The embattled ships were some distance off, but under her press of sail the *Themis* closed on them quickly.

The shattered gallery windows and stern of the French seventy-four became clearer as they neared. Their eighteen-pounders had inflicted more damage then Hayden had hoped. Beyond the French-man, Hayden could see *Majestic*, her rigging and sails in ruin, her topmasts shot away.

The French seventy-four had the much-vaunted weather gauge, but could not open the ports on her lower gun-deck because she was heeled overly by the rising wind. Pool's marines were shooting any men sent aloft to reduce sail, thus keeping her adversary at a disad-vantage. In response, the French skipper let sheets fly and some of his sails began flogging themselves to ruins.

Upon Pool's lee side, however, the French frigate was timing her broadsides to the crests, catching the British ship in a trough and causing slaughter across her decks.

"Mr Gould," Hayden called.

The boy jogged over, doing his manly best to appear untouched by what went on.

"Go down to Saint-Denis and inform him we will go straight for the French frigate and leave the seventy-four to Pool. I want to rake her once, then range up alongside and give her our starboard broadside."

The boy touched his hat. "Aye, sir. Straight at the French frigate, sir." He lumbered across the deck and down the companionway.

In the mist and rain beyond *Majestic*, Hayden found Bradley, who had worn ship and was running from the French frigate, his twenty-six twelve-pounders no match for thirty-six eighteens. The French captain was wearing ship to give chase. Beyond the smoke and chaos, Hayden could barely make out the nearest ships of the convoy, la-bouring heavily in the gathering seas.

The *Themis* passed the French two-decker at a distance, Hayden saving his shot. His gunners' attempts to disable the Frenchman's rudder shattered much planking in the transom, but the rudder head was intact—a nearly impossible shot in the best conditions.

A moment, and they were by the two battling ships. The stern of the French frigate came into view.

"Well, I'll be a god-damned, French papist," Barthe said. "She's afire!"

Smoke streamed from the shattered gallery windows, and Hayden could see men running about her deck and, as she had no boats, climbing madly aloft to escape the flames. Her guns were silent.

"Shall we order the gunports opened?" Wickham asked as he came up. He fumbled his glass at that moment, and bent to retrieve it from the deck.

"No," Hayden replied, shaken from his moment of surprise. "We may be forced to come to their aid. Let the French captain signa—"

A sun of lava-like flame erupted through the enemy frigate's deck, and then a thunderous crash. Hayden felt himself hurled back onto hard planks. A moment of stunned silence as he tried to comprehend what had just occurred, and then splinters rained down all around, some aflame. He staggered up, found no one at the helm, and made his way there, taking hold of the wheel, relieved to have anything to help him stand. Men lay strewn about the deck, moaning.

Glancing up, Hayden realised his topsails were gone, only a few bits of rag snapping and fluttering in the wind. A twitching, red-sleeved hand hung down from the tops, the fallen marine's shoulder barely visible. Of the rest of the company, none could be seen.

"Good God!" Hayden muttered. "Mr Hawthorne!" he called, searching about the deck. "Mr Hawthorne!"

A red coat stirred beneath a pile of faintly writhing men, and then a confused Hawthorne sat up, holding a hand to his face. Hayden could not leave the wheel, but Wickham had regained his feet, looking utterly disoriented but whole. "Go to Mr Hawthorne's aid, Mr Wickham, if you please—there away, forward." Hayden pointed.

The boy nodded dumbly and staggered drunkenly across the deck. Hawthorne was helped to his feet but collapsed against the rail, almost sinking down. Around Hayden others had propped themselves up and were sitting awkwardly; here and there men stooped or stood, hands on knees. Barthe lay only a few feet away, his eyes open and blinking, but he made no move and lay with his limbs thrown out oddly.

Some men came running up from below into a sudden awful silence, fragments of burning wood and tar lying on the deck and strewn across the sea. Floating among them, the dead, all of them naked, pale bodies rocking and lifting on the crests.

Griffiths and his assistant, Ariss, appeared, and on their heels Mr Smosh.

"Doctor!" Hayden called. "See to Mr Barthe there."

Griffiths hurried over, a quick penetrating gaze in Hayden's direction. "What in God's name happened?" he asked.

"The French frigate exploded—her magazine . . ." Hayden could not finish, words drying up in his mouth.

Archer appeared on deck, a party of men on his heels. He sent Dryden to relieve Hayden and began giving orders to clear the burning debris. Relieved of the helm, Hayden still stood there in a daze.

"Are you injured, Captain?" Dryden asked, and Hayden realised it was likely for the second time, and spoken rather loudly.

"My . . . my ears ring terribly."

"You have blood, sir!" Dryden said loudly. "It appears to be coming from your ear. The other one, sir."

Hayden reached up and found liquid on the lobe. Withdrawing his hand, he saw that his fingertips were crimson. But it seemed as though it had happened to some other. Blood coming from his ear worried him not in the least.

Hayden went to the weather rail and took hold of the shrouds, gazing about at the rising sea. Wind blew hard in his face but made almost no sound.

At that moment, Pool and the French seventy-four wore almost together, passed beneath the *Themis'* stern, and resumed their firing, which had been briefly interrupted by the exploding frigate. For a moment Hayden watched them go, and then the rain and cloud swallowed them. Only the garish flashes of their guns could be seen, flaring in the murk.

"Where am I to steer, Captain?" Dryden asked.

"We will go to Bradley's aid." Hayden raised a hand and pointed forward where the sterns of the two frigates could be seen. "We will run up to larboard of the French frigate and open fire."

Hayden looked across the deck and found Smosh helping Barthe to his feet. The sailing master swooned and would have fallen, but Smosh took him up and, unaided, crossed the slanting deck and bore him below. Even confused as he was, Hayden knew this was no easy feat, as Barthe was a substantial man.

Archer came up then, fixing an inquisitive gaze on Hayden. "Are you injured, Captain Hayden? You appear . . . bewildered, sir."

Hayden made an effort to speak with precision and clarity. "As are we all who were on deck when the frigate exploded." Hayden glanced up and saw there was still a marine either dead or unconscious in the tops. He pointed. "Send some men aloft to bring that marine down. All of his fellows were blown out of the tops and into the sea. I would go back, but we will never find them, even if they lived, and Bradley has need of us. I am more angry than I can say that we abandon our own people to rescue Bradley, who should never have been prize hunting on convoy duty to begin with." Hayden looked up again. "Find Mr Franks. We will need to bend our spare topsails. How many men have we who can work the ship?"

"All of the men on the gun-deck were untouched, sir. But the men who were above deck are either injured or . . . stunned, sir."

"Yes, let us hope we all recover quickly. I'm better, Mr Archer, you needn't look so concerned. You will not require Saint-Denis to take my place. We need to put our rig to rights and bend sails."

Archer nodded, satisfied that Hayden was still in his right senses, and went off gathering a party of topmen. There was much work to be done aloft, for the explosion and the subsequent debris had played the devil among their rig. Franks could now be seen hobbling about, giving orders, securing the loose falls of ropes. Chettle and his mates were abroad with their tool-boxes, mending here, lending a hand there. It was as though the crew had been all asleep and were just now stirring to find much to be done.

Hayden realised his shoulder and head throbbed from being hurled across the deck. He raised his arm and moved it in a painful circle. He could not turn his neck without a stabbing pain. A small price to pay. Some two hundred French sailors had lost their lives in the blink of an eye. Perhaps there might have been a few survivors—men high in the rigging blown clear—but they would perish in a quarter of an hour in the icy sea.

Men were being carried down to Griffiths, who had retreated to the cockpit again. Some could walk with a little aid, but others were carried, some senseless, others appearing half awake, but dumb and not responding to the entreaties of their fellows.

Wickham appeared, sheet of paper in hand. "I am not finished with my muster, Captain, but it seems we lost nine marines out of the tops and three seamen who were aloft. It was the greatest good fortune that Mr Hawthorne had only just reached the deck when the frigate exploded, or we would have lost him as well."

"And yourself, Mr Wickham?"

"Good as gold, sir. I had ducked down to retrieve a dropped glass, sir, so was behind the barricade at the time. A bit of good luck."

"Indeed. Have you counted the men in the sick-berth?"

"I have, sir, but the doctor is sending them out as they regain their reason. Most were merely stunned for a few moments and are recovering quickly. A landsman named Sterling was thrown into a gun, sir, and appears to have broken his collarbone. And the marine brought down from aloft was smashed against the mast and has only just come to his senses. Appears he has broken an arm."

"I am sad for the marines, but I fear they drowned before they could have regained their reason." Hayden shook his head.

An odd look came over Wickham's face. "The Frenchmen who were thrown clear—did you see them, sir? They were, all of them, unclothed. Or perhaps I was bewildered a moment and did not realise?"

"No, I saw it as well. I have heard of it before, men so near an explosion their clothes are torn off by the violence of it. What is more peculiar than that?" Hayden had a sudden vision of the pale men, bobbing in the rising sea—like a nightmare.

Turning his attention to the French frigate, Hayden made his way forward and ordered the starboard chase gun readied. Not too far off he could see Bradley sailing for the transport fleet, the French frigate on his larboard beam. They fired at one another with deck guns, to little effect, as the motion of the ships was now so violent upon the rising sea.

"I think we should fire a shot at the Frenchman, Mr Morris," Hayden said to the gun captain. "Let him know we are here."

"Aye, sir. It will be a miracle if we hit her, sir."

"Perhaps, but let us make our presence felt."

The gun was hastily aimed and, as the bow passed over a crest, fired. Hayden peered through a glass his servant had brought him and could just make out the French officers upon the quarterdeck, staring back. Three more shots were fired at Bradley, and then the French ship sheered off and ran toward the north-east. For a moment there was silence, and then the distant echo of a gun, and then another. The two seventy-fours were not finished, yet.

"Pass the word for Mr Archer," Hayden ordered, and scanned the sea in all directions.

The convoy was spread over a large area of ocean and was in danger of scattering. He could see the transports labouring in the growing gale, men aloft reducing sail. They should have come about onto the offshore tack before the wind had grown so strong, but there had been no one to make the decision, as Pool and Bradley were both prize hunting. Bradley would have to order it now, and hope all the ships could wear safely. Hayden guessed the fleet would need to heave-to immediately after wearing, and ride the gale out, trusting that no French squadron could reach them in this weather.

Debris dotted the seas to the west, all of it doused now, and beyond it, a dark, threatening horizon.

Archer approached, touched his hat, and waited.

"House the guns. Call all hands to prepare for this ill weather. Have the helmsman bring us into Bradley's lee, and find me Mr Barthe's speaking trumpet. I will have a word with Captain Bradley."

"Aye, sir."

Archer went off at a run, calling out orders as he went. Removed from the command of Captain Hart, the lieutenant was showing an uncharacteristic interest in his profession. Hayden was very gratified to see it.

It took a few moments for them to overtake the *Syren*, and when they finally did Hayden was distressed to see the damage that had been wreaked upon her. Her rig was torn apart, her sails cut to rags, and her hull and deck had been shot through in many places.

Hayden took Barthe's speaking trumpet and called out to the officers on the quarterdeck. "Where is Captain Bradley?" Hayden called. "We have much to do if we are to preserve our convoy."

"Captain Bradley is dead, sir," a lieutenant called back. The man stood at the rail, his jacket torn, face powder-stained, his manner entirely distressed. "Had you come but a little sooner you might have preserved his life, for he was killed by one of the Frenchman's last shots."

"I am very sorry to hear it," Hayden called through the trumpet. "We were almost thrown upon our beam-ends by the explosion. Our sails were blown away and we lost many of our own people. I could not reach you sooner. We must signal the convoy to wear, and collect them on the offshore tack. If this gale lasts a few days, they could come to grief as they are."

"Captain Pool is in charge of this convoy, Mr Hayden, and if he does not return, Captain Bradley has given command to me."

Hayden could not quite believe his ears. "Captain Bradley has no business giving the command of the fleet to a lieutenant. I am the senior officer, here."

"You were a lieutenant yourself but a few weeks past. Neither Captain Pool nor Captain Bradley had faith in your abilities, for so they both stated. I will obey the orders of my captain."

"Sir, we have no time to argue. We must preserve our convoy. I will order them to wear and heave-to on the offshore tack."

"No, sir. It was just this kind of malingering that Captain Pool wished to avoid. We shall not heave-to but force our way on. I will not end up back in Plymouth because of foul weather."

Saint-Denis appeared by Hayden's side.

Hayden spoke to him quietly. "Man the starboard battery, quietly. We will open the starboard gunports and run out the guns."

"You cannot be serious."

"I am deadly serious. This is mutiny and I will not stand for it. They cannot open ports on this tack, but we can . . . just. Do it now."

Saint-Denis did not move. "Mr Hayden, I must protest this action."

"Mr Archer!" Hayden called.

"I will do it," Saint-Denis said, "but I wish it noted in the log that I protested."

"Noted."

Hayden raised the speaking trumpet. "What is your name, sir?"

"Cole. I am acting captain of the *Syren*."

"Lieutenant Cole, I consider your refusal to obey orders as mutinous. I demand you comply or I will be forced to take action against your ship. Do you understand?"

"You would not dare, sir! I will see you court-martialled."

Hayden turned to Gould. "Have Mr Saint-Denis open ports and run out the guns."

"Aye, sir." The boy ran off.

Even with the ringing in his ears Hayden heard the ports open and the sound of gun-carriage wheels.

"Mr Cole!" Hayden called. "Will you comply with my orders?"

The men on the *Syren* backed from the rail, looking one to the other. Cole conferred with his fellow officers, urgently.

"This is not an idle threat, sir!" Hayden called. "I will fire into you."

Cole broke away from his fellows. "I will comply. But I will have your coat when we reach Gibraltar. And that is no idle threat."

Hayden turned away from the rail. "House the guns," he ordered. "Make sail, Mr Wickham. We must signal the convoy to wear, leeward ships first. Then signal McIntosh to draw near. I will have him relay my orders lest they are misapprehended. I will also make certain he understands who gives the orders until Captain Pool returns." Hayden looked about. "This gale is going to become a great deal worse before this day grows old. I am certain of it."

Seven

Three days the gale lived, forcing the convoy slowly west-north-west. Hayden and the other escorts had all they could manage to keep the ships together, and even then they tended to disperse by night. Two transports lumbered into each other in the midst of a squall, one so heavily damaged that her crew was taken off before she foundered. Hayden watched her fall beneath the waves, jade sea washing over her decks, and then only her masts thrusting up, the banner at the truck flicking once, like a whip, before sounding. Hayden imagined her gliding, ever so slowly, down onto the hidden, lightless mud of the Atlantic floor.

The escort captains and the masters of the transports all worked mightily to keep the convoy together when the ocean tried to tear them apart. Cole played his part, but Hayden could almost feel the man simmering upon his distant ship. No doubt he was hoping for Pool's return that he might have immediate redress—and Hayden feared, given Pool's opinion of his character, that he would comply only too happily.

Finally the wind dwindled, leaving the ships pitching and rolling awkwardly upon an unquiet sea. A liquid sun wavered up through a distant mist to deliver a surprisingly warm day. "Drying out" turned the ship into a laundress' nightmare. Hayden ordered the captains of the escorts to attend him, and watched the approaching cutters water-spider over the low swell.

In the course of half an hour all four officers heaved themselves over the *Themis'* rail, piped shrilly aboard by Mr Franks, who, to judge by his manner, appeared prepared to fire into any of their ships if even the slightest sign of disrespect was offered to his captain.

Hayden seated the officers and his first lieutenant around the newly acquired table but chose to stand at the head, gallery windows to his back, an unseasonally fair Biscay day glittering beyond. The irregular thumping and calling of men repairing the ship and renewing her rig filtered down the skylight, open to the warm, damp day. A gull swung by the stern windows, casting a slick shadow across the cabin sole and up over the faces of the gathered men.

All five appeared pasty-faced from fatigue, the strains of keeping the convoy together and afloat through the gale showing, but only Cole appeared sullen. He had cornered Saint-Denis upon coming aboard, a whispered conversation of such familiarity ensuing that there could be little doubt the two lieutenants shared a previous acquaintance.

Hayden cleared his throat and, when everyone's attention turned to him, began, "Thank you all for attending so promptly—"

Cole snorted. "And what choice had we? We should have been fired into had we refused."

Hayden noticed that the other men did not nod or show signs of agreement. They, at least, accepted the necessity of Hayden assuming command.

"I am still hopeful that Captain Pool will find us," Hayden continued, "but until such time we must make our own preparations. My midshipman is certain he saw a schooner hurrying north the morning we first perceived the French frigate. If it returns with a French squadron, we will be in a bad situation—especially if Captain Pool does not happen upon us." Hayden hesitated only a second, wondering if he should offer his plan as a suggestion, and hear the opinions of others, or if he should state it as the course of action he had chosen. A brief look around at the attentive faces and the single resentful countenance made up his mind. "The French will expect us to take the most direct route that weather will allow and shall seek us upon that course. For that reason we shall shape our course out into the Atlantic, at least thirty leagues, and proceed to Gibraltar so."

"Have you not considered, Captain Hayden," Cole asked, "that such a course of action will make it exceedingly unlikely that Captain Pool shall ever discover us? Or perhaps that is your intention?"

"Mr Cole, my intention is to preserve the convoy and to proceed to Gibraltar with all speed. We are, however, in a difficult situation, now: we have lost our most powerful ship. Our best hope lies in not being discovered by the French. There are few other courses open to us."

Heads nodded again.

"If I may, sor," McIntosh said, his manner unaltered from their previous gathering. "Perhaps we should disguise some few of our transports as armed vessels. We count in our convoy a number of ships of the very type the admiralty have, even recently, purchased and armed for just such employment. I am certain we can obtain enough uniforms to outfit their quarterdecks and then impress sailors from the other ships to give them numbers enough to speed their sail handling. They may not quite match our own vessels for sharpness, but they might fool a Frenchman."

"I had considered this, Captain McIntosh, but wondered if such a commonly used ploy would not be too easily detected. The French might take this as an indication of our true strength and be emboldened."

Stewart leaned a little forward, the better to be seen. "If we could keep our Trojan horses distant from any French ships that appear, it might answer, Captain Hayden."

Hayden was uncertain of the descriptor "Trojan horses" but not unimpressed by the argument. "So it might," Hayden conceded. "Let us enter three of our transports into the Royal Navy, temporarily. This was your idea, McIntosh; will you see it done?"

"I will, sor, if I might beg some old uniforms from yourselves— enough to outfit the quarterdeck of each ship."

The other officers nodded, even Cole agreeing at least on this— though Hayden suspected it was because the idea had not come from him.

"I shall write a letter and have copies enough made to send to each master. Best they understand our intentions perfectly. We will continue as we are: Captain Stewart shall remain whipper-in; McIntosh will convey messages and relay signals. Captain Cole, I shall ask you to take up the rear position, and Jones, you shall assume the forward. I will remain to weather where the *Syren* will join me if the French appear. Let us hope that a wind will find us this day and allow us to make some westing."

Transports were selected to masquerade as His Majesty's ships and some other small business quickly concluded before the officers returned to their vessels.

Hayden took the deck to see the captains off and stood at the rail watching their boats lurch back to their respective vessels. The *Themis'* cutters were dispatched to carry Hayden's letter to each captain and to enquire of any damage from the recent gale—the calm was too fortuitous not to be used. Mr Franks and Mr Chettle were sent off in the ship's barge to aid the vessel that had survived the collision, and two injured men were sent aboard the *Themis* and into the care of Dr Griffiths. All in all, there was much coming and going among the vessels of the convoy.

Surrounded by attentive midshipmen, Mr Barthe took the noon sight and reported their position, which had not been precisely known for the three days of the gale, though Hayden was pleased to see that the master's dead reckoning had not been far off the mark.

"How fare you, Mr Barthe?" Hayden asked him.

The sailing master pressed an open hand against the small of his back, having suffered some hurt when hurled across the deck by the explosion.

"My poor old frame was not made for such gymnastic manoeuvres, Captain, but it mends. Does your ear heal?"

"It causes no pain at all, Mr Barthe; bless your kindness for asking. The doctor assures me my hearing will return, by and by, though for the time being my good ear is doing the duty of two."

Wickham approached, then, to report on some repairs. Hayden informed them both of the decisions he had made and the response of the other captains, not mentioning the resistance from Cole, but did relate the man's fears that setting out west would make it less likely that Pool would find them.

"Cole has a point, Captain," Barthe agreed, "but it is still the right and proper thing to do. Pool has only his own rashness to blame for what occurred. Had he kept his place in the convoy, we could have made a better defense, as our numbers were about equal, though the French frigates were heavier than our own. Still, I think we could have driven them off or held them at bay as long as you liked."

Hayden decided on discretion, for a change, and passed over Mr Barthe's opinion without comment.

"Pool might find us, yet," Wickham stated. "He must realise that we would change our course to confuse the French."

Barthe glanced at Hayden, a silent comment on Wickham's youth and trusting nature. Hayden suspected that Mr Barthe thought as he did—assuming Pool drove off the French seventy-four, he would spend as little time as possible trying to locate the convoy but make all speed to Gibraltar, blame whoever had assumed control of the convoy for changing its planned course, and then proceed to Toulon to join Hood. Losing his convoy Pool would consider the greatest possible blessing. The senior admiral might admonish him for giving up his search for his charges so easily, but no more would come of it.

There would certainly be no court-martial. And if Pool took or even substantially damaged the French seventy-four, he would likely be congratulated if not rewarded.

Hayden climbed aloft, partly to inspect repairs in progress, thus saving poor Franks from making the journey with his injured foot, and partly to scrutinise the surrounding ocean. From the topmast trestle-trees he swept his glass slowly around the horizon. There was a faint, almost imperceptible dot of ruddy brown to the north-east— perhaps a sail, perhaps nothing at all.

Hayden called down to the men working below him. "Pass the word for Mr Wickham, if you please."

A moment later the converted middy clambered up beside Hayden, who passed him his glass.

Hayden reached out and indicated an unfortunately large area of the Atlantic. "Can you see that spot to the north-east, Mr Wickham? A sail, do you think?"

Wickham supported the glass on a hand clutched to a stay. For a long moment he remained very still.

"I believe it is a sail, Captain Hayden, but its nature and nationality are hidden from me. I can tell you this, though: That ship has wind."

"Damn! If the wind carries it up to us, we must hope it is Pool. But perhaps the wind will fill in before then and bear us out to sea. I wonder if he has seen us. You cannot make out her point of sailing, can you?"

Wickham raised the telescope again, gazed into its glassy depths for yet another moment, then shook his head. "I cannot, sir."

"Pass your duties on to Archer and remain here awhile, if you please. I should dearly like to know in what direction that ship shapes her course."

"Aye, sir."

Hayden took back his glass and examined each vessel of his much-dispersed convoy, all of them rising and falling slowly on the swell, some rolling more than they had any right to. They numbered thirty transports—losses remained a single ship to collision—but they still had many sea miles to go. A nod to Wickham, and Hayden climbed down, examining the rig as he went. The bosun, Franks, had been promoted unwarrantedly and then prevented from adequately learning his trade under his former captain, Hart. It was one of the many ways that Hart had found to oppress his crew: keep them in ignorance and yet abuse them for it whenever it pleased him. If not for Barthe and his mates, the *Themis* would likely have lost a mast, and, as it was, she had required replacements for the main and mizzen that had sprung due to her badly maintained rig.

Franks might not have warranted his position as bosun but, ever since Hayden had come aboard, had done everything within his powers to learn his trade. It was unfortunate that Franks learned but slowly, and with his broken foot was hampered from going aloft. Hayden was of half a mind to replace him but, given the man's good service and loyalty on the recent cruise with the despicable Hart, could not bring himself to do it. In fact, he could see the bosun on the deck watching him—worried that Hayden might find some deficiency that his mates had not seen or of which they had not made him aware.

Upon reaching the deck, he found poor Franks hobbling along the gangway, his unsmiling face set against the pain.

"There you are, Mr Franks. The cheek block of the main topmast staysail requires your attention, as the housing is cracked. And the same sail will soon need its spring stay renewed; best do it now while there is no wind and little sea. Your mates are not keeping you informed of the state of the rig, Mr Franks, and that cannot continue."

Franks looked much abashed by this, his face flushing. "It is not willingly done, sir. It is their poor understanding of such matters."

"It is an area in which poor understanding cannot be indulged. Let us consider a resolution to this problem, Mr Franks. We will speak of it again. Carry on."

Franks went off calling testily for his mates, and snarling at two men who suddenly were not working with enough energy; his rattan snapped down on the shoulders of one.

Hayden called for Mr Barthe and awaited him by the taffrail. The master came waddling stiffly along the deck, touching his hat as he approached.

"Mr Barthe, we cannot continue as we are with Mr Franks. It is intolerable that we haven't a proficient bosun."

Barthe became very serious upon hearing this. "Mr Franks is very attentive to his duties, Captain."

"And I would never suggest otherwise, but he has not yet mastered his trade, and that is not acceptable aboard a man-of-war."

"He has made great progress in his learning, sir. I have been witness to it myself."

"Yes, and if he were a bosun's mate, that would be commendable; but he is not."

Barthe made a sour face. "He will take it very hard, sir, if you send him back before the mast."

"I realise that, and it is not my intention—for whom would we replace him with? No, I intend to disrate Gordon, his mate, whom I would never have rated 'able' had I been in command. I will put a competent man in his place, which is why I am speaking of this with you. It is a great shame we do not have Aldrich to make bosun's mate, but is there not some other you would recommend?"

Barthe pressed a fleshy hand to his temple. "There are some competent seamen, sir—no doubt of it—but men that I could see one day as bosun . . . ? It is a position that demands much and returns little."

"Would you give up Dryden for a three-month, Mr Barthe? By then, certainly, Mr Franks will be walking properly again, and Dryden could do much to complete the education of both Franks and his mate, for though I shall remove Gordon, I will leave Coffey in place. It is an imposition, I realise, but sacrifices must be made for the good of the ship." Hayden thought of Admiral Cotton as he said this, and not without a little embarrassment. Hayden had not been too keen on making sacrifices for the good of the service when the admiral had demanded it.

Barthe considered this a moment. "Who will you give me to take his place?" Barthe asked reluctantly.

"Who would you have?"

"Mr Gould," the master replied without hesitation.

"Gould? He has barely got his boots wet. There must be some other who will fill the position more ably."

"Gould might be newly aboard, Captain, but I have never been witness to anyone learning so quickly. You never tell him a thing twice. By the time we reach Gibraltar, I swear, he will be quite ready to pass for lieutenant—but for his sea years, of course. I have never seen the like."

It was Hayden's turn to hesitate.

"To be a good officer, he must be proficient in all the duties of the sailing master," Barthe pointed out.

"Then you may have him, Mr Barthe, but he will remain a midshipman, only temporarily under you." Hayden considered a moment. "It will be a good education for him, I think. I will inform Mr Franks of our decision and you may speak with Dryden. I will pass the news to Gould as well." Hayden glanced out at the horizon where he and Wickham thought they had seen a sail.

"Is it Captain Pool, do you think?" Barthe enquired.

"That is my hope, Mr Barthe."

"That is mine as well," Barthe responded, then touched his hat. "By your leave, sir." The sailing master made his way forward.

A rumour of wind from the north reached them, a darkening ripple spreading southward, breaking up the surface into an irregular chop. The drying sails grew restive, wafted uncertainly, filled, fell slack, then bellied, the ship coming to life with a sigh. The usual disorganised scramble ensued as the masters brought their transports onto the same heading. The convoy began to make its way out into the Atlantic.

Very little time passed before Barthe had the men reducing sail to slow the *Themis* so the transports, heavily laden as they were, would not be left in their wake. Cole was signalled to tow the slowest of the transports—the *Hartlepool*, which had immediately fallen behind—to the fore of the convoy.

"That tub will be the end of us, Captain," Barthe growled as he came onto the quarterdeck, waving stubby fingers toward the *Hartlepool*.

"Nothing quite so dramatic, I hope, Mr Barthe, but she is going to slow our passage by several days." Hayden raised a glass and searched for the "smudge" on the northern horizon.

"Can you make her out, Captain?" Barthe asked, the thinnest edge of anxiety entering his voice.

"To be honest, I am uncertain." Hayden shaded his eyes and, looking up, called to the mizzen lookout. "Aloft there! Smithers! Can you make out a sail to the north?"

Wickham had returned to the deck some time before and Hayden had to rely on the perception of others not so farsighted.

"No, sir, Captain Hayden. She looked to be moving off to the east some time ago, and now I cannot make her out at all."

"Well, that is good news, I think." Hayden turned to Barthe, who had now a glass trained on the distant north.

The master lowered the brass tube. "Unless it was Pool."

"If it was, he could not have failed to make us out. We could perceive him from a lower vantage than the tops of a seventy-four and we are many sail clumped together. Whoever it was, they had no interest in us." Hayden stood a moment more staring toward the secret north, hoping his statement was true.

The day wore on, the convoy making slow but certain progress westward. After a warm day, the night arrived with an unexpected chill.

A large wooden frame was hauled aloft each night upon which lanterns could be lit in certain configurations to send signals to the convoy. It was an awkward bloody affair, too heavy by half, and heartily disliked by crew and officers. Hayden watched the men ready it for its journey up into the tops, the last light of a meagre sunset casting a cool, thin turquoise across the western horizon.

"Man halyards!" Mr Barthe ordered, overseeing the ascension himself. "Handsomely, Wilson. Handsomely!"

Hayden turned away, took a single tour of the deck, and then descended to his cabin. His steward, Castle, was lighting the lamps at that moment.

"I will be a guest of the gunroom this evening, Castle, so you have an evening free."

The man nodded. He was not the oldest seaman aboard but was certainly twenty years Hayden's senior, and had been at sea since he was a boy—an orphan, apparently. Words were not Castle's medium, not if a nod or polite throat-clearing would do. When he did dare speech it was whispered, halting, seeming wholly unfamiliar, as though he had only just learned, not just English, but any language, and was uncertain of its form. The man's entire manner was so opaque that Hayden felt he did not know him at all, yet by his deeds he appeared good-hearted, even generous. "Slinking John" the men called him, though his Christian name was Cyrus (if Cyrus qualified as a Christian name). Whenever Hayden spoke to him he appeared to draw back a little, without actually changing his position, and he listened like a man expecting, in truth *knowing*, that he would receive bad news.

Slinking John's place among the hands was difficult to understand. He shared a mess with Chettle and the carpenter's mates, who appeared to accept him without judgement. The other older hands tolerated him, which led the younger men to vague imitation, and though they might have called him "Slinking John" he was never mocked to his face—never bullied or practised upon. Being the captain's steward, of course, granted him a certain immunity, even privileges, but even the captain thought him an odd presence—almost more animal than human. Griffiths once likened him to a good hound "that lurked about and occasionally fetched." As a steward he was utterly efficient and unfailing, but Hayden wished sometimes that he might learn to be a bit more human and less canine.

"Rosseau knows I will not require dinner?"

Again the man nodded. He waited a moment until Hayden dismissed him, and then went padding off.

For a few blessed moments Hayden sat in his cabin, the day's final light draining ever so swiftly from the eastern sky. The transition from daylight azure, through topaz, sapphire, indigo, violet, then purple, and finally inky black, was a mystery he never tired of attempting to penetrate. Where did one colour begin and the other end? How could they bleed so seamlessly one into the other and alter so subtly that the eye could never really comprehend the moment of their transmutation?

A respectful knock interrupted his contemplation of nature's palette. Hayden called out for the marine to open the door.

"Doctor Worthing wishing to speak with you, sir," the marine said.

"Send him in." So much for being a poet, Hayden thought. *Blast*.

The look of sour injury that Worthing habitually wore was, if anything, more embittered and indicative of greater injury than usual. The man could press his lips together so that all blood appeared to be forced away, leaving them empty, hardened, thin.

"Dr Worthing. I hope I may be of some service." In truth, Hayden hoped the man would announce his complaint—petty as it might be—and be gone as quickly as possible.

"Mr Hayden, I hope, sir, that you were not party to this . . . contempt for church and crown."

"And what contempt might we be speaking of, Doctor?" Hayden asked innocently, sounding, he realised, too much like Smosh.

"You do realise that you have a Jew among your officers. . . ."

"I do not. Of whom do we speak?"

"Mr Gould, sir, as you well know."

"Mr Gould's mother is a Christian from a Christian family. Gould has attended church all his life."

"His father is a Jew. I have it on good authority."

"And what authority is that?"

But Worthing was not about to answer that question. "Do you deny it, Mr Hayden?"

"No. In fact I do not, but the religion of Gould's father is of no consequence. The Test Act requires only that Gould belong to the Church of England, and I assure you he does."

"Well, I am not reassured. Has he taken the sacrament—*publicly* taken the sacrament?"

"That is a question I cannot answer, Doctor, and nor is it a question I am prepared to ask."

"Not prepared to ask! Then I will ask it. I will see him take the sacrament before witnesses."

Hayden's temper flared. "Not aboard my ship. Only the admiralty has the right to impose such a demand—and you are not the admiralty."

"You *refuse* it?" The man's outrage attained new heights.

Hayden levelled his gaze at the parson and spoke with a clarity and firmness that he hoped would carry all the weight of his conviction. "There will be, Doctor, no Inquisitions aboard my ship."

"And what of you, Mr Hayden? Do you refuse it? Are you yet a papist, as the men are saying?"

"I do not think it is a matter of concern to my crew—nor even a matter of interest."

"In that you are wrong, Mr Hayden."

"Dr Worthing, if you sow dissension among my crew, I will confine you to your cabin for the duration of our passage."

"You would not dare! Do you not comprehend what the consequences would be?"

"I comprehend what they would be if I did not. There has been one mutiny aboard this ship; there shall not be a second. Provoke my crew no more, or I shall be forced to—"

Worthing interrupted this declaration. "I will not sit at table with a Jew."

"Then you may dine alone."

"I'm sure there are others who will join me."

"Not if they wish to remain officers aboard the *Themis*."

The two men stood glaring at each other, their impasse complete. It infuriated Worthing beyond measure that he could not impose his will upon Hayden, and Hayden was not about to bend on a single measure, no matter how small. He had known Worthings before— petty tyrants; given a county, they would demand a province. Worthing, unlike Hart, had only his ecclesiastical authority, which counted for very little aboard ship. "Thank God," Hayden almost added.

The man stepped suddenly a little nearer. "I believe, Mr Hayden, that you *are* a papist, and I will let this be known among my friends in the admiralty."

"I am sure your influential friends within the admiralty will be deeply shocked by such a revelation. The war against France will seem footling by comparison. No doubt all of their energies will be turned from defeating Britain's enemies and focussed where they should have been all along—on rooting out the secret papists and Jews in the Royal Navy." Hayden waited for the man to respond and when he did not said, "Do not come to me with such matters again."

For a moment Hayden thought Worthing would speak—or scream—but instead the man assumed the battered dignity of the solitary oppressed, and went almost silently out.

Griffiths was standing beyond the door, no doubt awaiting his turn, and the marine hesitated, not certain whether to announce the doctor at such a juncture or not.

"You wish to see me, Doctor?" Hayden enquired.

Griffiths nodded.

"Do come in."

The door closed behind the surgeon, who looked both embarrassed and angered.

"I fear you could not help but overhear at least some of what was said?" Hayden glanced at the doctor expectantly.

"Only that he accused you of being a papist and threatened to bring down the wrath of his 'friends' within the admiralty. An empty threat if ever there was one. How dare he make such an accusation? Is the man unbalanced?"

"Oh, it did not begin with me. It began with young Gould. Worthing learned that Gould's father is a Jew."

"Ah," Griffiths managed. For a moment he considered. "There is, Mr Hayden, the matter of the Test Act. . . ."

"Indeed there is. But Worthing may not apply it. Only the government or the admiralty may require it. I would not accede to his demand that Gould be forced to take the sacrament."

"Ah." The doctor took a seat on the bench before the gallery windows—thin fingers spread pale over meagre knees. "I do see your point, and understand your principle, but I cannot help but wonder, if I may be allowed an opinion on this matter, if you might not save yourself a great deal of . . . controversy by simply having both Gould and yourself take the sacrament. It will remove all the ammunition Worthing would employ to cause you trouble—which is more than his intention, it is his nature. You could even have Smosh do it, if that would lessen the sting."

"Though I esteem your opinions on all matters, Doctor, in this I cannot comply. Give in to that man and what will he demand next? Floggings for men who are not Christian enough? Trial by water? No, I will not allow him to test my crew in any way."

"He will use this to cause mischief, as I have said."

"But if not this, it will be something else. Give way to him once and I will be doing it the entire voyage."

"Religion, as you well know, is a fertile field for kindling resentments, animosities, even atrocities. He will spread the rumour that you are a papist. The crew all know you lived for many years in France. They will begin to wonder how you lived among the French as an Anglican. A conversion has been the cause of ruptures in many a family, and they will begin to wonder why your French Catholic relations were so accepting of your apostate beliefs." The doctor glanced up at him—almost a question.

"Are you suggesting, Dr Griffiths, that I have not been forthcoming about my own faith?"

Griffiths waved this idea away with a thin hand. "I am, like Mr Jefferson, a deist. Religions—all religions—are the creations of men and reflect all of man's worst instincts. The supreme being who created our universe, I am quite certain, has taken no notice of me or my petty aspirations. Which is by way of saying, Captain Hayden, that you could be either Catholic or Anglican or Mohammedan—it is all the same to me. But the crew might not share my enlightened beliefs."

"I am not going to explain my beliefs to my own crew. Next Worthing will be questioning my loyalty to England!"

The two were silent, uncomfortable, for a moment, both taken by their own thoughts.

"Did you wish to speak with me upon some matter, Doctor?"

"Only to say that one of the men brought aboard from the *Agnus* is very ill."

"I thought he came aboard with an injury?"

"So he did, but he has since taken such a turn that I am at a loss to explain it." Griffiths stood, crouched, reaching up an angular arm to take hold of a beam.

Hayden was alarmed by the doctor's obvious concern. "You don't think he has brought some . . . malady aboard, do you?"

"I did not a few hours ago, but now I cannot be certain." Griffiths leaned his forehead against a beam and closed his eyes a second. "I do not think he will reach Gibraltar. I-it came on with such rapidity. A fever, then cramping pains in his legs and back. He bleeds very freely from the nose, and his lungs are infused with fluid that he coughs up in a pink froth. The smell of his breath is unbearable, and his pain now so severe that I have given him laudanum, of which I have but scant supply. I should hardly be worried about this spreading, but he arrived recently from Portugal."

"They have not any contagion there, have they?"

"Not that we know of, but many a time a ship has left port bearing pestilence before anyone had become cognisant of the disease being there. Thus it is borne to some other port not yet alerted to the danger." Griffiths looked up at Hayden. "I would call this an influenza, but I have never seen it so severe in a man so young and apparently hale. Can we send a boat to the *Agnus* to enquire if they have any sick among their crew?"

Hayden glanced out the window. "It is too late this night, I think, but immediately it is light we shall dispatch someone. Will you send Mr Ariss, Doctor?"

"No. I think it best I go myself." Griffiths stood a moment, lost in thought.

"Is there any other course we might follow in this case?"

Griffiths shook his head. "No. That is everything." He glanced up at Hayden and tried to shrug off his obvious apprehension. "You are joining us for dinner?"

"I am."

"Until then."

"Keep me informed of this man's condition," Hayden said as the doctor opened the door to leave. "What is his name?"

"McKee." Griffiths opened his mouth as if to say more, hesitated, decided against speech, and disappeared.

Eight

The strained atmosphere in the gunroom brought to Hayden's mind a rope being stretched. He could almost hear the elongated "squeal." Both tradition and etiquette demanded that guests be accorded every possible courtesy, but the present guests—or at least one of them—had trespassed upon every convention the sailors held dear.

Hayden believed that Worthing must take great, if unacknowledged, pleasure in the present state of affairs. In this Griffiths was utterly correct: the reverend doctor found some perverse satisfaction in creating conflict and aggravation everywhere he passed. Having accomplished little in his life, he was resentful of all humankind for this state of affairs. *Why did they not see his natural superiority? Why did these foolish men sing the praises of others when they should be applauding him?* And so his resentments curdled, the tally of slights and offences multiplied, and his spite oozed bile until he became bloated with bitterness.

A number of attempts to generate polite conversation had sputtered and flickered out, and now the men seated round the table seemed intent on their food, on the motions of their glittering forks.

"How fare your patients, Doctor?" Smosh asked. The rotund little clergyman appeared the only one present unaffected by the disquiet in the gunroom.

"As well as can be hoped." Griffiths glanced Hayden's way. Neither had spoken to anyone else about his fears for McKee.

Smosh went on, apparently not recognizing the concern that passed between surgeon and captain. "I am unfamiliar with such matters, but it did seem to me that few were hurt in the action—at least aboard our ship. Was this true?"

Each waited for some other to reply, and after a few seconds of indecision Barthe answered.

"We were fortunate to lose so few"—he nodded to the marine lieutenant—"though Mr Hawthorne's men were not so favoured."

The marine lieutenant clumsily raised a glass, a dollop of claret slopping over the edge and slipping down his fingers and under-wrist toward his crimson cuff. "To the victorious dead," he said with excessive feeling. The marine was clearly numbing his emotions with wine that evening, for which no one blamed him. It was often seen that a single survivor of a slaughtered gun crew would feel more than just the loss of his mates; he would feel ashamed that he, no more worthy than any one of them, had been spared.

The men present raised their glasses and echoed Hawthorne's salute.

Immediately the strained silence returned—the rope stretching out, creaking like a rusty hinge.

"I wonder," Worthing ventured, making a small pile of potato shards with his fork, "if we would not have had greater losses had we gone to Captain Pool's aid." He then looked directly at Hayden, his usual air of lugubrious superiority less tolerable than ever.

"We did go to Pool's aid," Barthe said bluntly.

The clergyman offered a half-grimace and a shrug. "Upon our first pass we fired a few guns into the large French ship's stern, but upon our second pass we failed to engage the seventy-four, which I am told had the weather gauge on poor Pool. We sailed on, engaging no enemy vessels at all, though there were three to be had."

"Sir," Barthe began, his manners thrust aside, "it is apparent that you do not understand such matters—"

Worthing looked up sharply at Barthe and interrupted. "I understand that Captain Pool questioned Mr Hayden's courage, and that Mr Hayden then did not come to his aid when he had need."

If the man had not been a cleric in the Church of England, Hayden would have demanded he walk out with him.

"Doctor Worthing," Hayden said, his voice trembling with rage, "I fired first upon the frigate that had raked our seventy-four and had then engaged Pool upon his larboard side where he had no gunports open. I then raked the French seventy-four, brought my ship about, and came back, intending to engage the French frigate, which was wreaking havoc upon Pool's upper deck, the heel of his ship and the lifting seas making this deck vulnerable. The frigate exploded, likely due to our first cannonade. I did not feel a need to engage the French seventy-four, as I believed Pool was more than equal to that task, especially so as the French captain, though he did have the weather gauge, was fearful of opening his lower gunports due to the sea running and the heeling of his ship. I then went to the aid of Captain Bradley, who was engaged in battle with a frigate of superior force. No captain with common sense would have done differently."

"A well-rehearsed speech, Hayden," Worthing observed. "I hope the senior naval officer in Gibraltar is persuaded by it. Of course, he might have another story from Pool himself. Bradley cannot speak to it, as he departed this life—your 'going to his aid' being a bit late."

Hayden clutched his fork and knife in balled hands, like a child. Around the table the faces of the men appeared pale with anger. It occurred to Hayden that the company might fall upon the parson with their knives, for to speak to a captain so upon his own ship was unheard-of.

At that instant Hayden apprehended a flicker of pleasure flash over Worthing's sallow features.

Forcing his hands to relax, Hayden said in an easy manner, "Well, Doctor, you—and Captain Pool and anyone else—may make whatever reports you like once we reach Gibraltar. I am confident of my decisions." Hayden turned to Saint-Denis, the gunroom's senior officer and the man who should have been attempting to defuse such a situation.

"This is an excellent claret, Lieutenant. My compliments."

Saint-Denis nodded and tried to smile. An animal who had just heard the door of the trap slam behind him could not look more alarmed.

But Worthing could let no statement go unanswered. "I'm sure you are equally confident that Captain Pool will never overtake us upon this course," the reverend doctor said, "and you will retain your assumed rank of 'commodore' for a fortnight yet?"

Before Hayden could even consider a response, Smosh spoke.

"Your forthrightness must make you many a devotee," he said to Worthing. "I do admire it. I find myself perplexed that such insights have not gained you a living upon the land. But then, I am sure, Doctor Worthing, that you preferred to come to sea." He smiled quickly at the gathering. "Have we not all longed for a captive audience whom we might bless with our wisdom?"

Hawthorne turned his slitty gaze upon Worthing. "Yes, Doctor, why is it you do not have a living upon the land? A man of your learning—of your eminence—must have had many offers."

It was surprising to Hayden that a combatant so adroit in the art of opening wounds in others should allow himself to be injured in the same manner.

"I will tell you," Worthing responded in his haughty, put-upon manner, "I have been considered for many a position in my time; my particular talents have not gone unrecognised in all quarters. But others with more interest or better connexions invariably prevailed. When Lord Hood requested my services I felt that I was being called.

That I had been meant to minister among the poor, benighted sea-men of His Majesty's fleets. That, I believe, was the reason I have ever been passed over for positions ashore."

"Divine intervention . . ." Smosh said without apparent sarcasm, but unable to suppress a hint of a smile.

"Mock me if you will, but our Lord operates in ways we cannot comprehend."

"Indeed," Smosh responded. He raised his glass. "To the poor, benighted seamen of His Majesty's fleets."

Everyone raised his glass in reply, smiles not well concealed. "Hear," intoned one and all, though Hayden wondered if Griffiths had not said, "Amen."

Into this moment of levity Wickham's schoolboy voice enquired, "Is it your opinion, Captain, that Lord Hood will hold Toulon?"

Everyone turned to Hayden expectantly, and he had the feeling that his loyalty to Britain would be judged by his answer. But Hayden could not be dishonest, even so.

"Not if the French are determined to take it back, it pains me to say."

"Truly, Captain?" Hawthorne said, a bit surprised. "We have held Gibraltar."

"Yes, and no offence is meant to Lord Hood, but Toulon is situated so differently. Coming at it by land is simply less arduous. A concerted siege by a properly prepared army of adequate numbers and Toulon will fall. I shudder to think what will happen to the inhabitants after it does. I fear they will regret allying themselves with us."

"You have very little faith in Admiral Lord Hood," Worthing observed, "for an Englishman."

Hayden refused to be provoked, believing nothing gave the parson more pleasure than seeing that his arrows caused aggravation. "I have every faith in him, Dr Worthing, but I do not believe he can perform

miracles. We can hope the French remain so concentrated upon killing one another that they will spare Toulon for some time."

"It was audacious of Hood to assume control of Toulon in the first
place," Barthe spoke up before Worthing could frame another re-
proach. "But it says a great deal about the French form of government that the people of Toulon would surrender their city to us
rather than be governed by the Paris mobs. I have heard it opined
that this man—General Paoli—is uncomfortable with the Convention as well."

"He has fought for Corsican independence most of his life,"
Griffiths stated. "Did anyone really believe he would ally himself
with the French in the long haul? No. He will break his ties with
France at first opportunity."

"But Corsica is a small land, Doctor," Smosh said softly, "and
France is great, despite her present troubles. Or let us say that France
will be great again. They chased Paoli from the island once with little
difficulty. If Paoli chooses to break with the French, he will not keep
Corsica independent for many years, despite his admirable dream."

"I met him once," Wickham said, "General Paoli. At the home
of a friend of my father's during his years in England. I thought him
rather a sad sight—very dignified, almost noble, really, but even so,
like a figure in a play. Tragic, in the way that an exiled prince might
be so. People attended to his opinions with exceeding deference,
even some very great men who were present, but he looked terribly
out of place to my way of thinking. Briefly, he spoke to me—most
kindly—his English good but very simple, like a child's, and thickly
accented. His French was better and he seemed pleased to speak it.
He told me that one day he would return to Corsica, and if ever
I found myself there he would take me shooting in the mountains. I
thought he must control an excess of feeling just mentioning his
home." Wickham fell silent, indulging his memory.

"He is a great champion to many," Griffiths observed, "and not just within his own land. He was welcomed to Paris like a revolutionary war hero: the enlightened man—this after the Bourbons had forced him into exile in our own country for twenty years. Rousseau corresponded with him, and our own Dr Johnson welcomed him to his literary club. He has not lived the modest, anonymous life of a shopkeeper, though I did think it rather ungrateful of him to characterise the British as 'a nation of merchants' after we had sheltered him for two decades."

"He didn't say that, truly?" Barthe asked, incredulous.

"I have had it now from more than one source, so I believe it. Of course, it is not less cruel for being demonstrably true."

"And I thought us a nation of seamen," Hawthorne pitched in to small laughter, and then added, "And clergymen, of course."

"No, no," Smosh contended, "clergymen, one and all, have mercantile hearts. Some collect livings like stock certificates or manufactories. They call the managers 'curates' and collect a share of all the moneys, often investing it in land or other businesses. No, we are merchants as well. And a church, despite all its manifest and demonstrable value, is nothing more than a place of business. Our 'goods' are solace and salvation—excellent products, all must agree—and with the tithes and benefactions we build our shops, calling them churches and cathedrals. Increasing our trade is our avowed purpose. And is it not telling that we call a ministry a 'living'? Not a 'blessing' or even a 'duty.' No. We call it a 'living,' and what does that refer to but an annual income?" He placed a hand on his chest. "Beneath the pious breast of the cleric beats the calculating heart of a man of business."

"Mr Smosh, you should not make such jests," Worthing protested. "Even if you are being ironical, you should not say it. Such opinions are near to blasphemy, and there are people who might think you serious."

"But I am not being ironical," Smosh responded. "I am being truthful. I have not denied that many a churchman does great good within his parish, but then one can make the same argument about a cheese merchant or a banker. Merchants have their value and their purpose, as do we all."

Part of the satisfaction Hayden took in watching Smosh torture Dr Worthing was the little man's mental agility. Worthing was invariably at a loss for an answer, simply because he had never been presented with such arguments before, and when he did manage to mount a defense—invariably a tottering and faulty one—Smosh easily kicked out the braces and it came tumbling down.

Griffiths caught Hayden's eye at that moment and smiled cheerfully. Witnessing the torture of Dr Worthing could not help but bring a little warmth to even the most compassionate heart.

Hayden exited the gunroom, a bit befuddled by spirits. Wickham had gone before him and taken up a seat at the midshipmen's table, where he engaged in a conversation of such gravity that Hayden found himself stopping.

"Is something amiss, Mr Wickham?" Hayden enquired.

The midshipmen looked one to the other.

"I believe there is, sir," Wickham answered quietly, but appeared reluctant to say more.

Hayden glanced around. A few feet behind lay the gunroom, its door ajar. Forward the crew slung their hammocks and made up their messes.

"Come up to my cabin in a moment," Hayden said softly, nodded to the young gentlemen, and retreated up the ladder to the gun-deck.

His cabin was cheery, if cool. The gathered bodies in the gunroom had made it a place of warmth, if a little lacking in its usual cheer.

He lit several more candles, and a moment later the sentry let Wickham and the midshipmen into the cabin. Madison and Hobson deferred to Wickham, almost taking a step back.

"Something would appear to be troubling all of you?" Hayden began, looking at each of them in turn. "Mr Wickham, you seem to have been elected spokesman."

Wickham glanced at the others, who nodded, and he turned to Hayden. "It is Mr Gould, sir. A rumour has been spread among the crew that he is a Jew, sir, and has refused to take the sacrament."

Hayden felt his eyes close. Would Griffiths be proven right in this matter?

"And what do the crew make of this?" Hayden enquired, opening his eyes.

"I think to most it means very little, but they are being . . . whipped up, Captain. Resentments are being"—he searched for a word—"manufactured."

"And who is doing this?"

The middies all glanced at one another. "It is hard to be certain, sir, but it seems to have begun with Dr Worthing. He has befriended some of the men—if you could call it that—and they, in turn, are spreading his . . . preachings to the others. It is causing something of a division, sir."

Hayden heard himself sigh. "Damn the man!" he muttered. "And what about Gould? How is this affecting him? Where is he, by the way?"

"On watch, sir," Hobson offered.

"No man has refused to take his orders, Captain, but there are a few men who obey with some reluctance."

"We will have to flog one or two of them, Mr Wickham. The first time you apprehend a hand not jumping to when Gould gives them an order, put them on report. Let the men know what supporting Dr Worthing and his ideas will cost them. I will have a word with some of the older men—they should be talking sense to the others. And I shall speak with Worthing as well." Hayden felt his frustration mounting. Smosh might find some amusement in Dr Worthing, but Hayden thought him a dangerous nuisance. "I shall be forced to confine him to his quarters yet. Thank you for speaking of this with me."

The midshipmen, however, did not appear prepared to leave. There was an awkward shuffling and stalling feel about their manner.

"There is something more, I gather?" He raised an eyebrow at Wickham.

Wickham hesitated, then straightened and looked Hayden in the eye most directly. "Some of the men are saying that you crossed yourself when you saw all of the dead Frenchmen floating, sir . . . like a papist."

"I am sure I did no such thing."

"And I am sure you are right, Captain, but everyone was dazed and had not their wits about them, so no one can gainsay them. The men are suggesting that you had more sympathy for the dead Frenchmen than you had for our own injured, and that you should have gone back to search for the marines blown out of the tops."

"Blast this interfering clergyman to hell!" Hayden said with feeling. "You all know those marines would never have been found alive. If I had been blown over the side I would surely have drowned with that sea running—and I am a strong swimmer. At the same time, there was Bradley engaged with a heavy frigate. We could save more men there than marines in the sea."

"None of us questions your decision for a moment," Wickham assured him. "I am only telling you what is being said by the hands."

"Of course. Do pardon my outburst. Do you know, when the mutineers were hung, I thought that would be the end of trouble among this crew."

"There are a lot of new men, Captain," Wickham said, "and a man like Worthing . . . I think the crew are a bit afraid of him. No one wants to get on his bad side, sir."

"I am certainly evidence of that. Who are these men whom Worthing has . . . befriended?"

Here Wickham's reticence blossomed into near refusal. Seamen did not like to be known as peachers. Hayden was tempted to say, "You are a lieutenant now, Mr Wickham—no more schoolboy solidarity. Who are they?" but instead he waited, certain Wickham would work this out for himself.

"Weeks, sir, and Kitchen—"

"Chettle's mate?"

"Aye, sir," Wickham replied.

"He is awfully religious, sir," Madison added.

"No doubt triply true."

"Bracegirdle, Elliot, and Stephens."

Hayden was surprised that certain names were not included—troublemakers always seemed to find trouble. "Not too long a list. Bracegirdle and Stephens are new to the ship, are they not?"

"They are, sir, but Stephens grew up in the south-coast fisheries and then served in merchantmen. He is well-thought-of and liked, Captain Hayden."

"Well, he is up for a flogging if he tries to undermine my middies. Thank you, gentlemen. You may be about your business. I will deal with this matter."

Left alone in the chilly cabin, Hayden gazed longingly at his swinging cot, made up by his servant. A quick glance at his watch convinced him it was too late to confront Worthing this night. Morning would be soon enough. He wondered if he should take the deck and assess the mood of the watch—where Gould was on duty—but general exhaustion, drink, and repleteness pushed him toward his cot instead. All could be dealt with in the morning. That would be soon enough.

A sound so distant, so faint—a deep-chested booming—that it hardly registered. One element of a jumbled dream. Hayden sat up in his swaying cot and listened a moment; just the common sounds of a ship at sea, though the wind did seem to be making. He lay back down, the swinging of his cot swaying him back toward sleep. Again he was drawn back to the surface of dream by a heavy, hollow report.

"Thunder," he muttered, and let himself sink back down toward somnolence. Or was it the report of a gun? Again he sat up, calming his breathing so that he might listen. Feet came tapping, rapid-fire, down the companionway ladder outside his cabin. Before the sentry could knock, Hayden had swung out of his cot and was pulling on clothes, almost tumbling to the floor in his hurry.

"One moment!" he called, jerking on resistant boots. Snatching up a coat, he pulled open a door. Gould stood before him, looking perplexed if not worried, in the dim lamplight.

"Did I hear a gun?"

"We're not certain, sir," the boy answered—a quick, worried blurting. "Mr Archer sent me to ask for you, Captain."

They went immediately to the aft companionway ladder and up two rungs at a stride.

"Was it a signal?" At night there was a prearranged signal code employing guns, lanterns, and flares.

"I don't know, sir."

Hayden reached the deck a step ahead of the midshipman. A great distance off, lightning illuminated a cloud for an instant. Muffled thunder burst upon them. "Have we a ship in trouble, Mr Archer?"

Archer and Dryden, the master's mate, now mate to Mr Franks, stood by the larboard rail, Archer with a glass to his eye.

"We are uncertain, Captain Hayden," Archer replied. "South-east by south—Mr Dryden and the mizzen lookout thought they saw a powder flash, sir, but as it occurred simultaneous with a thunderclap and lightning, we cannot be sure."

"Did you see the flash, Mr Archer?" Hayden asked.

The young lieutenant handed him the glass. "I did not, sir."

Hayden turned to Dryden, the young man half a head shorter than he. "Was it a gun or not, Mr Dryden?"

"I wish I knew, sir. I just saw it out of the corner of my eye, like. If it were a signal, Captain Hayden, they've not repeated it."

Hayden began to lift the glass. "Where away?"

Dryden raised a hand, chose a point in the distant darkness, and indicated carefully. "There, sir, but well beyond the convoy."

Hayden put the night glass to his eye and gazed at the horizon, the sea suddenly up, the stars below, as the night glass inverted everything.

"Do you see anything, sir?" Gould asked, not yet fully accustomed to naval etiquette—only Hayden's senior officers or warrant officers of long standing would ask such a question while he was concentrating on a task.

For a moment Hayden meant not to answer, but then, remembering his conversation with Wickham and the other middies, he relented. "No, Mr Gould. We might have to call Mr Wickham to penetrate this darkness."

A thunder squall blackened the horizon. The weather had changed. "What is our heading, Mr Archer?"

"Sou-sou'west, sir. The wind has been veering slowly all this night. A gale would appear to be in the offing, Captain."

"Yes. Damn. I had hoped the northerly might hold for a few days."

The officers stood watching the spectacle, the night sky shattered by vague lightning, often buried deep within the inky blur.

"*Tonitrus,*" a voice intoned, and a scarlet-coated figure appeared beside him.

"If you insist on speaking Latin, Mr Hawthorne," Hayden said quietly, "the Reverend Inquisitor will have you court-martialled as a papist spy."

"And with my widely admired fluency in the French language, I will no doubt be accused of serving the Convention as well."

Hayden smiled. Hawthorne's abysmal French had almost gotten them killed on their last cruise. He lowered the glass.

"Well, I can see nothing but the lights of our convoy ships," Hayden concluded. "Have we lookouts aloft, yet?"

"We do, sir."

"Call them down, Mr Archer. If we have the misfortune to be struck by lightning, I want no one aloft. How long have we had this squall in view?"

"Some time, sir. It approaches but slowly."

Hayden continued to gaze into the darkness, hypnotized by the lightning. When it burst low and within the cloud, it did resemble muzzle flash.

"Was that a gun?" Gould asked.

"No. Almost certainly lightning," Hayden replied.

"Should we clear for action, sir?" Archer wondered.

It was the very question Hayden was contemplating. Only a moment he wavered. "No, Mr Archer. As no one is certain they saw muzzle flash, and the signal, were it one, has not been repeated, we will proceed as we are." Hayden looked back out into the darkness at the dim lights of the convoy ships. They undulated and guttered, floated up and fell, winking out here, blinking into being there—a field of drunken fireflies.

The officers stood at the rail, silent and contemplative.

"What is the meaning of *Tonitrus*?" Dryden asked suddenly.

"Thunder," Gould replied.

"Well done, Gould," Archer said. "You soon shall be rivalling Mr Hawthorne for classical learning."

"Well, as Gould appears to have your classical education in hand," Hawthorne said, "I will return to the rather pleasant dream I was having. Captain." Hawthorne touched his hat and disappeared into the darkness.

Archer went back to his duty as officer of the watch, and Hayden was left standing at the rail with Midshipman Gould. Hayden wanted to ask him if any difficulties had arisen due to his father's religion or his own race, but was reluctant to broach the subject—he knew not why. "How are you fitting in, Mr Gould? No problems, I hope?"

"None, sir. Mr Wickham has been most attentive in teaching me my duties, and now I'm learning the skills of master's mate. There is a great deal to take in all at once, but I feel I am making progress."

" 'Making progress' sounds a little modest, Mr Gould. The reports I've received tell me you are learning like no other." Hayden looked out at the swarm of lights again. "And how do you get along with the hands?"

He could feel the boy's hesitation in the dark.

"Well enough, Captain Hayden," he said too confidently. "As in everything, I have much to learn."

"Mr Barthe is an excellent sailing master, and a great seaman, but if you ever have need of some guidance in dealing with the hands, you might come to me." As soon as this was said, Hayden felt like a fraud. Was he not having his own problems with the crew—stirred up by Worthing? At least these had not yet become manifest in the running of the ship.

"Why, thank you, sir."

"Do not be embarrassed to seek advice in this matter. Like making a splice, governing a crew is a learned skill."

"Aye, sir."

"I will leave you to your duties."

Gould touched his hat and slipped quietly away. Much to his frustration, Hayden no longer felt the call of sleep—not that he wasn't fatigued, but he knew sleep would elude him this night. A desire for coffee came over him, but the stove would not be lit for some hours. Instead he paced the after quarterdeck, larboard to starboard, stopping occasionally to sweep his glass over the dark southern sea. No one would approach him there unless upon a matter of absolute necessity. In a ship crammed full of more than two hundred souls, he was blessed to have a cabin and the after quarterdeck as his own private estate. Even so, he missed the camaraderie of the gunroom, a

place he had become terribly familiar with since passing for lieutenant had granted him access to that little club. He missed the con-
viviality, the intense discussion, the wit of men like Hawthorne. He
had passed out of that particular brotherhood. Dinner in the gunroom
had brought that home to him. He was not only a guest, no longer
privy to the discussions that had been taking place, but he was the
captain—at least temporarily—the man upon whom everyone depended for his future in the service. Even more unsettling, he was
undoubtedly a subject for discussion around the table. Unlike that
scoundrel Hart, Hayden wanted no spies reporting such conversations to him. Better not to know. Far better.

The wind veered uncertainly southward, then steadied in the
south-west, sending the watch to sheets and braces and the ship sailing
obliquely back toward France. Perhaps two hours before first light,
sleep drove Hayden to his cot, but he was back on deck before dawn.

Wickham was officer of the watch and the midshipmen and Mr
Barthe were readying to take the morning sight once the sun lifted
a little higher. The squall had passed over them that night and left
them rolling in a small wind with a little more west in it. Broken
cloud bedraggled the sky, and the morning remained chill, the wind
eating into his woolen coat.

Across the eastern sky, a featureless band of pearl grey cloud slowly
blushed rose. The sun pushed upward into this miasmal haze, and
day overspread sky and sea.

"Aloft there," Hayden called when he judged the light adequate.
"Have you a count of our ships?"

Hayden could see the man sitting astride the top-gallant yard, a
glass slowly sweeping east to west. Lowering the glass and steadying
himself, the lookout peered down toward the deck.

"I can't be certain, Captain. Twice I've tallied twenty-nine and
once thirty."

"Blast," Hayden muttered, refraining from saying, "Damn your
eyes."

"I'll go aloft, sir," Wickham offered, and immediately clambered up onto the rail and began climbing the weather shrouds. Out to the end of the top-gallant yard he went, so sails would not obstruct his view. In a moment he lowered his glass and called down.

"I make it twenty-nine transports, Captain. All our escort vessels are in place, but McIntosh is beating toward us."

"You cannot see a ship in our wake, Mr Wickham, blown down to leeward, perhaps?"

"No, sir, but there is a low mist obscuring the horizon."

Hayden muttered another curse. Once the sun rose a little higher, his missing ship might be revealed, but it seemed now that there had been a gun fired, and it was, of all things, most likely a request for assistance.

McIntosh was soon sailing along within hailing distance.

"We have lost a transport, Captain Hayden."

"So we thought. What is her name?"

"The *Hartlepool*, sir."

"I knew that little tub would get herself into trouble," Mr Barthe complained. "Never was she fit for sea."

Hayden ignored this outburst. "Has anyone reported a signal from her? A gun fired about two bells?"

"No, sir, Captain. Shall I sail back and search for her?"

"Yes. Yes, I see no choice. Will you carry my surgeon to the *Agnus* as you go? I'll lower a boat and you can take the crew aboard and tow it behind."

"Gladly, Captain Hayden."

Hayden motioned one of the middies over. "Pass the word for Dr Griffiths, if you please."

The boy bobbed his head and set off at a trot.

It always seemed odd to Hayden that the boatswain was not the officer who had charge of the boats; that duty fell to the carpenter. Chettle and Franks were now in the process of launching a small cutter from a rolling deck onto a rising sea. Of necessity, some rather inexperienced men were involved in this endeavour, and their mates were schooling them in the usual genteel manner favoured by seamen. How Hayden missed Aldrich. He would have taken these bewildered landsmen in hand and with infinite patience turned them into sailors. Hayden would trade any ten of his present crew to have another Aldrich aboard.

Griffiths appeared at that moment, weaving down the gangway in response to the ship's roll. Clutched in one hand was a hat, in the other a small leather satchel. Griffiths' face was pinched and pale, and he glanced out at the rising sea with both animosity and dismay.

"You could still send Mr Ariss, Doctor," Hayden suggested.

"No, it is better I go myself." The surgeon watched the boat, now raised by tackles, as it tried to swing across the deck, poorly controlled by landsmen who were none too steady on the deck themselves. The experienced hands were aloft reducing sail at that moment, watching the antics on deck with ill-disguised amusement.

Griffiths was silent a moment, then seemed to make a decision. "I must tell you, Captain, I found that clergyman down in my sickberth this morning. Ariss had absented himself but a moment, and the man stole in. How he knew when to come I do not know."

"Worthing? I forbade him entry to the sick-berth."

"He heard me say that McKee—from the *Agnus*—was likely dying, and he slipped in with the intent of anointing the sick. Poor McKee would have none of it—he was horrified—but then he departed this life a few hours later. It has passed through the lower deck like consumption—the clergyman was in the sick-berth and a man died but a short time after. Who will come to me with their illnesses now? Did Worthing not comprehend the mischief he would effect?"

"I'm certain he did. It was explained to him most explicitly." Hayden removed his hat and ran fingers back through his hair. "And what of this man McKee? Do you know what did for him?"

The doctor shook his head, face folding into a grimace. "Let us hope I do not find the answer aboard the *Agnus*."

Childers had begun mustering his boat crew by the rail, and Hayden waved to him. "This sea is rising, Childers; take no green hands."

"Aye, sir."

"If you judge it unwise to return, remain on the *Agnus* and I will have McIntosh carry you back later this day."

Childers made a knuckle.

Gould appeared at Hayden's elbow. "Excuse me, Captain. Is it not common to send a midshipman off with the boat?"

"I am sending Madison."

Gould looked so very serious as he asked, "Might I go in his place? I have asked and he will not mind. He told me so himself."

Boys were always on the lookout for something resembling adventure. "Go on, then."

Hayden glanced over at Childers, who, overhearing the exchange, nodded. He would keep the boy out of trouble.

The boat was finally put into the sea with only superficial damage to the topsides and to the cutter itself, and the doctor was quickly ferried over to McIntosh's waiting schooner, where he and the crew were taken aboard. This vessel had not gone half a mile before the wind died away altogether.

"It is going to come around, sir," Barthe pronounced. "Blasted, fucking sou'wester!"

"Yes, I fear you are right, Mr Barthe. At least we made a little westing overnight. Our course will not be so very bad."

Barthe waved a small hand toward the ships of the convoy. "With this lot in tow, we shall be hove-to by dinner, Captain Hayden. Just see if we aren't."

Gibraltar had never seemed so very far away as it did at that moment.

Hayden made his way forward, wondering what he would do with Worthing. The man had defied him and had caused Hayden and Griffiths a serious problem as a result. As he walked his eye played over every part of the ship. This was not a conscious act, but something he had been trained to do since his days as a midshipman. The captains he had served had taught him that captains who missed no detail instilled high standards among their officers, who took pride in keeping up their parts of the ship to the captain's requirements.

Hayden found some landsmen coiling down ropes on the forecastle—a simple task any landsman should be able to master.

"These coils will not do!" Hayden informed them. "You must be able to pull them off their pins and have them run free. You can endanger both the ship and crew if these ropes foul in a gale." Hayden looked away from the surprised landsmen, who had never had the captain speak to them before. "Tawney!" Hayden called one of the foretopmen descending from the yards at that moment. "Show these men the proper manner of coiling down." Hayden turned back to the men. "You should have learned this your first days aboard. I expect better of you."

Hayden turned to walk away as Tawney jogged forward, but had not gone three paces when he heard one of the landsmen mutter, ". . . ing papist."

He spun around in time to see Tawney stretch the man out with one blow, the landsman striking the deck so hard that his head bounced like a ball. For a moment no one moved, the man on the deck still as the dead, but then he moaned and squirmed a little, limbs writhing weakly. Blood flowed from his nose onto the dark planking. Tawney had turned white with rage, and then awareness.

"I—I didn't realise what I was about, Captain," he stammered. "Man called you a fu . . . a papist, sir. . . ." His mouth opened, but no more words would come.

"Yes, and he shall be flogged for it, but it was not your place to punish him."

"I'm sorry, sir."

"I am sure you are. Jump down and get a cot from the sick-berth, and tell the master-at-arms the man shall be in irons as soon as Mr Ariss has released him."

"Aye, sir." The topman started to turn away.

"And Tawney . . ."

"Aye, sir?"

"No grog for these three days. Do you understand?"

"I do, sir. Thank you, sir."

Hayden was not about to flog the men who took his side, but Tawney could not go unpunished. A feud among the crew was the last thing he wanted.

Every man on deck stood, transfixed—apprehensive and curious— as they gauged what this meant to them, to their place in the ship. As Hayden began to make his way aft along the gangway, men shook themselves out of this and turned back to their duties with renewed energy. An angry captain was not to be provoked.

Reaching the quarterdeck, Hayden said to Madison, "Pass the word for Dr Worthing. I will be in my cabin."

Once shut up in his cabin, Hayden paced quickly the width of the ship, containing the desire to strike one of the deck beams—an unfair battle if ever there was to be one. Just when he was about to send a second man to fetch the parson, he heard footsteps coming unhurriedly up the stair.

He ordered the sentry to let Worthing in, and when the parson entered, Hayden stood with his arms crossed in the middle of the cabin. Worthing, not a man commonly attuned to the moods of others, took one look at Hayden and stopped sharply.

"I am informed that you were in the sick-berth this very morning against my direct orders, and I have just had a man call me a papist— within hearing!" Hayden began, no attempt at politeness being made. "Have you no comprehension what undermining the captain will accomplish? I am what stands between this ship and utter calamity. All my years of training and experience are what keeps this ship from foundering in a storm or being taken by the French. Do you not realise that subverting my authority puts you and every soul aboard in mortal danger? And this is not to mention that Griffiths thinks we might have a contagion aboard and you have just ensured, with your presence in the sick-berth, that no man will come to him except he is too ill to conceal it!"

"You have no right to speak to me thus!" Worthing replied haughtily. "You who are not even a captain. Are you accusing me—"

But Hayden would have none of it, raising his voice over the clergyman's. "Do you heed no voice but your own! This is a ship of war. We are crossing the Bay of Biscay—a sea plagued with privateers and French warships. I cannot, for a moment, tolerate dissension among my crew or allow any man to foster it. You, sir, for the duration of this voyage, are confined to your cabin. A marine guard will stand sentry outside your door. You shall be allowed out to eat your meals, use the heads, and to have one half-hour of air twice daily—under guard. You may speak to no one and have no visitors but Mr Smosh. That is all, sir. You may leave."

Worthing was positively twitching with rage, his face contorting and shivering. For a moment words eluded him, and then in a high quavering voice he began, "I am not some ignorant seaman you can call or dismiss at your whim!"

Hayden crossed the cabin in an instant, the clergyman stumbling back in trepidation. Opening the door, Hayden confronted the surprised sentry. "Escort Dr Worthing to his cabin and stand guard outside his door until Mr Hawthorne has you relieved. Dr Worthing is not to leave or have visitors. Is that understood?"

"I will not stand for it!" Worthing stated, but it was outrage without conviction. Hayden had frightened him and his shyness was now revealed. "You cannot—"

"Lead him off," Hayden said evenly, and then turned to Worthing. "You may proceed to your cabin with dignity, Dr Worthing, or be dragged. It matters not to me."

Worthing stood his ground only an instant, then went clopping out, stumbling, his shoes rushing to catch up to his ungainly body. He fell on the steps and required a steadying hand from the marine. Hayden stood a moment, gazing down the gun-deck at the two lines of blackened cannon, then pulled his door closed, retreated inside, and slumped down on the bench before the gallery.

A moment later a knock sounded at his door.

"Who is there?" Hayden called out, not rising.

"Hawthorne, Captain."

"Come in."

The door opened a foot, and Hawthorne's handsome face appeared. A moment he paused, and then let himself in. "I have a raging clergyman shut up in his cabin and a confused sentry standing outside his door not allowing him out. Your orders, I collect?"

"Entirely mine."

"Excellent. Bread and water? Floggings at dawn?"

"He may take his meals with the gunroom mess, but is to have no visitors or to even speak to anyone but Smosh."

"Which of the two gentlemen are we punishing?"

"It is not a matter for jest, Hawthorne."

"No. And it is past time that you took this step. I will see he preaches no more subversion among the crew. Leave it to me." Hawthorne paused a second. "Do you wonder how this might appear to the authorities when we reach Gibraltar?"

"Deranged, I expect. But what am I to do? The man is subverting my authority aboard my own ship. Spreading rumours that I am a papist. Telling utter lies, in fact. And this morning he went into the sick-berth against my orders. Never in this life have I met a man more prone to devilment—and I choose that word with intent. What ship will want such a parson aboard?"

"Lord Hood's *Victory*, I understand."

"Hood would be rid of the man in a week."

"So he would. I hear the crewman from the *Agnus* departed this life?"

"Yes. God rest his soul."

Hawthorne digested this a moment, then said quietly, "Do you think we have some plague aboard?"

It was a question Hayden did not even want to answer. "I pray not. The doctor has gone over to the *Agnus* to see if they have any others suffering fever."

"Griffiths has looked wholly distracted for more than a day. Distressed, even."

"Yes, he is concerned, but I take hope from the fact that he is yet uncertain. If McKee had yellow-jack or something like, the doctor would have known immediately."

"Yes, certainly. Barthe tells me we are in for a gale and we have lost a transport?"

"Both true, I regret to say. I have sent McIntosh to seek our misplaced ship."

"Have we a predator lurking near, or did this ship merely slip beneath the waves from general lubberly negligence?"

"I wish I knew, Mr Hawthorne, but I do now regret not looking more carefully into the sighting of what might have been a flare this night past." Hayden rose from his seat and fetched his hat.

He was still stiff and aching from being hurled across the deck. His ears rang—a high-pitched, relentless humming—and sitting for any length of time made him stiff again. Walking remained the best curative.

The wind was veering into the south-west as Hayden took the deck, crests breaking ineffectually on a steel-dark sea. Saint-Denis had begun preparations for a gale. Top-gallant masts were being housed and yards sent efficiently down to the deck.

"Saint-Denis? Have you doubled all the breechings on the guns?"

"Archer is seeing to the gun-deck, Captain," the lieutenant called loudly over the rising noise. "The weather-glass has dropped like a whore's under— Pardon me, sir. The weather-glass has fallen sharply."

"Yes, we are in for it, I fear." Hayden gazed out over the chaotic sea. All the ships within sight were reducing sail, sending down yards, and making the common preparations for foul weather.

McIntosh's schooner had reached the *Agnus*, and Hayden saw the *Themis*' cutter pulling over the mounting seas toward the transport. McIntosh had already reefed, and now set out to look for the missing ship, a task made doubly difficult, if not impossible, by the deteriorating weather.

"It is a damned foolish business sending out a convoy this late in the season," Barthe said as he approached Hayden and Saint-Denis on the quarterdeck. The sailing master appeared pasty-pale, a fragment of red hair, loose from his queue, wetly plastered to his forehead.

Hayden did not respond, but nodded. He was examining the ships in his convoy with a glass, appalled at how slowly evolutions were effected.

"Mr Hayden. Captain, I mean." It was Archer, still struggling to remember proper address.

"Mr Archer?"

The lieutenant sounded out of sorts, his habitual "recently awakened" manner thrust aside. "I have just sent Hale down to Mr Ariss. He was shaking with what I believed was fever, but professed himself to be perfectly well, sir."

"That loafer?" Barthe sounded surprised. "He asks to be put on the sick and hurt list if he can manufacture a sniffle."

Hayden lowered his glass and turned to Archer, who was very pensive, almost grim.

"What did Mr Ariss say?"

"Only that he hoped Dr Griffiths would return soon."

"Lieutenant," Hayden said to Saint-Denis. "Set a man to watch the *Agnus*. I fear this sea will become too great for our cutter to venture forth in, and McIntosh might not return before nightfall. The moment the doctor appears on deck, signal that we shall fetch him in the *Themis*."

"Aye, sir." Saint-Denis went quickly forward, calling for a man and a glass. For not the first time Hayden had to admit that the man, for all his flaws—and they formed not an inconsiderable list—was a passable seaman and officer. Hayden had seen many worse.

Ariss popped out of the after companionway, looked quickly about, spotted Hayden, and hurried toward him. The man's face was dark, jaw tight, a deep furrow appearing between his brows.

"How fares Hale?" Hayden asked him.

"That is why I have come, sir." He looked around at the listening men and fell silent.

"Excuse us, Mr Barthe," Hayden said, and motioned for Ariss to follow him to the taffrail.

Once there Ariss pitched his voice low. "Certainly you will want Dr Griffiths' more expert opinion, but I believe Hale has the same fever as the man from the *Agnus*, McKee, or so it appears to me." He lowered his voice even more. "And Pritchard, who has been in the sick-berth with a broken femur, is showing the same signs—high fever, sweats, aching joints, and his breathing is laboured and he has begun to cough up pink fluid, sir."

Hayden tried to hide his alarm. "We will fetch Griffiths back immediately and I will hear his opinion, though I do not doubt you are right, Mr Ariss. I will send a marine down to stand sentry. No one is to enter or leave the sick-berth without the permission of Dr Griffiths or myself. I wonder how many more men are feeling ill but will not come forward now."

"I have wondered the same thing, Captain."

Neither mentioned Dr Worthing, but he was clearly in their minds.

There was at that moment, from among the men forward, something like a collective moan of apprehension or despair. Hayden and Ariss turned to look.

Freddy Madison came running back along the heaving deck. "If you please, Captain," Madison spoke from a respectful distance. "You wished to be informed the instant the doctor appeared on the *Agnus*? Our cutter is away, sir, under sail and tacking toward us." He paused, swallowing once. "And, sir . . . the *Agnus* has just sent aloft the yellow-jack."

Raising his glass, Hayden found the *Agnus* wallowing upon a wind-driven sea. At her crosstrees shivered a yellow flag, the signal for yellow fever. For a moment Hayden stared, willing the banner to be some other signal . . . but it was not. He lowered his glass and took a long breath. Turning back to the surgeon's mate, he said softly, "Keep me informed of the state of Pritchard and Hale, Mr Ariss."

"Aye, sir," the man replied. He looked frightened, and that would not help settle the crew's fears. Hayden could hear the whispering.

The wind had settled, sou'west by west, which gave the convoy a more favourable slant than Hayden had hoped—the one bright point of the day—but the ships were hard on the wind and most were not as weatherly as the *Themis*. Hayden wondered if the wind would not veer a little more and force them to heave-to—luck was running that way.

"Mr Barthe!" Hayden called. "Let us bear off and take aboard our cutter." And then to the helmsman as Hayden made his way forward: "Prepare to shift your helm at Mr Barthe's order."

"Aye, sir."

"Mr Saint-Denis," Hayden addressed his first lieutenant. "Let us get our cutter aboard before this sea gets up any more. This wind has not finished making."

Saint-Denis nodded. "Aye, sir. It appears we have need of our doctor. . . ."

When Hayden refused to respond to this, on deck where everyone could hear, the young lieutenant went quickly off.

Hayden raised his glass again and found their cutter, double-reefed, the crew crowded to weather, and making heavy work of it. Two men were bailing constantly as spray broke aboard. Gould, Hayden noted, was assisting Childers with a heavy helm.

A rain squall overtook the *Themis,* and Hayden stepped into the lee of the mizzen to await the appearance of his oilskins, brought a moment later by a running servant. The frigate flew down upon the cutter, scudding before the gathering seas. In a few moments Hayden ordered her hove to and the crew of the cutter came up the side, only the doctor and Mr Gould having trouble catching the rhythm of the two vessels. Griffiths tumbled over the rail, caught by two seamen. He looked grim—even ill.

"As soon as you have found dry clothing, Doctor," Hayden said, "I will be in my cabin."

He left Saint-Denis and Barthe to beat back to their place in the convoy and took himself below to await the doctor.

A lengthy quarter of an hour crept by as Hayden paced, but then the doctor knocked and entered as quietly as ever.

"Three dead and half the crew ill," Griffiths announced—a no-nonsense diagnosis. "The master looks as if he will pull through, thank God, as the mate is a sot, if I am any judge. Why the man did not convey this information to us, I cannot even imagine. It is difficult to accept that anyone's understanding could be so diminished by drink."

Hayden had not allowed himself to hope for better—or so he had believed until hearing the doctor's pronouncement. His own dismay spoke otherwise, however. "And do you know what kind of contagion this might be?" he asked in what he hoped resembled a tone of calm acceptance.

Griffiths paused, his gaze flickering up as though he ticked off a mental list of symptoms. "Well, it is the strangest thing—it appears for all the world to be an influenza, yet I have never seen one so . . . violent. Including McKee, it has killed four young men in the prime of their lives, and that is not the way of any influenza of which I have knowledge. The *Agnus*, short of crew, took aboard two men in Portugal, one of whom has already departed this life. It appears these two, though British, had jumped ship from a Yankee merchantman. The Yank had unwittingly carried the fever from Virginia, and the two men, fearing for their lives, got themselves ashore by night and signed on to the first vessel leaving port—the *Agnus*. They were a sennight back to Portsmouth, with a gale behind them, and though one of them fell ill he did not suffer so greatly as the men on the Yankee ship. They must have thought they had escaped it, but the second man fell ill, just before they joined the convoy in Torbay. Even then they informed no one. But then that man died and the contagion began to spread throughout the ship. The survivor admitted this to me, and told me that, in Virginia, the horses became ill first and then the stablemen and drivers." Griffiths pinched the bridge of his nose, eyes closing. He had not slept much the previous night, Hayden conjectured, and bore a red-eyed, slightly unkempt look that day.

"And we carried it aboard our own ship . . . through an act of charity," Hayden said softly.

Griffiths paced to one side, agitated. "Yes, I cannot escape blame. I perceived he was fevered when I allowed McKee aboard but thought it merely a consequence of his injury. Corruption was my worry, not influenza, and even had I suspected influenza I should not have been much concerned, as it will not commonly strike down a man in good health. The sick, the elderly, consumptives—these are its customary victims." Griffiths stopped his pacing and met Hayden's eye, distress poorly hidden. "I have made a terrible mistake, Mr Hayden."

"No. I am confident that any doctor would have done the same. If only these bloody fools had had the common sense to inform the master of the *Agnus*. How did they get off the Yankee ship? Was it not quarantined?"

"I know not, Captain," Griffiths admitted. "I will have to inspect the crew, one man at a time. I can see no other way. The ill must be separated—immediately."

"Do you not worry that you have brought this miasma from the *Agnus* yourself?"

"We were aboard only a few moments. It is much more likely that I have it from McKee. But what else can we do? No one will come forward now that Worthing—blast his soul to hell—has been in my sick-berth and the man he visited has died."

"I am sure you are right. I will have Archer muster the men by their messes. Pestilence commonly spreads thus—through one mess and then another. We will build a quarantine berth for the men who have had close contact with the sick. Once he has done that, Chettle can make your sick-berth as large as you need."

Griffiths nodded. "Mr Ariss and I will hang our cots in the cockpit and take our meals there as well—for the time being."

Hayden almost shuddered at the thought of living among the sick, but Griffiths was right: He and his mate were the most likely to spread the disease, so must keep themselves away from the uninfected.

"Have the crew of the *Agnus* had commerce with the people of any other ship?" he asked, though in fact he felt a little swell of emotion at Griffiths' understated courage. Hayden would rather face a dozen battles than spend even an hour among the sick.

"I asked, but it seems they have not."

"We have that to be thankful for." Hayden might have said something about Griffiths' courage at that moment, but he knew the doctor would only be embarrassed and he wished to spare him any mortification. Griffiths was taking it hard that he had allowed an influenza aboard the *Themis*.

"Yes. If you will excuse me, Captain, I should see to the crew without delay."

"By all means." But then Hayden asked the question that preyed upon him. "How many of us do you think will contract this sickness, Doctor?"

Griffiths looked suddenly so exhausted that he might collapse where he stood. He reached up and clasped a beam. "If we act quickly, perhaps fewer than aboard the *Agnus*." He seemed to lose all focus for a second, but then managed: "One man in twenty has died, Captain."

"I trust, with your skills, Doctor, we shall fare better than that."

Griffiths nodded distractedly. "Thank you." Griffiths made a half-bow and hurried off, disappearing quietly below.

Hayden stood at the windows looking out at the gale-driven sea, the chill of the day seeping through the weave of his coat. One in twenty—ten men they could lose. They were separated from their most powerful ship and the commanding officer of the convoy, a transport had disappeared in the night, the weather conspired against them, and now this. . . . If half his crew went down with the contagion, how would he fight the French should they appear? What if he should become ill? Saint-Denis would not be his first choice to bring the convoy to Gibraltar or even to take command of the *Themis*.

A gentle tap on his door.

"Yes?" Hayden called.

The sentry opened the door only a little. "Mr Smosh to see you, Captain."

"Send him in, if you please."

The corpulent little cleric entered. Clearly, he was gaining his sea legs, for the ship was pitching overly and he stood without grasping any handhold.

"Mr Smosh. Is there some service you require?"

"I see you have confined Dr Worthing to his cabin. . . ."

"A measure that was forced upon me, I assure you. The man has a seditious character."

Smosh nodded. "Do not think I judge you, Captain Hayden. In truth, I approve it. As you say, he will cause mischief if it is at all possible. But that is not why I have interrupted your labours. It is being said that we have some plague aboard our ship?"

"I am afraid it is true. An influenza, the doctor conjectures, though a virulent one."

"I am terribly sorry to hear it. Might I offer to conduct a service for the crew? Often at such times men discover their religious nature. I am uncertain of its practical value, but it might ease the men's apprehensions somewhat."

"You have my permission. When should we arrange this service?"

"I suggest as soon as the doctor has finished seeing to the crew."

"Assuming the gale has not grown much worse, and crew can be spared, that would be perfectly acceptable. Thank you, Mr Smosh."

Smosh made a little nodding bow. "I am only too happy to do what little I can." The clergyman hesitated a moment. "It occurred to me that I might press one of your crew to assist me. . . . Could you spare Mr Gould, briefly?"

Hayden was surprised at this and about to say no when he realised that Smosh had not chosen Gould's name at random.

"Indeed. I think Mr Gould would be the ideal candidate."

Smosh held up a hand. "Do not discommode yourself, Captain Hayden. I will find Mr Barthe and the boy and inform them myself, if that is acceptable."

"Entirely, Mr Smosh, thank you."

The little parson smiled, made a leg, and let himself out.

"Remarkable," Hayden muttered after the door had closed. It seemed Hawthorne would be proven wrong and Griffiths in the right in the matter of Mr Smosh. Certainly Smosh had asked that Gould assist him for the very purpose of demonstrating to the crew that the boy was, indeed, a practising Christian. Hayden only hoped this would prove to be true.

Within an hour, unable to contain his anxiety about the spread of influenza, Hayden took himself down to the lower deck—the berth-deck—to discover how the doctor progressed. Griffiths was in the process of examining the men of number eight mess. Employing a narrow cylinder, the surgeon listened to them breathe, then looked into their ears and eyes, asked them numerous questions about their contact with the afflicted men and their general health. But above all he pressed his palm to their foreheads to ascertain if they were fevered and measured their pulse rates.

Seeing Hayden lurking nearby, Griffiths excused himself and he and Hayden retreated far enough toward the midshipmen's berth that they might speak privately.

"What is the verdict, Dr Griffiths?"

"I have not finished seeing the men, but so far we seem to be getting off rather too lightly. I fear there will be more cases in the days to come. The *Agnus* has half her crew down, after all, and I have only about six men who appear fevered."

"Perhaps we will be able to confine it, then." Hayden wondered if his relief showed.

"Such fevers spread easily and quickly, Captain. A low diet, in my experience, will accomplish more than anything else in resurrecting the sick, and I will bleed the men who require it. Physic will help soothe the nerves and the pulse, though we may need to speak with the *Syren*'s surgeon; my supply of antiphlogistics certainly will not be adequate—rosin of Jalap I possess in abundance, but vitriolated tartar I am certain is all but exhausted, and of mercurius dulcis I have but half a scruple."

"The moment McIntosh returns I will send him to Cole with a request for physic—if you could write me a list."

"As soon as I can put pen to paper." Griffiths made the smallest motion with head and body toward the gathered and wary men.

"I will leave you to your work, Doctor."

Hayden ascended the ladder to the gun-deck, where a group of boys—off watch—were playing at firing an eighteen-pounder, pulling on imaginary tackles, plunging the invisible swab down the unseen barrel. They ran their gun out with élan and, all as one, bellowed the report, BOOM!

"That's done for 'im!" one of the boys, the apparent gun captain, pronounced, gazing through the closed gunport at the battered French ship beyond. "She's a-sinking, lads."

"No! Not sinking!" one of the boys called out in dismay. "Wot about our prize money?"

The gun captain took a second, more carefully considered look. "Wait! No. She's not going down. Let's board her, boys!"

The gunner, not far off, replacing the flint on a lock, spotted Hayden and jumped up, alarmed. "Hey, you lot!" he shouted at the boys. "What are you about? Off you go and cause trouble elsewhere."

The boys started to protest, when one spotted Hayden and whispered loudly, *"Captain!"*

A scrambling of skinny legs and arms, the dreaded word *captain* echoing along the deck as the boys disappeared.

The gunner stood, abashed, teeth together, lips awkwardly spread— a sharp intake through teeth. "My apologies, Captain. They weren't doing no harm, sir, but I shouldn't let them play around the guns, I know."

"You certainly should not. And never again—even with the locks all covered and you present."

"Aye, sir."

Hayden found his oilskins and went up onto the deck. Wickham was standing by the mizzen shrouds, staring off to the north.

"Any sight of McIntosh?" Hayden asked.

Wickham seemed to be shaken from revery. "Sir?" he said.

"McIntosh . . . can you see him?"

"No, sir. He sailed into the general murk some time ago and has not returned."

"Hmm."

Hayden took Wickham's glass and examined the ships of his convoy. A gust struck the *Themis*, heeling her ponderously. Hayden could feel the ship resisting, the wind pushing back. A sea broke against the forward quarter, spray arcing over the rail and slattering down on the deck.

"The weather-glass has stopped falling, sir, but as yet it has displayed no inclination to rise."

Hayden lowered the glass. "This wind has not finished making, but I have seen winds defy the weather-glass before."

"No doubt, sir." Wickham was silent a moment. "How fares the doctor?"

It was an odd question, and Hayden glanced at Wickham, decided it was only an awkward attempt to ask after the sick, and said, "He hasn't done with the crew but has found fewer sick than feared." Hayden glanced at Wickham to see if his tone of optimism had been believable.

"That is good news, sir." Wickham appeared to relax a little, his carriage straightening. "The men have every faith in the doctor, Captain. He will pull us through."

"I believe their faith is well-placed."

"There, sir!" Wickham's hand shot up and he pointed into an inky squall that sagged low to the sea.

A glance through the glass assured Hayden that it was, indeed, a schooner and so almost certainly McIntosh. He passed the glass to Wickham, who confirmed that it was.

Hayden took a turn of the deck, stopping to speak with members of the crew, making a point of addressing the new men. At times like this a calm captain could soothe many apprehensions, and among such a superstitious community, dread of contagion was a fear as great as any but perhaps the sepsis. The term *plague ship* was whispered on all decks and the men set about their work, silent and grim. Everywhere he went Hayden assured the men it was not the yellow-jack or some other such scourge, but an influenza—a word that did not strike so great a fear into their hearts.

Hawthorne met Hayden as he returned to the quarterdeck, a weak smile flickering across the marine's handsome face. "Dr Griffiths has finished seeing the men," Hawthorne informed him, "though not the officers and guests." The marine leaned closer and spoke quietly. "Fourteen fevered, another half-dozen about whom he harbours fears. They have been separated from both the sick and the hale so that Griffiths might observe their state most closely."

"So many!" Hayden heard himself say, unable to hide his distress.

"Was the Good Samaritan so repaid for his charity?" Hawthorne wondered. "I have forgotten."

"A good Christian does not look for rewards in this life, Mr Hawthorne."

"Yet another way in which I have failed. But speaking of religion—we are rigging for church on the lower deck out of this bloody wind and rain. Mr Smosh is displaying uncommon energy in this endeavour, given his atheistic inclinations, and I must tell you, he has a most interesting curate this day."

"Mr Gould."

Hawthorne was clearly surprised that Hayden possessed this knowledge. "Indeed. I do hope the boy has actually attended church. It will only fuel the rumours if he is unacquainted with the common ritual."

"I believe Smosh chose Gould with the purpose of suppressing such rumours and will be certain he knows his part. Or so I hope." It occurred to Hayden at that moment that Smosh might have intended the opposite, but no, Smosh was not so inclined, he was sure.

"Let us pray," Hawthorne intoned.

Hayden kept the deck until McIntosh made his way, board by board, through the convoy and hove to within hailing distance of the *Themis*. The little schooner, tightly reefed, was a flyer and as weatherly as any two-sticker Hayden had ever known.

"*Nary a sign of our lost ship, Captain Hayden,*" McIntosh called from the rail. "*Not even a wee scrap of flotsam. If she went down, she had no time to launch boats.*" He shrugged, his look perplexed. "*I cannee explain it.*"

"*I've never known a ship to go under so quickly,*" Hayden called, "*lest she exploded. I do not think we can do more until this gale has passed, but I have a letter for you to carry to Captain Cole, if you please.*"

Hayden sent his servant down to Griffiths asking for the list of physic he required. This the servant produced in a quarter of an hour, and McIntosh eased sheets, flying through the ships of the convoy like a gull with the wind at its tail.

A gust struck Hayden on the back, pelting him with hard rain. A terrible flogging from above caused him to look up: below the cross-trees, the ochre Jack lashed itself into a frenzy.

Nine

Smosh, a slightly comical figure at the best of times, surprised Hayden by appearing positively dignified in his vestments. By contrast, Gould looked nervous, even abashed, his uniform, of excellent quality, so new he almost appeared to be royalty dropped into their midst.

The men sat upon the benches at each table, all turned to face aft, where Smosh prepared to address them. A group had gathered on the floor at his feet, and to one side the officers and warrant officers seated themselves on chairs.

If one had gone searching for a congregation of unrepentant sinners, certainly one would need look no further than the crew of a man-of-war. Yet, once church had been rigged, they became the most attentive and compliant group of absolute sinners one could ask for. They wore their best rigs, and sat like obedient schoolboys ready to take in a sermon on any of their cherished vices. One would think them a gathering of the most devout Christians rather than the tribe of heathens they actually were. Today, though, the men were more than solemn, a distressed, hunted look upon their wind-reddened faces. Hayden had never seen such torment, even aboard a ship about to enter battle.

Smosh cleared his throat loudly, awaited the cessation of shushing with great forbearance.

"O most powerful and Glorious Lord God, at whose command the winds blow," he began, and Hayden glanced over at Hawthorne, whose surprise equalled his own, "and lift up the waves of the sea, and who stillest the rage thereof."*

Hayden had been expecting a prayer for the sick, which would have been appropriate to their present situation, but this was a very well-known prayer to sailors, for it was often recited in the midst of great storms at sea.

Smosh's pleasant voice echoed within the wooden church. "We, thy creatures, but miserable sinners, do in this, our great distress, cry out to thee for help: Save us, Lord, or else we perish. We confess, when we have been safe, and seen all things quiet about us, we have forgotten thee, our God, and refused to harken to the still voice of thy word, and to obey thy commandments: But now we see how terrible thou art in all thy works of wonder, the Great God to be feared above all: And therefore we adore thy Divine Majesty, acknowledging thy power and imploring thy goodness. Help, Lord, and save us for thy mercy's sake in Jesus Christ thy Son, *Amen.*"

"Amen," repeated the miserable sinners in a manner most heartfelt.

"There is aboard our ship, this day, a thing of great evil—a pestilence that has struck down our friends and spreads among us. Some say that this is a judgement of God, but I do not believe that our merciful God has sent this contagion as punishment. It is a thing of evil and therefore not of our Lord."

Archer appeared at that moment, all a-lather. He looked about in the lamplit gloom, spotted Hayden, and, circling behind Smosh, came immediately to his captain. "McIntosh has brought our physic, sir, but he asks to speak with you, Captain, on a matter of the greatest urgency."

Smosh had stopped speaking as Archer appeared, and he nodded to Hayden very slightly and continued. Hayden was out of his seat

---

*From the 1662 Book of Common Prayer.

and upon the ladder in a moment—up to the gun-deck and then the quarterdeck, pulling on oilskins as he went.

The wind moaned in the shrouds, and the ship heeled, decks streaming dark rivulets that collected and sloshed against the bulwark, gushing out scuppers.

McIntosh stood at the rail of his schooner, head bent and half turned away from the wind, thinned brim of a threadbare sou'wester fluttering about his face. Seeing Hayden, he cupped hands to his mouth and called: *"Sor, just as I took my leave of Captain Cole his lookout spotted a ship to the north-east. A frigate, he believes, and perhaps another in the cloud. As soon as he had made she out, she dropped back into the murk, sor."*

Hayden muttered a curse. *"No idea of its nationality?"* he shouted back.

McIntosh threw his hands up and shrugged. *"None, sor."*

"They might explain our lost ship," Archer said loudly.

A blast of wind luffed Hayden's oilskins, and rain battered down with such force that for a moment no one attempted to speak over the rattle. As the gust eased and the howl quieted, Hayden called, *"I don't think signals can be seen in this bloody gloom, McIntosh. Alert the other escorts that they must clear for action. I will exchange places with Stewart."*

McIntosh, who Hayden was coming to appreciate was no fool, repeated Hayden's orders and called his crew to man sheets. Hayden did not wait to see him go, but turned to Archer.

"I am afraid Mr Smosh's prayers must be interrupted, Mr Archer. Call all hands. We will clear the ship but for my cabin, which can be left standing for the time being. We will man sheets and braces, wear ship, and, if we do not carry away our rig, exchange places with the *Cloud*. Lord knows how Stewart will come here." Archer turned to go when Hayden thought of something else. "Oh . . . and pass the word for Mr Wickham, if you please, Mr Archer. Ask him to fetch a night glass with him."

"Aye, sir."

A moment after Archer had hurried below, the men came pelting up, looking no less wicked to Hayden's eye—if anything, inordinately pleased to have escaped Mr Smosh's sermonizing. Without speaking, they hurried to their stations.

Barthe appeared, huffing out of the companionway, Archer and Wickham at his heels.

"Where is Saint-Denis?" Hayden asked, annoyed and not caring who knew it.

"I have just learned the doctor has sent him into the sick-berth, Captain," Archer answered.

"The sick-berth? Not the quarantine berth?"

"Pardon me, sir," Archer replied, shaking his head. "I misspoke. The quarantine berth, though much against his will."

"Ah." Would there be no end to his ill luck? Hayden wondered. Already he had too few officers, and even to lose one as disliked as Saint-Denis would place a greater burden upon Wickham and Archer, not to mention himself. "Well, Mr Archer, congratulations, it would seem you are acting first lieutenant. Ease sheets and braces and pilot us through the convoy. We will take up station in the *Cloud*'s place."

"Aye, sir." Archer turned to Mr Barthe and repeated the orders.

Hayden motioned to Wickham, leaning close so that he would be heard. "Mr Wickham, if you would search to the nor'east."

The boy nodded. "Cole saw a frigate, the men are saying. Is it true, sir?"

"That is what I am hoping you will tell me."

Wickham went to the rail, steadied himself, and trained his glass to the north, but in a moment the glass was lowered. He glanced at Hayden, embarrassed. "The lenses have fogged entirely, sir—within the tube."

"When do they not?" Hayden replied. "Your naked eye shall have to suffice."

A very passable evolution with reduced sail gave Hayden hope that he would have, one day, a crack crew—or, more accurately, some other captain would. The truncated November day waned as they made their way through the fleet, but Hayden was thankful even for the dull illumination that penetrated scudding clouds.

The *Themis* took up position to leeward of the convoy and near to the transports that brought up the rear. The *Syren* was not too distant—Hayden thought he could make out acting captain Cole standing by the mizzen shrouds.

"No sign of frigates?" Hayden enquired of Wickham.

"None, sir."

"Then I shall retire below, briefly." Quite chilled, Hayden slipped down to his cabin, which, though hardly warm, was at least dry and out of the wind. He sent his servant for coffee, and stared for a moment at a stack of papers requiring his attention—all neatly contained in a small, purpose-built, open-topped box made of cast-off white oak. The contemplation of this was brief before he settled on the gallery window seat, his feet spread wide to brace against the ship's motion. His situation never seemed to improve, but only grew worse with each day. Frigates to leeward, almost certainly not British, and given the proximity of the French coast, very likely of that nation. If his crew fell ill in equal proportion to the *Agnus*' he would be very hard-pressed to fight, and would almost certainly be reduced to bluffing, which would only work if the French force was roughly equal to his own. McIntosh's fraudulent fighting ships might actually aid their cause in such a situation. But Hayden feared clear skies and good light would expose these little masquerading men-of-war to any observant enemy—a good reason not to hope for a short gale.

Coffee arrived, and to Hayden's surprise, so did the doctor. Griffiths was not merely grey before his time but, at least in appearance, prematurely aged. This day he looked even more time's victim. About him hung an unwholesome air, as though proximity to the sick and injured had worn away at his own health. His face was powder pale, dry, and flaccid. Across the yellowish whites of his eyes branched fine lightning bolts of crimson. A naturally stooped carriage and angular frame never, even at the best of times, bespoke vigor, and as he entered, a vinegar-soaked handkerchief clapped over his mouth, he looked a figure of dejection if not ruin.

Hayden stopped, his fingers about to find the handle of a cup. "Dr Griffiths, I fear this will be a terrible trial for you. May I offer you coffee?"

Griffiths stopped, held out a hand, palm out. "Come no nearer." He took the cotton from his mouth, closed his eyes a moment, both body and face twisting in a tight grimace. In a few seconds he mastered himself and then said in a consciously steady voice, "I must inform you, most regretfully, Captain Hayden, that I appear to have contracted this contagion."

Ten

I will continue in my duties as long as I am able," Griffiths said, "but if my judgement becomes clouded from fever, I have ordered Mr Ariss to confine me to a cot in the quarantine berth. The sickness progresses rapidly, so I will be of service only a few hours more. I have given complete instructions to Mr Ariss for the care of the sick. I fear for Pritchard, who appears to have the pneumonia and is near to suffocating in his own fluids."

"This is the worst possible news," Hayden managed. "Mr Ariss cannot care for so many alone."

"I was about to say the same. We will need someone to act as his assistant. An intelligent man of steady nerve and kindly disposition. A young man is to be preferred, as influenza will compromise such a person's health less drastically, should he be so unlucky as to contract it."

"More than that, we need someone who is not afraid of the contagion." Hayden thought a moment. "Did Gould not claim his brothers were doctors?"

"I am not sure having a brother—or even two—in medicine is a qualification, Captain." Griffiths covered his mouth with the square of cotton and emitted a small, shocking cough, followed by a wheezing breath, indrawn.

"It might be the best qualification on offer, I'm afraid. Have you any other objections to Mr Gould?"

The doctor shook his head, his face at that moment turning red. He coughed again, more violently. "None." He fought for a breath and then pressed out, "He is, in every other way . . . ideal."

Hayden resisted the urge to clap the man on the back. "Then I will speak with him, but I am not certain that compelling a man against his wishes will give you the assistant you need."

"Let us hope that compulsion will not be necessary."

As he let the doctor out, Hayden spoke to the sentry. "Pass the word for Mr Barthe, and then after I will speak to Mr Gould."

Hayden threw himself down on the bench, gales and phantom frigates pushed out of his mind. The crew had been counting on Griffiths to see them through—*he* had been counting on it; how would they react when they learned that their surgeon had himself been afflicted with this sickness? For the most part they were a steady lot, but contagions had a way of creating a silent kind of panic that seemed to seep into men's hearts over time.

The stomping of Mr Barthe could be heard on the steps—even over the moans of the wind—and in a moment a rap on the door. The little sailing master hurried in and stood expectantly.

"Mr Barthe. I must take back Mr Gould, I am afraid. He is much needed elsewhere."

"But sir, he has only begun to learn his duties."

"I know it, but Dr Griffiths has more need of him than you, I fear."

Barthe looked confused. "What good could he be to the doctor?"

"The men will hear of it soon enough, but let us keep this quiet as long as we can. Dr Griffiths has been taken with the influenza. I need Gould to assist Mr Ariss, as strange as it may seem. His brothers are both physicians, you will remember, and he once contemplated taking up the study of medicine. I know it seems absurd to be employing a green midshipman in the sick-berth, but he is intelligent and levelheaded, and I hope his acquaintance through his brothers has made him less fearful of disease. The truth is, Mr Barthe, we are rather desperate."

The sailing master contemplated this a moment and then nodded. "What of Dryden? May I have him back?"

"Who needs him more, in your honest opinion, yourself or Mr Franks?"

It was difficult for the master to admit, but finally he said, "Franks."

"My feelings exactly. I will ask Gould if he will assist Mr Ariss. God knows I will understand if he does not wish to."

"He will not say no, Captain Hayden. So intent is he on succeeding in the service, I believe he would go into a flaming magazine if you asked him." Barthe turned to go, remembered himself, and said, "Is there anything else, sir?"

"Try to keep yourself away from the sick, Mr Barthe. I might be master and commander in rank, but prefer not to be so in truth."

"I will do my best, sir."

"Good. Send Gould in. I believe I heard him arrive outside."

A moment later Gould came through the door, made the proper salute, and stood awaiting Hayden's pleasure.

"Mr Gould, I have a rather difficult, perhaps even dangerous, position for you."

The boy nodded, waiting.

"It seems that Dr Griffiths has contracted the influenza, and Mr Ariss has need of an assistant. The men who are ill need much care— more than Ariss can manage—and another steady pair of hands is required."

The boy seemed perplexed for a moment. "You want me to be surgeon's mate?"

"It is more a loblolly boy, I think, but certainly you will be nursing the sick. It is not without danger, as you know—two men have died on our ship and more on the *Agnus*, but it must be done and you at least have the benefit of having read something of your brother's medical texts."

"I am likely as ignorant as the next seaman, sir, but yes, certainly, if you need me to do it I will."

"Report to Mr Ariss immediately. I have informed Mr Barthe that he will have to do without you . . . for the time being."

"Yes, sir." With only the smallest hint of hesitation, the boy went out. Hayden hoped he hadn't sent him to his death—a hope he held oftener than he would like.

There were, however, equally pressing matters requiring Hayden's attention. The unidentified ships seen in the fog, which had slipped back into the murk, were very likely not friendly; and unless they had, in the haze, mistaken Hayden's convoy for a fleet, they had not likely flown. No, they were out there, he felt, and perhaps accounted for the missing transport.

What to do about them—that was the thing. He stopped before the windows and looked out onto a dark, chaotic sea. Failing light made it all appear more ominous and threatening, but Hayden was no stranger to that. In truth he thought the wind was taking off a little, and with luck the gale would blow itself out in a few hours. Mind made up, he went to the door and spoke to the sentry beyond.

"Pass the word for Mr Archer and Mr Wickham, if you please."

"When Captain Pool suggested a similar plan, Mr Hayden, you opposed it, yet when it is a result of your own penetration, it is now a splendid strategy?"

A disgruntled Captain Cole hovered by the rail on a weeping deck, a dark and resentful silhouette. Hayden had sent him a summons and Cole had come aboard with only the greatest reluctance, refusing to go below out of the weather. Fear of contagion was great among seamen of every rank.

Though the wind had taken off noticeably, a heavy sea still ran and clouds would, intermittently, release their entire burden of rain upon the wildly moving ship. An indistinct, pale apparition sixty feet to larboard was a cutter from the *Syren*, holding position, that action being easier than trying to lie alongside a ship that both pitched and rolled.

Hayden had suffered one too many affronts from this man. "Captain Cole, I will take this opportunity to inform you that I find your tone offensive. You might not be pleased that I am in command of this convoy, but it is the case and I believe that the admiralty will uphold this. I do not wish to report that you were insubordinate, but I will do so. Is that understood?"

The man's face was invisible, but his frame appeared to contract a little. "It is, sir."

"I will explain why I have chosen to proceed in this manner, Captain Cole, if you will do me the honour of hearing me out." Hayden did not wait for the man to assent but went on. "Circumstances have changed utterly. Dr Griffiths visited the *Agnus* and that unlucky ship had half her crew down, too ill to stand watch. If the same fate befalls the *Themis*, that will leave your frigate and a collection of sloops to protect the convoy. Your own lookout saw a frigate and perhaps a second—not British, I would think, as they skulked back into the fog immediately. I have no proof of it, but I suspect they took the *Hartlepool* last night and will be looking to manage the same caper tonight, as the gale moderates. Last time it was the French who surprised us. This time we must surprise them. We have no choice—we must damage or drive the French off before my crew becomes too ill to fight."

In the pitchy night, Cole could hardly be distinguished, but Hayden was certain he perceived the man's carriage loosen, as though some of the inflammation of resentment were draining out of his very joints.

"I do take your point, Captain Hayden," he conceded, his tone moderated, "but we have seen conclusive evidence that this course is not without risks. What will be the result if these two ships are the French frigate and the seventy-four-gun ship that engaged our ships but recently?"

"Is it not true that your lookout thought the second ship to be a frigate, as well?"

"And he might have been right, but it was a ship in the fog, Captain. We cannot be utterly certain."

Hayden did not like the sound of this. A slight disorientation swept through him, as though he were falling. "The only reason they would be hiding from us would be out of fear that Pool had rejoined the convoy. They were likely trying to discern that very fact." Suddenly the risk involved in his planned action grew substantially. He hesitated, weighing all factors.

"Under any other circumstances, Captain Cole, I would never take such a risk, but my crew will only grow weaker. Our ability to fight will be continually diminished. Better we confront the French now, when we have surprise on our side, rather than later, at a time of their choosing, and in broad daylight."

He saw Cole nod in the darkness. "Which of us shall play the killdeer, then?"

"Killdeer?"

"A kind of plover, sir. It will drop a wing so that it appears injured, unable to fly, and then draw any creatures that might threaten its young away from the nest. Very clever, sir. It has a cry that sounds like 'killdeer.'"

"Ah. I've seen such a bird in Canada. *Gravelot à double collier,* the French call it."

"That would be it—a double black band about its throat. I think it should be my ship that plays lame, sir. If I can draw them to me, you can come out of the dark and take them by stealth."

"The *Themis* will claim that role. Better the heavier ship be attacked—our eighteen-pounders will be more of a match for the French. I'm sure you will come to our aid with all speed."

"You may count on it."

Hayden watched Cole go over the side, thinking that he was trusting the lives of his crew to a man who had accused him of not coming to his aid in time to save Bradley. Cole might resent him, but Hayden believed he was an honourable man. He would not abandon them if he could avoid it. No, Cole was the least of his worries. A seventy-four-gun ship lurking in the dark and pestilence aboard his own ship were on his mind now. Even contentious clergymen had been sent to the back of the ranks when it came to his concerns.

The coughing, liquid and suffocating, like men being throttled, could be heard through the thin deal-board walls that delineated the quarantine berth. The men who made up the watch below had gathered as distant from this little wooden cell as the confines of the lower deck would allow. When the door opened, Hayden peered into the dimly lit hell, men swinging in their cots, coverings cast off, skin a burnished rose, lips swollen purple. He clapped the vinegar-soaked cloth over his mouth and nose, inhaled, and choked on the fumes. For a moment he hesitated, eyes watering, but then gathered his resolve, pushed past the sentry, and entered the inferno. The fetor penetrated his protective veil even beyond the fumes of vinegar. For a moment Hayden thought he would retch. The men swayed in their cots, neat rows penduluming back and forth together, marking time. Some were still, drugged to sleep, Hayden thought, or at least insensate, though now and then one would choke, writhe briefly, perhaps prop up on an elbow, a confused, hopeless look upon his fevered face, and then sink back down. Gould perched on a stool and wiped a man's forehead with a cloth, leaving a smear of shiny liquid glistening on the skin. Nearby, in a bowl chocked off on a small shelf, Hayden saw crimson liquid washing back and forth in time with the rocking cots. Ariss had been bleeding the sick.

"Sit him up! Sit him up!" a horrible voice rasped. "He'll choke if you leave him like that."

At the end of the berth Hayden found Griffiths in a cot, eyes bulging and fevered. He waved a hand limply at one of the sick, barking irritable instructions at his mate.

"Mr Ariss," Hayden said as the mate caught sight of him. He was trying to prop a limp man up to a half-sitting position, arranging some bedding behind him with one hand, but the man was resisting, weakly. Hayden went to his aid, taking hold of the man's shoulder with one hand. He could feel the terrible, unnatural heat of his body through the palm of his hand.

"He is burning," Hayden whispered before he realised he should not.

"They're all burning, sir," Ariss replied sadly.

Griffiths sat up in his cot, swinging his legs over the side, but then he sat there, shoulders bent, gasping.

"You should not be up, Doctor," Ariss protested.

Griffiths only shook his head stubbornly. Hayden went over to him.

"You told Ariss to confine you to your berth when it became necessary, Doctor. I believe you should listen to him, now."

"But there is much to do," Griffiths hissed. "We must give them all a dose of . . . of . . ." The doctor's eyes, shining with fever, lost focus. He looked plaintively at Hayden. "There is some . . . thing . . ."

Hayden helped Griffiths back down into his cot, where he stared up at the deck-head somewhat fearfully.

"Mr Hayden?" he rasped.

"Yes, Doctor."

Griffiths waved a limp, long-fingered hand. "I believe Pritchard has departed this life. His earthly remains should be slipped over the side without delay."

Hayden was not sure if the doctor was in his right mind, but when he went to Pritchard's cot he found the doctor was almost certainly right.

"Mr Ariss, when you have a moment . . ." Hayden said softly.

Ariss glanced up, nodded, and when he was finished with his charge, crossed immediately to Pritchard. A quick search for a pulse, and then a small signal with his hand to Gould. The midshipman went to the door, spoke quietly with the sentry, and a moment later two frightened seamen came in, took Pritchard's cot down, tied the sides and ends firmly about its occupant, and then bore the dead man out. His cot, bedding, and clothing would all go over the side with him for fear of contagion. Only a few of the sick men took notice of this procession, but those watched in silent horror.

Five men, Hayden thought. This pestilence had claimed five men.

"Is there anything you might need, Mr Ariss?" Hayden asked.

"Cots, sir. I don't think any of the sick should be in hammocks, as it only makes breathing more difficult to lie bent in half. We have used all we could find."

"I'll have Chettle and Germain make some up immediately."

"Thank you, sir. That would be most helpful."

"And how fare you, Mr Gould?"

The boy, Hayden guessed, was terribly distressed but managing to keep it in check. "Well, sir. I follow the directions of Mr Ariss, or the doctor when he is lucid, and some of the men are on the mend, I think."

"You said the same of bloody Pritchard," one of the sick men muttered.

"He did rally for a bit," Gould said softly, "but it did not last, God rest his soul."

"God rest his soul," Hayden echoed. "Send word if there is anything that you require."

"Thank you, sir."

As Hayden turned to go he spotted Saint-Denis, hunkered down in his cot as though he hid. The man was clearly more wretched and unnerved than any other.

"Mr Saint-Denis," Hayden greeted him. "I am very sorry to find you among the sick, sir."

"I was not sick in the least," the lieutenant whispered. "But Griffiths put me in here with the afflicted, and now it has hold of me, just as he planned."

"I am quite certain you were fevered, sir. Griffiths would never make such a mistake."

"Mistake! It was no mistake! He wanted to do for me. But God saw what he was about. And look! Griffiths is taken with the fever. Now we will see who will live and who will be slipped over the side." This seemed to exhaust him and he fell silent, panting. Delirium had overwhelmed his mind—Hayden had seen fever do the same to many men.

"Mr Ariss will see you recovered, I am quite certain." Hayden nodded to the man and retreated from the cabin, pausing at the door to glance back into the dimly lit room, utterly relieved that this duty was done. The pale sailcloth cots acquired an ominous, death-shroud aspect in the warm light, like canvas coffins swaying slowly forth and back, rocked by some invisible force. Death was so present in the room that Hayden thought it could almost take shape, rise up, and devour the sick. He pulled the door quickly shut, nodded to the saluting sentry, and hurried up the ladder to the gun-deck, where the air seemed almost fresh and clean by comparison.

Hayden threw open his jacket and drew in great breaths of cold air. The quarantine berth had been so close that he felt fevered from just that brief exposure. For a moment he stood on the empty deck, leaning against the cascabel of an eighteen-pounder gun, mastering an almost overwhelming feeling that he had been touched by death.

As his breath calmed and his nerves were soothed, Hayden heard a small sound—a tiny sneeze, and then simpering. Stealthily he made his way down the gun-deck until, in the shadow of a great gun, he discovered one of the ship's boys, huddled with his knees drawn up and face hidden in the little square of his bent arms.

"Mick?" Hayden said gently.

The boy started, looked up fearfully, and sneezed three times, a pathetic little sound. He then began to weep like the earth's most wretched creature and hid his face again.

Hayden crouched down, observing the boy a moment. Not being a father, he was a bit out of his depth in such situations.

"What seems to be the trouble here?" Hayden enquired. "Has someone been ballyragging you?"

The boy shook his head, though he kept his face buried in the angular intersection of arms and narrow knees.

"I am the ship's captain, Mick, and when I ask you a question, you are obliged to answer. Did you know that?"

The mass of hair nodded.

"Then what is the trouble here?"

The boy controlled his weeping with effort and half raised his head, revealing crimson face and runny eyes. "I . . . I think I 'ave the fever, sir." His face disappeared again and he commenced weeping, shoulders convulsing, his misery complete.

Hayden put out a hand awkwardly and stroked the boy's shoulder. He let the boy's fury subside a little before he spoke.

"Have you the cough, then?" Hayden asked, trying to sound reassuring.

"No, sir, but I'm sneezing something awful."

"Ah. Well, we should have Mr Ariss look at you, but I am of the opinion that you have a cold. Just such a complaint came away with us from Plymouth and has been visiting one man after another. Your mate David had it not a sennight past, and his mate Paul has only just recovered. So I think you are preserved from the influenza. Let us go down to Mr Ariss and see if that isn't the case." Hayden patted him on the back. "Up we get, then."

He took the child's delicately boned hand and gentled him to his feet. The boy would not look at him, but wiped his nose on a shiny sleeve and came meekly along. As they walked, Hayden thought how frightening this must be to a child—he himself had been unnerved by it for a moment. How frightening this whole way of life.

In a moment they were down the ladder and Hayden asked Ariss to come out and see to the boy, not wanting the child to view the inside of the sick-berth unless there were no choice. Ariss pronounced him free of the influenza, which he referred to as "our new friend," and sent the boy off to his hammock to rest.

Hayden climbed up to his cabin, thinking how easily men were reduced to children in times of great distress.

By six bells the wind had moderated to a wholesome topsail breeze, and Hayden gave the order to drop back into the lee of the convoy.

"Do you think we are distant enough to fire our signal gun, sir?" Archer enquired. He seemed to be neither intimidated nor pleased to be acting first lieutenant, as though it mattered not at all.

The officers had all gathered on the quarterdeck, where they stared into the dark night. The fear that a seventy-four-gun ship might suddenly appear kept pressing into their musings, but so far no such calamity had befallen them.

"Seven bells will be soon enough," Hayden replied. "I wish to be distant enough from the convoy that we will appear beyond aid. Can you make out the *Syren*, Wickham?"

"I thought I saw her a moment ago, sir," the acting lieutenant answered from his position by the rail, "but it is difficult to be certain on such a night."

Cole's ship was somewhere off their starboard beam, awaiting the appearance of enemy vessels, or so Hayden dearly hoped.

"At least we shall be able to open our gunports," Hawthorne observed.

"So will the enemy, Mr Hawthorne," Barthe chided him gently.

"It would not be sporting otherwise," Hawthorne replied.

Low chuckles greeted this. Hawthorne was known for his wit in tight situations, and his remarks were often repeated at table. Hayden thought the marine had something of a reputation to preserve, now.

Hayden took a quick tour of the deck, speaking quietly to the men who waited silently by their guns on the quarterdeck. As he made his way along the gangway, he heard someone on the forecastle speaking very low, and was about to upbraid the man when he realised it was Mr Smosh.

"Ah, Captain Hayden," the parson said when he realised who drew near in the dark. "I was just reassuring the men that influenza quickly burns itself out. I have seen it before. In a few days we shall be free of it. Is that not so?"

"It does not cling to a ship the way the yellow-jack does, that is certain. A few days, as you say. Certainly we should be free of it by the time we reach Gibraltar." Hayden made a small motion with his hand, perhaps invisible in the dark. "Mr Smosh, could I ask you to accompany me? I have a matter on which I would seek your advice."

"Most certainly, Captain." Smosh excused himself graciously from his flock and walked beside Hayden.

When they reached the gangway and were beyond hearing of the forecastle, Hayden said, "Mr Smosh, although I appreciate your desire to give comfort to the crew at this trying time, it is our custom to preserve silence on the deck so that officers might be heard."

"I do apologise, Captain. I am unfamiliar with naval custom, as you can see."

"Do not apologise. Your efforts with the men are a great help to me, but we are in the midst of an action, or hope to be. Silence is the rule."

"Which I shall observe with all devotion in future."

Hayden was about to take his leave of the clergyman when Smosh spoke again.

"Forgive me, Captain. I have a request, if I may?"

Did the man not realise this was not the time for favours?

Hayden struggled to keep his tone moderate. "By all means, Mr Smosh."

"I do believe that Mr Ariss and young Gould have more sick than they can possibly minister to on their own. . . . I have been speaking with the men, sir, and after much discussion, I believe that if I were to remove my collar and forswear my duties—that is to say, I should not act as a clergyman in any regard—it would be acceptable to the men that I assist Mr Ariss in this time of need."

Hayden was utterly surprised and felt immediate remorse for thinking the man an annoyance. "I cannot begin to express my appreciation for this offer, Mr Smosh, but I do fear that the hands would not accept a priest in the quarantine berth."

"Forgive me again, Captain. I requested Mr Madison to enquire among the men, and begging your pardon, it seems they are quite prepared to allow me into the quarantine berth in a medical role. I am told that some parsons assist the surgeons in the cockpit during action? Is that not the case?"

"It is the case, but . . ." Hayden did not quite know what his next argument would be. "Would you allow me to speak to Mr Madison?"

"Indeed. Thank you, Captain."

As Hayden took his leave of Smosh and returned to the quarter-deck, a dark form stumbled out of a hatch and slumped down on the deck.

"Mr Ariss?" Hayden asked.

"Yes, sir, Captain." The man scrambled to his feet and made a quick knuckle. "I was in need of a breath of air, sir. I hope that meets with your approval, sir."

"By all means. No one deserves it more." Hayden stopped when he was two yards distant. "How fare you, Mr Ariss?"

The surgeon's mate sounded utterly spent, his voice devoid of emotion and scraping from exhaustion.

"I will manage, sir. It is only that the men keep falling ill. If there are any more, sir, I shall have to ask that the quarantine berth be made greater."

"How many do they number, now?"

"Twenty-two, sir." Ariss lowered his voice. "I must inform you, Captain Hayden, that the doctor is not faring well."

Hayden reached out and put a balancing hand on the capstan. "That is the worst possible news. Will he pull through, do you think?"

The mate hesitated. "I dearly hope so, Captain." But his hesitation said more than he professed.

"You have bled him, no doubt?"

"I have, sir, but it had little effect, which is highly uncommon in my experience."

Hayden was so distressed by this news that he wanted to slump down upon the deck himself.

Madison hurried over to him at that moment. "Captain Hayden!" came the boy's voice out of the dark. "Mr Wickham believes he has seen a ship to leeward."

Hayden wanted to tear himself away but did not. "Mr Madison, tell me quickly: Have you enquired among the hands about Mr Smosh serving in the sick-berth?"

"I have, sir. I believe the men will accept it, Captain, as long as he is not there in his capacity as parson."

"Then he is yours, Mr Ariss. Excuse me." Hayden took a step, then stopped and said to Ariss, "Please do everything within your power for Dr Griffiths."

"I will, sir."

Hayden walked briskly back to the taffrail, where the officers had gathered.

"No, no," Wickham was saying. "A point east of that."

No one spoke or made any sound as they all stared fixedly into the night.

"Are you certain, Mr Wickham?" Hayden asked.

"There is something out there, sir, I have no doubt of that."

"A frigate, do you think?"

"I could not say, Captain. It was just a mass of lesser darkness moving, perhaps, a little east."

Hayden turned to the first lieutenant. "Fire the signal gun, Mr Archer, then light the lanterns aloft."

"Aye, sir."

Almost immediately a gun was fired to leeward and the signal lanterns lit on the frame aloft. A green flare was also ignited and cast a lurid glow over the deck.

"Certainly only a blind man could miss that," Hawthorne said.

Hayden took stock of their situation. The wind had taken off until it was no longer blowing a gale but had begun veering into the north-west, and the temperature was dropping noticeably. An ugly cross-sea was beginning to develop and waves pressed by the north-westerly began to build and overlay the swell from the south-west. The ship was now running almost free, but had a terrible corkscrew motion.

"Enough to make a man-o'-war's man retch," Barthe growled. "It will have gone around to the north in another hour and the seas will become more confused yet. We have a cold, uncomfortable night ahead."

Hayden was about to agree when a meagre reddish glow appeared off their starboard quarter. Almost everyone noted it at once, which engendered a little choir of exclamations.

"It is a red flare, high up in the rigging," Archer asserted. "We are merely seeing it light the sails from abaft."

And then, as if to prove him right, a red flare appeared in a slot between the sails, and then a second, though how distant no one could gauge.

"A red flare!" the foremast lookout called. "A point off the larboard bow."

"We are between them," Archer said in consternation. He looked
about wildly, as though fearing such flares would appear all around.

"Two ships," Mr Barthe pronounced solemnly. "Let us hope there
is no third."

"Jump forward, Mr Wickham, if you please," Hayden ordered,
"and see if you can make out the ship."

"Aye, sir."

Wickham and Madison went running forward. A gust from
the north struck them then, and a little rain obscured all flares in the
blur. The squall seemed to race past, and the wind fell to lulls and
gusts. Some distance aft, the flares of the ship reappeared, setting
sails aglow and silhouetting a faint tracery of rigging.

An urgent rapping along the deck was Madison returning. "Captain
Hayden," he whispered urgently. "Mr Wickham believes that is a ship
of the line off our bow. At least a seventy-four, sir, perhaps greater."

"Is luck never to be with us?" Barthe demanded, his voice despairing.

Not another word was said among the officers on the quarterdeck,
but Hayden could sense their distress. He fought down his own panic
and misery. The thought that he had miscalculated, horribly, brought
on a moment of near blankness before he mastered his feelings and
brought order back to his mind.

"How distant?" Hayden asked, his voice dry.

"It is a difficult thing to measure in the dark, but Mr Wickham ventured a mile, sir."

Hayden took up his night glass and fixed it on the ship in their
wake. "Well, that is no seventy-four. It is a frigate, at best, and likely
the same that Bradley fell in with and we drove off. Is Captain Cole
to be seen?"

A moment of desperate searching—but no one could find the
British twenty-six.

"Mr Archer," Hayden asked, forcing his voice to something resembling normal, "have we red flares made up?"

"I'm certain we do, sir," Archer answered with admirable calm.

"Have someone fetch them, if you please."

"How many, Captain?"

"At least two. Half a dozen, if they are to be had."

"Aye, sir."

"Mr Hayden," Barthe whispered, drawing near. "I do not know what we can do. When the captain of this ship realises he faces only a pair of frigates . . . we will be dished. . . ."

Hayden could not have his senior officers losing their nerve, and he replied equally quietly to the sailing master. "Mr Barthe, guard your words, sir." And then to everyone present: "We have but one chance. Snuff every light, aloft and alow. Mr Barthe, we will slack sheets and let this frigate overtake us. Reload the guns with chain and bar and, on a roll, when well-heeled to larboard, fire at her lights and rigging aloft. If we can bring down her flares, and damage her rig enough to slow her, we will put the *Themis* between she and the larger ship, light red flares aloft, and go after the second Frenchman. I will speak the ship when we draw near and, I hope, confuse them long enough that we can sail across her stern and fire every gun at her rudder, wear ship, and attempt the same a second time."

"With these gun crews, Mr Hayden?" Barthe responded. "Half their musters are landsmen."

"The captains are all experienced gunners, Mr Barthe." Hayden heard a little frustration and peevishness creep into his voice. "If we can damage her rudder so that her helm no longer answers, she will not make harbour lest she is towed. And we might slip away."

"What about Cole, sir?" Archer asked. "I should hate to have him mistake us for a Frenchman or, worse, collide with us in the dark."

Hayden stared out into the night. Where the devil was Cole? "Captain Cole should be some distance to starboard and clear of us for a few moments yet. We shall have to trust to sharp eyes and providence to keep us apart."

"I will see to the flares aloft," Madison offered, and went off at a run.

"Douse the lanterns, then," Hayden ordered. "And we must have silence on the deck. Mr Archer, have the starboard guns reloaded, if you please, and be certain the gun captains understand what is expected of them. We have but one chance this night and can make no mistakes."

"I'll see it done, sir."

The quarterdeck gunners ran-in their carronades, wormed out the wadding, lowered the barrels as far as the carriages would allow, and, on the roll, coaxed out the ball. Bar and chain-shot were carried up from below and the guns quickly reloaded and run out, ready to fire. It was not accomplished in the most efficient or seamanlike manner, which made Hayden wonder if Barthe might be proven right, but they were in a corner and had only one very precarious track out.

The sails flapped as Barthe ordered sheets eased. A bitterly cold northerly was building, and kicking up a short, steep sea over the swell left by the sou'west gale.

"This ship is coming up rather quickly, Captain," Hawthorne whispered. "Can she see us, do you think?"

"It is rather close out here, but perhaps they have a French Wickham aboard whose eyes penetrate the dark."

The red flares appeared to illuminate more of the ship as she drew near, casting a devilish glow over rig and hull. Hayden could see her pitching and rolling on the confused sea, her flares making great, ponderous ellipses in the sky. Judging distances by night was always something of a black art, but Hayden guessed the Frenchman was no more than a hundred yards distant. An order, called out in French, drifted down to them. The sails shook in a frigid gust, the thrumming travelling down stays and shrouds to the very deck.

"I dearly hope this Frenchman catches us up," Barthe growled, "before our sails have flogged themselves to ruin."

"Another seventy-five yards, Mr Barthe," Hayden predicted. "Mr Archer? Open the starboard gunports, if you please."

"Aye, sir."

Wickham reappeared on the quarterdeck and Hayden sent him down to the gun-deck to oversee the gunners' efforts.

Another gust. A few drops of hard-driven rain clattered against the transom. Sails flogged, thrashing the air unmercifully. The French ship loomed up to starboard. She was a frigate now, not just a faintly glowing apparition. Hayden could almost make her out in detail. He could even see the obliquely angled gunports—open. The *Themis* would receive a broadside.

"Helmsman," Hayden whispered. "Port your helm. Bring her up two points to starboard. We will haul our wind, Mr Barthe, just enough to allow us to fire before she can bring her larboard battery to bear. Then we will bear off."

A slow turn to starboard, which gave the ship an even stranger motion as the seas struck them on the quarter. Hayden knew this would make the gunnery even more untenable. He stepped to the nearest carronade, crouched down, and sighted along the barrel. A dull silver filigree in the trough of the Atlantic was reflection from a smudge-moon that raced among tattered clouds. And then the ship began to roll to larboard, and pitch and yaw. The view along the barrel of the gun was sea, then slashed left to right across a great arc of sky. It would be a miracle if they hit any part of the French ship at all. They might be better to lie close alongside, pour in the broadsides that time would allow, and then return to their convoy and hope the French might be discouraged. But Hayden knew it was too late for that. He had made his decision—there was no losing one's nerve now.

"Mr Baldry," Hayden said quietly to the gun captain. "This will be a madly lucky shot, and I don't think you will get more than one. Crouch here and watch the progress of your gun so you can judge the path of it. You shall have to time your firing to a nicety, or you will be bringing down nothing but cloud. I will take the helm and try to position us so that we might have a chance. Good luck to you."

"Thank you, sir, but if I am not speaking out of place, we'll get more than one shot, sir. I promise you."

"I hope you are right."

Hayden relieved the helmsman of his wheel. His only hope was to keep the ship on her course; it was all but impossible under such conditions to counter the yaw caused by seas on their starboard quarter. If he could but give the gunners half a chance . . . They would have enough to do trying to predict the motion of the two ships and then pull the firing lanyard at the right instant. There was always a delay between the lanyard being tugged, flint striking steel, sparks igniting the powder in the pan, the flare of the touch-hole powder, and detonation of the charge in the barrel. Occasionally guns failed to fire at all or hung fire for seconds . . . or longer.

The seas coming from the north and the swell originating in the sou'west, though each of reasonable regularity, never seemed to converge at the same point—crest meeting trough, or two crests mounting up together. The sea was, therefore, chaotic, and the motion of the ship utterly unpredictable. It did not help that darkness hid the seas until they were upon the ship from astern, and Hayden was unaware of the sou'east swells until they lifted the bow.

"Gun captains," Hayden said loud enough to be heard across the quarterdeck, "fire when you have a shot."

"Aye, sir," the men answered up promptly but without confidence.

There was utter silence on the quarterdeck. Every man there knew what a mad endeavour this was. Gun captains crouched in the near darkness, sighting along their carronades, the dark shapes of their crews arrayed about them like standing stones. Hayden fought the wheel, trying to keep the stern from being pushed off to larboard. The mouths of the quarterdeck guns swept across the sky with such speed and unpredictability that no one dared fire.

"Mr Baldry," Hayden said urgently. "You have to take a chance. Mr Barthe, take the helm, if you please."

The sailing master crossed the swinging deck and took the wheel from Hayden, who went to the nearest carronade. There was a danger that the French ship would pass before a single gun was fired. The gun captain found Hayden's hand in the dark and placed the lanyard in his fingers. As Hayden crouched, a gun on the deck below fired to no appreciable effect, the shot blasted out into the dark sky.

"Damn," one of the officers swore.

Hayden tried to time the swing of the ship with the roll, yanked the lanyard and the gun, hesitated a second too long, and fired, hissing back along the wooden slide. He'd missed . . . utterly.

Other guns began firing then, the element of surprise lost. One struck the rig low down—too low down—but most holed only sky.

A little moonlight filtered down, and Hayden could see the French ship turning to bring her own guns to bear.

"We're going to receive fire, Captain," Hawthorne warned.

Hayden had jumped back to let the gun crew reload.

"Haul sheets aft, Mr Barthe," Hayden called, and the sailing master, unable to leave the helm, called the order to Franks.

A French gun discharged harmlessly down into the sea, and then a sporadic firing began from the enemy frigate, most of it missing, but one shot passed through the mizzen a dozen feet above Hayden's head and another thundered into the hull amidships—above the waterline, Hayden hoped.

The deep, jagged screech of eighteen-pound balls lacerating the air pimpled Hayden's skin. It did not matter how familiar—it was a horrifying sound felt in one's chest. Just the noise alone seemed capable of tearing away limbs.

The fire from the *Themis* was utterly ragged, and apparently without purpose or discipline, as the gun captains attempted to aim high into the rig of their enemy. The scream of spinning bar, as it went end for end through the air, tore apart the oceanic night, but only a few shots struck the French ship, and none produced the desired effect. The red flares still burned, their glow diluted by the faint moonlight.

Desperation was beginning to press up through Hayden's conflicting emotions. More and more he felt like a man in the grip of a relentless undertow, struggling to keep his head above water. He heard one of the gun crew whispering, *"Please, God. Please,"* with all the discouragement he felt.

The gun crew ran out the carronade and Hayden took the lanyard again, wondering if Baldry might not do better than he. Sighting one-eyed along the barrel, he realised that it would be a matter of the most complete luck to bring down the flares on their frame. He waited a second as the ship began to roll to larboard. The Frenchman's guns were firing as the roll brought them to bear, and they were beginning to damage the *Themis'* rig. Hayden tried to ignore it, concentrating on the motion of his own ship. Entirely by intuition he yanked the lanyard just as two other guns fired aboard the *Themis.* The red flares jerked suddenly forth and back, plunged, swung oddly aft, then checked.

There was a cheer from the men on the quarterdeck.

"We've shot away the forward halyard," Barthe called out.

The invisible frame hung oddly askew, the flares still blazing. Supported at only three corners, the light-frame flopped and swayed to the movement of the ship. More shots were fired from aboard the *Themis* but the flares persisted in their odd, jerky motion.

Hayden watched, mesmerised, expectant, wondering how quickly the French sailors could get hold of the wildly moving frame and rig a new halyard. The flares jerked suddenly, plunged a fateful yard, flailed madly, then swung down in a long arc, fetching up against the mainsail. Before the wet canvas could catch fire, the frame plummeted to the deck.

There was another cheer, and Hayden went immediately to the helm. "Mr Barthe, discover how badly our rig is damaged, trim sails, and chase that seventy-four. We will wear as we draw near, brace our yards, and sail across her stern."

The immense relief that Hayden felt could not be expressed, as though he'd made a last wager with all his resources on a worthless hand of cards and somehow, inexplicably, won.

Barthe was calling out orders, and the hands clambered aloft to repair damage.

"Shall I order the flares lit, Captain?" Archer asked. The sound of relief and elation in the lieutenant's voice could not be mistaken.

"Immediately." Hayden motioned to the helmsman to take the wheel. "Can you see the French two-decker?" Hayden asked the man.

"Aye, sir."

"We will run up on her starboard quarter, wear, and cross her stern within thirty yards—twenty, if we can manage it."

"I'll manage it, Captain."

"Mr Franks! Silence on deck."

"Aye, sir."

"Well done, Captain," Hawthorne said. Hayden could hear the grin in the marine's voice.

"That was the part most easily managed. Have you ever taken on a seventy-four-gun ship with a deck of eighteen-pounders?"

"No, but I once fought a rather large artillery corporal who offered offence at an inn."

"How did that come out?"

"Not at all well."

"Ah."

A fiery glow suffused the night, illuminating spars and rigging with a deep wine blush. At the same instant, a cold squall overtook them from astern, lobbing great dobs of rain down into the sea. The officers turned their backs to the weather, but Hayden could feel the massive raindrops battering his back and the cool water seeping through his oilskins and slowly saturating his woolen coat.

"Do you believe this deception will work?" Hawthorne asked quietly.

"If we reach the seventy-four before the French frigate; it was difficult to judge how badly damaged she might have been." Hayden turned, shaded his eyes with a hand, and tried to look astern, but the rain hid all and stung his face until he turned away.

The frigate was quickly gaining on the larger ship, which was clearly under reduced canvas in anticipation of action.

"Mr Archer," Hayden spoke to the lieutenant so no other might hear. "I will go forward and speak this ship in French. It is your responsibility to see that the helmsman brings us across the Frenchman's stern."

"Aye, sir."

"Mr Barthe? You are prepared to wear ship?"

"Every man is at his station, Captain. Mr Franks has been told to maintain silence on the deck."

"I will be on the forecastle."

Hayden careened forward on the strangely heaving deck. Rain continued to rattle against the planking, and a blast of wind luffed his oilskins like a stiff sail. Just as he stepped onto the quarterdeck the air exploded to his right and he fell hard on the slippery planks. Immediately he hauled himself up, awkwardly.

Around him men were cursing and clumsily finding their feet.

"Fucking Frenchman," someone growled.

"Shall we return fire, sir?" one of the gun captains asked.

"Only if you want to kill Englishmen. Those were twelve-pounders."

Hayden went to the starboard rail and shouted in French. *"Cole, you English bastard! You would fire upon your own brothers!"*

He hoped that he could not be heard upon the French ship they chased, but if he was, they might glean only enough to realise he spoke French.

Two more guns fired, one after the other, and then fell silent.

"Do they realise it is us, sir?" Madison asked.

"Let us hope someone speaks French." Hayden turned away, remembering that he had threatened to fire into Cole's ship but a day before. As he went to the forward barricade, he wondered if a second broadside would suddenly tear into his ship. With great effort he focussed on the swaying flares of the French two-decker as they appeared and dissolved between sails or impenetrable squalls of rain. How distant the Frenchman might be was impossible to gauge. The screens of rain would diminish for a moment and the chase would appear too near, but then the gale would close in again and the ship would be mysteriously pulled away.

"Mr Madison, when I give you the word I would have you run aft and order the helmsman to put his helm swiftly up. Do you understand?"

"Helm to starboard, sir."

"Yes."

The ship rolled so that rain and seawater washed across the deck, pressing about his ankles and seeping into Hayden's boots. Wind among the spars and shrouds ran down and up, then yet again up a minor scale. Rain, wind-driven and harsh, fell into the sea—a clatter like glass beads upon gravel. A long moment this persisted, began to relent, then recommenced. The men around him pulled in their necks and hunched shoulders, backs to the onslaught. A momentary lapse overtook them, and Hayden almost started. The French ship appeared out of the gloom, large and formidable.

"Run to the helmsman!" Hayden said to Madison over the din of the gale.

The stern of the two-decker rose up not twenty-five yards distant. Hayden could see the shapes of men gathered at the taffrail. On such a night he could not be certain of being heard, but cupped his hands to his mouth and shouted in French, *"There is an English frigate out here in the darkness bearing no lights."* But the ruse did not work this time. He could see officers pointing—likely at the position of the bridle ports or perhaps the figurehead. A stern-chaser exploded with flame and smoke, lobbing a ball among the rigging overhead to little effect.

"Prepare to fire," Hayden said in English. He felt the *Themis* begin a ponderous turn to larboard, a sea from the north heeling them far over in the opposite direction. Hayden grabbed the barricade to stop himself from sliding down the deck. A swell from the sou'west found them, an inky wave-top lolloping over the rail to douse carronade and crew.

The *Themis* began to round up, wind pressing her down even as the wave rolled her heavily to starboard. The stern of the French ship of the line was abeam, but no guns could be brought to bear as the ship rolled. Before Hayden could call out, Barthe ordered sheets to be let fly and the ship began to roll slowly back.

"Come up. Come up—damn you!" Hayden muttered. Barthe released the mizzen sheet, letting the sail flog, the gaff threatening to batter shrouds and any crew aloft within reach, but it allowed the helmsman to bring the bow a little to starboard; and as the ship rolled up, the gun captain of the nearest carronade yanked his lanyard. No explosion followed, the lock too wet to fire. Guns did begin to fire then, raggedly, some from the gun-deck below, others from the quarterdeck.

Shot struck the Frenchman's stern. At such small distance—twenty-five yards—Hayden could hear iron crashing into wood. The French crew kept firing their stern-chasers, and some men with muskets appeared at the rail. Hayden's own marines returned fire, but the *Themis* was quickly passing even as the French ship drew away.

"She's turning to larboard, sir," the gun captain declared.

Hayden had just registered the same thing. "Run back and tell the helmsman to wear ship immediately."

The man went off at a run.

Madison had returned from the quarterdeck, and Hayden called him over. "We will fire the larboard battery, Mr Madison. Go down to the gun-deck and inform Mr Wickham." Hayden called to the bosun. "Mr Franks. We will fire the larboard battery as we cross the Frenchman's stern."

Barthe was on the gangway ordering headsail sheets hauled to bring the ship's head around, the mizzen still luffed—it would soon do itself damage if it hadn't done so already, but they could not sheet it in now or it would resist their turn to starboard.

The French two-decker and the British frigate turned slowly in opposite directions, the French to larboard. The distance between the two ships had somewhat increased, as the Frenchman had been flying downwind, but the ships were still too near.

Barthe came huffing up the gangway. "I'm not certain we can wear without tearing away our jib-boom," the sailing master observed, measuring the slow turn of their ship and the small distance between the tip of the jib-boom and the larboard quarter of the French ship.

"The alternative is to take a full broadside from two decks of heavy guns," Hayden replied, all his attention fixed on the same sight. "I will risk our jib-boom."

The frigate was handier than the seventy-four and brought the wind across her stern more quickly. A carronade on the enemy's quarterdeck fired and the ball tore over Hayden's head and down into their ship between the gangways. A gust pushed Hayden bodily off balance and he clutched the rail. Rain all but obliterated the French ship.

"If we lose the jib-boom, Mr Barthe," Madison asked shakily, "will the foremast follow?"

"Not with the wind aft and our topmast housed . . . At least, not likely."

"*SAIL!*" a man called from the waist. "*To starboard! Upon us . . . !*"
Hayden almost fell, he spun so quickly. A dark mass issued out of
the tangled rain, so near that spray from its plunging bow slapped
over the *Themis*' rail, soaking hands standing mesmerised by their
guns.

"*Helm hard to starboard!*" Hayden shouted, the words nearly tearing
out his throat from sheer volume.

The *Themis* continued her turn, her jib-boom almost scraping the
French ship. Aboard the ghost ship, looming out of the darkness but
yards away, men shouted . . . in English.

"It's Cole, sir," Barthe said, turning to Hayden in astonishment.

Both British frigates lifted on the same sea and began to surge
forward, the *Themis* sheering to larboard, the *Syren* running straight.
The French seventy-four wallowed in the trough for an instant, and
as the *Themis* continued to turn away, Hayden watched the jib-boom
of the *Syren* shatter the stern gallery of the Frenchman, then tear
away as the bow of the frigate slammed into the settling stern with
a tremendous rending of timbers.

The two ships stuck fast as the sea passed beneath them, buckling
them upward, and then they tore apart with a splintering, wrenching
sound. Although the French ship turned abruptly to larboard, the
Themis was miraculously spared her broadside.

"She is stove in, sir . . ." Barthe said breathlessly, "the Frenchman."

"And the *Syren* is down by the head."

Hayden turned and made his way back along the swaying deck.
"Mr Archer! Haul in the boats. You will have command of the ship.
Keep us as near as you can to the *Syren*, but distant enough to be free
of her spars should she roll toward us." Hayden stopped on the gangway and called down into the gun-deck. "I need twenty-four men
to man the boats, Mr Wickham—no, twenty-eight; I shall employ
the jolly-boat as well. There are two hundred men to be rescued,
so the crews must be small. You shall have command of a cutter.

Madison another. Hobson the launch. Childers the jolly-boat. Mr Hawthorne! Two armed marines to each boat and one to accompany Childers. We cannot have boats overset by panicked men."

The boats were hauled quickly alongside, the crews mustered and sent down the heaving ladder. Hayden took his place in the largest boat—the barge—and grasped the tiller himself.

"Away boats."

"Pull, lads," Hayden called over the wind, *"the* Syren *is down by the head and will not swim long. We have two hundred souls to take away in this bloody gale. Let men say we broke our backs but none were lost."*

The boats set out over the confused sea, the dark shape of the *Syren* not too distant but slightly upwind. Although rain slashed down on them, as Hayden quartered the waves, the moon appeared between racing clouds, offering a cool, thin illumination of dark seas. The *Syren* was unquestionably down by the bow; Hayden could see her sails flogging as she turned beam-on to the wind. Steerageway had been lost. She was going to go down more quickly than he had hoped.

"Good God, sir," one of the oarsman swore, "is that the Frenchman?"

Hayden twisted around to look aft. In a pool of moonlight the French two-decker lay down by her stern, her bow rising unnaturally, spars strangely angled. She had begun a slow roll to starboard, and the ants teeming in the rigging were men trying to stay above the surface of the winter sea. For a moment Hayden could not look away, the sight so nightmarish, so preternaturally horrifying. And then he turned back to his business. He had his father's people to rescue. But for the few who might be preserved in the boats, his mother's would go down into the sea.

It seemed a long pull to the *Syren*. Hayden had kept the boat crews minimal so that they might have room to carry away as many as possible, but it meant they were undermanned for rowing to windward. He wondered what might await him as he neared the *Syren*. A scene of panic, or one of desperate order. In his short career in the Navy he had been witness to both. Good officers could make a difference, preserving both order and life. The *Syren* had lost her captain and Cole was untested. If there was a scene of panic, he would have to restore order before they could begin to take away the men. In his belt Hayden bore a brace of pistols that he hoped he would not be forced to use.

As they drew near the *Syren*, Hayden could see her bow was now just beneath the surface, her stern high. Men were clambering down into the boats from a gathering at the rail, someone calling out orders. No signs of disorder or mutiny could be seen.

"*Captain Cole,*" Hayden called. "*We have come with all our boats. We must get you off, sir.*"

"*God bless you, Hayden,*" Cole said with some emotion. "*We can put but a few more into our own boats.*"

"*Get them clear and have them pull for the* Themis." Hayden looked around and for a desperate moment could not find his ship. And then there she was, a nebulous glow of red from her flares. Archer had put her about and was working his way back up toward the sinking *Syren*, but Hayden was distressed to see how distant she was.

The *Syren*'s boats, overburdened for the weather, pushed off, and Hayden ordered his own boats alongside. Cole leaned over the rail; he held a pistol pointed at the sky. "Mr Hayden," he hissed. "I am not sure we can maintain order here. This ship will not be long afloat."

"Then let us get men into the boats and send them away." Hayden turned to his marine lieutenant. "Mr Hawthorne, come with me, if you please, and bring a marine from each boat."

Hayden clambered up the side, the red-coats in his wake. "I have twenty armed marines, Captain Cole," he lied loudly, "but I see we do not need them."

Cole looked uncertain and frightened, and Hayden did not have time to raise his spirits.

"Are there any ship's boys or sick left aboard?" Hayden called out. To his utter surprise, some boys and other men came out of the agitated mass of crew. Hayden ordered them down into the boats, a few of the sick requiring aid. He knew no names, but he began touching men on the shoulder and sending them down as the boats could receive them. To call for a number of men into the boats would have set off a rush, leading to men being hurt or drowned, boats overset.

He could feel the men swallowing down their panic, like choking bile. But they were not fainthearted, he could see that. Hayden went to the rail to be certain he had all the men the boats could bear and no more. "The best oarsmen must take up the spare sweeps. Pull like your lives depend on it."

"Captain Hayden, are you not going?" Cole asked, surprised.

"There will be time yet," Hayden said loud enough for all to hear. "We will all get off when the boats return."

The ship did not lurch, nor did it seem to rise or fall much with the passing seas. A sluggish, unrelenting drift down into the winter sea was its only motion. There was barely any conversation among the officers or men who remained, though several stared at the water as it inched up the slanting deck from the bow toward the stern. The passing waves washed aboard forward and sluiced across the deck, higher each time. Finally one ran up the forecastle planks and sloshed down onto the gun-deck through the great opening in the waist. The following sea did the same, and then water from below rose up to meet it. Even Hayden regarded this with growing horror.

He turned and gazed out to sea, wondering if the first boats had intercepted the *Themis* and how quickly they would return. Even a strong swimmer would likely perish before he was found on this foul night, for the winter sea drew the heat from a man's body and left him helpless in but a few moments. Once in the water they would be lost.

Hayden turned back to the gathered crew, now muttering among themselves, the mass of them creeping back up toward the taffrail like a multilegged creature.

"Cole," Hayden said, leaning close to the acting captain, "we should send the men up the mizzen."

Cole nodded, then leaned even closer to Hayden. "Will the boats return in time?"

"Let us keep up our spirits," Hayden replied, "for the sake of the men." He said this with confidence, but the entire scene seemed dark, a dream vision, the men all gathered silently aboard the sinking ship, the black, gale-driven seas rolling past. Hayden felt light-headed and wondered if he would wake.

Cole turned to the remaining crew and said, in a voice only slightly shaky, "We will go up the mizzen mast in an orderly fashion. There is no need to rush. Laughlin, take those dozen closest to you and proceed. Lay out on the yards and make room for as many as we can."

Hayden was trying to estimate the number of men—counting in the dark was impossible—and guessed there were perhaps sixty, and fewer than a dozen officers and warrant officers—more than he'd hoped. The men began to climb, and Hayden was impressed by their nerve, gathering at the shrouds on either side of the quarterdeck and going up, quickly but without any pushing or shouldering-aside. Bradley had had a good, steady crew, Hayden could see.

Cole and Hayden went up last, each bearing a lantern, climbing awkwardly one-handed. A small box with the ship's papers was passed up ahead of them, man to man, and the carpenter had the sense to send up axes to cut away the yards, in case it came to that; the men would have something to cling to in the sea while they perished of cold.

In the meagre moonlight, and the irregular smudge of illumination from smoke-stained lamps, Hayden could see the deck below contracting. It also angled a little more, forcing the men to cling to the tilting mast. The sailors did not speak, but clutched the rigging and one another, the stronger men aiding the weak, pulling them back to safety when they slipped or their grip gave way. Cole glanced at Hayden, his mouth a harsh line.

"Sir . . ." one of the men said. "Is that a ship?"

This caused a little hum of excitement among the men.

Hayden clambered up to the next ratline to look over the man nearest, and there, by moonlight, saw a dark hull and sails silhouetted against a moonlit cloud. The ship's stern lamps glowed unmistakeably.

"The French frigate," another pronounced, and Hayden agreed.

The men began to shift about as though they would protect themselves from musket fire or the great guns, but Cole and Hayden shouted over the noise, assuring the men that the French captain would not fire. Not, Hayden thought, upon men who were so soon to be dead.

Hayden could make out men at the rail as the ship went ghosting by—silent men, staring in horrified fascination. Who had ever seen the like? Six dozen men clinging to the rigging of a mast that appeared to jut out of the sea—all slipping inescapably away.

"Will they not save us?" someone asked in a tone of lamentation.

"No," an old sailor answered, his voice burdened with the sorrow of resignation. "No, they will rescue their own first, of whom there are so many more."

Air began bubbling up audibly from the sinking ship. Only the aft ten feet of the stern remained dry, the foot of the mizzen already submerged. The ship began to go down more quickly now as the air boiled out of the hull. Men began pressing themselves higher, doubling up, but still no one was forced off as they were looking out for one another. Hayden felt oddly proud of them, sticking together under the most desperate circumstances. Most of the men could not swim.

"Who has the axes?" Hayden called out. "Prepare to cut away the cross-jack yard. I don't want yards falling on the men below, so await my order."

Hayden stared down into the dark waters, the seas rolling past.

Already the rail was under and the water approaching the futtock staves. Like all the men, he searched the seas toward the *Themis* but could see no sign of boats.

The men had crept up so that most were astride the cross-jack yard or above on the tops or in the rigging of the top-gallant mast, which had not been housed. Hayden and Cole were the lowest men, perched on the ratlines just below the yard. Two men with small axes sat astride the mast just above them, looking anxiously from the rising water to Hayden. A sea rolled by beneath them and the water seemed to have risen half a dozen feet.

"By God, we're going down quickly now," Cole whispered to him.

"Can you swim?" Hayden leaned close and asked.

"A little," Cole answered after the briefest hesitation.

"We will have to get clear of this yard so it can be cut away. Pass up your lamp."

The two lamps were sent up and Hayden and Cole climbed over the men above so that they might cling to the mizzen-top platform.

Hayden spoke loudly so that all the men might hear. "When the yard is afloat, it will not support all of you if you try to mount it. Remain in the water and put your arms around it only." The water reached Hayden's feet; even before it ran into his boots he could feel the cold of it through the leather, which was pressed around his foot and ankle by the pressure. Immediately his foot began to ache.

"Cut away the jeers," Hayden said to the axemen, "and the lifts below the blocks so that we have some rope to hold on to."

The axes began to rise and fall with urgency.

The few strokes required to sever the ropes were only just completed a moment before the water reached the yard, so that the spar, with all of its riders, plunged fewer than three feet but spilled all of the men aboard into the frigid sea. A wave broke upon the last men clinging to the sinking mast and Hayden was torn from his precarious perch and flung into the icy sea. The cold knifed into his flesh, cramping muscles and prying apart his joints. He broke the surface gasping, looked around, and saw a boy astride the mast, balanced precariously and holding aloft a lamp—their only hope of discovery and salvation. Grabbing a flailing sailor by the scruff of his jacket, Hayden swam the few strokes to the yard, just awash from all the bodies clinging to it.

Leaving the rescued man gasping, Hayden swam out again as he could hear men crying out. A sea lifted him as he reached a man. The sailor grasped for Hayden, pushing him under, but Hayden surfaced behind the man, took hold of him strongly, and on his back dragged him to the yard. After that he was spent utterly, barely able to hold the yard as the sea lifted them.

"Call out!" Hayden shouted. "All at once or we shall never be heard. *Here . . . !*" he called. *"Here . . . !"*

Men joined him. *"Here . . . !"* they called from lips so cold they could barely form words. *"HERE . . . !"*

A sea broke over them, battering Hayden down into the frigid waters, though he somehow kept his grip on the spar. When he surfaced again, the man to either side of him was gone, as was the boy holding the lantern.

"Call out or we're lost!" Hayden cried. *"Here . . . !"*

Fewer men took up the cry this time, and with less energy.

By luck Hayden found the foot rope, which had remained with the yard, and this allowed him to bear himself up a little more easily, though his leg soon trembled with the effort of supporting his weight even in the sea.

Men began to fall away, as though blown by the wind or some current in the sea. The man nearest Hayden slipped under, gasping. Reaching out, Hayden found the man's coat sleeve but his fingers could not close on it. The last he felt was the man's stone-coarse hand scrape by his own, neither able to take hold.

It became increasingly difficult for Hayden to keep his head from sagging into the water, the muscles of his neck no longer obeying his commands. He leaned his temple against the arm thrown over the spar. An urge to retch washed through him, the cold penetrating deep into his bowels. No one called out. The moon broke free of the clouds and cast its chill glow upon a glassy ocean of irregular seas crested in moonlight. A few stars, scattered among the clouds, shimmered in the heavens. Hayden knew that he would not endure ten minutes more and thought of his father upon a ship, so many years ago, foundering in the winter Atlantic. Often, he dreamed of his father drifting in the depths, asleep until the sea gave up her dead. Hayden would soon begin his own slow descent, leaflike, to join the elder Hayden.

"Sir?"

Hayden's eyes had closed, and he opened them with effort. A small boy, lips bruised and eyes sunken, pushed at the shoulder of his jacket.

"Sir."

"Yes?"

"I thought I 'eard s-someone cry out."

"Where away?"

"Don't know, sir."

Hayden tried to make his addled brain work. "Let us get you up on the yard. Can you manage?"

"I don't think so, sir."

"I will help. Crook up your leg and let me get a hand under your knee."

The boy did so, but when he put weight on Hayden's bent wrist, Hayden nearly went under, his arm giving way. The ocean had sapped all his strength.

"Sorry, sir."

"You are not to blame. Listen carefully. I'm standing on the foot-rope. I will duck under the water and you will step on my back, climb up, and straddle the yard. Do you understand?"

"Are you sure, sir?" the boy asked.

"It is the only way. Ready?"

The boy nodded and Hayden let the water close over his head, holding the yard with his wrists, fingers fused and useless. A knee thumped into his temple, passed by, and a small foot pressed down on his shoulder, almost sending Hayden into the depths. A long moment he bore the weight, and just as he was about to give way, there was a sudden push and the foot was gone. Floating to the surface, Hayden might have drifted off, but the boy took Hayden's arm between two wrists and helped pull it over the spar.

"Cry out," Hayden gasped.

"Here," the boy squeaked. *"Themis!"*

Over the roar of the gale no one would hear him, Hayden despaired.

"Here!" the boy managed, a little louder—a little more desperate. *"Thee-mis!"*

The wind answered with a gust, spume flung upon them from the streaked surface.

"Did you hear, sir? S-sir?"

"No," Hayden thought he answered but was not certain. He felt as though he were slipping into a dream.

"Hold tight, sir. *H-here!"*

The sea no longer felt cold, but warm, inviting. How easily he could depart this life for the sweet dream that beckoned—Henrietta drawing him into her arms, his father whispering his name in joyful awakening. A jumble of memories and emotions. Then voices. What were they saying?

He was hauled bodily over a hard edge and tossed down on some unyielding surface. The voices kept yammering, words unfathomable, and then someone said, "Is he alive? Mr Wickham! Is he alive?"

He surfaced into warmth, a soft weight pressing him down—like a covering of warm snow. For a moment Hayden lay still, uncertain, afraid to open his eyes. And then he did. A reddish glow illuminated a small circle, and within it, distant but a yard, crouched a figure on a stool.

"Wickham?" His voice came out parched and harsh.

The figure stirred. "Captain Hayden!" Of an instant, the boy was on his feet. "We thought when you stopped shivering that meant either you recovered or . . ." He chose not to complete this sentence.

"What in the world is in my cot?" Hayden asked, hardly able to move under the weight. "And what has me bound to my mattress?"

"We have every blanket the officers possessed, or nearly so, to cover you. And Jefferies heated nine-pound balls in the stove and we placed them all around you—it was Mr Gould's idea. Mr Barthe and Mr Franks ran several ropes up to the deck-head to bear all the weight. We have been exchanging the balls for newly heated ones as they've cooled. But here you are, sir! Alive!"

Hayden thought the boy would weep.

Hayden found his mind was a jumble of half-remembered images. "There were others. . . ."

"From the *Syren*, sir? We preserved the lives of all who made it into the boats but for two who were found floating near to you, Captain. All the men who first came away in the boats we kept separate from our crew, so they should not be exposed to the influenza, and have placed them on other ships in the convoy."

"Cole?"

Wickham lowered his voice. "Never found, sir."

"The French?"

"We have not caught sight of them since their seventy-four went down."

"How long have I been . . . asleep?"

"I do not know if you have been properly asleep, Captain. There has been a great deal of muttering and incoherent speech, and opening your eyes. You were in a delirium, like, but lacking the fever. The opposite, in truth, for you had the life nearly drawn out of you."

"How long?"

"Most of a day, Captain." Wickham brightened. "I shall inform Mr Hawthorne and Mr Barthe that you are awake, sir. They have been terribly concerned, and in and out of your cabin every bell."

"What of the sick? Griffiths?"

Wickham took his gaze from Hayden's face and shook his head just perceptibly. "We've lost more men, sir. The doctor is with us, yet . . . but is most grievously ill."

There was a moment of silence between them.

"I shall tell Mr Hawthorne that you have survived, Captain, if you will excuse me."

Before Wickham reached the door, Hayden had slipped into a dream—the warmth of a female embrace.

Fatigue hovered ever near. Hayden found he could not stay upon his feet long and required sleep after even a brief period out of his cot. He continued to eat the diet Ariss had prescribed; even so, his strength was returning but slowly.

Archer and Barthe were more than able to command the *Themis*, but there was an entire convoy that required the direction only a single, decisive commander could provide, and Hayden could not slack for a moment if he hoped to bring his charges safely to anchor in Gibraltar.

For this reason he was on deck as often as he felt able and, when abroad, found himself regularly passing by the quarantine berth. As much as the place unsettled him, he could not stay away. Enquiries about the doctor's condition were met with hopeful words but disheartened looks.

Upon one of his rounds, Hayden happened upon Mr Gould sitting at the aft mess table. Realizing that Ariss, Gould, and Smosh must periodically have fresh air and a few moments' respite from their labours, the starboard aft mess had been designated for their use alone—not that the crew needed to be encouraged to keep their distance.

Here he found Gould seated at the table—"slumped" would be a more accurate description—and before him, a dozen paces distant, stood a small gathering of hands.

"Will you have more, Mr Gould?" one of the men asked.

Gould managed a shake of the head. Hayden could see only his back, but clearly he was bent over, engaged in the act of eating.

"Mr Jefferies has been saving some cheese . . . ?" another wondered. "Shall I fetch you a slice?"

To this a nod of the head.

The crewman went off at a trot.

Seeing the captain, the men all made their knuckle.

"How fare you, Mr Gould? No, do not rise. Eat while you may. Lord knows you will be called away soon enough."

"I am well, sir," Gould responded, hurrying to chew and swallow that he might answer his captain.

The man returned with cheese on a wooden plate at that moment and, reaching out to his farthest extreme, set it upon the table and then scurried back to stand among the men attending the midshipman.

"You are in good hands, I see," Hayden observed.

"Yes, sir. The men have been most kind, Captain."

"I can see that, and well deserved. Carry on." And Hayden passed by, feeling the greatest sense of relief he had in many days. The hands would forgive a courageous officer many offences or shortcomings. He had seen it oftener than he could say. And there was nothing the men feared so much as a pestilence—with the possible exception of sepsis. Aiding Mr Ariss in the quarantine berth had won Gould the admiration and appreciation of the older hands, no doubt, and the rest would follow their example. Gould would have no troubles with the hands for a very long time, and Hayden was very pleased to see it. Very pleased indeed.

Eleven

They lowered the dead man, twisting slowly in a crude sling, the noose he had used to hang himself still tightly encircling his delicate neck. Two of his messmates caught him as he neared the deck and guided the body, almost tenderly, to the hard planks. He lay there unnaturally, limbs stiff, strands of fine, youthful hair drifting about a bloodless face.

Hardly more than a boy, Hayden thought.

The men, gathering silently, removed their hats and stared as though they had never seen a corpse before. Hayden hardly remembered the boy alive, but thought, now, he would never forget the sight of him in death, his slack mouth, swollen, purple lips, traceries of crimson across his cheeks where blood vessels had ruptured.

Griffiths came forward, still so weak that he braced himself on a walking stick, and, unable to sustain a crouch, thumped down awkwardly on his knees by the boy's side. He loosened the noose, a badly made knot that had slipped tight and tighter, suffocating him finally. An abrupt examination of the boy's hands, his neck, then the doctor nodded to the men who stood by with a cot.

"Carry him down to the sick-berth," he said hoarsely. "God rest his soul."

"*God rest his soul,*" echoed in ripples across the deck, repeated by each man in turn.

Setting his stick and placing two hands upon the knob, Griffiths hauled himself up with difficulty. A quick, direct look at Hayden and the acting captain fell in beside the surgeon, the two making their way to the taffrail.

"Please, sit, Doctor," Hayden insisted, and Griffiths, a little out of breath, did so gratefully, tumbling down onto the little bench. Hayden leaned back against the larboard rail and waited.

"I will examine him more thoroughly," Griffiths said, a little out of breath from even these small exertions, "but almost certainly it was self-murder."

Hayden shook his head—the second such death since he had come aboard the *Themis*. A memory of the haunted look of Giles Sanson as he cast himself into the sea came to him—another face never to be forgotten.

"I . . . I hardly noticed him when he was alive. One of the impressed men, I believe . . . What could have led one so young to so rash an act, one must wonder."

Griffiths took a handkerchief and wiped perspiration from his face, still gaunt from recent illness. "I will attempt to determine if any . . . unnatural acts were forced upon him."

A muttered curse escaped Hayden's lips. "Perhaps the men who knew him can cast a little light on this matter."

"If anyone knew him. Even so, I doubt you will learn anything that causes the least surprise; a young man, likely of sensitive disposition, impressed against his will, thrust into a harsh world he neither knew nor understood, taken to sea by winter, threatened and unnerved by terrible winds and seas, an enemy he knew nothing of trying to kill him with savage guns, and even his own crew likely hostile or at least uncaring, mayhap even cruel. I have seen melancholia sink its claws into men subjected to less. 'Self-murder' you will write in the log, but the boy was murdered by the Royal Navy. That is the truth."

Griffiths was so fragile and peevish since his illness that Hayden chose not to argue this particular point. He thought it more likely that the boy was being ballyragged or even buggered, and that was a fault to be laid at the feet of the officers, of whom there were too few, and of those only a handful had enough sea miles to know their business. He himself felt shame that this had happened aboard his ship— that the boy, friendless and despairing, had been driven to take his own life. Hayden felt the failure was his and his alone.

"The good news," the surgeon said, "if there can be good news on such a day, is the port doctor has declared us free of influenza. We may lower that cursed yellow flag and even venture ashore." Griffiths turned his gaze upon Hayden, who felt that the doctor had slipped a little away from life after his illness, and when one looked into his eyes he seemed to be somehow deeper inside, as though the man's essence were falling into a dark and narrow well.

"Then let us have it down this instant." Hayden looked about for the officer of the watch. "Mr Archer? Haul down the quarantine flag, if you please."

"Aye, sir!" Archer responded, as though he had never been given such a gratifying order in all of his life.

"Do tell me if you find anything out of the ordinary regarding . . . the dead boy." Hayden had already forgotten his name, but then, his poor brain had not been quite the same since the Atlantic had nearly drawn all the life out of him. "I am called away. To report to the admiral, don't you know. I pray it will be more productive than my last such encounter."

Hayden went quickly down to his cabin and gathered up the diverse papers he would need—a list of those who had died of influenza, and those who had been lost in the foundering of the *Syren*. Requests for stores and water would go to the commissioner.

In a moment he was in the stern-sheets of the ship's barge, Childers at the helm, and setting off across the harbour, the little town of Gibraltar bathed in sunlight some distance away.

Admiral Joseph Brown sat at a writing-table. Across the stern gallery, curtains hung, precisely drawn, so that the Mediterranean sun slanted down upon his desk, leaving all of his considerable bulk in shadow but for powdery white hands. Thick spectacles and a puzzled squint suggested to Hayden that the man's sight was failing. Not looking up from the report Hayden had submitted, the admiral said quietly, "How many men were found with you after the *Syren* went down?"

"Six, sir . . . though two of those passed on soon after." Hayden did not say that he had almost been among them, hanging between life and death for several hours, the furnace of his body having been quenched by the winter ocean.

For a moment Hayden waited for the admiral to say more, but the man read on, as though he had not received the report some weeks previous, for the *Themis* had been lying a month in Gibraltar Harbour, quarantined, land tantalizingly near. The influenza had burned through Hayden's crew like a fire, spreading from man to man, felling one, then another. Twenty men the disease had claimed— one in ten—unheard-of for such a contagion. Those who had fallen ill recovered slowly, a lingering cough, shortness of breath, and loss of vigor common. And now, in the aftermath, the crew seemed haunted, silent, wary, as though the angel of death had walked among them, invisible, unmerciful, touching this man upon the brow, then that. Even those who had escaped illness altogether appeared, some-how, convalescent.

Brown laid the letter aside and turned in his chair, a shuffling of the feet, a brittle twist of the shoulders. He removed his spectacles and for a moment contemplated Hayden. "The *Syren*'s only surviving lieutenant informs me that you threatened to fire into his ship. Is this true?"

Hayden felt his mouth go dry, and when he spoke his voice

was thickened and harsh. "Captain Bradley seemed to have believed he possessed the authority to appoint one of his lieutenants to command of the convoy. Certainly he did not. As senior officer the responsibility fell to me—by all practises of the Navy. Cole must have known this, and his actions were insubordinate, verging upon mutinous. I acted as the situation dictated to establish the proper chain of command."

"You did not mention this in your account to me. . . ."

"Cole was dead, sir. I saw no reason to attach this unfortunate incident to his otherwise good name."

"It was *his* name you were attempting to protect?" Brown's sarcasm was clear.

"Indeed, sir, it was."

"Pool informed me that he had little faith in you."

Hayden shifted in the straight-backed chair. "I assure you, Admiral Brown, I gave Captain Pool no reason to hold that belief."

Chalky fingers drummed upon the mahogany table. "The service is a small community, Mr Hayden. Men's reputations precede them."

Hayden felt his face flush. "In my particular case," he replied heatedly, "it is the reputation of one of my former commanding officers that precedes me."

The drumming stopped, and Brown's head cocked slightly to starboard. "Are you suggesting, sir, that one of your captains is responsible for your character within the service? Is that your idea of loyalty?"

Hayden shut his eyes a moment. *Fool,* he berated himself, Hart has many friends both in and out of the service.

"I did not mean that, sir," Hayden offered lamely.

"Then I cannot comprehend what you could have meant." The admiral glanced at his hand, still resting on the table, flexed the waxy fingers, and resumed his staccato drumming.

"The Reverend Dr Worthing has written me—three letters!—

complaining of his treatment at your hands. Did you confine this gentleman to his quarters?"

"I did, sir. He was provoking unrest among my crew and would not desist even after being warned."

"So say you. Dr Worthing believes you are dangerously inexperienced, if not subject to delusions."

"You may enquire among my officers, Admiral. I don't believe you will find one who shares Dr Worthing's opinion." As though Worthing might divide good officers from bad—the man had never previously been aboard a ship!

But Brown seemed little interested in enquiring among Hayden's officers. "Do you deny this as well?—after asserting your control of the convoy, against the wishes of Captain Bradley, you then relinquished your ship and command of the convoy to a junior lieutenant so that you might go on an ill-prepared rescue mission? Did you not comprehend where your responsibilities lay?"

"I did, sir, fully, but my senior lieutenant was ill with the influenza, my third lieutenant was a midshipman of sixteen years temporarily promoted, and my second, though an excellent young officer, lacked experience. There were two hundred souls at risk, and I had no one else I might send."

Brown raised his greying brows a little. It was clear he remained unconvinced by this argument.

"If I may, sir," Hayden managed, struggling to keep his tone mild, "we did bring the convoy through under difficult circumstances, rescued most of the *Syren*'s crew, and sank both a frigate and a French seventy-four—"

The hand banged down flat on the desk, gripping the edge with an arthritic thumb. "Mr Hayden, the seventy-four-gun ship sank due to collision caused by incompetent execution of a poorly contrived plan. The frigate went down when her magazine exploded—which, for all that is known, was likely due entirely to the mismanagement of the French crew. I will give you no credit for sinking ships by *chance!*"

The admiral rose from his chair, walked stiffly to the stern gallery, and drew back the curtain, undamming a deluge of stark sunlight. It raced across the cabin deck, enveloping Hayden so that he lifted a hand to shade away the pain in his eyes. For a moment the admiral stood, gazing out, and Hayden realised he was mastering his anger.

"I have no captain to take your place—none who would take your ship, at any rate." Brown spoke calmly and turned his head but little in Hayden's direction. "I will send you as escort to a few transports to Genoa, and then on to Toulon. Do not tarry in Genoa; indeed, once the transports are safely in harbour, you need not even anchor. Dr Worthing and . . . this other parson must go with you. Allow me to give you some counsel in this matter, Hayden: Confining parsons to their cabins for sedition is likely to make you something of a subject of . . . merriment within the service. I suggest you not do it again. Good day."

A moment later Hayden was in the warmish sunshine, wondering if he would ever leave an interview with a superior not feeling as though he had been ill-used, insulted, his actions subject to flagrant misrepresentation, and his motives questioned. Pool had abandoned his convoy, leaving Hayden without adequate means to repulse the French squadron, and for this Pool had apparently received not the smallest censure—though he had managed to impugn Hayden's character while explaining away his own dereliction of duty. Hayden brought his convoy—Pool's convoy!—across Biscay through difficult winter conditions, repulsed an enemy squadron of superior force, sank two French vessels—one a ship of the line—and for this he was mocked and told that his reputation had preceded him! It was more than a saint could bear.

The trip across the busy harbour passed slowly, Childers, sensing Hayden's mood, silently glancing his way occasionally. Hayden's stomach, not his best friend under perfect circumstances, growled like a terrier. As Childers brought the barge alongside the *Themis*, Hayden stepped onto a rung of the topside ladder and climbed quickly up, barely acknowledging bosun and marines as he gained the deck. In a moment he was in his cabin, sealed orders slapped down upon his writing-table, and pacing angrily larboard to starboard.

A half-hour of this fruitless activity did little to reduce his choler, but Hayden believed he might, at least, be capable of concealing his frustration from others. He sent for Saint-Denis.

The first lieutenant arrived a few moments later, haggard, thinning hair lank and faded, his entire carriage bespeaking fragility. It seemed to Hayden that Saint-Denis grew weaker, in fact was relapsing into illness. Along with this, his character appeared to be breaking down—at least his arrogance had been compromised.

"Are you well, Lieutenant?" Hayden enquired.

Saint-Denis nodded stiffly. "Well enough." Then: "I recover but slowly, Mr Hayden."

"It appears to be true of those who were most ill. I worry that Griffiths' health has been broken."

"It is an irony that he came nearer death than any who did not succumb. If not for young Gould I believe we would have lost the doctor." He touched a hand absently to his temple. "Lost any number of us, in truth. He nursed us back to health. I never expected to be spoon-fed like a babe at this time of my life, but so I was."

"We all owe Gould, Ariss, and Smosh a great debt of thanks."

Saint-Denis nodded, his manner intense but unreadable. Since his recovery he appeared to be in confusion about Gould—as though disdain and gratitude had commingled to form some strange emotion for which men had no name.

"How went your meeting with Brown, sir?" the lieutenant enquired, mastering himself.

Hayden felt the wound in his pride bleed a little, but he attempted to show no sign of it. "We are to escort seven transports to Genoa and then proceed directly to Toulon. Presumably, Lord Hood will find a captain for the *Themis* . . . and all will be well with the world."

"When do we sail, sir?"

"In a few days. We must water and take on powder and shot."

"Very good, sir."

A golf match was arranged by Wickham, to be held in a pasture just beyond the isthmus. Hayden thought it a strange idea, but it seemed to animate his officers and—given their recent states of both mind and body—that was no bad thing. The players would be Saint-Denis, Dr Worthing (hardly to be left out, as he possessed the only clubs), Mr Smosh, and Wickham. Hayden, who had never even seen the game played, declined an invitation but agreed to observe. A good part of the ship's company also planned to join the audience, and food and drink were quickly organised, the whole enterprise taking on something of a holiday atmosphere. Interest was so keen that Hayden suspected wagering had slipped into the matter, and he only hoped that none of his crew would be ruined, given the precarious state of most seamen's financial affairs.

The chosen day presented itself, warm, windless, the vault of the Mediterranean without cloud and flawlessly blue. Boats carried the party of sportsmen ashore, landing them near the town. The goodness of the day, the gaiety of his companions, and the sense of hardships past put Hayden in a mood of benevolent contentment. All that remained for him to feel utterly at peace with the world was the presence of Henrietta Carthew, and though this was clearly impossible, he allowed himself to fall into brief reveries in which his memories of Henrietta were so palpable that the emotions he felt in her presence were recaptured entirely, giving his feelings of tranquility a luxurious edge of yearning, which was not at all unpleasant.

As the crew of the *Themis* proceeded along the street, some of the

locals were drawn into its sphere: a few young men looking for diversion, and a number of young women of dubious occupation, who
immediately found themselves the object of much male attention. To
Hayden's surprise, Griffiths seemed interested in these girls, and then
Hayden realised it was one particular girl that drew the doctor's eye.
She was, Hayden noted, very comely, her skin delicate, hair shining
coppery in the sun. Her behavior was so modest that Hayden wondered if she was not a sister of one of the young men who had joined
the party (and he wondered at the young man's judgement to bring
his sibling into such company), when he noticed the girl had but a
single hand—the left being missing. The scar of her surgery was still
pink and fresh upon her wrist.

"Do you see, Doctor?" Hayden said quietly. "That young woman
has lost her hand."

Griffiths nodded, taking his gaze away, flushing a little with embarrassment. "Yes, and an ugly job the surgeon made of it."

They continued to walk, saying nothing more. Hayden, Hawthorne, and Griffiths made a small party within the party, strolling
along the street among sailors, inhabitants, and soldiers. The three
seemed happy in one another's company, as they had been when all
were residents of the gunroom, and this alleviated some of the isola-
tion Hayden felt as captain.

This peaceful state, however, was interrupted by great alarm from
down the street. People could be seen dashing into doorways and
bolting up side alleys, and a few seconds later, shouts of *"Mad dog!
Mad dog!"* reached them. Faces appeared at upper windows, leaning
precariously out to stare down into the suddenly chaotic street.

A black mongrel dodged among the flying bodies, muzzle thick
with drooly froth, snapping at any who happened in its path. Hawthorne looked quickly about and snatched up a barrow handle that
leaned against a wall. He strode to the centre of the narrow way,
spread his legs, and hefted the handle like an axe. Before him the sea
of people seemed to part in a swirl of skirts and frock coats, children

being swept up and thrust through open windows into waiting arms. Without warning, the dog tacked to starboard, chasing after a corpulent man who, in his alarm, ran first toward a closed door and then clumsily changed course. The mongrel snapped at his ample buttocks as he turned but then carried on toward Hawthorne, who barred its way. In a moment it was done, the barrow handle flailing down, a sharp crack, and the brute lay on the cobbles, his limbs twitching faintly. Hawthorne fetched him two more blows to the skull and the mad dog lay limp and still.

"I am bit!" the corpulent man cried. "I am bit!" He pulled at his breeches, twisting around awkwardly in an attempt to see an area of his bulk that had not been in view for some years. "My God, the brute got hold of me!"

Griffiths took charge, galvanised by need. He and Hawthorne peeled the man's breeches down around his ankles right there in the street, the crew of the *Themis* and emerging residents crowding round.

"It is a scratch, only," Griffiths pronounced, crouched by the man's bulging derriere. "The teeth did not penetrate the skin." He turned to a group of locals. "Is there a smith?" he demanded.

"I'll fetch him, sir," a young man offered, and went off at a run.

The corpulent man had grown somewhat pale and Griffiths had him sit down on the ground, and then lie down when he did not show signs of recovery. The dog was an object of almost equal curiosity, people collecting around it but keeping a little distance in the event it was not wholly dead. A pock-marked boy prodded the beast with a stick, the dark skin mounding into creases where the point pressed, but the dog did not respond otherwise.

A smith appeared, running down the street with a pair of tongs in one hand. The crowd opened a narrow corridor to let him pass, and he stopped over the mad dog's victim.

"Who is the doctor?" he asked.

"I am," Griffiths answered, reaching out to take the offered tongs.

This sight caused the corpulent man to stir, but Hawthorne and two crewmen pinned him, squirming, to the ground before he could escape.

"Do not move!" Griffiths ordered, and, with only the slightest pause to take aim, applied the glowing-hot coal to the man's buttock. A hissing sound and the smell of burning flesh caused everyone to draw back, some covering their noses and mouths.

"Done," Griffiths announced, returning the tongs to their owner. Griffiths turned his attention to several people who seemed to be the victim's friends. "He must be submerged in a cold bath for as long as he can hold his breath—as many times as he can bear—then whipped with towels. I believe we applied the coal in good time and he will be preserved from the madness."

Griffiths hauled himself to his feet using his walking stick. "Shall we carry on?" he said testily, embarrassed by his physical weakness.

"By all means," Hayden replied.

Griffiths might have been put out of sorts by the incident, but it was clear the rest of the crew thought it a most diverting entertainment and talked of nothing else as they made their way down the street and out of the town. Occasional cries of *"Mad dog! Mad dog!"* produced immediate alarm and much laughter for a short stretch, but then the novelty wore away and these ceased altogether.

Through a gate in the stone wall the golfing party emerged into the pasture. The bullocks, carried there from Morocco to feed the British fleet, could be seen collected in a distant corner, where herdsmen with dogs had agreed to keep them. The habitually dull-rummy, and today confused, looks in the eyes of the cattle as they observed the progress of the sportsmen and their entourage seemed appropriate to Hayden. As human endeavours went, golf did seem to be one of the oddest. Around him seamen partook of coarse Spanish wine, which could be had cheaply from any merchant in the town, and already they were none too steady on their feet. It did not help that several weeks upon a moving deck made the land seem to sway about—a strange phenomenon familiar to any man who had gone to sea.

"It is rather like the links land at Saint Andrews," Worthing observed, surveying the area. "Have you played the old course?" he enquired of Saint-Denis.

"Twice only," Saint-Denis replied, frustrating Worthing, who seemed certain that in this he would prove superior.

Worthing sported a bright red coat, an object of apparel which had originally been adopted by golfers to give warning to strolling families who might otherwise find themselves in a cannonade of small missiles. This garment had apparently been made to fit a slightly smaller man or perhaps had been purchased some years earlier when the worthy doctor had been youthfully slim, for now it seemed to pull his entire form upward, fitting tightly around his small belly and forcing back his shoulders.

A few feet behind walked Worthing's servant, a particularly devout hand whom the crew had nicknamed "Dismal Johnny." He bore, under his right arm, with shafts pointing aft, a small array of play clubs, spoons, putters, and diverse curious and exotic-looking implements, some of which appeared to be tools especially manufactured for cutting hay or perhaps pounding beef.

The procession stopped at the first teeing-up place and stood about wondering what would happen next, the sailors looking on faintly bemused. Saint-Denis retrieved one of the play clubs and hefted it knowingly. He flexed the ash shaft, sighted along its length, then, taking hold of the sheepskin grip, waggled it back and forth.

"A most excellent club," he pronounced it. "Who is your cleek maker, Doctor?"

"Jarvis, in Edinburgh," Worthing said, perhaps a bit defensively.

"Jarvis? I have not heard of him."

"He is not so well-known as some, but does excellent work and has made a number of clubs to my own design."

Saint-Denis drew the club back slowly, a little above waist height, then whipped it fiercely around his body, sweeping the ground before him and continuing through, the club making a most satisfying and impressive *swoosh* as it went.

"Ah, I wondered. Several of these were unknown to me."

"This I call the 'mishleek,'" the reverend doctor said proudly, handing the lieutenant an object that looked like a small garden hoe fixed at an angle on the end of a wooden shaft. "For playing out of sand or soft dirt."

Saint-Denis waggled this one. "Of course. I can see its utility immediately."

Worthing retrieved another. "The globmudge, for playing out of ditches."

Saint-Denis smiled broadly as he received this one, returning the mishleek. "I have needed such a club many times but had none." He turned to his student in the gentleman's game. "Do you see, Wickham—for ditches in which a little water might lie. A globmudge," he said admiringly. "I possessed a mud-flinger for a time but found it unsatisfactory in all ways."

"Oh yes, the mud-flingers were poorly conceived and deficient in every way that mattered. You will find the globmudge its superior for unditching the ball and getting it down the links. Many a player who has seen me swing my globmudge in a little rivulet of mud and the ball almost miraculously flying up has hurried off to Jarvis to possess just such a weapon of his own. I hope we will find a ditch in which I might demonstrate its handsomer qualities."

"So do I. Three putters you carry?"

"Yes, one can hardly do with fewer, and God knows I have tried. And I also have this." He took yet another club from those on offer. "I haven't a name for it yet. The 'new-cleek' I have been calling it until inspiration supplies better."

"Let us make this an object of our day—to find a suitable name for your new-cleek." Saint-Denis took it to hand and gave it a half-swing. "For long grass?"

"No—"

"Mud holes?"

"By no means. It is for driving one's ball out of the sheep dung while preserving one's apparel. You will see, there is hardly any splatter at all."

"Mr Smosh?" Saint-Denis called, making a slow circle.

The Reverend Mr Smosh was at that moment standing among a gathering of sailors and tipping the contents of a near-empty wine bottle down his throat.

"Do you see? Dr Worthing has another career as an inventor of cleeks."

"Indeed, I have been most attentive," Smosh replied, running some vowels into consonants just perceptibly. "I have no doubt the modge-glub will prove its uses before the day is out. When do we begin?"

"Let us not waste this perfect day," Saint-Denis said. "Dr Worthing . . . I believe you should have the honour of first ball."

Wooden tees and "featheries" were produced from a canvas sack and distributed to the sportsmen. Wickham turned his feathery over in his hand, squeezing it, then tossing it up a few times as though gauging its weight or ability to fly through the air.

"I am surprised to find Worthing could afford those," Hawthorne whispered.

"Are they dear?" Hayden asked.

"Quite. And one needs several for every match."

"What kind of wood are they?"

"Not wood at all. Leather stuffed hard with soaked goose down that expands as it dries. Quite hard, and then painted to preserve the leather."

The course, five holes, had been set up by Wickham and Saint-Denis the previous day, playing back and forth the length of the vaguely L-shaped pasture and once, narrowly, across it. The pasture was more flat than not, surrounded by a stone wall, overgrown in various places. A few shade trees dotted the field proper, and half a dozen more grew just beyond the wall, their canopies spreading over the grassland.

Worthing selected a levelish area, free of cow dung, and pressed his tee down into the cropped grass. Taking a broad stance, his manner almost solemn, he made a stiff practise swing, whipping a play club around his body and thudding it into the ground, tearing up a chunk of turf that went tumbling along the green.

"Damn!" he muttered, and tried the same again, this time to his satisfaction. Stepping up to his ball, he addressed it in his splayed stance, club waggling behind the sacrificially mounted feathery. After a moment of indecision, he drew back his club, and as he leaned left, about to begin his swing, the ball tottered off the tee, made a small bounce, and rolled half a foot.

"Damn this ball to hell!" the reverend doctor spat out.

Bending awkwardly in his tight coat, Worthing snatched up the ball and set it delicately back upon its tiny perch.

He went through the same motions, waggling his club, his belly thrust forward, shoulders pulled back. The club began its circuit about his frame, hovered thoughtfully a moment, then lashed forward, striking a glancing blow upon the unsuspecting feathery. The little sphere went spinning off, not ten feet above the trampled turf, drawing a low arc toward the stone wall. It struck the ground obliquely, bounced once, altering its path even more to starboard, found the ground again, and fetched up almost immediately against the wall, where all progress stopped with a dull, vowelless *thump*.

Worthing dashed the head of his play club against the turf and cursed like a sailor. He thrust the grip at Wickham, who was next to stand up, and stomped off to the side. While laying out the course the previous day, Wickham had received instruction from Saint-Denis and had the opportunity to strike a few featheries, so he was not completely unprepared for what was to follow. Pushing a tee into the ground and mounting his ball upon it, Wickham took his stance as previously instructed. He waggled the clubhead behind the feathery threateningly, drew the club back, his face set all the while in perfect, childlike concentration. His stroke was not nearly so fast as the doctor's, but it was apparently more true, for the ball shot off the tee, cleaving the air low over the pasture, landed at such an angle that it did not bounce but only rolled for forty yards, spinning to a stop in what appeared to be a clump of thistle.

Saint-Denis offered his student congratulations and a few small corrections to his technique, then insisted Mr Smosh be next to the tee. Smosh handed his bottle to a ship's boy, unbuttoned his jacket, rotated bent arms at the shoulders to loosen his muscles, stepped forward, and planted his tee. He stood upright, short legs straight, lower lip thrust out, face almost aglow from drink. Apparently he felt no need of a practise swing, but went straight to business. He lined his club up behind the feathery, measuring its precise position with one eye closed, as though he aimed a fowling piece. A moment he stood thus, arranging his club in exactly the right attitude, then yanked the club back and high up into the air. With a strange motion, somewhere between splitting wood and scything hay, he drove the ball up into the sky. Off it went, hissing through the warm Mediterranean air, a small white dot against the perfect blue. For an impossible time it seemed to stay aloft, as though it had sprouted wings and hovered like a shrike. And then down, down it tumbled, gathering speed until it struck the ground no little distance off, bounced froglike, and settled out of sight.

"You have a . . . *unique* swing," Saint-Denis observed, clearly not approving, perhaps even a little amused.

Smosh made a small bow, proffered the club to Saint-Denis, and, to a round of spontaneous applause and some catcalls, retrieved his bottle and resumed his place, indifferent, apparently, to the fate of a little leather sphere stuffed with goose down.

Saint-Denis then took the stage. His usual vanity and bravado had been much eroded by recent illness, but he still clearly took pride in his golf prowess—had bragged about it at table—and now was forced to perform before a gathering, not all of whom called him friend. His stance was not unlike Dr Worthing's, but his limbs, frail from influenza, seemed as thin as the shaft of the club he held. His stroke, though well schooled, lacked potency, and the ball set off but slowly, lofting low over the ground, and was soon rolling to a stop not much beyond that of Dr Worthing's, though in open ground.

The party set off, the gallery chattering and laughing in their wake. As Dr Worthing's ball was "away," he was first to play, and found his feathery in a clump of weed not a yard from the stone wall. After a moment's deliberation of the ball's situation, and a thoughtful assessment of the distance to the hole, Worthing selected a spoon. He took careful measure of his backswing to be certain of clearing the wall—there would be no cleek-maker in Gibraltar to mend a broken club—and took his odd stance upon uneven ground. A moment he concentrated his mind, then drew the spoon back and thrashed the air, sending the ball sputtering along the ground, where it fetched up fifty feet distant. This time there were no oaths, but he lifted the head of the club and inspected it with much disapproval.

"Bloody cleek-maker," he muttered, then tossed the offending stick to Dismal Johnny.

Saint-Denis, much to his wounded pride, was next away. Having learned from the doctor's example, he chose a different club, flexed and hefted it, then stepped up to his ball. He drew the club back once, succumbed to indecision and returned it to hovering aft of the ball, drew it back again, and made an awkward slicing motion. To his obvious surprise, this sent the ball rocketing toward the hole, so that it fetched up not forty yards distant from the vertical staff that marked the cup.

"You see, Wickham," he said, "it comes back to me, though I have not played in some time."

"It seemed a perfect stroke," the midshipman observed.

"By no means perfect," the lieutenant answered, "but very near."

Poor Wickham was forced to make his shot out of a stand of vicious thistle, which would have been difficult enough, but Saint-Denis, encouraged by his recent success, insisted on giving much instruction, correcting Wickham's stance and grip and adding abundant criticism of his swing.

With all of this tutelage, much of it contradictory, Hayden thought it a wonder that Wickham could swing the club at all. But swing he did, and even managed to make a decent shot of it, flaying thistle flesh and scattering prickly leaves all about. The ball did not fly far, but it soared true, rolling to a stop in open ground.

"Well done, Wickham," Saint-Denis pronounced. "Mr Smosh . . . Mr Smosh?"

The chaplain's name was repeated by various members of the crowd, and a moment latter Smosh staggered out of the party, his neckcloth half undone, face crimson, eyes nearly shut. He took a club, seemingly at random, from the servant, and stepped up to his feathery. Again he took his strange, high swing, struck the ball a resounding *smack*, and lofted it high into the air. It shrank smaller and smaller until it was petite, then minute, minuscule. . . . It began to fall, gathering speed, gathering size, until it thumped dully down onto the ground and bounce-rolled up to within a few yards of the thin spar marking the first hole.

The crowd reacted with great acclaim and many a thump on the sportsman's back. Smosh was absorbed into this cheering mass, which supported him, embraced him, and encouraged him to drink to his success.

Griffiths glanced Hayden's way, all unsaid. It was a holiday, Hayden thought, and Smosh had no duties aboard ship. Let him indulge himself.

Worthing was next to play, and seemed even more determined to make a good show of it. This determination, however, increased his self-consciousness and banished all ability to focus his mind. Twice he drew his club back and lost confidence returning the club to address. Flushed a little with embarrassment, he resolved to make a stroke, drew the club back, thrashed it through the air, and missed the ball completely, though it rolled an inch off the nubbin it perched upon, as if avoiding the doctor's attack.

A string of oaths, that would have made Mr Barthe proud, followed, causing much surprised laughter among the crew. Again the chaplain addressed the ball, drew his club back with exaggerated care, and flashed it forward. The ball this time had the decency to stay in place and take its proper thrashing. It flew forward, hardly two feet above the grass, and then began a series of long, low bounces, almost loping over the ground, until it rolled to a stop eight yards short of the hole and three dozen feet to the left.

"Excellent shot, Dr Worthing," Saint-Denis offered cheerfully, to a dark stare from the clergyman.

The gathering trudged on, though a good number broke off to seek the shade of a tree that overhung the enclosing wall. The young ladies who had attached themselves to the sailors accompanied this party, the pleasures of golf apparently not the diversion they sought. From the sounds erupting from this group, Hayden was sure a certain variety of commerce had been contracted, and not with much privacy, either—something the sailors were well used to. The young lady who had so recently lost her hand could be seen hovering, unhappily, upon the fringe of this gathering. From all sides she was urgently besieged by sailors, and the other women mocked her reluctance.

"You're not above it, now, princess," one of the whores called out.

The sailors had begun tugging at her arms and the sleeves of her dress. Without a word, Griffiths broke away from Hayden and Hawthorne, striding stiffly toward the shade tree, swinging his cane, shoulders taut with apparent anger.

Hawthorne glanced at Hayden, a smile quickly giving way to a look of alarm. Hayden took a step to follow the doctor—drunken sailors were capable of much trouble—but Hawthorne held up a hand to restrain him.

"I think we shall have fewer floggings if the captain remains here," he said. "If I may . . . ?"

Hayden nodded once and watched Hawthorne set off in the wake of Griffiths, a few marines taking up positions in his wake. Griffiths reached the girl first, waving his cane at bemused and then, almost immediately, indignant sailors. They squared up to the advancing doctor but then noticed the small party of marines quickly converging. Hawthorne was much admired among the hands, but he also had a reputation as a man not to be trifled with. The sailors backed away resentfully, giving up their prize, and Griffiths rather quickly led the young woman away, toward the town.

"Isn't it just like a surgeon to take a fancy to a woman with one hand removed," Hawthorne said as he rejoined Hayden.

"All a bit out of character," Hayden replied. "But then the doctor, I am sure, is much like many another man in this regard."

"Indeed," Hawthorne agreed. "Who is to play?"

"Wickham." And both men made a show of turning their attention back to the golf match.

The midshipman's ball squatted in the open on a sparse patch of flattened grass and dried mud.

"A good lie, Wickham," Saint-Denis pronounced. "Not quite so good as being raised up a little by grass, but not so very bad. You will not need a baffing spoon here, or Dr Worthing's estimable glob-mudge. A simple spoon will do, eh, Doctor?"

Worthing selected a club from among those on offer and thrust the grip in Wickham's direction. "This will suffice for a player of your experience."

Saint-Denis did not seem to approve of the selection but apparently felt he could not gainsay the owner of the clubs.

"A vigorous half-swing, Wickham, no more. Just as I demonstrated yesterday."

Wickham made a practise swipe at an imaginary feathery.

"Quite acceptable," Saint-Denis said, nodding his head, "but keep the club low throughout the backswing and do not, for love of God, raise your head. All the authorities agree the player who lifts his head shall be damned to golfers' purgatory for all eternity."

"And, pray, what does golfers' purgatory look like?" Hawthorne enquired innocently, causing laughter among the thinning audience.

"At the deepest level, Mr Hawthorne, there is no golf at all, and at the intermediate levels the courses are devised by cruel madmen determined to ruin a sportsman's every pleasure. Sand there is aplenty, rain daily, holes so far apart that days must be set aside to play but a one." He grimaced. "It unnerves me even to speak of it." He turned to Lord Arthur. "Mr Wickham."

The middy stepped up to the ball and with a deft, shallow swing sent the ball lofting upward and then down near the hole, where in three bounces it approached then passed the cup, rolling to a sudden stop three yards beyond.

"Well struck, Wickham! Well struck!"

Saint-Denis' ball was quickly found, sitting in a little depression like a solitary egg in a bowl.

The sportsmen, minus Smosh, formed a triumvirate to contemplate this terrible lie, no one offering an opinion for a moment, silenced, perhaps, by the utter horror of it.

"A spoon will not scoop that meal out," Wickham said at last.

"No," Saint-Denis agreed, his brow furrowed in frustration. "An iron is called for. A track-iron, I wonder?"

Smosh approached at that moment, a look of cherubic delight upon his chubby face. He tacked back and forth a half a yard as he came, but appeared unaware of it. He fetched up where his fellows stood in conference, looked down at the ball in its nest, and pronounced, "Nulick."

"What are you saying, Smosh?" Saint-Denis asked, clearly offended by the clergyman's state.

"Nigleek," Smosh ventured, but then shook his head in frustration. He raised both hands to shoulder height and lowered them in pace with his next, deliberate pronouncement. *"Nib-lick,"* he enunciated in a vain attempt at precision.

"Are you saying 'new-cleek'?" Wickham asked.

Smosh nodded vigorously, clearly unwilling to risk more verbalization.

"Pass me the 'niblick,' then," Saint-Denis said. "I shall give it a go."

The new-cleek was handed forward and Saint-Denis took his stance over the ball, which lay almost entirely below the level of the ground. A quick joggle from one foot to the other and then a violent swipe at the ball sent a small clod of earth and roots in a tumble along the ground. The ball, however, had been but jostled by the effort and lay, mockingly, in the same spot.

"That counts a stroke," Worthing announced for all to hear.

Smosh clearly agreed. *"A stork,"* he echoed.

A second, more violent, attempt produced an explosion of dirt, but out of it the ball materialised, plopping down three yards distant, dirt and stones raining all around.

"You could not have managed *that* without my new-cleek, I'll wager," Worthing crowed.

"No," Saint-Denis said heatedly, "the niblick is a device of utter, bloody genius." He turned and stomped off, leaving an offended Worthing in his wake.

Smosh caught the clergyman's attention and held up the club, which Saint-Denis had all but thrown at him. "Niblick," he said tentatively.

Worthing drew himself up, a look of unmitigated contempt upon his face. "And you call yourself a man of God," he said in disgust, and turned away.

His ball still farthest from the hole, Saint-Denis was forced to take another turn. This time he did not tarry over it but grabbed a club seemingly at random from the servant and took a swipe at his ball, sending it in bouncing, erratic flight over the harsh terrain. A moment of this jackrabbitlike behavior and it hopped past the hole a good thirty yards, then spun five more for good measure. It was Saint-Denis' turn to curse, which he managed as coarsely as any foremast hand. The spectators erupted into applause, whether at this display of golfing prowess or his newly revealed talent for profanity, Hayden could not be sure.

The players and their entourage set off again.

En route to his ball, Smosh actually stumbled and would have fallen but for the intercession of Hawthorne, who managed to catch him by the arm. This caused much laughter among the thinning gallery. Approaching Smosh's ball, a disgusted Saint-Denis retrieved a club from the caddy and, holding it by the head, tapped the drunken clergyman on the arm with the grip. Smosh took the club without comment or even looking, stepped up to the ball, closed one eye, turned his head to assess the distance to the hole, then pulled the approach putter back, somehow maintaining his balance, and made a clean, even swing. The ball performed a gentle, balletic arc toward the hole, not rising above a foot, landed with nary a bounce, rolled five feet, and stopped within inches of the cup.

Wild applause from the small audience. Smosh turned to them, made an elaborate and solemn bow, pivoted back to his ball, tripped on his own feet, and sprawled full length. His putter, thrust out before in an attempt to save himself, made slight contact with the ball and rolled it softly into the cup.

Overwhelming huzzahs from the bystanders.

Smosh was dragged ungently to his feet by the crowd, and almost carried off in their enthusiasm.

Both Worthing and Saint-Denis were away, and as the reverend doctor's ball must be passed to reach the other, Saint-Denis insisted the clergyman be first. With perhaps forty feet to the cup, Worthing elected to use his approach putter. As making this shot would tie him with Smosh—whom Hayden expected he did not want to lose to under any circumstances—Dr Worthing spent some moments examining the terrain, deciding where best to land his ball and how far it would carry and break.

"What does he mean, 'break'?" Hayden enquired of Hawthorne.

"The amount it will deviate to either starboard or larboard dependent on the slope of the ground," Hawthorne answered.

"Have you played this game before, then, Mr Hawthorne?"

"Only once or twice, but I have friends in London who are overly . . . zealous. I have been subjected to a great deal of their talk."

"You did not speak up when Wickham was looking for players," Hayden noted.

"Between us," Hawthorne whispered, "I would rather be whipped around the fleet and marched barefoot back to London. Have you never attempted it?"

Hayden shook his head.

"It is a game perfectly contrived to induce the greatest possible frustration and test one's mastery of choler to the utmost. I have seen men of the mildest character dash a play club to splinters on a tree in a passion that would befit an especially violent lunatic. No, never take up this cursed game unless you have the disposition of a saint, the patience of a nun."

"Or the skill of Mr Smosh," Hayden added. "Do you believe our reverend guest is so proficient? And he is completely foxed, forced to close one eye lest he see more than one feathery."

The marine lieutenant laughed. "Yes, which to hit, that is the question."

Saint-Denis had come over to discuss with Worthing his situation and use it as an opportunity for instruction with Mr Wickham.

"His lie is perfectly good, though perhaps a little below the level of his feet. Easily accommodated by a bend of the knees. The ground, however, slopes away to the left and the ball will break toward this natural incline. Dr Worthing will play the ball 'high,' or to the right, to allow for this slope. But the principal objective of such a shot is to get the ball into the air somewhat, for rolling over uneven ground the ball may find any little hillock or hollow and deviate off in some unpredicted direction. Are you ready, Doctor?"

Saint-Denis and his student withdrew, leaving the clergyman to contemplate his shot in solitude. After crouching down to examine the lie of the ground yet one more time, Worthing stood up to his ball, arranged his stance, rocked a little from one foot to the other, eyed the target, and drew back his putter. A slow, pendulum motion and the ball was propelled up, not quite a foot, and sailed unerringly wide of the hole by a mere inch, landed, and rolled a dozen feet.

The clergyman checked his cursing before it began but walked purposefully to his ball, his face a mask of denied fury. He took the putter used for holing out and again examined his lie, plucking a small stone out of the path as he did so. Taking a stance over his ball, both arms and legs rod straight, he pulled his club back and brought it forward again with a slight wobble. Contacting the ball too high, it sputtered away, rolled and bounced toward the hole, and at the last second curled a little to larboard and lost all way two feet beyond its intended berth.

A collective "Ohhh" escaped the crowd.

Worthing marched over to the feathery, bent, and struck it with a pop. The response of the gallery was quite wild as the ball fell into the hole, but by smiles on faces it was clear that sincerity was lacking.

"Well done, Doctor!" and "Purely struck!" were heard among the huzzahs.

The doctor did not even deign to glance toward the audience, but thrust his putter at the servant and walked a few paces off, fairly twitching from suppressed rage.

Saint-Denis was sizing up the situation of his feathery and did not appear to be in any hurry to draw a conclusion. After a minute examination of the ground near the hole, and some consideration to most of the terrain in between, he selected a spoon. The eyes of the masses upon him, Saint-Denis was suddenly all manufactured authority, standing up to the ball with great resolve. Every movement was made with deliberation, apparent concentration. He waggled the club strongly, set it behind the little feathery upon the cattle-cropped grass, drew it back with utter focus, and flashed it forward in a low, sweeping stroke. The ball went winging off the toe of the club, avid in its desire to avoid the hole. Struck so obliquely, however, it did not travel far, so the distance to the hole remained much the same, though the direction had changed utterly.

Saint-Denis muttered an oath under his breath, shook his head, and stomped off toward the offending ball that had so brazenly defied his authority. Again the ground was examined foot by foot, the lie evaluated; he even threw a pinch of dry grass into the air to assess the direction and strength of the wind—which seemed like an over-abundance of caution, given that a dead calm prevailed.

Another stroke and the ball this time relented and went where it was told, rolling up within six feet of the cup.

Wickham then two-putted from ten feet and Saint-Denis holed out in one. The first hole went to Mr Smosh, who was nowhere to be found but was finally carried forth, his frock coat gone, his neckcloth missing, and his collar open. A hint of powder lay upon his cheek—a chalklike dusting—and a trace of rouge was smeared around his mouth. Thus made up, the clergyman took up a play club, addressed the feathery teed up by the servant, and with astonishing precision, given that he swayed while he stood, sent the ball sailing off toward the next hole.

And so the match went, Worthing and Saint-Denis becoming more and more determined not to be outplayed, which undermined their ability to focus the mind. Wickham's natural athleticism combined with his low expectations allowed him to relax and actually enjoy the match. Smosh, drunker at every hole, continued to hit the ball with perfect balance and grace, sending the feathery wherever he liked, though seeing the hole became more and more difficult.

"Mr Smosh . . . You are aiming the wrong way. No, traverse more to larboard. . . . More yet. Just so. Flail away."

By the seventh hole Smosh had opened up an impossible lead on the other players. But on the eighth he stood up to his ball, bent over, and vomited horribly upon his feathery. He then stood, drew back his club, and sent the befouled ball off in a splatter of half-digested breakfast.

Inevitably, featheries fluttered down into pancakes of soggy cow dung; Dr Worthing's ball was the first to find such a nest. He strode up to the ball, confronted it with hands on hips, lips pressed thin, and then called for the new-cleek, which caused a rise in excited chatter.

"He's going to hit out of the shit with the niblick!" voices were saying. An expectant hush settled over the pasture.

Grasping the club, Worthing took his stance, waving the niblick in the direction of the ball, which lay in the centre of the flattened mush like the yolk in the middle of an egg. Thrice he drew the niblick back two slow feet, then brought it forward with equal speed, careful not to sully the club in the manure. Then, to everyone's horrified fascination, he drew it fully back, whipped it forward, and in a storm of green-grey shit, sent the ball skittering along the ground, spinning off the foul material as it rolled. The niblick was not quite as effective at preserving the player's boots and breeches as the designer had boasted, but it did propel the ball along proficiently.

Each player took his turn at extracting a ball—or two—from the manure piles, though depending upon how long the dung had aged it could be more or less messy. Wickham fared best in this, though Smosh, at one point, lost his balance and sat down in dung without being even the least aware of it.

By the tenth hole the gallery of spectators had retired to the shade and were almost all passed out on the grass, a few famous snorers serenading the cattle. Only the officers remained interested in the match, the smart money backing either Smosh or Wickham, depending upon the gambler's faith that Smosh could actually finish the round. Despite being clearly befuddled and hardly aware that he played golf at all, Smosh continued to amaze with his unerring ability to strike the ball cleanly and get it down in the fewest strokes.

On the fourteenth hole he was beginning to falter, standing for an impossible length of time over his ball, as though unsure where he was or what he was to do. Just as Saint-Denis stepped forward to prompt him, Smosh drew back his club, struck the ball with customary authority, performed a complete pirouette, and toppled, face-first, to the ground, where he lay still as a corpse.

Mr Ariss was wakened, and he pronounced Smosh alive, though no effort to bring him back to consciousness produced any effect. Finally, the clergyman was taken up and propped against a tree, watched over by his servant lest he choke on his own gorge. The match was abandoned after eighteen holes, the players too fatigued or disheartened to continue. Worthing gathered up his clubs and strode off toward the town, clearly offended by all that had occurred. Saint-Denis told one and all that he would certainly have played much better had he not been so weakened from his recent illness, but congratulated Wickham on learning the game so quickly, pointing out that solid instruction was the key to golf.

"And what thought you of the match?" Hayden asked Hawthorne as they walked back to the boats.

"Not so interesting as a hanging, but more diverting than old women at cards." Hawthorne was pensive a moment, then smiled. "Let me pass along a bit of drollery from my golfing friends. It is a rusty old saw, but perhaps you have not heard it. Two gentlemen went out upon the links one fair morning to indulge in a match. At the third hole, one of the gentlemen, by the name of Herald, sustained an attack upon his chest and fell down instantly dead. Upon returning home that evening the other man, when asked by his wife how went his play . . ."

Griffiths returned to the ship at an uncharacteristically late hour. Upon boarding he visited the sick-berth, briefly consulted with Mr Ariss on several cases of near-fatal poisoning caused by excesses of cheap wine, and then presented himself to the marine sentry at the captain's door. Immediately he was admitted, and found the captain and Mr Hawthorne seated within.

"I do apologise, Captain, for my tardiness," he said formally.

"Not at all, Dr Griffiths. I trust you have left Mr Ariss with all necessary instructions. Your hour of return is your business." Hayden trusted his officers, even his warrant officers, to police themselves, and given that they were, to a man, responsible and dutiful, this system worked perfectly well. "Mr Hawthorne and I are about to indulge in coffee, Dr Griffiths. Would you care to join us?"

"Thank you, sir."

The three men took chairs at Hayden's table, an unusual and awkward silence settling among them. Hayden thought that Griffiths was about to break this silence when a knock on the door announced their coffee.

The steaming liquid was poured, the perfume of it filling the cabin.

"Did you enjoy the golf match, Doctor?" Hawthorne enquired.

"The little I saw. Who was the victor, pray?"

"Wickham," Hayden answered, "but only because Smosh became insensible from drink. Saint-Denis was too weakened by his recent illness and should have retired, I think, and the reverend doctor too prideful and was punished for it."

"Even clergymen are subject to divine censure," the doctor declared. "Vanity is often our undoing." He seemed to grow even more solemn. He was a man whose mind was clearly on another matter— a matter of some gravity. He took a long breath, hesitated, and then plunged. "No doubt you saw me effect the rescue of the young lady this day?"

"I did and thought it most noble of you," Hayden said, and Hawthorne nodded his agreement.

Griffiths shrugged. "She did not seem to me . . . one of the common port Sallys, and you noted yourself that she had lost a hand. . . ."

Hayden remembered that he had.

"I had seen another similar circumstance—or so I imagined—when I was undergoing my surgical training. A young woman came to the hospital—a seamstress—and a more captivating creature it would be difficult to conceive of. She had run a needle through the thenar eminence, missing the first metacarpal, here, at the base of her thumb"—he held up a hand by way of explanation—"and it had become infected—very badly so. The corruption had quickly spread. After consulting with another student on the matter, it was decided to remove her hand to save the arm, and likely her life. This was done successfully, the delicate young woman, not more than two and twenty, suffering the agony of amputation with nary a complaint. I made as neat a job of it as I could, and under my careful eye, for I will admit she seemed very fair to me, a full recovery was made. She was sent home, and not a fortnight later I learned, upon making enquiries, that she had drowned herself. It transpired that, having lost her only means of livelihood and having no family or connexions, she chose death rather than debasement. I cannot recount to you, gentlemen, the nights I lay awake, haunted by what I had done to this poor girl. My teacher in anatomy and surgery assured me that there had been no other possible course and that what I had done had saved her life, but it was little comfort. My feelings of shame over this have hardly lessened over the intervening years. And then, today . . . I was confronted with another young woman in what I perceived might be similar circumstances. You know what next I did. Some time it took to coax her story forth, but believing me, after many assurances on my part, to be a gentleman interested only in her welfare, she did relent and tell me. Her hand had been crushed by a wagon in the street after she had been knocked down by some drunken lout. Unable to save it, the hand was removed— and poorly so—by a local surgeon. Until that unfortunate event, Miss Brentwood, for that is her name, had been employed as a maid of all work by the chief carpenter in the Navy shipyard. This . . . man had made improper and unwanted advances to her for some time, which she had always rebuffed. Once she had lost her hand, and he knew she could not find work elsewhere, this man informed her that she must accept his attentions or she would be put out in the street. She left his employ that day. But a maid of all work with only one hand has no prospects, and her savings were small. Today we saw where it led. . . . She contemplated debasing herself rather than go hungry, but in the end could not. I came along just as she had resolved that starvation would be preferable." Griffiths availed himself of his coffee. He looked more than a little mortified by this admission. "I think I have found her a position with a family I know through an acquaintance. Certainly she would be better off in England, and if I can manage it, I will contrive to send her hither."

"I hope these good deeds do not go unrewarded." What Hayden really hoped was that Griffiths had not fallen prey to a woman more cunning than pure.

Hawthorne said nothing.

"It is, I realise, an unusual thing to do for a stranger, but I could not allow the same fate to befall a second young woman were it within my power to intercede. I have lived these many years with my remorse over the previous affair; I could not bear to have it doubled."

A knock on the door stopped Hayden from answering. His sentry opened the door at a call from Hayden.

"Beg pardon, Captain. Mr Ariss is urgently seeking Dr Griffiths. One of the men who was ill . . . seems to have gone a bit mad, sir. Screaming somewhat about spiders, sir."

Somewhere below, Hayden thought he could hear shouting.

Griffiths excused himself and hurried out.

Hawthorne fixed Hayden with a look, difficult to read.

"You appear to have some opinion of this matter, Lieutenant?" Hayden ventured.

For a moment Hawthorne contemplated, took a sip of his coffee, and then began. "I believe, Captain, that there are two romantic . . . 'myths,' as I have come to think of them—one rather natural to women and the other to men, though neither exclusively so. The romantic myth common to women is a belief in the transformative power of love. I have, over the years, witnessed women give themselves, body and soul, to men most unlikely to ever bring them happiness either by nature of their character or due to impossibly different hopes and desires in life. It was the belief of these women, most often to their everlasting sorrow, that the men would fall so impossibly in love with them that they would transform themselves simply to retain the affection of such a perfect female." Hawthorne again had redress to his coffee. "I have also been witness to many young women rebuffing men who were in every way deserving and compatible, only to then marry a man who was neither. But a man who would completely transform himself to be worthy of her love—now, there was a man worth having—not some poor sod who simply adored her and wanted the same life." Hawthorne turned his gaze to the windows a moment. "The male romantic myth," he continued, "is rescuing the maiden in distress, and this is equally fraught with danger. Rescuing a young woman from a bad situation or circumstances might seem entirely noble, but gratitude, too often, has proved a poor foundation upon which to build a marriage—compatibility of temperament or a large fortune, apparently, are to be preferred. Gratitude, in my experience, flowers briefly and then withers into resentment. Let us hope that our friend does not suffer another disappointment, for his character is such, in these matters, that he will not easily withstand it."

The ship's bell rang at that moment, and Hawthorne rose to his feet.

"If you will excuse me, Captain, I have duties."

"By all means."

Hayden found himself alone, contemplating upon the deed of Dr Griffiths, and the observations of Mr Hawthorne, who in matters of the heart was greatly experienced, and clearly more thoughtful than Hayden would have predicted. Certainly Hayden agreed that the doctor's character was delicate in such matters, although he was not certain why he believed this. Even so, it was a noble and generous deed, assuming the woman's story to be true, and Hayden honoured Griffiths' sentiments. Still . . .

Hayden gazed at the cold, muddy liquid remaining in the doctor's coffee cup, and the sight unsettled him in some way he could not explain.

Twelve

A late-December dusk blew in from the east, carrying with it a fleet of aggrieved gulls, mourning and grumbling pitifully in the ruins of the recent gale.

"Fucking levanter," Mr Barthe pronounced the wind. He lowered his night glass but continued to stare into the darkness. "Can you make out anything at all, Mr Wickham?"

Wickham, who stood at the forward barricade with a night glass pressed to his eye, answered softly, as though they approached the harbour of Toulon by stealth. "There are no ships in the roads, Mr Barthe."

"What said you?"

"I do not believe there are ships anchored in the roads, Mr Barthe," Wickham repeated, raising his voice only a little.

"Mr Wickham, either I am gone deaf or you are whispering."

Wickham raised his voice. *"There are no—"*

". . . ships in the roads. Yes, yes. I heard that. Ah, Captain Hayden." The sailing master touched his hat as Hayden mounted the forecastle. "There don't appear to be any ships—"

". . . in the roads, or so I have heard. The eastern gale has no doubt made that anchorage untenable. They have all shifted their berths to the inner harbour."

"If I have learned anything of the bloody Mediterranean in winter, it is that this weather is not done with us yet," Barthe offered. "A little calm means only that worse approaches. I am quite confident I can con us in, sir. The wind could not be better suited to such an endeavour, and there is moonlight enough."

"If you are certain, Mr Barthe. With another gale in the offing and these confounding currents setting us first one way and then another, I do not mind telling you, I would rather be safely at anchor this night."

"Then we shall be, sir. Mr Wickham has volunteered to see through the dark for us, and it is an excellent, spacious plot of water, sir. I shall have us all sleeping sound within the hour, Captain Hayden. See if I don't."

"Then you are appointed pilot, Mr Barthe—take us in."

This simple proposition, however, was not so easily effected, as the east wind and confounding currents conjoined forces, the wind dropping away to a mere breeze and the current setting them in the same direction. Several anxious hours saw them weathering Sepet Point and even dropping anchor once to hold them off the shore as the wind died away altogether. It was nearing midnight when a small but steady breeze, originating in the east even then, began making. At the same time, the current appeared to subside, and, setting sail, the *Themis* passed slowly over a glassy, dark sea toward the entrance of Toulon Harbour.

Eight bells sounded as they crossed the outer roads, echoed distantly by a more numerous chiming within the nearing city—twelve bells upon the land.

"Midnight," Hawthorne announced. "Will this wind carry us in, do you think, or will it leave us wallowing in the roads?"

Hayden shrugged. "Despite all appearances, Mr Hawthorne, I am not the god of the seas. What the winds might or might not do is a mystery to me."

Hawthorne chuckled. "I do apologise, Captain. In the dark I mistook you for Neptune."

"Easily done, Mr Hawthorne. No need to apologise . . . except, perhaps, to Neptune."

A small presence materialised to Hayden's left—Rosseau, his cook. *"Toulon, Capitaine?"*

"Oui, Monsieur. Toulon."

"If . . . if we fall into the hands of the . . . our people, Capitaine," Rosseau said hesitantly in French, *"would you be so kind as to tell them I am a prisoner—not your cook."*

"I will do that, monsieur," Hayden answered in the same language, *"but do not be concerned. Toulon is yet in the hands of Lord Hood."*

In the vague moonlight Hayden could see the man—could even perceive his anxiety. The administration of Toulon had, some weeks previous, invited Admiral Lord Hood to assume control of the city and port—and the French Mediterranean fleet, which was lying there. As in other parts of southern France, the citizens were in rebellion. Hayden had been told Lord Hood had demanded the city fathers swear allegiance to the Bourbons, but that they had done so reluctantly. It appeared that the citizens of Toulon were in rebellion against the excesses of the Convention and the Committee of Public Safety rather than rebelling because they favoured the former royal family. It was, Hayden thought, a tremendous gamble they took, but the benefit to the British could hardly be overstated. The French Mediterranean fleet on a platter! Despite the clear advantages to Britain, Hayden could not help but feel some concern for the people of Toulon—despite the war, the French people remained dear to him. If the revolutionary government took the city back, there would be reprisals, and everyone, even his cook, understood what form these would take.

Hayden and Barthe returned to the quarterdeck, leaving Wickham on the forecastle to part the darkness.

"Turn up the hands, Mr Franks," Hayden ordered, "let us hand all canvas but topsails, and then make ready to bring the ship to anchor."

The crew took the deck at a trot; bringing the ship into a new harbour was always an event of interest, and doubly so in this case, as it was a French port in British hands—a sight not often to be seen.

To starboard the Grand Tower could be made out, looming over the entrance. A few lights were likely from the city, almost due north. The wind kept backing until it bore down on them from Toulon.

"Do you smell that?" Barthe inhaled deeply. "An old, smoggy stench of charred wood and powder smoke? They have been under terrible siege, I would venture."

Hayden could smell it—rain somehow brought out the pungent odour of burned wood. He felt for the people of Toulon. If the revolutionary army took back the city, Hood would never be able to remove them all.

Leaving Barthe on the quarterdeck, Hayden went forward. Even though he knew Wickham had far better sight in the darkness, he was becoming anxious about the situation.

"Why are the siege guns silent?" he muttered to himself as he hurried along the gangway.

"There are ships at anchor nearer the quays, Captain," Wickham reported, "and a little brig not so distant before us. We will not weather her, sir."

"Let us pass beneath her stern, Mr Wickham," Hayden replied, "and work our way up toward the town where our own ships will have come to anchor." Hayden turned to Gould, who, as usual, was acting as Wickham's shadow. "Mr Gould, would you pass the word to Mr Barthe to set foresail and driver. We will tack as we pass beyond the two-sticker."

"Aye, sir," Gould answered crisply, and hastened off toward the stern.

Out of the darkness came a voice, speaking French. *"What ship?"* a man called from the brig.

"We are His Majesty's Ship Themis." Hayden replied in the same language.

Over the still waters voices drifted, conferring in his mother's tongue, but the words were torn apart on the little breeze and arrived in slurred syllables, shattered vowels; he could not splice them back together.

Mr Barthe came hurrying along the gangway, giving orders for sails to be set. Hayden was not reassured by his manner, which seemed suddenly to lack its former resolution.

"What is this about a Frenchman . . . ? Ah."

As the stern of the brig grew more distinct, Hayden called out in French, *"Where does the English admiral anchor? Where is Lord Hood?"*

A muffled conference seemed to take place. *"You are an English ship?"* someone called. Hayden could almost make out a shape at the taffrail.

"Oui. Une frégate anglaise."

More talk, incomprehensible to Hayden.

"Can you make out what they're saying?" Mr Barthe asked, attempting not to reveal his growing anxiety.

"I cannot. Can you, Mr Wickham?"

"Somewhat about sending a boat to the admiral, sir. *Amiral* must mean 'admiral,' does it not?"

"Luff!" came a cry from the French brig. *"Luuuff!"*

"Helm hard down!" Hayden cried along the deck. "Dryden! Hard down! Let us have the lead . . . *handsomely.*"

The *Themis* began a slow turn in the little zephyr. Hayden could hear the men aboard holding their breath, as everyone made thwarted little gestures, a strained twist to the right, as though they could help bring the ship's head around.

"She will not tack in this small wind, sir," Barthe whispered.

"Back the foresail as she luffs, Mr Barthe," Hayden ordered, but the wind fell away to nothing even as he spoke.

Before the sailing master could repeat Hayden's order, the ship shuddered once, heeled a little to starboard, and abruptly lost all way.

A foul oath escaped Mr Barthe. "There is no shoal on my chart."

"Send the men aloft with all speed," Hayden ordered. "Clew up and hand the sails. We cannot be very hard aground with so little way on. Mr Franks! Swing out two cutters, if you please. Mr Landry, the kedge and two hawsers for the boats; we shall warp ourselves off."

Men began hurrying this way and that, but Hayden was pleased to note that there was no panic. Men waited in silent expectation for orders and then went coolly about their business.

"A boat is away from the brig, Captain."

"Perhaps they have gone for help," someone offered, only to be silenced by Archer, who had come forward.

"Kedge and hawsers on the way, sir," Archer reported. "Boats will be afloat in but a moment."

Hayden looked aloft. Sails were being handed with dispatch, the crew galvanised by their predicament—aground by night in a strange harbour. A pennant at the masthead began to waft at that moment.

"There is a bit of wind coming down the harbour, sir," Barthe said, hope present in his voice.

Hayden went to the forward barricade and stared down into the water. "Drop the lead to the bottom and tell me if we make stern-way," Hayden called to the man in the chains.

Only a moment did he wait for an answer.

"Making stern-way, Captain," the leadsman called.

"Hoist the mizzen staysail and driver, Mr Barthe, if you please. Keep the sheets to windward so we might be carried away from this shoal."

Hands jumped to the halyards before orders were given, sails flashing aloft in the miserly light of a haze-hidden moon. The wind lasted only a moment, blowing a few loose strands of hair about Hayden's ear.

"We must not, now, drift onto another shoal. Let go the best bower, Mr Archer, and we will discover our situation, here."

"Aye, sir."

The forecastle men hurried to their places to drop the anchor.

"Mr Archer. We have no time for niceties. Let go the shank painter. We will make repairs to the planking at another time."

The shank painter was let go, whipping about the anchor shank with a buzzing sound and snapping against wood. The upper anchor fluke scraped down the topside planking, men grimacing all around.

"Let go the ring stopper," Archer ordered, and the anchor plunged down into the water with an unmanageable splash. The cable flashed out through the hawse hole on the gun-deck, a crewman pouring water on it as it passed so that it would not cause fire. But before a few fathoms of cable had been veered, the anchor found bottom. Hayden let only a little more cable run—not really enough—and ordered it checked.

The leadsman began sounding by the bow.

"Five fathoms and one half, Mr Archer," he called.

A general relieved murmuring flitted around the deck, but the motion of the ship did not comfort Hayden.

"Sound the stern, if you please," Hayden ordered the leadsman, who quickly coiled up his line and went trotting aft, lead swinging from his right fist.

"Sir," Gould called as he bustled down the gangway from the quarterdeck, "the helm does not answer. It is seized fast, sir."

Barthe swore.

"We are aground aft, I am sure, Mr Archer," Hayden announced, then went to the starboard rail to see if the kedge and hawsers were aboard the boats.

"Mr Archer, you will go with the boats, if you please. Set the anchor there"—Hayden pointed to the northwest—"so that we might pull free of this shoal. Sound as you go so you will know how much cable to veer. The anchor must hold, Mr Archer. Five times our depth in cable at the least—seven would be better."

"Aye, sir," Archer replied, going down the side at a dangerous pace.

"Away boats." And the boats went off into the cool darkness. At that same instant and from the same direction a boat appeared, hailing them as the *"frégate anglaise."* Immediately it came alongside and a party climbed over the rail, two apparently naval officers, though in the darkness it was difficult to be certain.

Introductions were brief, most of the French party not brought forward. None of them spoke English and were clearly relieved when Hayden responded in flawless French.

"Capitaine Hayden," one of the officers began, *"it is the order of the commanding officer that you perform ten days' quarantine. With us we have a pilot who will guide you to the quarantine berth."*

"Is this the order of Lord Hood?"

"It is the usual procedure for foreign ships entering Toulon. I apologise for the inconvenience."

"Will you carry a letter to Lord Hood for me? I must alert him of our arrival at the earliest possible moment."

"Certainly. It will be our pleasure."

"Captain," Wickham whispered, touching Hayden's sleeve. "Look at their hats, sir. They wear national cockades, I am certain. . . ."

Hayden turned back to the party of Frenchmen, all of whom looked unsettled or out of sorts, though they made great effort to hide it. The poor light turned all colours to near greys, but Hayden was sure, after a moment, that Wickham was right: The Frenchmen wore tricolour cockades. The feeling in his heart at that moment was not unlike the feeling he had known when his mother had first informed him of his father's death. An overwhelming, numbing distress.

"I believe I will send my own boat to Lord Hood," Hayden announced, watching the reaction of the visitors carefully.

The two French officers glanced at each other and nodded.

"Soyez tranquille," one said, *"les Anglais sont de braves gens, nous les traitons bien; l'amiral anglais est sortie il y a quelque temps."*

Wickham cursed—which Hayden hardly ever remembered him doing.

The men at the capstan bars began to strain at that moment, hauling taut the cable that led to the kedge.

Hawthorne leaned close to Hayden and whispered, "What did
they say, sir?"

Hayden spoke equally quietly. "We are their prisoners. Toulon has
fallen." A cooling little breeze touched Hayden's face at that moment
as it rippled the waters all around. "Gather your sentries, Mr Hawthorne. I will endeavour to get us out of this predicament."

Several of the visitors, sensing that things were not going as they
had hoped, began to draw swords, only to find themselves surrounded
by a party of sailors, many hefting belaying pins threateningly. Hawthorne's marines were quickly there in support, muskets levelled.

"Take them all below, Mr Hawthorne, if you please," Hayden
ordered. "Mr Barthe, send the hands aloft. Prepare to make sail."

"Aye, sir. Lay aloft if you don't want to rot in a French jail."

The hands ran to the shrouds as though they raced for a gold piece.
The men at the capstan strained, veins bulging at their necks as they
stamped and hmmphed, forcing the bars around and the ship forward
by brute strength and will.

"Mr Saint-Denis, set two men to cut the bower cable this instant.
We will cut the kedge hawser upon my command." Hayden made a
silent prayer to no god in particular that their rudder might not be
damaged.

"Aye, sir."

Barthe was ordering yards braced around and was disposing of
the crew to set the most sail possible as quickly as could be humanly
managed.

Hayden was using the French brig to gauge the *Themis'* progress
but noticed now there was a bustle aboard the enemy ship—they were
readying their guns.

"Mr Barthe, we cannot haul ourselves much further. Loose sail."

"Loose top-gallants and clear away the jib," Barthe ordered. *"Man top-
gallant halyards and sheets."*

"Lieutenant," Hayden called, "cut the kedge hawser. If this breeze holds, we will have way on immediately."

Sails came rippling down or shot up their respective stays—a display of seamanship that any officer would admire. Sails filled, the ship answered, swayed a little to leeward, then gathered way.

"Mr Wickham, have you sight of our cutters?"

The boy hesitated a second, searching to the north-east, then his hand shot up. "There! Not too distant, sir, and pulling like they are being chased by the French navy entire."

"Lieutenant Saint-Denis!" Hayden called, and found his first out on the beak-head, crouched, making certain the kedge hawser did not foul.

"Sir," Saint-Denis replied smartly, though he struggled over the barricade, still weakened by his illness.

"As soon as the hands are off the yards we will clear for action. The brig will bring her guns to bear as we pass. I should like to return fire." Hayden looked up at the sky, which appeared almost empty of clouds for the first time in three days. "Bloody moonlight," he muttered. "It will see the end of us." Hayden turned a slow circle, examining the French positions bearing on the harbour. In a moment the *Themis* would be under fire from both sides of the harbour mouth. If the wind died away at that point—as it had several times this night—they would be at the mercy of the French guns.

"Cast off the French boat, if you please, Mr Gould," Hayden ordered the young middy.

Before Hayden's own guns could be run out, the brig fired a small broadside with her six-pounders, all aimed up into the rigging in hopes of retarding or ending the *Themis*' progress. Musket fire began, much of it directed toward the *Themis*' quarterdeck.

"Mr Hawthorne!" Hayden called, seeing the marine lieutenant mustering a party to go aloft and return fire. "Keep your people on the deck, for the moment. This brig is intent on bringing down our spars." Hayden had lost enough marines in the tops; he could afford to lose no more.

Hawthorne appeared disappointed. "Aye, sir. Shall we return fire from the deck, Captain?"

Another salvo fired from the brig just as gunports opened on the *Themis.*

"Yes, you shall, Mr Hawthorne."

The *Themis* fired her broadside at that moment, battering the brig unmercifully, for she was not three ship lengths distant. No guns sounded in return.

Archer's boats caught the *Themis* up, and the men came huffing over the rail opposite the open gunports and threw themselves down upon the deck, too spent to stand. Even Archer was utterly done for, as he had clearly taken up an oar with the hands.

"Do not stream the boats," Hayden ordered the coxswains. "Cast them free. Let us have nothing to impede our progress."

A report from a battery on the eastern point, and a ball sent up a splash just short of the *Themis.*

As they were now sailing almost free, the wind gave the appearance of having dropped away to a zephyr, but the sails were full and Hayden could see by the land that they moved . . . slowly. If the wind would but hold for half of the hour, they would slip away. If . . .

They sailed very near the brig, now, and would be past in but a moment. Musket fire came from that quarter with renewed energy, balls cracking off carronades and burrowing through the air with a deadly *hiss.*

Gould, who stood but two paces off, looked despairingly about at the others. Hayden feared the boy might lose his nerve. A reassuring hand on his shoulder from Saint-Denis—an uncharacteristic show of compassion—and the first lieutenant took a step forward and sideways, interposing himself between the musket fire and the midshipman. Saint-Denis had only just moved when he stumbled back as though pushed, a look of utter surprise and confusion on his face. He fell against Gould, who grasped ineffectually at him, half pulling off his coat and breaking the tumble only a little.

Immediately, Gould crouched over the prostrate Saint-Denis, who blinked up at the sky as though his vision had been suddenly compromised. He took hold of Gould's arm and said something lost beneath the booming of guns. A liquid breath, and he choked out a little blood.

"Captain Hayden!" Gould cried. "There is something . . . amiss with the lieutenant."

Wickham went to the fallen officer, but a dark and growing stain on his white waistcoat told all. "Bear the lieutenant down to Dr Griffiths," Wickham ordered three seamen, who came forward and took up the wounded officer. "You there, support his head. Just so. Handsomely, now."

Among the musket fire, which continued unabated, the officers watched Saint-Denis being borne below, his arms hanging limp and joggling, hands bouncing along the deck.

"My God, sir," Gould managed to no one in particular, "the lieutenant only just survived the influenza and now he has been shot through. Will he die?"

Before anyone could answer, the *Themis* fired a second broadside, smoke blooming up and slowly spreading over the rail. All musket fire from the brig ceased. From diverse points along the shore, cannon began spouting flame, heavy balls rending the air.

"Mr Archer, we will direct fire toward the shore batteries as our guns can be brought to bear. Perhaps we will prevent a little shot from finding us."

"Aye, sir."

As they passed beneath the Grand Tower, the tiny breeze that bore them on sighed once, then fell away. Sails hung limp as pelts, but the ship drifted onward, carrying her way over a star-festooned sea.

"Blast this wind to hell!" Barthe pronounced. "We shall sit here and be cut to flinders if we cannot sail."

Hayden cursed himself for cutting free the boats. "Mr Franks," he called, "launch the barge. We will warp out of range of these batteries, if we must."

"Aye, sir," Franks answered. "Lay aloft! Lay out!"

Galvanised by fire from all around, the men went quickly about their business, the barge swinging up into the air in record time, two men aboard hurriedly arranging its gear. Hayden could feel the ship losing way, like a boat run up on soft sand.

The wind gasped, wafting the sails, the highest aloft bellying an instant, then all went slack and restive.

Barthe turned to Hayden, his manner very brittle. "We are for it, now, Captain," the master said gravely.

Hayden did not reply but turned to Archer. "Extinguish all lights . . . and let us pray for a cloud to cover the moon."

But the few clouds abroad that night appeared to be going about their own business without a thought for the moon or British frigates adrift in Toulon Harbour.

Balls began to land in earnest all around or to tear open the air above. Just as Franks ordered the barge to be lowered a ball struck it amidships, blasting out the larboard side and showering the men with splinters and shards of planking.

In the silence that followed, Franks could be heard hollering, *"Childers? Price?"* The bosun gazed up at the shattered hull. Childers emerged, staggering in the swaying craft. He stumbled two steps aft and threw himself at the falls of the tackle, grasping hold and clinging there as though he thought the boat would break apart and drop him to the deck. The other man, more frightened yet, came over the side, grabbed a guy rope, and flew down to the deck hand over hand.

"We shall have that ruin of a hull down on the deck, Mr Franks,"

Hayden called, "and the launch over the side—smartly! Have the small kedge brought up from the hold, Mr Madison."

The barge, all but broken-backed, thumped down, and the tackles were transferred quickly to the launch, which swung aloft with all speed.

"If those bloody Frenchmen do not manage to shoot that one away . . ." Barthe grumbled, gazing up at the boat hanging from the yard tackles.

For a moment all held their breath as the boat was swung out, then quickly lowered by squealing blocks down into the calm sea. The kedge went next, swung out on tackles, and then the hawser, followed by the remaining crew. Archer and the still-shaken Childers clambered into the stern. Immediately the boat pushed off, a flaw of wind came down the harbour, bellied the sails, pressing the *Themis* forward. Shot continued to fall all around, the scream of it tearing at every man's nerves. Two heavy balls smashed into the hull forward, but the ship gathered way, her own guns replying. A dense cloud of smoke enveloped the ship and hung over it, carried on the same wind. Wickham clambered out to the end of the jib-boom, more or less out of the smoke, and conned them out.

As the Grand Tower fell behind to larboard, Hayden felt a little wave of relief pass through his knotted muscles.

"We are out, Captain," Hawthorne pronounced. He raised a hand as though he would clap Hayden on the back, remembered his position, and turned the gesture into an awkward wave toward the shore.

"Throw a rope to the launch and we will take her in tow," Hayden ordered. "I do not want to heave to so we can bring them aboard if this wind keeps making."

As they passed out of the inner harbour, the breeze, which had been blowing from nor-nor'east, came around to the east.

"We will not weather Cape Sepet on this slant, Captain," Barthe observed. The sailing master stood by the binnacle, scrutinizing their heading. "If we are forced to make several boards to weather the cape, the French might stir themselves to give chase."

"The wind has not settled itself yet, Mr Barthe. Let us hope, when we travel further from the land, that it will back a little more."

"Which it might manage, Captain," Barthe agreed. "We have had some luck this night. Let us pray it will sail with us but a little further."

Shore batteries along the peninsula opened fire and Hayden ordered that fire be returned. The ship barely had enough way on to answer her helm at times, and then the fickle wind would pick up and hurry them on, allowing a more favourable course. Archer's boat was drawn alongside and the crew retrieved. Hayden could not lose another boat, so they took it in tow, even though it slowed them a little on such a small wind.

The quarterdeck was a silent place, the French batteries landing shot all around but little of it finding its mark. Barthe and Franks had men aloft repairing damage to the rig, and the gun crews were kept busy returning fire, though largely to obscure the *Themis* from view with clouds of smoke. The leadsman cried out his soundings—minor proclamations of the ship's safety—until the bottom began to shoal.

"Mr Barthe?" Hayden called to the sailing master. "How go your repairs, sir? I believe we shall be forced to tack."

"We can clear away in a moment, sir," Barthe replied from the waist.

"Then let us coil down and make ready."

Before the order could be given to tack ship, the wind backed a little more, and more yet, and the leadsman found the bottom dropping away. The darker mass of Cape Sepet moved farther to starboard as the ship's heading altered, and tacking ship was delayed for the time being.

The leadsmen worked furiously as the *Themis* skirted the edge of the bank, calling depths over the crash of French guns. In the midst of this Griffiths appeared on deck, a grim, greying presence, consumptively spare.

Hayden, whose eyes ran from powder smoke, saw the doctor as though through a pane of flawed glass, distorted and dulled.

"Doctor," Hayden said as Griffiths approached.

"I am very sorry to report, Captain, that Saint-Denis has departed this life," the doctor stated, but haltingly. "The musket ball found his heart and he bled his pitiful life away." The doctor paused a moment, clearly not finished, though Hayden wondered what more there could be to say. "He asked for pen and paper at the end, but had not the firmness of hand to write. Mr Ariss kindly offered to take down anything he might speak, thinking it would be a letter to his family or perhaps a final will." Again Griffiths paused as though wondering what to say. "It was, instead, a letter to Mr Gould. Saint-Denis thanked him for saving his life during his recent illness. . . . He also asked his forgiveness for persecuting him. I must say, I was rather surprised. Very near the end, Saint-Denis managed to ask, 'Have I wholly wasted my days?' Mr Ariss assured him that this was not the case, but Saint-Denis would not hear it. 'Perhaps Gould can make something of himself,' he said, 'where I could not.' Those were his final words."

Hayden could not hide his surprise. "It seems Saint-Denis was more honest with himself than we might have presumed."

Griffiths' facial gesture was unreadable. "It is passing strange," he ventured. "I have misliked Saint-Denis since first we met, but these past weeks I have had a change of heart toward him. No doubt his brush with death caused him to reexamine his place in this world— and shewed him that it was not nearly so high as he had believed. He was humbled, but as a man is humbled before God, if I may say it. Putting himself in the way of musket fire to preserve young Gould was likely the first time he had ever placed another before himself." Griffiths stood a moment, lost in thought, shook his head, then wandered away without remembering to touch his hat or even take leave.

Hayden stood at the starboard rail looking out toward the shadowed coast of France—a distant world divided from him by a narrow river of sea—and the booming of guns suddenly seemed a salute, as though someone great had passed who was mourned and honoured.

Wickham came quickly up, touching his hat. "Mr Barthe says we shall double the cape on this tack, Captain."

"Yes, I am quite certain he is correct. Saint-Denis has just died."

Wickham said nothing for a moment, and then "God rest his soul," the midshipman said softly. "I am very sorry to hear it."

"Do you think Mr Gould will have any particular . . . sentiment about this? Were he and Saint-Denis friends?"

"Given that Saint-Denis persecuted him relentlessly upon learning he was a Jew, I would think not, but Saint-Denis seemed to suffer a sea change after Gould nursed him back to health. Did they become friends? Gould has a desire to think the best of any man, or so I believe. He forgave the lieutenant his trespasses, but . . . Well, Captain, I should not speak for Mr Gould."

"Yes, certainly."

The guns ashore stopped firing at that moment, and on the *Themis* they fell silent as well. After the great guns had been exercised, Hayden often noted that the ensuing quiet was somehow deeper, more complete, or perhaps more profound. The night wrapped itself around them as the ship's almost silent progress carried them seaward. Hayden felt a deep melancholy settle over him, for some reason he could not fathom. Perhaps because Saint-Denis' life had been so misguided and cut short before there was any chance of redemption. Perhaps it was relief at their narrow escape from Toulon. He did not know, but he felt as though, were he alone, he might weep.

"We shall have daylight in a few hours, Captain," Wickham observed.

"Not for us all. Ask Mr Smosh if he will read the service when we commit Saint-Denis' body to the depths."

"Aye, sir." Wickham touched his hat and turned to go.

"And Mr Wickham?"

"Sir?"

"You are acting second lieutenant now."

Wickham nodded and touched his hat. "Yes, sir. Thank you, sir," he said softly. For a moment he stood as though he might say more, and then made his way forward like a man in a daze.

Thirteen

At dawn, a British frigate, blown off station in the gale, appeared to leeward. She was desperately beating toward the *Themis*, and signalling for her to hold position.

Hayden and Hawthorne stood at the rail, watching her bob through a streak of sunlight. A bracing easterly pressed against their backs and shook pennants overhead. Neither man had slept after their escape from Toulon. After they had come so near to losing their ship and being made prisoners, their minds had been left in such a turmoil as to prohibit repose.

"I believe this was the ship charged with preventing British vessels entering Toulon," Hayden ventured.

"They made a bloody poor job of it." Hawthorne's voice had a harsh, hollow tone—his throat abraded by exhaustion.

"And I shall not shrink from telling them so."

In under an hour the two frigates rolled, hove to, side by side, the respective commanders calling to each other through speaking trumpets. Hayden refrained from upbraiding the man before his crew but let it be known that it was something near a miracle that they had escaped Toulon with the loss of only a single man and three ship's boats, and sundry minor damages. The frigate's captain felt such guilt at hearing this that he offered Hayden a cutter, which was gladly accepted. It was only later that Mr Gould pointed out the frigate had four cutters, as well as the usual complement of ship's boats, so could easily afford this act of apparent generosity.

Admiral Lord Hood, it transpired, had been driven from Toulon with his various allies by the republican armies, and though the crew of the *Themis* were aware of this from the previous night's altercation, to hear it spoken still brought a groan from one and all. The British fleet had shifted its berth to Hieyres Bay some small distance down the French coast. The wind, brisk and blowing north-east by north, would not allow them to sail along the coast but dictated a course of east by south—not so terribly bad, Hayden noted, but they would not find the admiral that day. The worst of it was, they must have sailed past the British fleet by night, distant enough that they had been unaware of its presence.

As it was likely his last night as commander of the *Themis*—a thought that left him troubled and anxious about the future—Hayden decided to invite some of his officers and guests to dinner to take his mind off such matters. This impending loss of command removed some sense of his obligations as senior officer, and he decided not to invite Worthing but to invite the other ecclesiastical guest, Reverend Smosh—an unforgivable snub, but Hayden did not care. Worthing had not only attempted to undermine him with his crew but had done the same while in Gibraltar. Undoubtedly he would continue in this endeavour once they found Lord Hood. Inviting such a man to his table was beyond even Hayden's sense of duty. But when Hayden's guests arrived, Worthing was among them, having assumed that the invitation to Smosh included him. Despite his near hatred of the man, Hayden could not then send him away. Another chair was quickly added and a setting produced, so subtly that almost no one noticed.

Reverend Smosh, Hawthorne, Archer, Wickham, Barthe, and Dr Griffiths were all in attendance, as well as midshipmen Madison and Gould (Hobson was officer of the watch, the ship being short of senior officers), Mr Ariss, the surgeon's mate, and Mr Franks, the bosun.

The atmosphere at this dinner was subdued, though Hayden was not sure why. Perhaps it was the near loss of their ship the previous night or the British retreat from Toulon. Hayden wondered what had become of all the thousands of Toulon residents who had supported inviting the British into the city. Certainly Lord Hood could not evacuate them all.

"What do you think will become of them, Captain?" Barthe asked, referring to the very people who were so constantly in Hayden's thoughts.

Hayden was forced to shake his head. "One would hope for a trial, but the country is in the grip of . . . bloodlust, it seems."

"A trial!" Worthing said. "Do wolves make trials? Have we not all read the reports of what transpires in that accursed country? How the guillotine is active night and day? The queen executed. The Duc d'Orléans executed. The Girondin leaders executed. Marat murdered. Madame Roland, Bailey, Barnave . . . The French are not a people, they are animals."

There was an uncomfortable shifting about the table, but before Hayden could reply, Griffiths looked up from his dinner, fixing his much-darkened gaze on Dr Worthing.

"I was once taken to a hanging, Doctor, by the man who taught me surgery and anatomy . . . an English hanging. The criminal was a young woman of perhaps five and twenty—no more. She had been given a trial, or so I understood, and convicted of stealing a few loaves of bread. No guillotine being available, she was brought to the gallows in a cart, drunk, I suspect out of pity. With her was a boy"—he nodded to Wickham—"half a dozen years younger than Mr Wickham, who was to be half hung for his crimes.

"The woman staggered onto the gallows before the usual crowd of civilised English men and women, many nobles in their carriages, the

ladies turned out very fine for the occasion. They cheered unreserv-
edly when the young woman blew kisses to the bucks in attendance
and indulged in some drunken banter with the executioner, who
turned her off in the midst of a laugh.

"The boy was then dragged onto the gallows, weeping and begging hysterically not to be killed, to which the audience all cried
'Shame!' at such a show of cowardice. They had not come to see that!
The executioner threw the boy down and put a knee upon his chest,
then proceeded to loop a cord around the child's neck and to strangle
him until insensible. When this criminal lay utterly still, the cord
was removed and the boy brought back to this just world by the
agency of a bucket of cold water dashed over him. He was then carried, silent and stupefied, to the cart that had borne him there, stripped
to the waist, and tied to the tail, where he was to be whipped about
the town for his crime, which was, if I have not already noted, begging. We then learned that the woman who had been hanged was
his mother, and many of the people present voiced the opinion that,
no doubt, this would prove an excellent lesson for him. The dead
woman was then delivered to her father, who stood by with a barrow. As the man wheeled his daughter away he had the misfortune
to impede the progress of a man and his wife in their carriage, so
incensing the wife that she snatched up the whip and beat the man
so that the barrow overtipped, tumbling the poor dead girl into the
dirt." Griffiths took a sip of his wine with a shaking hand and then
went on. "I make it sound as though I was innocent in this affair—
a mere paying bystander—but two nights later my teacher sent, by
moonlight, myself, two of my fellow students, and his man to disin-
ter the body of this young woman so that we might have her fresh
corpse for our anatomy class. Lots were drawn, and I got to dissect
the head and broken neck. We have little to recommend us over the
French, or any other people, I believe."

There was a silence around the table.

Worthing appeared not the least chastised by this account. "I am uncertain of your exact meaning, Mr Griffiths. The woman was a criminal, tried and found guilty. She was punished according to the laws of the land—the same that apply to you and me. My only disagreement is with the poor benighted people who believed the boy would learn from this example. I can tell you with utter assurance that he will not. Half hung he may have been at ten years, but fully hung he will be before he is two and twenty. I have seen it times too numerous to recount—entire families with no moral principles to guide them. But half hanging this boy was our society's attempt to preserve him from what awaits if he continues down his mother's path. What is half hanging and being flogged compared with the torment of eternal damnation? It is a mercy. The good magistrate who stood in judgement no doubt hoped the memory of the noose tightening about the boy's neck and the slipping into darkness would stay the child's hand when next he was tempted to steal bread . . . or your coat or boots. It was an act of compassion, if entirely misplaced."

"Certainly we flog men with regularity upon our own ship," Franks said, clearly in agreement with Worthing, even if such agreement was not to his taste. "And I have been known to start many a man. The hands would not be inclined to work smartly or even obey the officers' orders without such encouragements."

"Surely that is true, Mr Franks," Wickham said, "but many of our crew are not sailors by desire; they were impressed. It is not a life they have chosen"—he waved a hand around the table—"as we have chosen it."

Worthing appeared to suppress a small smile of affection. "When you are a captain of your own ship, Lord Arthur, I hope to sup with you again and hear your views on this subject. Time may alter your opinions in ways you cannot expect."

"Perhaps, Dr Worthing," Wickham replied, clearly misliking being patronised, "but I doubt human nature will change appreciably in so short a time."

"Am I given to understand, Acting Lieutenant," Hawthorne said, "that you believe you will make your post in 'so short a time'?"

"That was never my meaning!" Wickham protested, actually blushing.

"There are a few lessons yet to be learned," Mr Barthe added. "Spherical trigonometry yet to be completely mastered, working a ship over a bar, predicting tides . . ."

"Shaving," Hawthorne said wickedly, causing much laughter.

"To Mr Wickham making his post," Madison offered, raising a glass. Everyone lifted their wine in response.

"To Mr Wickham making his post," the guests responded, as well as, "To Captain Wickham."

Wickham laughed and coloured at the same time.

Hayden thought Wickham's statement was more truth than boast—Lord Arthur would likely make his post before Hayden, especially as things were progressing. Already Hayden dreaded reporting to Lord Hood, who had, no doubt, received reports of Hayden's character from Captain Pool when he joined the admiral several weeks earlier.

"I think we should have a toast to Captain Hayden," Mr Smosh suggested, "who has brought us this far through storms, groundings, attacks by the enemy, abandonment by our comrades, pestilence, and most recently by preserving us from a French prison."

"*Hear,*" the others responded. "To Captain Hayden."

Despite knowing this was done in good faith and out of concern for his impending loss of command, Hayden thought to deflect this attention from himself. "I believe we should drink to Mr Ariss, Mr Gould, and Mr Smosh, who saved so many lives through their ut- terly tireless efforts. Saint-Denis believed that he and the doctor would both have died without you," Hayden added, nodding to Gould and Ariss. He lifted his glass. "To your tireless efforts."

And so they toasted. But after this a silence fell on the assembly and Hayden thought that it would be his last such dinner with these men, for in a day or two at most he would be removed from his command and likely waiting for a ship to return him to England.

He resembled, to a remarkable degree, engravings Hayden had seen of George Washington. The same nose and elongated chin. The high forehead, kindly, intelligent eyes. Hayden would not allow himself to be misled by the eyes: Lord Hood was the commander in chief of His Majesty's fleets in the Mediterranean and had not achieved this position in life through the agency of kindness. The Lord Admiral sat upon a large, almost thronelike chair, coatless, his silk waistcoat as white as sea foam on a summer's day. His long, almost melancholy face was tanned like a plowman's, his massive hands the same. For a moment he regarded Hayden, his look, if anything, appearing to grow sadder, which alarmed Hayden no end.

"Captain Hayden," Hood said, his voice strong and surprisingly melodic, "I have had several letters, posted at Gibraltar, from Reverend Dr Worthing, and another from Captain Pool, all mentioning your name in less-than-benevolent terms. Dr Worthing especially appears unable to contain his venom."

It had been driven home in his conversation with Admiral Brown that one could never be certain who might be acquainted with whom in the service, so Hayden decided to be circumspect. "I am sorry, sir, for any aggravation such letters might have occasioned."

The admiral chose not to answer this but only raised his thick brows a little. He lifted his cup of coffee from a small table, found it either empty or not to his taste, and, with a sour look, returned the dainty china to its saucer.

"Am I to understand that you were left with Pool's convoy after he was separated from it?"

"Yes, sir. Captain Pool could not discover us, apparently."

"And given how soon after he arrived in Gibraltar, I cannot say I am surprised." Hood turned his gaze on Hayden. "I should like to hear your accounting, Hayden. Be candid; I mislike modesty as much as vanity."

Hayden was not sure if he could walk a road so narrow, nor was he certain that Hood wanted the truth. The admiral's small slight of Pool, however, gave Hayden some hope and he began a retelling of the story of his convoy across Biscay, holding back only matters relating to Worthing. It seemed he hurried overly, for Hood kept interrupting with questions, finally leading Hayden to relate almost every circumstance—the French squadron, influenza, the accidental ramming of the French seventy-four, the loss of the *Syren* and poor Cole. He ended with their near capture in Toulon, at which Hood sat silently, as though turning over the events Hayden had related.

"Dr Worthing wrote that you confined him to his quarters?"

"That is true, Lord Hood. I do apologise for treating your chaplain so."

"He is not my chaplain," Hood stated firmly. "I have not met the man above three times—at the home of a friend—but it is the curse of command that everyone asks favours . . . and then never returns them in kind. A relative of Worthing's—a surgeon—delivered my niece of a child in the worst circumstances for either mother or child to survive, let alone thrive, and brought them both through—subsequently, I promised to find Worthing a position aboard ship." The admiral shrugged as though to say, *What other course could there have been?* "It seems you have had a rather adventurous time of it, though one would hardly call the influenza an adventure. Never in all my years have I heard of one so severe. It was the influenza? Your surgeon was not mistaken?"

"He is an excellent surgeon, sir, and he had seen influenza before. I would be very surprised if he were wrong."

The admiral made a little gesture with shoulders and face that seemed to say, "Perhaps." "Admiral Cotton has requested I find a captain for the *Themis*, which has had infamy attached to her name, unfortunately. I shall have to give this matter my full consideration. For the time being, Hayden, I shall leave you in command. I understand you are short of officers?"

"Yes, sir. My first lieutenant was killed in Toulon, and I have only one lieutenant and a midshipman acting. He is a precocious young middy, sir, but has only been two years in the service."

"I will give this some thought as well. I might have a lieutenant for you. He is aboard my ship and hoping for promotion, but I believe a year or two in a frigate would benefit him greatly." The admiral fell into thought again.

Given the demands on his time, Hayden was surprised Hood had spent so much time with a mere master and commander.

"Worthing wrote that one of your middies is a Jew—or so he claimed. Is this true?"

"His father is a Jew, sir—a reliable Plymouth merchant—but his mother is not. The boy has been raised in the Church of England, as Reverend Smosh—the second chaplain I have brought you—will attest."

"Ah. Do you know Captain Schomberg? Isaac Schomberg?"

"Only by reputation, sir." Hayden knew the Schombergs were a prominent London Jewish family, though the sons were said to have been raised outside of their faith.

"A sea officer of great ability. Should you feel it necessary, I believe Captain Schomberg would take this boy on. I would ask it of him myself, on your behalf."

"I believe Gould has won the respect of the crew, sir. He is well-placed for the moment."

"As you like." Hood looked up at Hayden and almost smiled. "Do I understand, Captain, that you have something of a gift for languages? Remember, I mislike modesty."

"I speak several well enough, sir."

"Italian?"

"There are numerous dialects, sir. I should do well enough in Genoa."

"I think that will answer nicely. You also speak French?"

"Yes, sir."

"I would have you make company with several Army officers. They all travel with Sir Gilbert Elliot to Corsica to treat with General Paoli. Do you know him?"

"I know to whom you refer, sir. One of my midshipmen, Lord Arthur Wickham, was acquainted with him in England. Apparently the general promised to take him shooting should he ever visit that island."

Hood chuckled. "Is the boy of a . . . practical nature?"

"Indeed, sir. He is mature beyond his years and I believe has a great future in the service."

Hood contemplated this only a second. "I wonder if his presence would please General Paoli—he is a stubborn old man, I will tell you."

"Wickham wins over all around him, sir. I don't know if General Paoli would be any different."

"Take the boy as your aide. We cannot hope to drive the French out of Corsica without Paoli's supporters." Hood appeared to gather his thoughts a moment. "We shall need to transport and land troops on the island, Hayden, and I want to be certain the Army officers do not concoct some plan dependent on us landing troops in some untenable situation. I expect you to speak up and be certain any such landing places will be acceptable to the Navy."

"Aye, sir."

"I have prevailed upon Dundas to send Colonel John Moore." A little amused smile appeared on the admiral's face. "He is too perfect by half, but one of the more capable officers I have met—capable of sizing up a situation and drawing a plan without dithering. A very decisive sort. Not unlike you, Hayden. You shall either be like brothers or loathe each other utterly." This made the admiral smile, but then he again slipped into his thoughts.

For several long moments the admiral did not speak. Once Hayden was sure he would but Hood appeared to change his mind.

Finally Hayden asked, "Is there any other service I might perform, Lord Hood?"

"No," the admiral said softly, shaking his head. As Hayden rose to his feet, the admiral asked, "How old would your father be now, Hayden?"

Hayden could not have been more taken aback, and for a few seconds could not answer. "Fifty-one, sir," he managed, "this coming June."

Hood did not look at Hayden but brushed at something on his breeches. "He might have had his flag by now. Imagine. And your mother, Captain . . . she is well, I hope?"

"Very well, sir. She has removed to Boston."

"Boston!" Hood repeated, clearly surprised. "You have more of your mother's features, though you have the carriage, even the gestures, of your father." The admiral looked up at Hayden. "You have heard this before?"

Hayden nodded. "I have been told I have my father's voice and habits of speech."

"So you do. It is a bit unsettling for any who knew him. Good luck in Corsica, Captain Hayden."

"Thank you, sir."

Hayden turned and went to the door, but just as he put his hand on the handle, the admiral spoke again.

"I wonder if I shouldn't assign Worthing to Captain Pool's ship? Does that seem a good match?"

Hayden tried not to smile. "I believe they would get along famously."

"Then it is done. And this other parson . . . what was his name?"

"Smosh, sir."

"Aye, what a name! I wonder who will deserve him. . . ."

"If you have no ship in need, sir, he might serve aboard the *Themis* for the time being. We would welcome him."

"Then he is yours, Hayden." He raised a finger. "I have almost forgotten. This evening I shall have the captains of the fleet to dine. I hope you will join us."

"It would be my honour to do so."

"And bring this middy we are sending to Paoli. Until then. Good day to you."

"Good day, sir."

Hayden exited the cabin in something like shock. As he had so often left such audiences in a rage, it was utterly strange to feel that he had been treated both kindly and with justice. He had only needed to travel a few thousand miles from England to find this. Lord Hood had known his father! Had known him and held him in high regard, perhaps even affection. A remarkable stroke of good fortune . . . for a change. He emerged into the sunshine with these thoughts whirling in his head.

Upon the *Victory*'s deck Hayden found the same scene that had greeted him earlier. French families, gathered in small groups, endeavouring to stay clear of the sailors working. British Army officers formed their own squadrons. Children played chase-me around the capstan, laughing as though on an adventure, unaware that their parents had relinquished everything to escape Toulon. By the expressions on the adults' faces, however, Hayden knew this innocence did not extend to them.

A well-dressed gentleman, clearly English though with excellent command of French, was surrounded by supplicants, and Hayden could hear him promising over and over that the English would not abandon them. Hayden hoped that this would prove true, as these poor refugees had sided with the British against the excesses of the Convention. The loss of Toulon had left them without a country.

As I am, Hayden thought. This idea came to him unbidden and engendered a little vertigo of distress.

Hayden stopped and stood by the rail, observing his own ship a moment. It had not occurred to him until then to feel any sense of relief—he had not been cast free by Hood and replaced, but still had his post ship, though without his post to accompany it. Still, he had much to be thankful for, though there was no way of knowing if and when Hood would decide to replace him with some other. It was ever his situation that uncertainty could not be banished, but hung on the horizon like an irresolute gale that might at any time sweep down upon him, bearing with it utter disaster.

As Hayden turned to cross the deck, a small child rammed him, head foremost, in the thigh, and fell upon the planks with a look of confusion upon her face. Immediately he knelt.

"Are you injured?" he asked in French.

The girl, about five years, gazed at him as though he spoke some foreign language.

"Are you in disguise?" she whispered in the same tongue.

"In disguise?" He could not imagine what she meant.

"I won't tell," she said, sitting up and whispering even more quietly. *"I am Princess Marie, and I am escaping from the Jacobins. Will you help me?"*

"Yes, my princess," Hayden replied. *"I am the Comte de le Coeur, and I have been sent to find you."*

"I knew you would come," she whispered passionately. *"Will we go by ship?"* She jumped to her feet and stared Hayden in the eye.

"Yes, by an English ship—the Victory. *I have it all arranged. The admiral is one of us."*

"That is why you are dressed as an English officer. Very cunning, Monsieur le Comte. When I am returned, one day, to my throne, I shall reward your bravery and loyalty."

Hayden stood, swept off his hat, and made an elaborate bow. *"I am humbled by your generosity, my princess. Certainly, the admiral has prepared a cabin for you and will have you to dine this very evening. But I must be off; there are so many who require rescue."*

"Yes, yes. *Rescue as many of my subjects as you are able. My people have suffered terribly under the Jacobins."* And with that, she glanced behind, turned, and dashed off.

Hayden realised that two women had been watching, and both smiled. Charmed they might have been by the little play, but this did not entirely mask the distress in their lovely faces.

"You speak French perfectly, monsieur," the older woman observed in heavily accented English. Both were so handsome that, for a few seconds, Hayden could not think what to say. Undoubtedly, they were mother and daughter—the younger woman's countenance claimed that she could be no other—though the elder did not look thirty. This was an obvious impossibility, for her daughter was in the first bloom of young womanhood—one and twenty, Hayden thought.

"Thank you, madame," Hayden replied, making a slight bow. "My mother is French." Hayden found the young woman so comely that he struggled not to stare.

"Forgive me, monsieur, but from what region?"

"Paris and Bordeaux."

"We are from Toulon," the woman informed him, "but, no doubt, you understood that."

"Yes. I am very sorry so many have been driven from their homes." Hayden felt a small pang of guilt that the English had not held Toulon—as though they had somehow acted in bad faith with that city's citizens.

The woman pressed her lovely lips together and made the slightest nod of agreement.

Dismay was so clearly written upon their faces and in their carriage that Hayden felt his heart go out to them.

"Pardon, Captain," the woman said to Hayden, struggling, but insisting on speaking English, "do you know the idea of Lord Hood for what will 'appen to . . . ourselves?"

"I am sorry, madame," Hayden replied in French, *"but Lord Hood has not confided this information to me."*

But the woman continued to speak English. "We fear that Lord Hood intends to place . . . us . . . Is that correct? 'Us'?"

"Yes."

"He intends to place us in Genoa or Naples. This will not do. The army that drove us from Toulon will very soon march south—that is what everyone say—and we will be force to flee again or be capture and on the guillotine for our assisting of the English. We must be taken somewhere safe—England or Canada."

Hayden thought their fears could very likely be borne out. There was much talk among the British officers that the Jacobin army would press on into the northern Italian states, and sooner rather than later.

The woman curtsied. *"Pardon, monsieur.* I am Madame Bourdage and this is my daughter, Héloïse."

"Charles Hayden. *Enchanté.*"

Madame Bourdage's gaze wandered to Hayden's left, and she and her daughter both curtsied very low. "Sir Gilbert," she said.

Hayden turned to find the Englishman he had previously seen surrounded by supplicants. The man nodded to him but addressed the women.

"Madame Bourdage. Mademoiselle. As I have told everyone, I have yet no answer as to where you will go. Very soon, I hope. Very soon. You have not been forgotten, I assure you." Sir Gilbert's manner was very courtly and charming. Clearly the beauty of the two women had not gone unnoticed by the gentleman. Age, Hayden had observed many times, did not dampen this particular appreciation among males.

The two women were swept up into his wake, curtsying quickly to Hayden as they went, other men and women drawn into the gentleman's orbit as he made his way along the deck.

Hayden stood a moment, watching them retreat.

"Sir Gilbert Elliot," a voice informed him.

Hayden turned to find a young Army officer smiling and nodding toward the English gentleman, who was again afloat in a sea of forlorn orphans.

"The friend of Burke?" Hayden wondered.

"The very one." The young man made a small bow. "Colonel John Moore."

"Charles Hayden, captain of the frigate *Themis*."

"So I thought. You are to accompany us to Corsica?"

"Yes, and very happy I am about it, too. I have just come from Lord Hood, who informed me of this decision, but I confess, I know little more about it."

A conspiratorial smile made Moore appear even younger. "It is fortunate that I have had several conversations on this matter with Sir Gilbert, General Dundas, my superior, and Lord Hood." He waved a hand forward. "Shall we take a turn around the deck and I will recount what I have learned?"

Hayden immediately agreed. There was often distrust, if not animosity, between the two services, but Moore showed no signs of this in his manner—of course, they had just met and he might have reasons of his own to be speaking so kindly to a Navy man. Hayden was certain he would find out soon enough. In appearance, Moore was rather Hayden's opposite—yellow haired, blue eyed, though Hayden's height and well made in much the same manner. If calmness and animation could be combined into one person, Moore appeared to be that person. Hayden's immediate impression was of a man very content within himself—unusual in one so young.

"No doubt you have heard that there has been a rebellion against the French on Corsica," Moore began, "and that General Paoli and his supporters have shut the French into a few strongholds along the northern coast?"

"I had not."

Moore glanced Hayden's way, perhaps a bit dismayed at how uninformed he was.

"I have but lately arrived from England," Hayden offered in defense, "and was several weeks in Gibraltar in strict quarantine due to an influenza contracted en route."

Moore appeared a little relieved by this. "News does not travel quickly enough—unless it is bad news, of course."

"Even bad news travels too slowly. We learned that Toulon was lost when we sailed into that harbour by night and barely managed to withdraw."

Moore drew back a little and looked at him anew. "That was your ship? I have heard several sea officers voice the opinion that the captain of that vessel must be a most skilled seaman."

"Most lucky, I think," Hayden corrected. "The wind favoured us or we would be guests of the French, yet." Hayden stepped around a running child whose attention was fixed elsewhere—perhaps another miniature noble fleeing the Jacobins. "You were speaking of Corsica . . ."

"Yes. It seems that Paoli has written several letters to Lord Hood requesting British aid or perhaps an alliance. Sir Gilbert even speculates that the Corsicans might put their land under British protection. A naval base so near the northern states of the Italian peninsula would serve our interests well, especially now, as there is a significant Republican army in Toulon, only a few days' march from the borders." He paused here, as if awaiting Hayden's agreement, so the Navy man nodded.

Moore, Hayden thought, had understated the importance of a naval base on Corsica. The British desperately needed a safe port east of Gibraltar, nearer the Italian states. The Mediterranean was large and Gibraltar isolated at the western extreme. But a Corsican port could be used to resupply ships blockading the French ports, not so far away, or to carry aid to the numerous Italian states that might find themselves fighting the French—sooner rather than later.

"We are sent to Corsica to discover if, indeed, the French have been driven into their few ports and towers, and if so, if it is possible to dislodge them—and how best this might be accomplished. As this enterprise will take the efforts of both Navy and Army, representatives of both services are to be sent." He gestured to himself, then Hayden. "We will be accompanied by Lieutenant Major Kochler, I am told." Moore glanced at him. "You look surprised."

"In truth, I am astonished. Lord Hood knows nothing of me. That he would not choose an officer with whom he was more familiar, and in whose abilities he had greater faith, is a puzzle."

"Apparently, he does not lack faith in your abilities, Captain," Moore ventured. "Lord Hood took the time to show me a map . . ." He glanced at Hayden and grinned at his mistake. "A *chart*, I suppose you would name it, displaying all the environs surrounding San Fiorenzo Bay and the supposed French positions. We are to make a closer inspection and recommend a plan of operations. I will rely upon your expertise in knowing how best the Navy might be used to cannonade French batteries—there are at least two strong towers and greater fortifications at San Fiorenzo. The city of Bastia has extensive fortifications, I am given to understand, and Calvi is also invested. Landing places must be found. . . . Well, certainly I don't need to explain such things to you, Captain." They had stopped at the rail, where Hayden's boat awaited. "We are to present ourselves to Captain Davis aboard the *Lowestoffe* tomorrow morning at daybreak. Until then."

Hayden went over the side thinking that Moore was either a consummate actor, a politician, or a rather singular specimen of an Army officer. That he would appear so open to co-operation with the Navy was highly unusual. Hayden had barely got his anchor down, earlier that day, before receiving an acquaintance who informed him that Hood did not get on with the senior Army officers and thought them ditherers if not outright cowards. Moore had struck Hayden as neither of these things, but then time might change his opinion of that.

Hayden sent Wickham to inform Dr Worthing of his new situation, for he was determined to be rid of that vexing provocateur at the earliest possible moment. A note was composed in haste and Hayden had his coxswain carry it, immediately, to Pool's ship, informing the good captain that his new chaplain would be arriving posthaste. Worthing was ordered to pack up his belongings, golf clubs and all, and to be ready to shift his berth to the *Majestic* upon a moment's notice. Hayden could not erase a small smile—it might better have been described as a smirk—at this turn of events. There was no one, with the exception of a certain Captain Hart—now retired from the service—to whom Hayden would rather send the good doctor.

Hawthorne intercepted Hayden climbing to the gun-deck. He, too, sported a poorly disguised expression of satisfaction. "Am I given to understand that the good Dr Worthing is being sent to minister to Captain Pool and his crew?"

"Lord Hood felt that Captain Pool would benefit from the . . . efforts of a chaplain of Dr Worthing's particular talents."

"How would such an idea occur to Lord Hood, I wonder," Hawthorne asked, smile turning to a grin.

"I had no part in it," Hayden protested. "The idea, splendid as I might think it, originated entirely in the mind of Admiral Lord Hood. He did elicit my opinion on the matter and I endorsed it most heartily, but to suggest that I made interest for this happy turn of events would be utterly false."

Hawthorne laughed, unable to hide his delight at this news. "I shall run down to the gunroom and offer to help the man pack. With my own hands, I will bear his belongings onto the deck, though I suppose I will not be alone in offering the parson a helping hand over the side."

"No, I would guess we will not be the first congregation to be happily rid of him."

The grin wavered into a genuine look of concern. "Where is poor Smosh to be sent? To a more likely captain than Pool, I hope?"

"How likely the man is I cannot say, but Smosh is to be chaplain aboard the *Themis* until a more appropriate position is found for him. And, oddly, I am to remain in command of the same ship until Lord Hood appoints a proper captain, though I am to be sent away for a time—I cannot say how long. I will leave Mr Archer in command. Lord Hood has said he will send me a lieutenant—he has one to spare, apparently—but I do not think I will install this new man over Archer, who has shown a marked increase in zeal for his profession these last weeks."

"Every man aboard has shown a marked increase in zeal for their profession since the departure of Captain Hart. It is remarkable how disheartened we all had become under that little tyrant."

Hayden nodded absently.

"And where is it you go—or should I not ask?"

"It will be known soon enough, though I ask you to confine this information to our officers. I am for Corsica, if you can believe it, where I hope to meet General Paoli. Sir Gilbert Elliot is sent to that place to treat with the general, and I am to accompany him with two Army officers to discover if it is, indeed, possible to drive out the French."

"Army officers," Hawthorne said darkly. "You have my sympathy in that."

"Not at all. One I have met, and he is a man of excellent judgement who did not even seem aware that my coat was blue and not crimson."

"Let us see if this innocence of fashion can last more than a few days. The services are ever at crossed purposes in my experience."

"Which has long been my view, Mr Hawthorne, though with the

caveat that I believe that neither service fully understands the other's field of operation. Army officers do not understand why ships cannot make progress into the teeth of a gale or why we cannot land their troops on a lee shore with a sea running. Likewise, seamen misunderstand how armies are best utilised on a given landscape or why they march so slowly."

"I hope such misunderstandings are few, then."

Moments later Hayden and Hawthorne stood at the rail while the disgraced Reverend Dr Worthing watched his belongings being lowered into the boat. He did not look at Hayden or offer to make any sort of good-bye but simply climbed over the rail. As his head was about to disappear below the level of the bulwark, he stopped, unable to leave without having the last word.

The chaplain eyed Hayden darkly, his sour mouth turned down and pressed thin. "Lord Hood might have been easily convinced of your innocence in your mistreatment of me, but the Lord God will not similarly be deceived. It is on your soul."

The man disappeared down the ladder, and Hawthorne turned to Hayden, a great smile of disbelief overspreading his handsome face. "Well, there you have it. God will punish you for confining his chaplain to his cabin. All of the mischief he intended was no doubt the will of our Lord."

The crew were not so kind as Hawthorne and laughed openly at this final threat, the mockery in their voices unmasked. Even the oarsmen in the barge that bore him, sitting stiffly in the stern, grinned openly. A few men began to call out taunts, but Hayden had Franks put a stop to that—out of respect for Worthing's position, not his person. Hayden had seen justice so seldom in his career in the King's Navy that he could hardly tear his eyes from the sight of Worthing borne across the open bay to Captain Pool's *Majestic*. It was unseemly to gloat, so he displayed a mask of utter neutrality—or so he hoped—but secretly the thought of all the troubles that would soon befall the captain who had been maligning him from Gibraltar to Toulon, caused him more than a little satisfaction. It made Hayden wonder if, on occasion, God did not intervene in the affairs of men to arrange a higher justice.

A few gulls circled over the retreating barge and the erect form of the eternally wronged clergyman. They called out—mockingly, Hayden thought. Worthing waved a dismissive hand in their direction, but this only seemed to excite their malice.

Hayden could not help himself: he laughed.

The admiral's cabin aboard the *Victory* seemed a palace to Charles Saunders Hayden, who had, only a few weeks before, been marvelling at the scale of his own cabin aboard the *Themis*. The table, which stretched almost the width of the ship, put his newly acquired dining table to shame, not only by its scale but with its grandeur. Twenty-two men were seated without the least crowding, and the table, six feet in breadth, bore a collection of silver candelabra and plate that Hayden's meagre salary could not have purchased were every ha'penny saved over the course of several decades. White-painted deck-head and ceilings reflected the candlelight, and the white linen and waist-coats of the officers seemed contrived to set off the blue sea of the gathered officers' best coats.

Hayden sat a little uncomfortably at the table, placed only one down from Lord Hood on the right, Lord Arthur immediately to his left. Many officers senior to him were seated farther down the table, and Hayden felt them looking at him, wondering who he could possibly be that Hood would show him such favour. It was not a situation to which Hayden was accustomed.

To the admiral's left sat Sir Gilbert Elliot, whom Hayden had seen earlier that day, and to his right General Dundas. Directly across the table from Hayden sat Admiral Hotham, whom Hayden had never met but knew by reputation, although this could be said of many a man dining with the admiral that evening.

Hood, as his appointment of Worthing to Pool's ship had indicated, had a wicked sense of humour, though at the same time was very droll, never laughing at his own jests so that the more junior captains, or those who were unfamiliar with this characteristic, did not know whether to laugh or keep silent.

"Admiral Hotham," Hood said after the dinner had been properly launched with appropriate toasts. "Does this young officer seated opposite you not have a familiar cast?"

Hotham gazed at Hayden for a few seconds. "I dare say he does, Lord Hood. I knew just such a man, these many years ago. A promising young officer whose career was too soon ended; let us hope the apple has not fallen too far from the trunk."

"Did you know my father, Admiral Hotham?" Hayden asked.

Hotham, whose manner was both stern and formal, denied this appearance each time he opened his mouth, for he was entirely amiable and pleasant in all his discourse. He was also known to be the cautious second in command to Lord Hood, whose recent taking of Toulon was typical of His Lordship's boldness.

"Indeed I did, Captain Hayden. I was a newly passed lieutenant when he entered the midshipmen's berth aboard the old *St George*. I knew him all his life and esteemed him greatly. But you must often hear such things said."

"Not at all, sir. I had begun to think that men who served with my father had all retired the service, so infrequently have I encountered them."

Hotham laughed. "There are yet a few of us who have not been cast upon the beach." He glanced Hood's way—almost a wink. Turning his attention back to Hayden, he continued. "Lord Hood tells me that your dear mother has removed to Boston. . . . What has taken her so far away, pray?"

"She remarried, sir—a prominent Boston ship owner." Hayden

was not surprised that every man familiar with his father remembered his mother—she had been known within the service for her considerable charm.

"Do remember me to her when next you meet. I wish her all the happiness in the world, for when your poor father was lost she was utterly disconsolate, I will tell you. If she had not had a fine young boy to raise, I fear she might have faded away from sorrow." Hotham tried to smile at Hayden but did not quite succeed. "But here you are, looking much like both your dear parents, which warms my heart and makes me think that your father did not pass from this world entirely." He fell silent at that moment, almost sorrowful.

Just then, a slight man in the uniform of a captain caught Hayden's eye. He reminded Hayden a little of Landry with his small chin and sloping forehead—not a handsome man at all—but there was such animation in this face that Hayden could not help but smile in return.

"Was it you, Captain Hayden, who escaped Toulon so recently?" the man enquired.

"It was, yes, though I have heard some others were not so fortunate."

"Yes, some transports slipped in there and were taken. Bad luck. Handsomely done on your part, though." He raised a wineglass in Hayden's direction and they toasted. "You must have a steady crew to have managed so well."

"Yes, they acquitted themselves nobly, I must say. Not a man among them shirked or shied." Hayden was so used to hearing his crew maligned—Hart's crew maligned—that he felt an unusual gratitude toward this man.

"I am sorry, sir," Hayden said, "but we have not been introduced. . . ."

"Nelson. Horatio."

"Of the *Agamemnon*?"

Nelson nodded. "And who is this young middy who has fallen in among all these terrible captains and admirals?"

"Lord Arthur Wickham, Captain, though acting third lieutenant at this moment."

"A great pleasure, Acting Lieutenant Lord Arthur Wickham."

"It is an honour, sir," Wickham replied quickly, clearly impressed with this young officer. "I have heard much about you, Captain Nelson."

Nelson glanced at Hayden, a little smile playing about his mouth. "Never believe all the stories you hear in the Navy, Lieutenant. We are all terrible liars when it comes to our own accomplishments."

Hood broke into the conversation then. "Captain Nelson, am I to understand that you are calling all the officers at my table liars?"

"Oh, no one at this table, Lord Hood. It is quite well-known that we are the most modest gentlemen in the Navy, never writing even in our private journals of our exploits. No, sir, advancing our own causes never enters our thoughts. Why, have you even heard me mention my recent success off Sardinia?"

"Not above a dozen times," Hood replied, this exchange causing much laughter among those near enough to hear.

"You see, Lord Arthur," Nelson said, "it is unseemly to bring your accomplishments to the attention of your superiors more than a dozen times. Do not forget that and your future in the service will be assured."

"I shall remember your advice, always," Wickham answered. "All the details of our recent escape from Toulon I shall keep to myself, though my own part in the affair was quite worthy of a knighthood— or so everyone present claimed."

This charmed Nelson, and Wickham was never addressed by anyone for the rest of the evening by anything but "Sir Arthur," which pleased and embarrassed him at the same time.

It was a convivial affair, given that the gathered company had so recently been driven from Toulon. There were, at table, a few officers who did not seem to partake of the joy; General Dundas had only the most stilted conversation with anyone, especially, it seemed, their host. And to Hayden's satisfaction, Captain Pool, seated far down the table, could not help but glance Hayden's way with both envy and ill-disguised indignation.

The conversation, however, was not all pleasantries, as much was said about the recent evacuation of Toulon and the survival of the greater part of the French fleet—a fact that both distressed and chagrined everyone present.

"If I had known the Dons would betray us, I would have fired a dozen more ships," a handsome young officer proclaimed. "Without the least doubt, the Spanish will make peace with the Jacobins any day and reveal their true colours."

Hayden could not help but notice Nelson's reaction to this, how he caught the eye of another captain and both appeared to be controlling their anger or perhaps disdain.

"Sydney Smith," Hotham whispered, seeing the question on Hayden's face.

Smith was another Hayden knew by reputation. Most recently, he had been naval advisor to the king of Sweden, for which the king had granted him a knighthood, and he now went about insisting that everyone address him as "Sir Sydney." Although Sir Sydney was well-known for his courage and enterprise, he was boastful and ever a promoter of his own career even at the expense of others, by which means he had made many enemies. Perhaps for this reason his real accomplishments were ever denigrated by some, who deemed them nothing but puffery. It was also known that Smith was never shy when it came to arrogating powers unto himself that his superiors had not conferred. The term "loose cannon" could not be misapplied to the vainglorious Sir Sydney.

The Army officers, of whom several were present, including Lieutenant Colonel Moore, whom Hayden had met earlier, and Lieutenant Major Kochler, who also was to accompany them to Corsica, fell sullenly silent when the subject of Toulon and its loss were discussed. Hayden had heard from various sources that the senior British general had advised Lord Hood against taking Toulon, as he had never believed it could be held. The naval officers, meanwhile, believed it could have been held had the officers commanding the Army committed themselves fully to the project. It was no secret that Hood thought General Dundas timid and indecisive—two traits of which no trace could be found in the character of Lord Hood.

Hayden wondered if Moore would ever be coaxed into expressing his own opinion on the matter, for Hayden, though predisposed to believing the naval point of view, had long thought that Toulon could not stand against a determined siege by a large, well-equipped force.

Sir Gilbert Elliot was a man of parts, Hayden quickly realised, fluent in several languages, articulate, thoughtful—a bit of an idealist, perhaps, but Hayden felt there was a place for idealists in this world. They set the goals for which others then strived.

"Have you visited Corsica previously?" Sir Gilbert enquired of Hayden.

"I have not, sir, but I am anxious to see it for myself. The people have chased their freedom for so long that, I confess, the thought that we might aid them is gratifying."

Sir Gilbert smiled his approval, nodding vigorously. "Yes, and again yes. It is my hope that we can provide a political structure, not unlike our own, but with certain modifications that will better suit the Corsican character. And Lord knows our own system is not perfect. Perhaps we might step a little nearer perfection in this case."

Lord Hood listened to this exchange, his look thoughtful, perhaps amused. "If the good Lord had meant us to mount the sky, Sir Gilbert, he would have given us wings. He did not. We are destined to remain on the ground and muddle through as best we are able. Perfection is not in the nature of our species. What serves us best today will not do at all tomorrow, yet we will attempt to continue as we were, not casting aside the things that once served but no longer. Perhaps, if we are wise, we might modify yesterday's ideas or institutions so that they half function. Or we will cast them aside and adopt something that is no better or perhaps worse. No, perfection, if we even attain it for a moment, will be entirely a matter of good fortune, not good planning, of that I am quite sure. It is my belief that, in life, as in military matters, things change more quickly than we comprehend and our knowledge of events is ever inadequate. We make our decisions based on rumours and guesses. Sometimes they turn out well—sometimes ill."

"Well, I will continue to hold out hope that in the matter of Corsica they will turn out well."

"And so will I!" Lord Hood seemed surprised that he might be expected to think otherwise. "How could I not? The events of this world are predicated upon forces that we only vaguely perceive. Toulon might have been the core of a rebellion that encompassed all the southern part of France—which would have been much to our advantage. It was not impossible, even if somewhat improbable. But this did not come to pass. We may never fully understand why. Corsica may one day be a prosperous and peaceful province of the British Empire, or it might make common cause with our enemies despite our best intentions." He threw his hands up. "All things are possible."

"I shall endeavour, with all my powers, to make Corsica a land both prosperous and peaceful, and, it is my hope, kindly disposed toward our own people."

"As long as we do not try to make the Corsicans into little Englishmen," John Moore offered. "It is a mistake we British have made too often."

Sir Gilbert nodded apparent agreement, though he said nothing. "Captain Hayden, was it you I heard speaking today with Madame Bourdage?"

Hayden admitted it had been.

"How is it that you have such perfect command of the language, for I confess, I have not heard an Englishman speak it so well."

"My mother is French, Sir Gilbert. I spent some time in that country when I was a boy."

"It must be very difficult for you, Captain, at war against your mother's people."

"I am an Englishman, Sir Gilbert," Hayden answered, aware that others were listening. "I know where my loyalties lie."

Hayden could not help but notice a few of the officers within hearing glancing one to the other, as though some unspoken language was shared among them but unknown to outsiders like Hayden.

When dinner ended, and the gathered officers and guests stood to leave, Hayden found John Moore on a course designed to intercept him. In tow, he had another Army officer, rather a contrast to Moore, who was tall and fair, for this man was dark and somewhat replete, though not much shorter than either Hayden or Moore.

"There you are, Captain," Moore addressed him. "May I introduce Major Kochler. Captain Charles Hayden."

Kochler returned Hayden's bow with a slight, impatient nod. "Your servant."

"As we are all off to Corsica on the morrow, I thought you should meet."

Kochler acknowledged this with what appeared to be more of a grimace than a smile, apparently more interested in the jostling officers as they exited the cabin.

"I am much looking forward to arranging our efforts in whatever way will best serve to expel the French," Hayden responded, trying to save the moment and not embarrass Moore, who clearly had not expected such discourtesy from his fellow officer.

When Kochler did not respond to this, Moore said, "And I am sure we are all of like sentiment, Captain." He glanced at Kochler, whose attention seemed to have been drawn elsewhere. "Until tomorrow."

Hayden was swept out with the tide of officers, who ebbed onto the gun-deck and then up the ladder into the autumnal, winter night. Navy men flowed into pools of blue, chatting amiably, while the Army officers all drained redly down into a corner of the fore-castle, where their muted conversation could not be distinguished.

By order of the officers' seniority, boats arrived to bear away the admirals and various captains. As a mere master and commander, Hayden's own barge would be very near the last, so he found a small section of rail to lean against and stood drinking in the warmish, winter night.

"Ah, Captain Hayden . . ." Sir Gilbert appeared in the lamplight. "I thought you might have slipped away. May I have a word?"

"Certainly, sir."

Elliot motioned Hayden to accompany him and, finding a small, unpopulated area of deck, began speaking so softly, Hayden had difficulty hearing.

"You had, this day, the good fortune to meet Madame Bourdage and her daughter. . . ."

"I had only just made their acquaintance."

"It occurred to me, this evening, that you must have family in France . . . on your mother's side?"

Uncertain as to the direction this conversation might take, Hayden agreed rather reluctantly.

Sir Gilbert pressed on. "If you were to discover some members of your family among the Toulon refugees, it might be possible to send them on to England, and safety. I do not know if Bourdage is a name found in your family tree . . . but then, no one else would know, either. Certainly I would never question such a claim."

"I am quite certain, Sir Gilbert," Hayden answered, as pleasantly as he was able, "that Bourdage is not a name to be found in my family, at any remove."

"Ah." Sir Gilbert looked rather more surprised than offended at Hayden's response. "If, upon further reflection, you find that you have made a mistake in this—no one's memory is perfect—do not hesitate to inform me. I can hardly imagine the joy of your relations to find themselves sent safely on to England. Were someone to perform such a service for me, I know I should feel uncommon gratitude."

When Hayden was finally in his boat and being rowed across Hieyres Bay toward the *Themis*, the single event of the evening that remained in his thoughts was his private conversation with Sir Gilbert Elliot. Was Madame Bourdage—or her beautiful daughter— Sir Gilbert's mistress? Or was there some reason, other than the obvious, for him approaching Hayden? Hayden also wondered if he were not putting too fine a point upon his honour in this matter. If it were within his power to rescue two of the refugees cast adrift by the British failure at Toulon, should he not take the opportunity to do so? The thought that these lovely women might eventually be discovered by a French army and put to death was rather unsettling.

Upon reaching the *Themis*, Hayden immediately retired to his cabin, doffing his coat and neckcloth. He had indulged rather too freely at dinner, and his miserable stomach was not about to allow him to lie prone. It was also true that wine had muddled his brain more than a little, so he sat listlessly on the bench beneath the gallery windows, propped uncomfortably on pillows and folded blankets.

The near silence of the ship was interrupted by a sentry challenging a boat that had ventured too near, and then footsteps came swiftly down the ladder. A hushed conversation outside his cabin was followed by the most discreet knock upon his door.

Thinking that he could never be left in peace, Hayden crossed the cabin and pulled open the door. Two apprehensive marines stood beyond, one his sentry.

"My apologies, sir, but I could see there was yet a light. Two women are asking to speak with you, if you please, Captain . . . a Madame Bourdage and her daughter, I believe."

"At this hour?" Hayden replied. "Well, I suppose you should bring them to me."

"Aye, sir."

A moment later the two women were shown into his cabin.

"A thousand apologies, Captain Hayden," Madame Bourdage began. "I was informed that you might sail at first light." She appeared so utterly distressed, her eyes rimmed in red as though she had wept only recently.

Hayden directed them both to chairs, but Madame Bourdage could not sit still, such was her agitation, and she rose immediately, taking Hayden by the arm and then clutching his hand.

"We are," she stated in French, *"as you see us, utterly desolate and dependent for our very survival upon the good-will of others, men who have counted our people among their enemies for many years. I know that Sir Gilbert has spoken with you, and that he has asked a great favour. In truth, he has asked you to compromise your honour and say something that is not true . . . that will see us to safety. I should never ask this of you for myself. . . ."* She gestured almost tenderly toward her daughter, and her eyes glistened. *"But for my daughter I would beg. Please, monsieur, if you could find it within your heart to aid us . . . we should be in your debt, always. I have a necklace— not a fortune, certainly, but enough to pay our passage to England. In London we have friends . . . who escaped there at the beginning of the troubles. They will not turn away from us, I am certain."*

Hayden glanced toward her daughter, who gazed at him with such a mixture of hope and dread upon her beautiful face that Hayden felt utterly bewildered.

A moment he vacillated, first this way, then that, the two women appearing almost to hold their breath. "I shall inform Sir Gilbert that you are a cousin of my mother."

Immediately Madame Bourdage released such a flood of tears and began kissing his hands. *"Oh, monsieur, monsieur,"* she repeated over and over. Her daughter rose up from her chair and, grasping his right hand, began doing the same.

"Merci, monsieur," she said with feeling. *"Merci beaucoup."*

When the two women had mastered themselves, Hayden asked, "The little girl . . . the one who collided with me on the deck. Who was she?"

"The daughter of Monsieur and Madame Mercier," Héloïse informed him in French.

"Have they money to take them to England?"

Mother and daughter looked at each other and shrugged.

"I cannot say for certain," replied Madame Bourdage, "but it is possible."

"I will inform Sir Gilbert that they are also related to my mother . . . and to you, if you don't object."

"No, of course not." She realised, at last, what Hayden intended. "We will see them to England, Captain Hayden—somehow. Though they are five altogether. We will find a way."

Hayden escorted the women onto the deck and to the rail, where a bosun's chair had been rigged to return them to their boat. All the while "Thank you, thank you" rained down upon him, and he saw them off with a feeling that he had never told a lie in so good a cause. Afterward, Hayden went to his cot with a warm glow in his heart and feeling rather proud of himself, which he realised he did not feel nearly often enough in this wretched, soul-destroying war.

Fourteen

From the sea, Corsica appeared fair and green, the crests of her mountains dusted with snow that reflected coral and gold from the dawn sky. The frigate *Lowestoffe* carried a fair wind toward the island's northern shore, and Hayden stood alone at the rail, a strange emptiness in his stomach. Were it a time of peace, this island would look idyllic, even romantic, against the morning sky, but today it appeared enigmatic at best, menacing if one dwelt upon the morbid possibilities.

"So what think you, Captain Hayden?"

It was Moore appearing at his side, crimson jacket not out of place against the morning sky.

"I was not expecting snow."

"I am told it is only on the tallest peaks of the inner mountains. It should be no concern to us."

"That is some relief."

"You have been pondering the charts and maps?"

Hayden nodded. "As we need an anchorage to land your troops, it would appear that San Fiorenzo will answer in that regard. The western shore of the bay has been invested with cannon and is fortified, but once the French have been driven thence, I believe the citadel on the eastern shore will capitulate, after a hasty display of resistance."

Moore nodded his agreement. "Yes, Bastia and Calvi shall prove the more difficult shells to break, but San Fiorenzo will take a co-ordinated effort of both Army and Navy." He hesitated a second. "Do you think our superiors will be able to make common cause, or will this matter go the way of many another where both our services have been engaged?"

The lieutenant colonel had not attempted to affix blame for such difficulties, which Hayden approved.

"At least let us hope that *we* might make common cause, Moore, without bickering and thwarting one another's efforts," Hayden offered.

"Yes, by all means. Let us attempt that, Hayden." Moore turned to face him. "It is of the greatest consequence not to make enemies of one's friends."

"Then let us shake hands on it," Hayden suggested, and they did, most heartily.

"Did I say that my brother, Graham, is a Navy man?" Moore asked.

"You did not. Graham Moore?"

Moore regarded him with a little surprise. "Yes."

"I am quite certain we met—in Halifax, some years ago. I believe he told me he had a brother named Jack."

Moore laughed. "So I am known in my family. The service is both great and small, is it not?"

"So it is." This explained a great deal—a brother in the Navy. Hayden felt his small distrust of the man evaporate, as though they were almost brothers themselves.

The captain's barge rocked over the small swell, the bottom visible through glassy clear waters. The Ile Rozza, actually a peninsula, lay between the French positions at Calvi and the Bay of San Fiorenzo.

It was understood to be under the control of General Paoli. Both Moore and Hayden hoped this would prove true, for it seemed possible that the old general was misrepresenting how much of the island he controlled so that driving out the French would appear to be an easier task than it actually was. Certainly, without British aid in the form of guns, powder, and soldiers, he would never manage it.

The shore was a patchwork of eroded cliffs, extending rocky shoals, and sandy beaches. These beaches and the mouth of the occasional small stream would make ideal landing places, but some of the low shoals of monolithic stone would do if the sea was calm. Tides in the Mediterranean were so small as to be unmeasurable, which simplified matters considerably. How many times had he heard of armies asking to be put ashore at some propitious time, only to have their plans thwarted by inconsiderate tides?

The boat rounded a rocky point and a small bay opened before them—their chosen landing spot. Hayden could see a crowd gathered on the shore, but the distance hid all details.

"Wickham, have you your glass to hand?"

"I am sorry, sir," the boy replied, "but I have it packed away."

Moore, Sir Gilbert, Major Kochler, Hayden, and Wickham took passage in the barge, and though Hayden was certain everyone, including Sir Gilbert, possessed a glass, no one had thought to leave one accessible—a situation almost more amusing than embarrassing.

"And we call ourselves professional soldiers," Moore said, and shook his head, smiling.

Oars dipped into the limpid sea, then emerged to make dripping arcs through the air, little rings forming between the larger swirls. Between each oar-driven surge, the barge slipped forward gently, surged, then slipped.

Wickham rose suddenly to gaze intently at the shore. "Sir . . . these men appear to be dressed in the French national uniform."

"Are you certain?" Hayden stood, as well, but his eye was not so keen as Wickham's, and no one else could tell, either.

Kochler tossed some baggage aside and, in a moment, dug out his glass, which he fixed on the shore. Hayden guessed he was not a man given to harsh language, but a mild blasphemy escaped him and the glass was passed to Moore and then to Sir Gilbert, who both confirmed that Wickham had been right. Before Sir Gilbert could offer it to Hayden, Kochler requested its return.

Men, similarly dressed, began to appear along the cliff to their right, much to everyone's distress, for these men bore muskets.

"But we were to meet Paoli's representative here . . ." Sir Gilbert protested with great indignation.

"There is nothing for it now," Moore replied with remarkable equanimity. "If we turn about they will have us."

As retreat was impossible, there were no dissenting opinions.

Wickham looked anxiously at Hayden, as though his French heritage might allow him to intercede on their behalf.

"What will they do with us, do you think?" Wickham asked quietly.

"The French are not a savage people. They will not mistreat us." And though Hayden believed that this was likely true, the thought of being held prisoner for months or even years filled him with a barely containable frustration. That he should finally have found a superior officer who seemed prepared to believe in his abilities and then that he should almost immediately land in a French prison was unbearable.

The Englishmen remained silent as the boat approached the beach. Hayden watched the party ashore for any evidence of their intentions, but they showed signs of neither hostility nor welcome. Their utter neutrality was most madding. Moore glanced his way, no doubt thinking similar thoughts.

As they neared the beach, Hayden clambered forward through the oarsmen to the bow, hoping this act would not be interpreted as a threat, but the men gathered ashore did not seem to care one way or the other. As the boat ran up on the sand and Hayden stepped over the gunnel and into ankle-deep water, one of the men raised his musket, fired it at the sky, and called out, *"Viva Paoli, la patria e la nazione inglese!"* Around him others echoed his act and words, filling the still air with acrid smoke.

Hayden turned back to Sir Gilbert and the others, who almost to a man breathed a great sigh of relief. Sir Gilbert released his hold on the gunnel and surreptitiously flexed cramped fingers.

The Corsicans came forward then and aided the sailors in dragging the boat up the beach a few feet so that Sir Gilbert and the others could disembark on dry sand. Suddenly the previously dour Corsicans were all animation, smiling and speaking at once. Muskets were fired in the air and decidedly British huzzahs shouted. Immediately the Englishmen's baggage was carried ashore and taken up by the inhabitants, who would allow no one to aid them.

Signor Leonati, the Englishmen were informed, was already on his way to meet them.

"Who is Signor Leonati?" Hayden enquired, pleased to find that his Italian was readily understood, and that he comprehended most of what was said to him if he could but convince the speaker to slow down a little.

"The nephew of the general," he was informed. *"General Paoli."*

"And where is the general?" Sir Gilbert asked, his command of Italian equal to that of his French.

"Not far," he was told. *"Not so very far."*

Although General Paoli was "not so very far"—and in English miles this was true—it took the remainder of the day, the day next, and half of a third day to reach him. The ruggedness of the countryside was unrelenting, and Hayden had the impression of a dusty, dry island, sparsely covered with hardy scrub and stunted trees, relieved only by deep valleys where rivulets greened the parched landscape in snaking narrow bands. Hayden wondered if there was a place on the entire island where rock did not thrust up through the ground. But when he asked this of Sir Gilbert he was surprised by the answer.

"There lies, on the eastern shore, a coastal plain that is very fertile. And high in the mountains you will find areas where the ground is moist and covered by ferns beneath very tall, straight pines. It is a more varied landscape than our small view of it reveals."

As they traveled, snakes darted out of the bush and, just as quickly, slithered off, but the local men assured the visitors that these serpents were not venomous; indeed, they hardly paid them any heed. Even more numerous than snakes were what looked like salamanders, not the length of a man's hand, and they were everywhere—soon to be victims of the serpents, Hayden suspected.

At one point Wickham asked Hayden, "Why are these people dressed as Frenchmen?" and Hayden, in turn, asked this of the nearest Corsican.

"Ah," Hayden responded when the explanation was made. "Most of the people wore the French national uniform while the French were in control of the island, and out of economy continue to do so; though it is not the best economy, I am informed, for several men have been mistaken for Frenchmen and shot during skirmishes."

"Are the French yet abroad?" Wickham wondered. "I was informed that they were shut up in their few strongholds along the coast."

Moore, overhearing this, answered the midshipman quietly in English. "So we have been told, Mr Wickham. Whether it is strictly true . . ." He shrugged.

Hayden did note that as they traveled, parties were constantly sent ahead and often reported back. Small companies occupied the heights, nearby, and the visitors were led along paths that wound along the valley floors. Very infrequently did they find themselves in exposed positions, upon hillsides or ridgetops, and when they did, the Corsicans hurried them along.

Hayden was concerned that the countryside might prove too difficult for Sir Gilbert Elliot, who appeared to be at least two decades older than the military men, but this worry was soon put away. Sir Gilbert's claim that he walked often and far was certainly true. Rather like John Moore, the diplomat had a manner that was very refined, his understanding great. As they walked he gave the plants their names, both Latinate and common, and plucked leaves here or there to examine and to show his companions.

"See! *Juniperus oxycedrus.*" He bruised a leaf with his fingers and insisted the others inhale the scent. "And here is myrtle," he observed, plucking a leaf to show them. "The French tower on the Bay of San Fiorenzo sits on Mortella Point, which is to say, Myrtle Point."

If Sir Gilbert had a flaw to his impressive character, it was that he felt his understanding was superior to that of other men, though this was carefully veiled behind excellent manners and a cultivated modesty.

On their third day on the island, the convent of Recollets, abandoned since the revolution, was reached shortly after midday. Walls, manned by armed Corsicans in numbers, loomed out of the trees, and the moment they perceived the Englishmen and their escorts they all cheered most heartily. This was the largest building Hayden had yet seen on the island, old but in good repair despite falling into disuse a number of years earlier. Gladly, the visitors gave up their mules to eager boys, who, with their dark, clear eyes, stared openly at the visitors. Hayden suspected they had never seen an Englishman.

Wine and various fruits were offered for refreshment, but as they were all anxious to meet Paoli, it was decided that they should demur on this offer and go immediately to an audience with the general.

They were led up stairs through the old convent and into a small cell, where Paoli sat by a window, book tilted toward the light. Immediately they entered, he rose, with some difficulty, to greet them most cordially. His English was good but softly accented, his once powerful frame becoming frail. In both his voice and manner there was about him an air of delicate sorrow, as though he were in mourning. Sir Gilbert had told them that the general had lost a well-loved brother a year previous, but somehow Hayden did not think that was the cause of his sadness. Paoli had dedicated his life to achieving independence for Corsica and his people, yet despite all that he had done, this freedom seemed as distant as ever it had.

"Do you remember Lord Arthur Wickham?" Sir Gilbert asked the general.

As the old man seemed perplexed, Wickham spoke up. "You once proposed to take me shooting in the mountains should I ever visit Corsica."

Paoli laughed. "I fear I have grown too old to keep my promise, but I will certainly arrange for some other to fulfill my obligations in this matter."

The visitors were offered chairs, and they and a few of Paoli's followers crowded the small room, some leaning up against the plastered stone walls. A letter from Lord Hood was produced by Sir Gilbert and offered to the general, who appeared to regard it with suspicion or displeasure. The old man opened it with a small blade and read thoughtfully. For a moment he stared at the page, his face exhibiting mild consternation. With the page shivering faintly, he laid the letter on a small table that held his books and spectacles, then turned his attention to Moore, Kochler, and Hayden. Immediately he began to talk of the terrain and the kind of attack that he believed would succeed on the nearby fortifications.

At the first opportunity Moore interrupted him. "I must tell you, General Paoli, that Major Kochler, Captain Hayden, and I are under Sir Gilbert, who is the king's senior commissioner in the Mediterranean. Until you have had some previous conversation with Sir Gilbert, we are unable to enter into a discussion of our mission."

This did not please the general. "I have grown tired of ministers and negotiations," he declared, not hiding his disappointment and frustration. Asking first some people in the room to withdraw, he turned to Sir Gilbert. "It pains me to find in this letter that Lord Hood remains inexplicit and diffident of me. In affairs of this nature I have found that it is always best to be open and candid." Even as he said this his voice grew thick with emotion, so that he spoke only with difficulty. "Long ago I wrote to your king and his ministers; I have also repeatedly written to Lord Hood that I and my people wished to be free, either as subjects of Great Britain, which I know does not want slaves, or free under the protection of Great Britain, as the king and the country may hereafter think most convenient to adopt. Having said this, I do not know what else I might say. Why, therefore, does His Lordship tease me with more negotiations? Has he not already injured me sufficiently with promises of succour which he has always withheld? If it is meant to include *mes compatriotes* in any arrangement which may hereafter be made with the Bourbons, I can have no hand in it. I shall retire. All I wish is to see, before I die, my country settled and happy after struggles that have lasted three hundred years. Under the protection or government of the British nation, I believe my countrymen will enjoy a proper degree of liberty. I have told them so, and they have such confidence in me that they believe me and wish to make the experiment."

No one had deigned to interrupt the general as he spoke, even if some of his expressions with regard to Lord Hood were less than polite. Clearly he felt himself wronged, but Hayden guessed that the general's desire for peace for his people was obviously so great that emotion made his words intemperate.

"My dear general," Sir Gilbert began, "I am sure that it was never the intention of Lord Hood to take even the smallest advantage of you or your people. I have been sent, and it is to this end that Lord Hood has written, to discover if there is any method, by assembling the states or otherwise, of receiving assent from the people for what you have so eloquently stated was their wish."

This only seemed to aggrieve Paoli more. "How can this be done while the French are still present? They must first be expelled; then it is my intention to convene the states. Until such time I know what is their wish and can speak for them."

This seemed a less-than-perfect solution to Sir Gilbert, or so Hayden thought from the sour look upon his face, but he threw his hands up. "Then we must first expel the French," he declared.

At that moment, dinner was announced, and they made their way down to the refectory. The fare was simple but flavourful, as though the food that grew upon the parched island had its essence concentrated and not diluted by an overabundance of moisture.

The general begged their indulgence and retired soon after the meal's end, saying that his aging body must have its sleep. Convent cells were prepared for the visitors and they found themselves with the luxury of separate beds, even if there were two to a room.

Moore sat upon his cot, face warmly illuminated by candlelight. "The general appears much broken since last I saw him," the soldier observed. "Leonati told me that he had an attack upon his chest but a few months ago, and that learning what has transpired in Paris has reduced his health even more. That, as much as anything, led him to turn against the French. Let us hope he lives to see his people free."

Hayden hung his jacket upon a wooden peg in the wall. "Yes, I should like to see that as well. It appears to me that the Corsicans have a strong case for wanting their independence but have not the strength militarily of achieving, or at least maintaining, it in the long term." Hayden paused, the earlier conversation repeating in his mind. "I did not think Sir Gilbert and Paoli were in sentiment with one another. . . ."

This appeared to distress Moore a little. "I thought the same. Let us hope they soon pass beyond the difficulties of their first meeting. Paoli clearly felt that Lord Hood had done him some injury, but it is the responsibility of Lord Hood to first consider the interests of Britain—not Corsica, however worthy her people might be." He folded his jacket and laid it on a chair and then began to pace the three steps allowed by the small room. "I hope tomorrow we might begin to reconnoitre the French positions. I am not well suited to diplomatic missions."

"Nor am I," Hayden agreed. "I should rather be on blockade, and that is saying a great deal."

The conversation appeared to be at an end, prompting Hayden to wish the soldier a good night of rest, when Moore spoke again.

"I do apologise, Captain, for the lieutenant major's incivility. . . . It is an attitude much ingrained in our service—and regrettably so. Kochler is, I believe, an excellent officer, and I do hope that, in not too short a time, he will have his opinions of the Navy altered by mere observation of your service's zeal and capabilities."

"There is no cause for you to apologise," Hayden replied. "I am well aware that the same attitude perseveres in the Navy. Jealousy and mislike of your service are ever two of the sentiments that bind sailors together. A regrettable state of affairs, I believe."

Moore had stretched out on his bed and lay staring up at the ceiling, thick hands locked behind his head. "I do despair, at times, for our race. It is as though we are ever trapped in adolescence and never reach our majority. How do we make a world when we are forever children?"

Hayden was surprised to find Moore sounding positively melancholy—perhaps it happened only at day's end when fatigue overcame him.

"I do know what you mean," Hayden said. "Perhaps some of us never even reach our *lieutenant majority*."

"Oh, Hayden, you have no shame." The colonel laughed. "Even for a sailor."

Hayden woke early and slipped out of his room before dawn. Descending the stairs, he intended to walk out into the soft, morning air. Instead, he found General Paoli, sitting at a candlelit table, eating bread and cheese and drinking warmed milk.

"It is, as you English would say, salubrious"—a crease appeared between heavy brows—"from the Latin *salubris*. It is one of the great advantages of the English language—adapting words from every tongue without distinction." He smiled, perhaps a bit embarrassed. "My stomach is not so hardy as once it was," he explained, and invited Hayden to join him. A jam made of figs was being applied to bits of cheese with a spoon, and at the general's behest, Hayden soon found himself doing the same.

"What ship is it you command, Captain?" Paoli asked.

Hayden was quite certain that the general had spent enough time in English society to realise his visitor did not wear a post captain's uniform.

"I hold the rank of master and commander, only," Hayden answered, "and am in temporary command of a thirty-two-gun frigate—the *Themis*."

Paoli nodded. "The goddess of order," he observed. "What will become of you when the admiralty appoints a captain to take your place?"

"Lord Hood was to do that when I arrived here from England, but he has chosen to leave me in place instead."

Hayden thought the old man's face darkened a little at the mention of the admiral, but he did not show it in his voice.

"Perhaps His Lordship will decide to confirm your command of this ship. Would the admiralty not support his decision?"

It was more than Hayden would allow himself to hope. As commander in chief, Lord Hood *could* appoint him post captain and grant him command of the *Themis*—or any other vessel, for that matter. In such situations, the admiralty almost invariably confirmed the admiral's choice—though Hayden knew of exceptions.

"Perhaps they would, but I am no favourite of the admiralty, I must tell you."

"Ah. I have been told that your recent service has been exemplary."

Apparently the general had been uncovering information about the men Hood had sent to treat with him. Hayden did not think Paoli had survived in politics to this age by being obtuse.

"I do my duty to the best of my ability." Uncomfortable speaking of his own accomplishments, Hayden chose to change the subject. "How strong a resistance do you believe the French will mount, General?"

The old man spread a little jam on his cheese with unsteady hands. "One can say many things about the French," Paoli observed softly, "but one cannot call them cowards. Even so, no man likes to give his life in a cause that is lost. Corsica is lost to the Jacobins unless they can carry an army here, and presently your navy prevents that. French courage will not fail, but I believe their commitment will falter a little more as one fortification after another falls. It is akin to pushing a cart lodged in the mud: difficult at first, but once it begins to roll it grows easier. I am content to see it take as long as it takes. It is one of the great benefits of age; life teaches many lessons, but patience it reminds us of most often. Almost all of my life I have struggled to see my people and my homeland free from foreign domination; I can wait a little longer. Twenty years the French have been here. Before that we enjoyed ten years of freedom, of self-government. The Americans are so proud of their republic and their democracy, as though they invented these things. No, we, a simple people on a small island, achieved these things before them. All we had to do was spend three hundred years driving out the Genoese! But in 'sixty-nine the Bourbons sent their armies and we could not stand against them— they were too great—and our experiment in self-government was brought to an end. That is why we need to ally ourselves with England. Corsica is not strong enough to stand alone. That is our tragedy. But it is the other great lesson of age—compromise. We are not great enough to stand alone, so we must ally ourselves with the country most likely to respect our independence—your nation, Captain, where I spent twenty long years in exile."

Hayden did not know quite what to say, and so stammered, "Perhaps your long-held dream of independence can yet be achieved, guaranteed by Britain."

Paoli shrugged. "Before I die, I should like very much to see the fate of my country settled. Let the next generation of Corsicans spend their days pursuing the common pleasures of this life—love, children, the scent of *maquis* on the morning air—instead of constantly being called out to fight one enemy after another. For so many years we have struggled that now we ask little of life. We do not want wealth or empire or military glory. Just peace and to decide our own affairs . . . And some more fig jam," he said, scraping the last dollop out of the jar. But then he paused and regarded Hayden, his manner somber. "That is enough for my people."

"It should be enough for anyone, I believe," Hayden responded, touched by the sincerity of this man.

Suppressing a charming smile, Paoli touched Hayden's arm with a large hand—a stonemason's hand. "Then let me find us more of this jam, Captain." He rose stiffly and went to a cupboard, moving things about inside and muttering. "Ah!" he said, snatching up a jar with not a little triumph. Returning to the table, he sat heavily in his chair, as though at the last instant his legs betrayed him. "Do you have children, Captain?"

"I do not, General, though I hope to one day."

"To most I say, 'Do not hurry,' but to military men I say, 'Now is not too soon.' It is a life of great uncertainty, the one we have chosen. I myself have been most fortunate to have survived so long when many of my comrades have given their lives for our cause. A priest once told me that God preserved my life so that I might bring independence to my people. I do not believe that God is so concerned with the fate of Paoli, or that another man could not do what I have done or might yet do. No, Paoli is not so important that God has taken notice." He lifted his cup, but before it reached his mouth he paused, meeting Hayden's eye. "Is this not pleasant, to be alone without a crowd always pressing? I rise so early for this, and this alone— a few moments of peace."

"I hope I have not interrupted your . . . solitude, General."

"Not at all. It is a pleasure to speak English with an Englishman. I will tell you, in the greatest privacy, that there are times when I wish my own people were as practical and—what is the word?—*pragmatic* as yours. But no: Corsicans are passionate and impulsive people, very quick to take offence and to anger. That is our curse, Captain. But it is a greater curse to be without passion, I think."

Hayden was not allowed to respond to this observation, which he thought might have been levelled at his father's people, for the other visitors came downstairs, then, and followers of Paoli appeared bearing food. Clearly they had been staying quietly away from the general for some time. Breakfast quickly became a social event, attended by many of the general's followers. Hayden found himself feeling a little sorry for the old Corsican, who bore the burden of his people's aspirations upon aging shoulders.

Perhaps Sir Gilbert had sensed the growing impatience of his young companions, for once he had them alone he proposed an alteration in plans. "I think it best," he told them, "that I spend today in private conversation with General Paoli. I have asked and received permission for you, Colonel, Major Kochler, and Captain Hayden to visit the area of San Fiorenzo where the French hold several prominent positions. One of the general's people will accompany you."

"Am I not to go with them?" Wickham asked, disappointment clear in his voice.

"You, young Lord Arthur, are to be taken shooting this day; the general arranged it himself."

"Shooting!" Wickham responded in dismay.

"Exactly so," Sir Gilbert said, and then, very quietly: "But do not let the Corsicans hear you respond in this manner. The general is showing you great favour, and that means everything to his people."

"I am not ungrateful," Wickham answered, chastised, "I only hoped to assist the other officers in any way I could."

"Today you may assist them by going shooting. And you may assist me later by returning for supper and telling the tale of your day to the general, who believes you are to be a great admiral one day."

The military men did not linger over their preparations but quickly gathered together what effects they might need and went down to the courtyard. Here they were met by the young man whom Paoli had appointed as their guide and interpreter, Pozzo di Borgo.

Di Borgo had, at the commencement of the revolution, been elected a deputy to the National Assembly in Paris, there to represent his people, and he had much to say of what he had witnessed during his time in that city—which had been the first occasion of his life to leave the island.

As they rode out, di Borgo told them of all the recent events that had led the general to break with republican France. "It was distressing enough that Jacobins ruled in Paris, but the Committee of Public Safety . . . that was a different madness. What dismayed the general most was that Corsicans, primarily Saliceti, had conspired against him, blackening his name before the Convention and accusing him of treason. The general was then invited to the mainland to 'discuss' the situation in Corsica, but he had no delusions about the Convention's intent. Very wisely, he did not refuse the Jacobins' invitation but simply wrote to say that his health would not allow such a journey. The situation on our island grew ever more fractious, several factions vying for control, all to their own ends. Only General Paoli put Corsica first. The break with Jacobin France was inevitable."

As they rode and talked, Hayden noticed that their escort occupied the peaks ahead and abreast, companies constantly being sent out before, leapfrogging one another, to maintain their vigil.

"You have known the general a long time?" Moore asked.

"Not so long as I would like. Even in exile he was an inspiration to our people. It is sad to see him finally return, so broken in health." He shook his head. "But now, perhaps, with the aid of your nation, he can see our people free and retire from active life, as I know he wishes to do. All of our people wish him happiness and rest. No one deserves it more."

Hayden thought di Borgo was rather too ardent—perhaps eager— in his desire to see the general retiring, despite his tone of respect-ful sorrow. It was not something new to find young lions standing by, impatiently, when the old lion showed signs of failing. Paoli had been the leader of the Corsicans' revolt for so long that younger men of ability had, for decades, been thwarted in their ambitions.

"We learned," observed Moore, "after the evacuation of Toulon, that the general there had been a Corsican."

"Bonaparte." Di Borgo said this as though he spat out dirt.

"You've heard of him?"

"He is well-known among my people. Once he was a lieuten-ant colonel of the Corsican Volunteers, but his intemperance and arrogance led to a near insurrection in Agaccio. Bonaparte's father had once been General Paoli's secretary; the general introduced him to the woman who became his wife—Letitia. But the brothers Bonaparte . . . they will intrigue as long as they can draw breath. It is no secret that the general thought Napoleon Bonaparte unprincipled and ambitious. General Paoli has always put Corsica before any aspi-rations of his own, and he looks for men of like character. Thwarted here, Bonaparte offered his services to the Jacobins. He is now seen as a man the French might send to invade our nation and imprison the general. I am ashamed to say that the Bonapartes have their sup-porters here, but people who love Corsica know them for what they are—a family of opportunists."

They had ridden perhaps three leagues when musket fire began on the hill above them. Di Borgo tried to turn his charges round and

herd them back, but as soon as cries of *"The French. The French!"* and
"Jacobins!" were heard, both Moore and Kochler dropped from their
mules and, muskets in hand, began toiling directly up the rugged
slope. Hayden took up his own firearm and went in pursuit. The hill
was a litter of large, broken blocks of stone and low bramble, making
progress difficult. As the Army men were not commonly confined
to ships for months on end, they were not so easily winded and
quickly put distance between themselves and Hayden. By the time
he reached the crest, Hayden worried the skirmish would be over,
but in fact, the firing grew hotter the higher he climbed.

As he mounted the hilltop, Hayden found the Army men crouched
behind a table-size stone, both reloading their muskets. Around them
the Corsicans kept up an erratic fire.

"Kind of you to join us, Hayden," Kochler remarked, earning him
a dark look from Moore.

Under the circumstances, Hayden chose to let the remark pass,
though it stung him more than he knew it should. Below, in a narrow
valley—almost a ravine—a company of French soldiers advanced from
rock to rock, a disciplined fire being returned first from the right, as
soldiers advanced on the left, and then reversing so that the right might
advance. The scattered Corsican militiamen fired as the desire struck,
often not at the men who advanced but those who had gone to ground.

"This will never do," Moore announced, and sliding back a few
steps so as to be out of the line of fire, he began exhorting the Corsicans to concentrate their fire and not waste it. Leonati lent his voice
to Moore's, and in a few moments, under the colonel's direction, the
French were sent retreating down the slopes. The Corsicans would
have jumped up and given chase—some did leap up to do just that—
but Moore managed to put a stop to this, and instead moved his force
down the slope in a concentrated, ordered manner, not letting them
get spread out so that the quick could range too far ahead and become isolated from their fellows.

For nearly an hour they chased the fleeing French, until, finally, the enemy managed to outdistance the militiamen. A single wounded man was the only Corsican casualty, and the British escaped all injuries but for scratches and bruises inflicted by the island of Corsica on the unsuspecting visitors.

Moore was examining a bloody gash across the back of his hand as Hayden joined him.

"The inhabitants do not seem to have suffered as we have," Hayden observed, inspecting his own small injuries.

"Apparently they know which bushes bear thorns. Look at what I have done. . . ." Moore held up his hand. "A bayonet could not inflict such injury."

Twenty feet off, the Corsicans were stripping a dead French soldier of his valuables—including his uniform. As most of the locals bore only fowling pieces, the dead soldier's musket was a great prize, claimed, unfortunately, by more than one. Di Borgo was forced to step in and confiscate the musket until it could be properly decided where it should be bestowed, as several claimed to have fired the fatal shot.

Upon the instant that this small dispute began, the Corsicans assembled into two distinct parties, each supporting a claimant, and the discussion quickly grew heated.

As they began the walk back to their mules, a frustrated di Borgo joined them.

"It is always thus," he said in French, though quiet enough that only the British could hear. "No matter that they swear loyalty to the general and the cause of Corsican independence, the moment there is any dispute or sign of conflict, they form into clans, and old resentments and disputes from three generations past bubble up as though these things occurred only yesterday. I am ashamed for my people. They are like children in this."

In his anger and frustration he ranged ahead of the visitors, leaving Hayden to look around and notice that the militiamen no longer

mingled freely as they walked but stayed in two antagonistic groups
that had formed only a quarter of an hour before. They muttered
among themselves and cast resentful glances at the others. Hayden
had the feeling that if di Borgo had not been so close to Paoli, he
might not have been able to end this dispute. Blood could have been
spilled . . . seemingly *over a musket.* How were the British ever to
drive out the French with such allies?

A plague on both your houses, Hayden thought.

The French scurried about like industrious insects digging a nest
into the grey-brown earth. Seven hundred feet above and some eight
hundred yards distant, the British officers—Army and Navy—fixed
glasses upon the earthworks being thrown up below.

"They call it the Convention Redoubt," di Borgo told them.

Colonel Moore gazed down upon this scene through his glass.
"Given that the French are cutting off the heads of anyone not sufficiently ardent in support of the revolution, it could hardly have been
christened otherwise," he observed, keeping his eye fixed on the efforts below. "That is Fornali Bay, then, to the right?"

"Yes," di Borgo agreed. "There is another battery just beyond the
trees." He pointed to the hillside above the little bay.

Fornali Bay formed an irregular narrow triangle that cut back into
the island between two hills—an inlet opening onto the much larger
bay. Anchored fore and aft, near to the northern shore, were two
frigates, both well under cover of the guns above. On the hill to the
right, or south, of the bay stood a small stone tower with but a single
gun visible. Below this and to the left, just to be made out through
a stand of trees, a battery had been raised on a meagre near-level
shoulder. To the left of the little bay the French were busy construct-
ing their redoubt with the industry of men expecting imminent

attack. All of these positions were arranged to repel assaults from the sea, and were open at the rear—a fact not lost on any of the military men gazing down on this scene from above. The French, Hayden realised, were confident that no guns could be carried to the hilltops behind, and it was easy to imagine why.

Across the larger bay, perhaps a mile and a half-distant, grey buildings apparent in the sun, stood the town of San Fiorenzo and the old stone fortress where most of the troops, according to the Corsicans, were stationed.

Pivoting in his place, Hayden turned his telescope to the north, following the undulating coastline until he found the tower on Mortella Point. This was of an entirely different nature than the small tower below—which was only a watchtower, really. Round and squat, the tower of Mortella reputedly had walls fourteen feet thick. Captain Linzee had taken it the previous October with a single frigate, but the Corsicans, to whom it had been delivered, were unable to hold it, and the French had taken it back.

"So that is the Martello Tower," Kochler said, his own glass following Hayden's.

"*Mortella*," Hayden corrected before he thought better of it.

"Did Lord Hood not say 'Martello'?" Kochler protested, glancing at his comrade.

"He did," Moore agreed, "but one can hardly correct an admiral."

"Unlike lowly majors," Kochler noted indignantly.

Hayden might have apologised had not Kochler been so continually discourteous to him.

Kochler glanced up at Hayden, making clear his silent affront, then back into his glass. "The *Martello* Tower fell rather easily to a frigate, I am told. It must have been manned by French sailors."

"I don't know who manned it," Hayden replied, "but Captain Linzee took it in a hard-fought exchange."

"Hard-fought?" Kochler said, and looking up at Hayden, he waved a hand toward the Convention Redoubt. "You will be up against

French Army regulars now, Captain, not sailors; do not expect them to break and run the first time you fire a gun. You will actually have to fight them."

Before Hayden could respond to this insult, Moore literally stepped between them. "Is it not enough that there can be no accord between our superiors? Those of us who will actually fight these battles cannot afford such pettiness. I do beseech both of you to remember that such antipathy can only aid our enemies and create ill will among ourselves."

"If there is ill will, it did not begin with us," Kochler responded, his choler rising. He turned his gaze upon Hayden, anger overriding his judgement. "Your admiral has passed up no opportunity to smear the reputation of the Army. We were blamed for the loss of Toulon, though the general told Hood the city could never be held. And now, if Corsica is not emptied of the French, and quickly, the Army will be condemned—though if we succeed, it will be the Navy who will claim the victory."

"Major!" Moore said forcefully. "This will never do! Captain Hayden has made every effort to aid and befriend us. This criticism is misplaced. I will not have this in my command. If you cannot work in harmony with the Navy, then tell me so and I will return you to Gibraltar."

Hayden felt his own heart pounding, for he had taken such offence at the man's manner and words that he had been about to demand satisfaction. Moore, however, ever the voice of reason, was right, and the part of Hayden that was not in a rage knew it.

Kochler made no answer to Moore, nor did he offer to apologise to Hayden for a moment, but then relented a little. "For the sake of this enterprise," he said, clearly neither mollified nor repentant, "I shall refrain from speaking the truth regarding this subject. Do accept my regrets, Captain; clearly this is not the time to bring forward such matters."

"Bring them forward at a time of your choosing, Major, and I shall be happy to satisfy you upon every count." Co-operation with the Army, Hayden was willing to attempt, but he would not suffer such offences.

Kochler made a little half-bowing nod of the head in Hayden's direction.

Moore was clearly unhappy with both of them and said, in a tone of exasperation, "There is much to be done. Let us move down toward the tower on Mortella Point. I should like to see it closer to, and discover if there is a place where the major thinks a battery might be erected."

Beneath an air of strain, the British officers walked nor-nor'west, among their honour guard of Corsicans, toward the mouth of the larger Bay of San Fiorenzo. The walking was not easy, up and down rugged slopes, and Hayden was soon hot from exertion.

The line of hills they followed paralleled the nearby shore, more or less, and to their left lay a deep valley with a narrow stream hidden at the bottom. Both Moore and Kochler had remarked, unable to conceal their concern, that moving guns over such a landscape would be arduous if not impossible.

"Certainly we can drag a small howitzer or two up here," Kochler observed, though he did not sound confident even of that. He turned in a small circle so that he might examine the landscape, his mouth turned down and gaze half-focussed.

"What think you, Captain?" Moore enquired of Hayden.

"I am quite certain that sailors could manage it," Hayden replied, and immediately felt both foolish and childish.

"I am sure each of you will toss a pair of howitzers in your pockets and stroll up here over the course of a leisurely morning," Kochler said.

"Major Kochler . . ." Moore intoned a warning.

"I am but jesting, sir," Kochler responded, "in an attempt to ease all misunderstandings with Captain Hayden. I have no doubt the sailors will surmount all difficulties and bear guns up to the appointed outlooks. Their zeal cannot be questioned. Their officers without parallel."

"I do understand your disdain for sea officers, Major," Hayden responded. "We are clearly all fools. How else could you describe a man who spends ten years at sea, in all seasons, to become a mere master and commander? An intelligent man would simply invest six and a half thousand pounds to procure a commission in some fashionable regiment, remove to London, and while away his evenings at White's."

Kochler did not reply but walked quickly on, stopping now and again to quiz the shore and the lay of the land with his glass, lingering over every shrub, every outcropping of weathered stone. If he had heard Hayden, and certainly he had, he made no sign of it other than a slight stiffness to his posture and his refusal to look in Hayden's direction. Apparently, Hayden's riposte had struck too close to home, and Kochler knew there was no denial to be made; it was a matter of common knowledge that wealthy young gentlemen did purchase commissions and then spent little or no time with their regiments, but preferred to disport themselves in London's clubs and less reputable establishments.

For a few moments they stopped to rest and drink water, staring out over the azure bay to the town and hills beyond, and back toward the higher mountains where clouds hung, as though unable to find their way between the rugged peaks.

"Landing troops should not prove difficult here—is that not true, Captain Hayden?" Moore asked, trying to make some conversation rather than gain real information.

"These beaches are ideal for our needs," Hayden replied, beginning to regret his response to Kochler. Moore's professionalism shamed him. "Beyond the tower on Mortella Point there is a beach of such scale that we could land all of Britain's armies at once, and with excellent anchorage in the roadstead beyond. The beaches this side of Mortella Point are commanded by the French batteries; we cannot use them except by night, and even then it would be a danger."

"Do you know, Major," Moore said to Kochler, clearly trying to jolly the man out of his ill humour, "with the French largely shut up in their towers, I think the taking of San Fiorenzo shall be no great thing. With the aid of the Navy we shall manage it most expeditiously."

"So men said at the beginning of the American war," Kochler growled, touched his hat, rose, and walked away.

Fifteen

Hayden had arrived at the appointed hour, met at *Victory*'s rail by a marine who led him below out of some rather unpleasant weather. Shedding oilskins, Hayden took the offered chair outside the admiral's day cabin and composed himself to wait.

"Lord Hood has the general with him," the admiral's secretary informed him. "I shouldn't think they will be much longer."

Hayden, whose hearing had not yet been compromised by the din of cannon fire, could distinguish the admiral speaking within—and though Hood clearly made an effort to keep his voice low, he was not addressing his guest in the most gentle tone.

"These three days past it was artillery that was lacking. Now it is camp equipage. Tomorrow it will be the season that will not permit it."

Dundas' voice equalled Hood's in discretion but exceeded it wholly in umbrage. "I will not send my men into the field without the necessary artillery so that I may satisfy your desire for reputation!" His hissed whisper shivered with anger. "Nor will I send them without food to eat nor proper clothing. We make all haste, but the swiftness of our retreat from Toulon left all things in disorder—guns on one ship, infantry on another, equipage . . . who knows where."

"I do not serve my king for personal glory, sir," Hood returned, the anger palpable even in such hushed tones. "I seek only to expel the French before they have time to fortify their positions. How many more men will be lost due to delay? That is what I wonder."

"There is more to this than stowing some furniture, knocking flat a few bulkheads, and running out the guns," Dundas whispered, his voice thickening.

"There is a great deal more to it!" Hood shot back. "I could ready my own sailors for such an expedition in a tenth the time it has taken the Army."

"And look where this impulsiveness has led you!"

"Whatever do you mean, sir!"

"Toulon could never have been held. It was the height of folly even to consider it."

"It would have been the height of folly to not take such a chance— the French fleet offered to us on a platter."

"A fleet that is largely afloat and in Jacobin hands!"

An even more heated exchange followed, voices rising, and then Dundas suddenly burst out of the room, stormed by the admiral's stricken staff, and disappeared. The door was closed softly from within and Hayden waited, no one daring to announce him. An hour passed before the secretary finally worked up enough nerve to knock timidly upon the door.

Hayden was ushered in to find Lord Hood standing, hands behind his back, staring out the gallery windows at the unsettled sea. He turned as Hayden entered, complexion still high from his recent anger.

"Captain Hayden," he mumbled, and then stared at the junior officer a moment as though unable, for the life of him, to remember why Hayden had been sent for. His gaze cleared and he crossed to his worktable, snatching up several sheets of paper. "I would have your opinion of this." He thrust the papers at his visitor. It did not

escape Hayden that for a man of advanced years and still in the grip
of outrage, Lord Hood's hand held remarkably steady. "It is from
Colonel Moore. Read it with all due care; I wish your most considered judgement."

Hayden took the letter, composed his mind a moment, and began.

Lord Hood:

*Agreeably, to Your Lordship's order, I landed in Corsica and waited
upon General Paoli. The following is my report upon the different
heads of instruction delivered to me by Lieutenant-General Dundas.
The first object seems to be the possession of Martello Bay [Hayden
took note of the spelling—Moore was more of a courtier than he ex-
pected] for the security of the fleet, and to enable it to co-operate effectively with the Army when landed. The works which defend the bay
are a stone tower with two or three light guns (4-prs) at Martello Point,
another of the same kind at Fornali. The fort of Fornali consists of a
strong battery immediately under the tower, and a redoubt open in the
rear lately erected on a height between the towers of Martello and Fornali. In the last there are four guns of different calibres. One hundred
and fifty or two hundred men from the garrison at San Fiorenzo guard
these different works. They are chiefly designed to act against shipping
but are commanded by heights in their rear. If these are occupied with
cannon, the works must be abandoned. The road leading to the heights
has generally been thought impracticable for cannon. It is, however, by
no means so for light guns or howitzers. I annex a detailed plan, concerted with General Paoli for an attack on the works of Martello, by
landing a body of 500 men with light field pieces at the northern point
of the bay, and marching by a path that has been reconnoitered, under
cover of the hills, to a place called Vechiagia, which commands within a
few hundred yards the new redoubt and the tower of Fornali. The possession of this bay having been secured for the fleet, General Paoli*

points out the bays of Vechia and Nonza upon the eastern side of the Gulf of Fiorenzo as places proper for the landing of the troops, provisions, ordnance &c.

The Army, immediately upon landing, will have to move with a few light guns about a league into the country.

There followed a detailed account for attacking the cities of Bastia and Calvi, which Hayden thought would likely fall to others. Toward the end of the letter, which was long and of impressive detail, Hayden found Moore's opinion of the Corsicans, which was very different from that of General Dundas.

The French and the few Corsicans in their interest are confined to the posts I have mentioned by the inhabitants attached to General Paoli who call themselves "patriots" and give the others the name of "Jacobins." Paoli's men are armed, in general, with fowling-pieces, and turn out voluntarily with provisions on their back and serve without pay. When their provisions are expended they return home but are succeeded by others in the like manner. Thus, though the individuals fluctuate, a body of men is constantly kept up sufficient to stop the communication of the enemy by land. General Paoli can command at any time for a particular service a considerable body of Corsicans, but he thinks that 2000 will be sufficient to embody as a permanent corpse to act with the army. To enable him to do this, he requires £4000 immediately, 100 barrels of powder, with proportion of lead and flints, and if possible, 1000 stands of arms. He will endeavour to provide provisions himself, and only wishes that when his people are detached with the British they may occasionally receive rations.

The Corsicans seem to be in general a stout, hardy, and warlike people, excellent marksmen and well adapted to the country they have to act in. They will be particularly useful in possessing heights, and by surrounding our posts prevent the possibility of surprise.

Hayden returned the letter to Lord Hood, who gazed at him with his sorrowful eyes. "And what think you of Moore's plan?"

Hayden held both Moore and Paoli in the highest regard, but had a single objection to their design. "I believe it is an excellent plan, sir, and would admirably have answered, given the situation in San Fiorenzo when last we were there."

Hood nodded as though he had almost expected Hayden to say just this. "There have been the inevitable delays, some unavoidable—weather, finding the guns, which were loaded in haste at Toulon—but there has been a great deal of . . . hesitation that cannot be explained away so kindly. What do you think will await us when finally we land Dundas' troops?"

Remembering Kochler's claim that the Navy never passed up an opportunity to damage the reputation of the Army, Hayden chose his words with care. "The French were cognisant of the British military presence on the island, sir—they could not help but guess why. Certainly all of their fortifications will have been strengthened so that they cannot be so easily attacked from the rear. That is what I would have done."

"Then this plan, in which Paoli and Moore and Kochler have invested so much energy, will not procure the bay for us?"

"Not if the French have been employed as I have suggested. The plan will need to be adapted somewhat, but I have utter faith in Moore. And General Paoli had a most sound grasp of all matters military—we all thought so."

"You did, did you?" Hood paced a few steps, head down, then turned back to Hayden. "That old rascal could talk a viper out of her eggs. I have never met his like. But Paoli commands the Corsican militia—we cannot hope to prevail without him . . . alas. I have little faith in these Army men and even less in Paoli, I will tell you. If we hope to see the French driven out of Corsica—in our lifetimes—our own service may be called into action . . . and sooner rather than later."

It was a scene of great industry and order, Hayden thought. The ships' boats ferried ashore soldiers or provisions, guns or equipage; all landed in the small surf without calamity. Tripods—often to be heard called "triangles"—were erected to sling the guns out of the boats and onto carriages that rolled up tracks hastily constructed of makeshift fascines laid upon flour-soft sand. The Royals, 25th and 51st Regiments, were all under the command of his friend, Lieutenant Colonel John Moore, who attempted to meet every boat as it landed and direct its cargo, human or otherwise, to the appropriate section of the beach. Seven hundred men—one hundred and twenty of them sailors under Hayden's command—formed into orderly companies.

A bright, Mediterranean sun illuminated this scene, while to the east, a press of clouds streamed rain in ribbons down upon the mountains' green slopes. Three weeks had passed since Hayden left Corsica with Moore to report to Hood and Dundas. It astonished Hayden. A naval attack would have been prepared in hours, if necessary, though one must admit that ships of the Royal Navy left their home ports ready to clear for action at any moment. The Army did not have the luxury of a vessel of war for each of its brigades—in this, Dundas was correct.

Out of the ordered chaos appeared Major Kochler, who did not seem to be regarding the scene with the same sentiments as Hayden. He stood, hands on hips, and was clearly judging the spectacle rather severely. Glancing to his left, he noticed Hayden.

"Can we not land men in one place and equipment in another? I should like to see the crews engaged in unloading guns, not tripping over the men packing victuals."

Hayden took a deep calming breath, to little effect. "It is only this single boat," Hayden explained, waving a hand at a cutter drawn up to the beach. "All others have landed on their assigned plot of sand." Hayden was chagrined to have his efforts criticised. Kochler would happen by when this single boat landed out of place!

Kochler seemed rather unimpressed by Hayden's claim, and went back to watching the operation with apparent disapproval.

Remembering his decision to follow Moore's example and attempt co-operation with all officers of the Army, Hayden said, "I had been told you still kept company with General Paoli?"

For a moment Kochler did not answer, and then finally he replied, "I have only just arrived . . . and brought your Mr Wickham with me." The officer looked around and then shrugged. "I don't know where he has gone." He paused, and Hayden thought he had finished speaking when Kochler offered, "Are you ready to bear our guns up onto the hills?"

"One in each pocket, sir."

Kochler turned and gazed at him. "What pockets you must have, Captain," and with that he marched off down the strand.

"Ah, there you are, Wickham." Hayden spotted the young man stepping out of the way of sailors bearing eighteen-pound balls ashore. "How went your shooting with the general?"

Wickham looked very pleased to see Hayden, breaking into his boyish smile. "It went well, sir. To have been given an opportunity to spend time in the presence of that great man is something I will always be thankful for."

"Well, your shooting holiday is over. I am going to put you in charge of landing the powder. Do not blow yourself up and spoil everyone's high opinion of you."

"Aye, sir," the middy replied, suppressing a smile. "Once a man's character has been blasted, it is almost impossible to remake it."

Despite the most concerted efforts of both services, the better part of a day was required to ferry all the men and equipment ashore. A frustrated Colonel Moore ordered the men to lie upon their arms that night. As there were no tents—these had either been lost in the retreat from Toulon or not yet located—the men slept in the open, but the evening was so fair that no harm came of it.

Hayden supped with the Army officers and then sat by their fire afterward sipping port and cursing the fickle smoke, which seemed to chase him wherever he moved.

"At least we are ashore and ready to march at first light," Moore observed. Hayden noted that the man was unable to remain down-hearted for any span of time but was soon finding something with which to be pleased.

Hayden excused himself momentarily to see to a small matter and upon his return overheard the Army men speaking quietly.

"The general has given our plan his fullest support?" Kochler en-quired of his companion in the most discreet voice, though, betrayed by the stillness of the night, the words carried to Hayden.

Burning wood cracked loudly, a spray of sparks exploding up among the cold stars. Realizing that his approach had not been perceived, Hayden was about to make some noise, but instead stopped, perfectly aware that this constituted an unforgivable breach of manners.

In the firelight, Hayden saw Moore take up a stick and begin rear-ranging some of the burning logs, his face appearing very thoughtful in the flickering light. "So I believed, until the final moment," he offered, lowering his voice, "but last night and this morning again I had to press him to land the troops, as he found every excuse not to do so. The weather was not right, the plan should be reconsidered, were we certain of the French numbers?" He shook his head. "But we are ashore now, and let us hope we can conclude our business with dispatch."

Hayden thought Kochler looked more than a little troubled by what Moore had said; in truth, Moore did not look less distressed. As much as he might like to, Hayden did not dare reveal the conversa-tion he had overheard between the senior officers of both services. It did satisfy him a little, however, to find that both Moore and Kochler appeared to share Hood's perception of Dundas. When he went to his own blankets to sleep, Hayden realised that Moore was in greater need of his aid than he had previously realised. Not only did Dundas not support his efforts as he should, he actually appeared to oppose them.

At first light, Moore and Kochler went ahead with the Royals, the 25th and 51st Foot, leaving Hayden to bring forward the guns. The track the Navy men took, much aided by the Corsicans' knowledge, was nothing more than a goat path that twisted through the broken blocks of stone and coiled among stunted trees. Nowhere was it wide enough for the guns to be rolled upon their carriages, and Hayden was forced to have his carpenters build narrow sledges that were dragged by harnesses of men, and pried upward by bars so that they went forward half a foot or a foot at a time. The path was so winding that only a few men could be sent to the ropes to pull, there never being enough length of path to allow more. Seldom could blocks be employed, though here and there a strap was wound around a rock and the ropes run off so that a purchase could be gained, making the whole frustrating enterprise, briefly, a little easier. A crew went ahead, clearing bush and trees with axes and filling in depressions, building the path up here, levelling there. Hayden hurried back and forth between the different parties, giving instructions, mulling solutions to difficulties in concert with his officers. Always he was thinking that he wanted to acquit himself well so that the reputation of the Navy should not be injured, but the island of Corsica did not much care for the reputation of the Navy and thwarted him at every turn.

Anywhere the path passed too narrowly between stones, the sledges had to be gotten over, so fascines were employed to make bridges. Here and there the stones were higher than a man and a path around had to be found.

Hayden took up a pry bar himself, in his turn, setting the bar beneath the sledge runner. "One, two, three . . . *Heave!*" The gun grated forward three inches. *"Again."*

As Hayden was digging his bar in beneath the sledge runner yet again, the boom of a distant cannon reached them and an almost constant fire ensued.

"Ship's guns," one of the men pronounced. "Attacking the Martello Tower, I would imagine."

Wickham looked over at Hayden, question unspoken.

"I do believe he's right. But it is no concern of ours. We have our own task to complete."

Late in the afternoon, Hayden received a request from Moore to join him at the forward position. Leaving the guns under the able command of Wickham and a more senior lieutenant, Hayden took up his musket and field-pack and hurried forward to find Moore.

The lieutenant colonel was not with his men, who had reached the site of their proposed encampment near Mont Rivinco, but he was directed toward a neighboring hilltop, where Moore and Kochler were discovered gazing through field glasses onto the French positions at Fornali Bay.

This was not the first sight that struck Hayden, though; instead, his eye was drawn to the bay immediately before the stone tower on Mortella Point. Here a seventy-four-gun ship and a frigate—*Fortitude* and *Juno*, Hayden believed—were anchored fore and aft so that they fired broadsides continually upon the tower, which, at a much slower rate, returned fire. From this distance Hayden could not perceive any damage to the French stronghold, and the ships were so thickly shrouded in smoke from their guns that their state could only be guessed at. For a moment his eye lingered on this distant drama and then he turned his attention to the scene directly below.

Hayden did not need to look through a glass to immediately perceive that the concerns he had voiced to Lord Hood had been more prescient than he had hoped. The French had not wasted the three weeks the English had been absent. All of their positions had been enlarged and strengthened. The small tower above Fornali Bay had embrasures in every direction and a closed battery had been thrown up in front of it. The battery below the tower boasted a mortar and several new guns. Perhaps the most changed was the Convention Redoubt, which lay across Fornali Bay from the tower and had been much enlarged, enclosed in the rear, and better armed. Men could be seen completing the earthworks even as the British officers looked on.

Moore said nothing beyond the briefest greeting, his jaw tight and entire manner stiffly controlled. Retrieving his glass, Hayden examined the works below in some detail. With every moment he felt his frustration increase tenfold, and it was not moderated in the least that he had been proven right. Their carefully drawn plans had been made obsolete by the length of time it had taken to organise the attack and by the energies of the French. The urge to speak some ill of Dundas was almost irresistible.

Hayden lowered his glass and addressed Moore. "I will defer to your more expert opinions in this matter, for war on land is not my province, but it does appear that our previous plans will no longer answer. Am I not correct?"

Moore nodded. "You are absolutely correct. These positions are too strong for our small force and a single howitzer and six-pounder. What think you, Kochler?"

Kochler sat down upon a stone and dug out his drinking water. "I should curse these bloody Frenchmen, but of course we have no one to blame but ourselves." He looked up at Moore, frustration, even anger, contained in every gesture. "Our entire force shall be needed, and how we shall manage it even then I do not know."

"I will write to General Dundas and acquaint him with the situation."

"It would be best if he would come ashore and view the French positions for himself, if he can be so convinced," Kochler responded, not able to hide his consternation. "Perhaps that will galvanise his actions."

"I shall urge him to do so in the strongest possible terms. Our provisions will now be inadequate and we shall have to land and carry forward more food."

"I shall see it done," Kochler stated tersely.

Moore turned to Hayden. "Bringing the guns forward will no longer be necessary. They will do us no good."

"Shall I return them to the beach?"

"I am afraid the answer is yes. We are not ungrateful, however, for your efforts, Hayden."

Before he left to return to the guns, Hayden aimed his glass at the tower and the two British ships. Beyond, he could see the transports and other ships anchored and still engaged in landing men and equipment. He would much rather have been aboard ship, firing on the tower, but he reminded himself that at least he had employment in this matter. Many sea officers did not.

Hayden hiked back to his men, wondering at Dundas' apparent reluctance to come ashore. Hayden was used to the traditions and duties of the Navy, and this reluctance seemed peculiar to him. Certainly Moore and Kochler were perfectly capable, but even so, when fleets went into action, admirals put their own ships into the line of battle and stood upon the quarterdeck among the other officers.

The rest of the day was committed to hauling "the damned guns" back to the beach, which Hayden and his sailors managed sometime after midnight, whereupon they tumbled down upon the sand and passed into unconsciousness. Hayden himself fell into a stupor and did not wake until the sun was up and the crash of distant guns penetrated his dreams.

He propped himself up on one elbow and, with dirty fingers, rubbed at his eyes, causing one to sting terribly for a moment. The Army was in motion, food being prepared and consumed in orderly fashion. His own men were not quite so smart—an exhausted, bedraggled-looking lot, to be honest—but they were mustered and then went about breaking their fasts, lieutenants and midshipmen bringing order to what might have been chaos, though of a rather subdued nature. Taken off a ship and out of their usual routines, the sailors appeared a little lost.

"There is news, sir," Wickham said, arriving with a cup of murky black liquid that smelled vaguely like coffee. "*Fortitude* and *Juno* were forced to sheer off, sir. *Fortitude* was set afire from hot shot, and she lost above sixty men. *Juno* was not nearly so badly mauled but hauled herself out of range as well. Very little damage was inflicted on the tower." Wickham took a seat upon a little stool. "I would not have expected them to have a furnace for heating shot, sir. It had not been the case previously."

"Clearly, the French were better prepared, on this occasion," Hayden answered, glancing around at the soldiers, embarrassed that the Navy had failed. He then tasted his coffee, which was more bitter than he had expected.

After a Spartan breakfast, Hayden retrieved his glass and hurried off to the distant hill overlooking the French positions. As he expected, he found Moore and Kochler, with some of their senior officers, all staring off toward the tower of Mortella. Smoke blossomed up from the low hill behind the tower, and a fragment of plaster or stone was blown away from the stronghold.

"They've established a battery ashore," Hayden said, realizing immediately that he was stating what everyone already knew.

"Yes," Moore told him, "and to damned little effect. Our only advantage appears to lie in the fact that, even if our guns are not inflicting perceivable damage, the French cannot traverse their guns to fire upon our position at all. A small comfort."

"Has General Dundas agreed to come on shore?" Hayden asked.

"We hope that he might arrive this very morning," Kochler

replied. "If we show you a position not too distant from this place, Captain Hayden, can you tell us in perfect honesty if you believe large guns could be got up there?"

"How 'large' do you mean?" Hayden asked.

"Eighteen-pounders."

Hayden was stunned by this. "Naval eighteen-pounders?"

"The Army has no guns of that size, Captain," Kochler informed him.

"Hauling a six-pounder and a howitzer over this godforsaken landscape was almost more than we could manage." The idea of eighteen-pounders being brought to even the base of the hill, let alone carried to the top, seemed absurd to Hayden; they weighed forty hundredweight! His professional pride, however, silenced his immediate objections. "But, by all means, let us look."

Although the hike was not far, the roughness of the landscape made progress slow. It was some time before they had traversed the half-mile. A slightly down-sloping shelf of brown-grey stone seemed an ideal place to mount a battery.

"It is perfect," Moore muttered.

Hayden knew from dragging small guns along the path behind this ridge that the landward slopes of these hills were steep, rugged in the extreme, and an arduous climb for men unencumbered by anything at all, let alone guns weighing four thousand English pounds. Certainly a plunging fire from this place would soon drive every man from the Convention Redoubt or the batteries of Fornali. It was difficult to imagine that any gun could be elevated to return fire, but even if it were possible, it would be dismounted by the British guns in moments.

Moore was gazing through his glass at the redoubt. "Eight hundred yards," he announced. "Do you agree, Hayden?"

"Within half a cable's length, yes."

Hayden turned away from the view across the Bay of San Fiorenzo and walked a few yards over the crest. Traversing a little to the north, he found a promontory from which he could inspect the greater part of the hill's vast, arcing back. The landscape on this side of the bay was all of one piece—ubiquitous lichen-stained, greyish-brown stone, much of it broken away from the mother rock and tossed about in blocks. Overspreading this, a sparse underwood of myrtle and what appeared to be stunted arbutus. It was no wonder the French, and the Genoese before them, largely abandoned the inner mountains and the west coast to the inhabitants and left them to govern themselves. Moving troops over such difficult terrain was all but impossible, and ambushes could be laid anywhere.

In a way it would have been better had the slope been steeper. Then cables could be run from top to bottom and the guns hauled up the cables, as his men had hauled the guns up a small cliff the day previous. But this slope would not allow that, for any cables run must sag so much that the guns would be always on the earth.

"What think you, Hayden?" Moore asked, approaching the promontory upon which Hayden crouched.

"There is," Hayden said, pointing vaguely, "down to the left, a wide and very shallow gully. Do you see? Perhaps 'gully' is not the proper description. It is the only place that is not clearly impassable—which is to say that it is only very likely to prove so. I will climb down and see what is to be seen." He turned to Moore. "Can it be managed without guns?"

Moore looked very pensive. "You have seen the effects of grape at short range?"

"I have."

"Then you know—the loss of life would be very great, and even then I am not certain the French positions could be carried."

Hayden nodded. "Let me climb down. If it is within the borders of human strength and endurance, I will attempt it."

Moore made a little bow toward him. "Thank you, Captain. Lord Hood chose well in you. I will speak to the general."

Left on his own, Hayden scrambled across the slope and began to pick his way down. To his left and right the terrain was impossible. There was simply no way a four-thousand-pound gun could be borne over it. Men were not strong enough and the gun would present a grave danger should it slide.

He climbed down the draw, tacking side to side, examining every foot of terrain. The gully itself was an extremely shallow trough, nearly thirty yards broad—and though green with sparse vegetation, no more impassable than any other part of Corsica that he had yet seen. Though Hayden could not put a name to the rock that formed these hills, it had clearly been eroded by the ages in such a way that it offered jagged edges and was everywhere coarse and abrading. For a moment he stopped and gazed back up the slope, and his heart despaired. "Blast these damned hills," he muttered. "Why do these Army men insist on guns?"

He resumed his descent, which even unencumbered was perilous, and he was forced, here and there, to climb hand over hand. The vegetation was so hardy that he used it for handholds without the least worry of it giving way.

When he reached the bottom, Hayden turned and stared again up the forbidding slope. Perhaps halfway down, Moore picked his way among the rocks, eyes focussed on his footing. In a quarter of an hour he reached Hayden, who sat upon a rock, training his glass over the backs of the hills.

"What think you, Captain?" Moore asked as he reached the bottom. "Is it at all possible?"

"I must be truthful with you, Colonel, I don't believe it can be managed." Hayden removed his hat and wiped his forehead with a handkerchief. "But I am willing to make the attempt, even if I am doubtful of its outcome."

Moore took a seat beside him, gazing up the hillside.

"There is a reason the French did not occupy the hills," Hayden observed. "Nor did they build their fortifications to be protected from that quarter—they believed it to be beyond human endurance to carry guns to such heights."

Moore turned to Hayden with a look of utter sincerity. "I hope you can prove them wrong, Captain. It will save many lives among my men, for which I would be grateful beyond measure."

"I will tell you this, Moore: I know my men; they will break their backs before they will give it up."

Moore made another little bow of thanks in his direction. "Let us find Kochler. He believes there might be a second gun position—not so perfect as this, for it is further off, but of easier access."

"I should like to examine this slope once more. I expect it will reveal more of its impediments while I ascend than it did when I climbed down."

"I will come with you, and offer what counsel I can."

The climb was not more encouraging, every yard appearing more impassable than upon his first examination. By the time they reached the top, Hayden felt he had been too confident by far in his prediction. Only a miracle would see success.

They set off along the ridgeline in the wake of Kochler, who could just be seen in the distance, a red coat in the grey dusty landscape.

"This terrain is so rugged," Moore declared, "that moving men over it in a timely fashion will be one of our greatest obstacles. To mount a surprise attack while moving so slowly would be impossible."

"I have noticed the Corsicans do not suffer in this matter as we do," Hayden ventured, wondering even as he said it if it was true or simply a misperception.

"I have observed the same," Moore agreed. "I must speak with them and have an explanation, for surely this would greatly aid our efforts."

They caught Kochler up at the jagged crest of a hill. He was staring down into the valley below, where a stream drained into a small slough, parted from the sea by a sandy beach.

Moore pointed down the slope below. "This is almost a natural ramp beneath us."

Kochler nodded thoughtfully. "I thought the same." He turned and gazed off toward the fortifications around Fornali Bay. "Certainly we are not more than a thousand yards and, with this height, in range of eighteen-pounders."

"Do you agree, Captain?" Moore asked Hayden.

It was difficult to be sure of the distance—Hayden was much better at estimating such things over water—but he thought Kochler's measure quite close.

"Yes, a thousand yards—not fewer."

Moore gazed back down at the slope below—a green triangle of vegetation angling steeply up from the slough; to the right a ridge, craggy and broken, taking the same attitude. "If guns could be hauled to this height, I don't know where we would mount them, and this last section would be difficult to climb, let alone bear guns over."

"The engineers would have to build up a platform, here." Kochler pointed. "Is this the Old Pivot?" he asked, giving Dundas' nickname. He fixed his glass on a not-too-distant point.

A company of Corsicans and British soldiers hurried along the very path where Hayden had borne the guns. It struck him how much more quickly they moved unburdened by cannon.

Moore confirmed that this was their commanding officer, and the three set out to intercept Dundas, who was no doubt coming at Moore's request. There was no easy or direct way down from this peak, so it was only the greatest good fortune that someone in Dundas' party spotted them.

An hour later they were toiling up the hills again, with Lieutenant General David Dundas in tow. At nine and fifty, Dundas seemed a sorrowful and greying presence, mounting the hills slowly but without pause, until the top was reached. There, out of breath, he required a moment to recoup, then followed the others to the best vantage. Moore pointed out the changed situation around Fornali—the British battery adding punctuation in the background as the cannonading of the Mortella tower continued.

Hayden thought the lieutenant general looked ill as he directed his glass to each salient or embrasure, and every battery in turn. After this catalogue was completed, Dundas stood staring down at the French positions, saying nothing, his two senior officers waiting for him to pass judgement. "Perhaps we can bombard them from the sea?" he finally offered, with little conviction.

"We agree with Captain Hayden that the batteries all are well fortified on their seaward side, and could withstand any number of broadsides, while nothing will impede the French from returning fire, to great effect. We saw what damage was inflicted on *Fortitude* and *Juno* but yesterday."

Dundas nodded. It had seemed a slim chance, but he had, perhaps, been hoping his officers might simply defer to his opinion—something that Hayden suspected they were becoming less and less willing to do.

"We have discovered two excellent positions on the heights where batteries could be advantageously erected," Moore offered.

"And is there some road I am unaware of by which you would carry your guns up to these positions, Colonel Moore?"

"There is not, sir, but Captain Hayden believes it might be managed, all the same." Moore glanced Hayden's way, clearly embarrassed at having misrepresented Hayden's opinion so. There was no doubt in Hayden's mind, however, that Dundas would never allow the attempt if he were not assured, perhaps repeatedly, of its success.

Dundas continued to stare down upon the shore, where the tricolour shimmered in the soft breeze. Just as Hayden thought Moore should repeat himself—perhaps in the belief that Dundas had not heard—Dundas nodded. "Let us survey these positions, then."

For the second time that day they made their way along the line of hills, stopping at the first proposed battery. "Certainly it is an excellent situation," Dundas agreed, "but eighteen-pounders . . ." He trailed off, clearly doubtful of the feasibility of the idea.

They then showed the lieutenant general the route proposed to carry the guns to the crest, which appeared to unnerve Dundas altogether. "Over the course of several campaigns I have witnessed attempts to bear guns to such eminences—many easier of access than this. Almost without exception these attempts ended in failure." He turned to his officers. "This is simply not possible, Moore. . . . That is why the French have not occupied these hilltops. Guns cannot be raised here."

"Sir," Moore said reasonably, "you have seen the strengthened French positions for yourself. Storming them will cost many lives, and success is by no means assured. Certainly we may fail to bring guns to these heights, but it will cost us nothing in lives and only very little time in delays to allow the Navy to make the attempt."

Dundas did not seem pleased by this and turned to Kochler. "You have not offered your opinion, Major," Dundas observed, though this seemed, to Hayden, merely an attempt to avoid making a decision.

Kochler hesitated. Hayden thought he would agree with Dundas, for certainly the man had little faith in the Navy to accomplish this task.

"It is my opinion that we should allow the Navy to attempt it," Kochler declared, "but success or failure of our enterprise shall be upon their heads. Admiral Lord Hood must be made to understand that."

Hayden's surprise was quickly overwhelmed by resentment and chagrin. For a moment he even wondered if Moore had conspired with Kochler in this, but could not bring himself to believe it of the colonel. In a very real sense, Hayden had committed the Navy to this nearly impossible task, and the success of the operations in San Fiorenzo Bay would now depend upon him raising guns to the heights. Failing that, the Army would claim the French positions could not be stormed without such batteries, and place all blame for failure upon the Navy—upon Hayden, in fact. Hood's good opinion of him would be lost.

Dundas brightened visibly upon hearing this. "If the Navy have agreed to take on this responsibility . . ." but he could not, even then, bring himself to make the commitment.

"Perhaps we might leave Captain Hayden to consider the possibilities, here, and discuss the present circumstances among ourselves," Moore suggested.

The Army officers retreated back to Moore's encampment, leaving Hayden to fume upon the heights. In frustration, he walked over to examine again the slope up which he had proposed to haul the guns. "Well, there it is," he muttered to himself. If he failed, all hopes that Hood might grant him a post ship would be lost. And then he wondered if he were becoming one of those men who put success in his career above all. What of Corsica and the hopes of Paoli? But the Army had created a situation in which he must almost certainly fail, blasting all of their hopes—British and Corsican alike.

"Damn you both," he whispered, Kochler and Dundas being the objects of this profanity. He walked slowly back to the encampment, hoping above all things that Dundas would not allow the attempt, all the while wondering if his new "friend" had betrayed him most cunningly.

Before he had begun the actual descent, the cannonade, which had gone on ceaselessly throughout the day, suddenly fell ominously silent. Walking back up a few steps, Hayden fixed his glass on the distant tower. A great feather of dense smoke swelled up into the hazy blue.

"It is a tower of stone," he muttered. "How can it burn?"

But there could be no other explanation for such quantities of smoke, and certainly the men within must surrender or suffocate. As he turned to proceed down the hill he was met by Moore hurrying up.

"They have broken off firing," Moore stated, though it was half a question.

"Yes," Hayden said testily, but then added in a more civil tone, "It seems the tower, or something within, has caught fire." Hayden indicated the smoke rising above the shoulder of the hill.

"One would think the place was packed with straw!" Moore observed. "I can't imagine why it should burn so."

Hayden nodded agreement, his resentment rising.

"I must tell you, Captain," Moore said, turning away from the sight and fixing his attention upon Hayden. "Kochler throwing all responsibility for the success or failure of our enterprise upon the Navy was as much a surprise to me as to you, and I do deplore it."

This was said with such utter sincerity that Hayden could not help but hope the man was telling the truth.

"It was never my intention to commit the resources of His Majesty's Navy to this endeavour," Hayden said. "Only Lord Hood may do that. I meant merely to indicate my willingness to make the attempt. If Dundas represents my willingness as an offer, I shall be in a difficult position with my commanding officer."

"I will speak with the general and represent your situation to him most adamantly. It is utterly unfair to place the entire success of our enterprise upon your shoulders; we must bear it all together."

"Thank you, Moore."

Sixteen

Two days were wasted as Dundas attempted to decide upon a course of action. In frustration, Moore wrote him a letter again begging that Dundas allow him to attempt to move the necessary guns up to the heights, and the general finally relented and gave his permission. Whether Hood had been informed of this, Hayden knew not, and as he had no directions from that quarter he accepted the task of moving the guns, as his previous orders had been to give all support and aid to the Army in this enterprise. He was not, however, pleased with the prospect, and not at all due to the difficulty.

There was, now, one advantage that had not existed formerly—the guns could be landed on a beach much nearer to their final objective. This was made possible by the fall of the tower on Mortella Point, the guns of which had previously traversed the beach to its south. The landing would have to be made by night, as the batteries at Fornali were near enough that they could lob shot down onto the beach, but once the guns were moved inland fewer than a hundred yards, they would be completely sheltered from any fire the enemy could mount.

Four eighteen-pounders, one ten-inch mortar, and a single eight-inch howitzer were shifted into boats from a ship by day and readied for their journey ashore. Once this had been accomplished, Hayden made a visit to the stone tower on Mortella Point. An aide of General

Dundas' was there drawing a plan of the fort and taking careful measurements. He showed Hayden why the tower had smoked so magnificently—the parapet had been lined to a depth of five feet with bass junk, which had caught fire when the British had thrown heated shot into it. The tower itself mounted but a single gun and contained a small furnace for heating shot. The walls were thick— perhaps fourteen feet—and there was but a single small entry high up in the wall. Its weakness had been its inability to fire in any direction but out to sea and toward the nearby beaches. The battery erected inland had been able to prosecute its cannonade with impunity. "It seems an excellent design for shore defenses," Hayden observed. "Did the Corsicans erect it?"

"I don't believe they did. But whether it was the Genoese or some other I cannot say."

As the day drew to a close, Hayden put off for the ship, from which the guns had been shifted, and as soon as darkness was deemed complete, he returned with them to shore. The beach was the very same one Kochler and Moore had been speculating about from the heights—backed by a small freshwater lagoon. Hayden's intention was to land the guns in the usual manner—using tripods—drag them on sleds across the beach, pull the boats across, load the guns back into the boats, and then ferry them over the lagoon. They would then be landed in two separate locations. Two eighteen-pounders and the ten-inch mortar would be dragged up the ramp to the nearest position. An eight-inch howitzer and two eighteen-pounders would be transported down the valley, following the path Hayden had previously employed, then moved to the crest directly behind the Convention Redoubt. It all sounded rather easy if stated quickly.

The boats lumbered heavily through the water, thin starlight offering the most meagre illumination. Each eighteen-pounder equalled the weight of twenty-five men, so the boats with their crews and a single gun sat low in the water. The carriages were borne in their own boats, so that a small flotilla was needed to carry all the artillery, shot, and powder. A dark, ragged line that blotted out the stars marked the crest of the hills. In this poor light they seemed much higher than Hayden remembered, as though only darkness revealed their true stature.

The boats landed silently, the beach having been occupied previously by the Corsican militia and a company of Royals. Erecting tripods was the work of a few minutes, though slinging out the guns took longer. Before the guns could be lifted, the crack of musket fire sounded above, and lead balls began thumping into the sand. A man standing near to Hayden was struck in the calf and collapsed onto the sand, howling.

"Douse torches and lamps!" Hayden called out, forcing himself to hold his place and stand tall in the centre of scrambling men.

The Corsicans were off at a run to engage the French, and the Royals began returning fire. In five minutes the French, who had sallied forth from one of their batteries, were in flight.

Moore, who had come to observe the landing of the guns, found Hayden in the dark. "Have you any wounded?" he asked.

"One man shot through the leg, another through the hat. I'm not sure the hat will live, but I think the man will survive. What of your men?"

"Unharmed, thank God. Do you think the French will try to find us with their guns?"

Hayden had wondered the same thing. The beach was a good distance from their batteries, but not impossible. He hoped to be off the beach long before first light, and under cover of the hills. "We might hope they do; it will be a wasted effort. The more shot and powder they use, the less will be preserved for their defense."

After the French attack, the British would only risk dim lanterns, and these were shielded as much as possible so that their light did not spill out where it was unneeded.

The guns were raised, the boats slid out from beneath, and gun carriages pulled into place. Guns were lowered carefully onto the carriages. To cross the narrow span of sand, fascines were laid the width of the carriage trucks apart, and staked in place. Ropes were attached to the carriages and the hands took hold of these. The sheer deadweight of an eighteen-pounder gun was difficult to overestimate, but slowly they went up the sloping strand and down the other side, only to have the process reversed: tripods erected, guns raised from their carriages and lowered gently into the boats.

The waters of the lagoon were so shallow that the boats bearing the great guns sat on the silty bottom and no crews could climb aboard. Instead, the boats were heaved, a few inches at a time, until they swam, and then floated by wading sailors, who pushed them across the inky surface. All the while men kept looking about, listening, fearing the sound of musket fire again.

There was very little speech, by order, and what little was needed, whispered. Hayden himself waded across the lagoon, his hands on the gunnel of a barge. A sailor with a torch went ahead; the sound of his legs washing through the cool waters was all that broke the silence. In less than half an hour landing places were reached, and the easy part of the task was over. Guns were slung out and lowered onto crude sledges, officers and bosuns carefully overseeing the rigging of tripods and tackles—dropping a forty-hundredweight gun could maim a man or worse. The guns were dragged a few feet up from the waters lest a sudden downpour in the mountains swell the stream and sink their guns, and then the order was given for the men to lie upon their arms for the remainder of the night. The Corsicans and some of Moore's men stood guard, and Hayden bundled into his blankets and fell into a strange dream, where hands reached out of the ground as he walked and took hold of his feet and ankles, so that a single step required more strength than he could muster.

Before dawn, the men assembled and were released to break their fasts. Had it been somehow possible to lift an eighteen-pounder without mechanical aid, it would have taken forty souls, but that number could not find purchase on the gun at one time, so the cannon were dragged, sometimes upon the ground, at other times upon wooden tracks hastily constructed. Everywhere it could be contrived, even for the shortest distances, tackles were rigged using the largest ship's blocks Hayden had been able to procure. With pry bars and muscle the guns were inched over the unyielding terrain, over rocks and gullies, men straining so that veins bulged blue and faces turned crimson. Two men were carried back to the surgeon at the beach camp beyond Mortella Point, both with what Hayden suspected were hernias. A third collapsed in the forenoon, writhing on the ground and clutching his back, and he, too, was borne away on a litter.

Despite the brutality of the work, no one complained. It had gotten about that the Army intended to blame the Navy men for the failure to take the French positions if the guns were not carried to the heights, and no sailor was willing to live with that. Injured backs and hernias be damned.

Having seen the guns on their way along the valley, Hayden went quickly to the ramp, where the second set of eighteen-pounders was being readied to haul. This slope, though gentle-appearing from a distance, was not so upon closer inspection. It was also far more rugged than any had realised. The slope had the distinct advantage, however, of allowing block and tackle to be used to haul the guns the majority of the distance to the top. Very heavy cables were being long-spliced together and a purchase created by rigging massive ship's blocks. Men were clearing away brush and small trees in a direct line up the slope, and arguing over ways to get the guns over rocks. Hayden struggled up the slope to see how the blocks were being attached at the top, and here he found Wickham overseeing the men as they ran ropes several times around rocks.

"How go your efforts, Lieutenant?" Hayden asked. Wickham always seemed to colour a little with pleasure each time he was addressed as "Lieutenant." He had doffed his coat and was in the thick of the work, hair plastered to a sweaty forehead.

"Well enough, sir. I don't think we can manage more than two-to-one purchase, but I'd rather haul twenty hundredweight than forty, so it will do."

"We can put as many men to hauling as there is rope to take hold of, so I dare say it will answer."

"How go your own efforts, sir?"

"It is a slow business, Wickham. But if it cannot be managed yard by yard or foot by foot, then we shall press forward inch by inch. Perhaps the French will run out of victuals before we get the guns to the top."

Wickham smiled. "Little worry of that, Captain. We shall drive them from their redoubt, yet. I am certain of it."

Hayden climbed up then, to look at the place Kochler had proposed to mount the guns. To the left of the ramp, up which the guns were to be hauled, a jagged ridge of broken stone inclined steeply downward to the beach. Although this ridge provided protection, both from the prying eyes of the French and from their cannon, the guns would have to be raised to its top before they could be employed, and this, Hayden despaired, might be their undoing. Even the climb up this ridge was difficult, and Hayden once found himself unable to proceed but not quite sure he could descend, either.

Casting about for a hand- or foothold, Hayden felt his legs begin to shake from the strain, and his fingers were cramping. He fought down panic, searching with a foot beneath him for any kind of toehold.

"Bloody island," he cursed under his breath, "shall be the death of me."

But then his boot encountered a small ledge, hardly wider than his thumb, and he lowered his weight onto it, quickly finding lower handholds, and from here he was able to climb quickly down.

A few moments he rested and contemplated the rock, until he discerned what he believed to be an easier route of ascent. Steeling his nerve, he tackled the rock again and was soon pulling himself over the top. Here he found an officer of the engineers and a crew at work on levelling ground for the battery. At least someone thought it possible the guns might reach the top, and Hayden was quite certain he knew who it was not.

An hour saw Hayden returning to the other guns, finding them sooner than he had hoped. Progress was always frustrated on this rugged, little goat path. An image of British infantrymen charging the French positions into a hail of grapeshot occurred to him. This he found so horrifying that it made him recoil almost visibly, and he tore his mind away from such thoughts and back to the guns that lay, massive and indifferent, upon hoof-hardened ground.

Winter days were short, and the sun soon plunged into a pool of cloud on the horizon, setting it afire. Torches were lit and the men kept to their task. Conversation grew less and less frequent and more and more terse when it did occur. Finally, at about a quarter of eleven, it was apparent that the men were too exhausted to continue, and Hayden called a halt to all work.

A rough camp had been readied for the men, and they rolled into blankets around fires, watched over by dutiful Corsicans. Sleep was easily found by one and all. Even Hayden collapsed and was insensible in moments.

Late in the night he opened his eyes to find a moon riding high, adrift in a hazy sea of black and blurry stars. The fire had burned low, and he was cold. That was what had wakened him. For a time he remained prone, hoping some other would rise and feed the fire, but when no one did he roused himself and piled wood on the coals. He stood near the heat, surrounded by the dusky cocoons of men wrapped in woolen blankets. The fresh wood began to smoke, then caught with an aspirated *whoop*. A moment Hayden stayed, warming himself. His body was stiff and aching from his day's labour, and he felt a deep sense of exhaustion.

"Sir?"

Hayden turned to find that one of the cocoons had risen and was lumbering toward him.

"Mr Wickham. Did I wake you?"

"I don't believe so, sir. I was but half asleep." The boy pulled his blanket closer about his shoulders.

Hayden had spent enough time around Wickham, now, that he knew his moods, and tonight he was not reassured by the tone of the midshipman's voice. "Has something troubled you, Mr Wickham?"

The boy said nothing a moment, moving to stand over the fire so that he might warm himself. "I had several conversations with General Paoli, while you were away, sir. And as many with Sir Gilbert . . ." The boy's decision to speak appeared to dissolve.

"These conversations distressed you?"

"They did, sir, though I am not certain in what way." He said nothing a moment more. "I do not hold out much hope for this enterprise, in the long run."

"Raising the guns?" Hayden asked, confused.

"No, sir . . . our presence in Corsica—British presence."

"Why is that, pray?"

Wickham brushed back his hair with a hand mittened in his blanket. "Sir Gilbert is an intelligent man, and certainly he has the best interests of the Corsicans at heart, but he does not seem to understand how . . . life is arranged on this island. It is not in the least like England, sir, nor are the Corsicans like us. They are strongly divided into clans . . . and the bonds of loyalty exceed our own loyalty to family or friends. Although General Paoli has tried to eliminate this, the Corsicans kill each other over perceived insults, and then go on killing each other . . . sometimes for generations. When one clan gains any kind of political office, it is expected, by everyone, that they will look after their own people at the expense of others. It is not even thought wrong. The idea that you might appoint the most capable person to a position is unknown, here, as is the idea that justice should be meted out equally. Leonati told me that when the general first came to power a relative of his was arrested. Everyone expected that Paoli would see him pardoned of his crimes—but he did not. He

let the man suffer the fate decreed by the courts. It was unheard-of.
Our ideas of justice, of fairness, do not hold here. Paoli binds all the
clans together because he understands them and they respect him. I
am not sure that Sir Gilbert comprehends this. He seems to perceive
Paoli as an impediment to the creation of a perfect state. I think Sir
Gilbert is a little like Mr Aldrich in this: he believes that if something
seems reasonable to him, it must seem reasonable to all. But what is
reasonable in Corsica is that you look after your own . . . and they
will look after you when their time comes. Only Paoli and a few
others see the need to rise above this. They believe that the Corsicans
will learn this lesson, too . . . in time. But not overnight. I fear Sir
Gilbert is in such a hurry to create perfection that he will try to push
General Paoli aside. And if so, he will quickly lose the trust of the
Corsicans. He does not know the history of the clans' alliances, of
their grievances one against the other. He cannot smooth over the
indignation of one clan toward another, for he does not understand
the source of the indignation to begin with. We are strangers here. It
is as though we have traveled to a place where the laws of nature
are different. Gravity does not pull bodies down when they fall—
instead, they rise or tumble sideways."

Hayden wanted to protest this—after all, Sir Gilbert Elliot had
traveled widely and seen many cultures—but everything Wickham
had said seemed disturbingly true, as though the boy had given voice
to fears Hayden shared but could not previously acknowledge. To
admit these things aloud, though, made the present enterprise appear
somewhat futile.

"All we can do, Wickham, is drive out the French and hope that
Paoli and Sir Gilbert can work out their differences." But Hayden
could not maintain this pose of neutrality and hope, and let out a
long breath. "Lord Hood did not trust Paoli, either. He seemed to
think him an old scoundrel."

Wickham turned to him, his face flickering in the firelight. "Oh
no, sir. General Paoli is a very wise man. With all respect, Lord

Hood and Sir Gilbert are much mistaken. The general is a man of great integrity and broad understanding. It is true that he does not always reveal all of his intentions, but a lifetime in politics has taught him some painful lessons. Betrayal is not unknown to him."

"No doubt, Wickham. No doubt. Let us, at least, not betray his trust. We will drive out the French as we have promised. That is our part of the bargain. If others fail, we can say that we held true."

"Aye, sir. If we can carry these guns to the hilltops, the French will not tarry in their batteries."

"Indeed. The French, the Corsicans, and the British Army do not believe guns can be carried to such heights, but I believe we shall prove them wrong."

"So do I, sir. And then"—Hayden could see him smile—"we shall have to carry them down again."

Hayden laughed softly. "You could have been a dandy in London society, Mr Wickham, but you, rather rashly, I think, chose the Navy instead. Our tasks are Promethean, our rewards intangible—"

"Our boots are smoking."

"Oh, damn! Look what we've done! Baked our boots in the service of England. What more can be asked of us, Wickham? What more?"

After his conversation with Wickham, Hayden had barely closed his eyes when it was time to rise, form up the men, and then eat breakfast. Sunlight had not offered even a suggestion of its powers when they were back at the guns, hauling again on ropes, Hayden feeling that, indeed, they had been cursed and set an impossible task. The sunken-eyed faces of his men, slick with sweat and dirt, appeared haunted in the torchlight.

The sun announced its intentions by illuminating the underside of a cloud that hung low over the eastern mountains, turning it

various hues of ember red, before a shaft of filtered light pierced
between two peaks.

"It's a sign from the almighty!" one of the men jested.

"We's all to go 'ome and 'ave tea, lads!" another announced.

It was one of the things about sailors that endeared them to
Hayden: he had heard them make jests, sometimes very black in nature, at moments when any sensible man would have been frightened
into utter silence or too exhausted to speak. They found ways to keep
their spirits up under any circumstances.

As soon as it was light enough, Hayden left his train of guns and
hiked over to find Wickham. The first eighteen-pounder, on its
sledge, had been fastened to the rope, and the men were set to haul by
walking down the slope, all the weight they could manage hanging
on the cable.

Wickham stood by the gun, holding a pistol.

"Are you expecting a mutiny, Mr Wickham?"

"No, sir. The men hauling are too far off to hear my commands,
so I'm signalling with guns and flags, sir. When I fire my pistol they
are to leave off hauling and belay."

"Most ingenious, Lieutenant. Be certain you kill no one."

"There is no ball in the pistol, sir."

"I was jesting, Wickham."

"Of course you were, sir."

A flag was raised by a midshipman and the men commenced hauling, the gun inching up its prepared path. In a dozen feet the sledge
reached a gap between rocks too narrow to allow passage, and Wickham fired his pistol into the air. Hauling ceased, and the sledge came
to rest, as though waiting.

"We shall have to build a bridge over," Wickham called to the
lieutenant, who came jolting down the slope at that moment.

"I will leave you to it," Hayden said, and set off to rejoin his own
party.

Hiking up over the crest of the hill, Hayden could soon perceive his own crews below, massing about each gun like predators at a carcass. Along the hilltops to his left, Hayden could see Corsican militia and companies of Moore's 51st, making certain the French remained in their redoubt and did not attack the toiling sailors—a thought that lay in the back of every Navy man's mind.

Picking his way down the slope, Hayden quickly caught the crews up.

"How goes it?" he asked the *Juno*'s bosun, a quietly competent man named Germain.

"Lead Arse is always slowing us down, but the others move along handsomely."

"'Lead arse'?"

The bosun laughed, a bit embarrassed. "The men have given the guns new names—christened them with dirt, sir. The eighteen-pounder at the fore is 'Swift' because . . . well, it's always in front, so it's winning, like. The other eighteen is 'Lead Arse,' and the howitzer is 'Bill's Sweetheart,' because . . ." The bosun coloured and fell silent.

"You needn't explain that one," Hayden replied.

He turned his attention to speeding up their progress, but it was nearly futile. Coaxing Lead Arse twenty yards could take an hour. At times, an hour did not see the guns progress twenty feet!

But despite Corsica's efforts to thwart Hayden and his crews at every turn, by day's end the three guns lay at the bottom of the slope up which Hayden had proposed to drag them. The mood of the hands was much improved, and enough grog was carried from the beach to give every man a taste before supper. Hayden thought it less than they deserved.

Before darkness could settle in, Hayden hiked back to see how Wickham and the lieutenant fared. To his great relief, he discovered the first eighteen-pounder at the top of the slope, ready to be slung up to the peak, but the second, though halfway up the ramp, lay among the ruins of its sledge. Hayden made his way down to this gun, where he found Wickham at the centre of the gathered men.

"Mr Wickham. Your gun seems to have run afoul of Corsica."

"Yes, sir. We were pulling it over these rocks by means of a wooden bridge when the bridge collapsed. We shall have it all put to rights in a few moments."

Indeed, men could be seen already bearing wood up the slope, and the gun was being readied to sling as soon as a tripod could be firmly erected above the irregular slope. Two hours Hayden spent seeing the gun remounted on its remade sledge and guided over the rocks, everything managed to a nicety.

It was, by then, thoroughly dark.

And out of this darkness came a familiar voice. "I have wagered all my savings that you shall not be thwarted in your efforts by anything so minor as a mountain. After all, it is only a small one, as these things go."

Hayden turned to find Hawthorne grinning at him in the torchlight.

"Mr Hawthorne!" Hayden said, genuinely happy to see the marine. "How is it you are here?"

"You have surely been too busy to notice, but your ship lies anchored in the bay beyond Mortella Point."

"The *Themis*?"

"None other. I asked Mr Archer's leave to come ashore and protect my investment. If these guns are not perched atop some mountain by the day after tomorrow, I shall be pauperised, and my children after me."

"You have a very strong back, Mr Hawthorne, which makes you doubly welcome. How fares our crew and officers? Is our new lieutenant finding his way, do you think?"

"Ransome, sir?"

"Ransome?"

The marine lieutenant laughed. "Yes, the poor man is named William Albert Ransome. William Albert Ransome the Second, we have discovered. Other than his impressive moniker, he appears to be an excellent officer, if a little eccentric."

"And he is eccentric in what way?"

"He has some very odd beliefs, Captain. Transmutation of the species is one of his several hobbyhorses. He told us all at dinner, this two nights past, that ships would one day sail without wind and that the sailors' arts would be confined to pulling levers and steering, though reading a chart and navigation I doubt will go out of fashion. A very peculiar sort of man, but we have all taken a liking to him just as men always do the village idiot."

Hayden was very anxious, suddenly, to see his ship, and, a few moments later, he and Hawthorne were striding along the beach toward the tower on Mortella Point. Hardly more than an hour saw them boarding the *Themis*, which rode to her anchor on a calm sea.

The officer of the watch was Gould, who greeted Hayden with genuine affection—and perhaps a little relief. It made Hayden realise that Gould was yet not confident of his place on the ship and was happy to see back aboard the officer who first supported him.

Mr Barthe met Hayden as he descended to his cabin.

"Captain Hayden, sir," the sailing master began, "have you set your guns upon the hilltops?"

"Not yet, Mr Barthe. I hope you have not been wagering, as well," Hayden teased. "You know Mrs Barthe's feelings on this count."

Barthe, whose passion for gaming had all but ruined his family in the past, looked suddenly chagrined, and he cast a resentful look at Hawthorne. "You needn't worry, Captain Hayden," Barthe offered, a little abashed, "I will not fall back into my old ways. I am quite determined."

A sense of disquiet crept over Hayden—perhaps it was the fact that Barthe did not deny that he had been gambling, but Hayden did not want to embarrass the sailing master by pursuing this further with others present. Barthe had finally freed himself of debt as a result of the prize money earned on their last cruise; to see him take his family back into those straitened circumstances would distress Hayden more than a little, not to mention that gambling was not officially permitted aboard ships of the Royal Navy. Hawthorne, Hayden assumed, had been jesting about his own wagers.

Mr Archer appeared, and he and Barthe informed him of all events aboard the *Themis* since he had departed. As they spoke, Griffiths announced himself at the door of Hayden's cabin and was invited in. Medical matters were quickly dispensed with and port was produced, the officers all pleased to find themselves back in one cabin. It occurred to Hayden to tell the gathering that he considered himself fortunate to have such excellent officers and companions, which they all drank to most heartily.

"We have not told you about our recently departed parson," Hawthorne said, breaking into a grin.

"Is Mr Smosh no longer with us?"

"Most happily, he is still aboard, but Dr Worthing . . . there is another story."

Laughter and shaking of heads all around as the gathered men waited for Hawthorne to continue.

"Our dearly departed parson had not been aboard *Majestic* a week when he ran afoul of his new captain—Pool. Letters were sent off to Lord Hood—by both Worthing and Pool, Worthing asking that his captain be replaced for incompetence, and Pool begging that Hood relieve him of this vexatious man of God." A finger pointed at the deck-head. "We have all of this from a friend of Ransome, who is a lieutenant aboard *Majestic*. Lord Hood, however, has refused to honour either request, and has informed both gentlemen not to aggravate him more with such petty matters." Hawthorne's smile grew even larger. "I only regret that I am not allowed to observe these proceedings more closely that I might extract the fullest measure of contentment from every exchange."

"If you were observing it that closely, Mr Hawthorne," Barthe informed him, "you would be marine lieutenant aboard *Majestic* . . . and I do not think that would provide you with such 'contentment.'"

"Lord preserve me from that."

There was a moment of silence—there being, perhaps, so much to say that no one knew where next to proceed.

At that moment the new lieutenant arrived and was introduced. He was, by manner and address, unmistakably from a better family than anyone aboard save Wickham. Although he was not remarkably handsome in any way, he was a pleasant-looking young man of perhaps twenty years, with auburn hair, pale skin, uneven teeth that somehow formed a disarming smile.

As soon as he had been introduced, he looked at Hayden rather closely in the lamplight. "You do have differently coloured eyes!" he blurted, to much laughter. Ransome looked around, embarrassed. "I am sorry, Captain. I believed I was being practised upon when they told me that you had one blue eye and one green."

"No, I am afraid you were being told the truth. Would you join us in some port?"

"It would be an honour."

Conversation strayed a bit, as though it could not find its wind.

"I understand, Captain Hayden," Ransome said after a moment, "that you have a gift for discovering the French and bringing them to action."

Hayden laughed. "Now, there you *have* been practised upon. And, to be honest, I think of getting into action as being rather bad luck." Hayden wondered what was being said about him in his absence.

"You do not think of it in that manner at all," Griffiths interjected. "I have never known a man so pleased by the prospect of action."

"We are all pleased to do what we joined His Majesty's Navy to do," Hayden protested, "engage our enemies. But I believe the lucky captains are the ones who never seem to have an opportunity to engage the enemy. Think how seldom they must write home to a family to inform them their son or husband or father has departed this life. I cannot tell you how much I should like to be relieved of that particular duty."

"It is odd, is it not?" Barthe observed thoughtfully, "how some captains do always seem to be in some kind of action or another, while others can go a whole war and never catch sight of a French ship."

"It cannot simply be a matter of luck," Ransome said, looking around as though asking for agreement.

"In truth, Lieutenant," Hayden said, "I think it can be attributed to precisely that: chance and nothing more."

"But not in your case, Captain," Hawthorne protested, suddenly serious. "You understand the enemy better than anyone else as a result of having lived among them. Perhaps it is not cognisance on your part, but, instinctively, you know what the French will do, where they will be, even. You understand the French mind."

"Oh, Mr Hawthorne," Hayden protested. "I know where the French will be at mealtimes—at table—but, otherwise, where a French ship will be is as predictable as where an English ship will be. Measure tide, wind, and the proximity of threats and perils, couple those with some contemplation of the enemy's intent, and you will know as much about the French mind as do I."

"Protest all you like, Captain," Hawthorne stated, "but *you* knew the French frigate was signalling a ship over the horizon, while Pool and Bradley did not—which cost Bradley his life. *You* knew the French frigate and seventy-four were lurking out in the fog, and just how to draw them out—which led to the seventy-four's destruction. You may protest, Captain, but we all know better."

The others nodded heads, which disconcerted Hayden, for they were certainly attributing abilities to him that he did not possess.

Hayden turned to Ransome. "How are you adjusting to life aboard a frigate? A little different than *Victory*, I should think." This obvious change of subject made his companions all smile a bit too knowingly.

"I am finding it much to my liking, Captain Hayden. Do you think it possible that we shall again be sent on a cruise?"

"The intentions of the admiralty are a mystery to me, Lieutenant. I was sent here to deliver the *Themis* to Lord Hood so that he might find her a captain. It surprises me, yet, that he has not done so."

"Then you are under the command of Lord Hood?" Ransome enquired. "When he spoke with me, I was given the impression that you were not . . ."

"No one wishes to claim the *Themis*, it appears. I fear, at times, that we shall spend the war sailing about with neither orders nor purpose, shunted from one admiral to another, turned away from port after port." Hayden had meant this in jest, but his words silenced the gathering and distress surfaced in every face—every face but Ransome's.

The new lieutenant actually brightened with pleasure. "Well, if we are without orders, I suppose we might consider ourselves to be privateers—in all but name." He rubbed his hands together comically. "Think of the prizes that await us."

This made the others laugh, and a toast was drunk to becoming privateers.

The gathering broke up soon after, but before he took himself back to shore, Hayden wanted to have a word, privately, with some of his officers, beginning with his senior lieutenant.

"It is true, sir, what you said." Archer appeared a bit dismayed. "Lord Hood doesn't seem to have duties for us, even though, I am informed, he has written frequently to the admiralty requesting frigates. I was ordered to anchor here and offer support—to whom was never made clear."

Hayden felt as though he were falling, his stomach ballooning up. The Mediterranean was a massive theater; surely, Hood had employment for any number of frigates. To leave the *Themis* adrift seemed more than peculiar.

"What is in the mind of Lord Hood, I cannot tell," Hayden responded. "But surely he will have some duty for us shortly. He must."

Archer did not appear convinced, but nodded rather hopelessly.

The last officer to be spoken with was the doctor. Though the Mediterranean sun had darkened his flour-pale complexion, Griffiths still appeared frail and unwell. Hayden worried that the doctor had gone back to his duties too soon but had not yet recovered enough to execute them. Enquiries after his health Griffiths brushed aside, claiming that he recovered apace and that Hayden need not concern himself. But Hayden was concerned, and resolved to have a word with Ariss about the doctor at first opportunity.

The medical condition of the crew Griffiths reported as good. Almost everyone had made a full recovery from the influenza, and apart from a mild bowel disorder that had passed through the crew the week previous, the men were hale. He did, however, have more to say about one man, and this was not of a medical nature. "He has shown a distinct interest in our recent prizes and the amount of prize money we might realise from them," Griffiths reported, speaking of their new lieutenant. "We learned that Hood had been trying to place him in a frigate for some months, believing that this would be a great boon to his education as an officer, but he has always managed to make some excuse or argument that spared him this fate. Likewise, he was not in favour of joining the *Themis* . . . until he learned of our recent prizes. It appears that our new lieutenant has a passion for money that is barely controlled and poorly disguised. His family was attempting to marry him to a suitable fortune in London this past year, but apparently this was being effectuated rather too obviously and the suitable fortunes withdrew. Avarice, of course, is hardly uncommon, but I came to my senses in this matter a day ago. Do you know the name Samuel Albert Ransome? No? Well, he was once an extraordinarily wealthy man, but an untimely investment in the South Seas Trading Company brought him to a complete and humiliating ruin. He died not long after, and it was widely suspected, though his family vigorously denied it, that it was by his own hand. Lieutenant Albert Ransome is this unfortunate man's grandson." The doctor shifted uncomfortably in his chair. "That is the first part of the story. Since arriving at Corsica but a day ago, he has been much engaged in a . . . certain enterprise in which he has embroiled a number of crew members. It seems that a rumour has been circulated among the men of the Army that a certain Captain Hayden, a brash and rather arrogant young officer, told the Navy that though *they* might not be capable of carrying guns to the hilltops, certainly *he* could do it. This rumour engendered no little resentment among the Army men, and was followed by a rash of wagering with some of the officers of this very ship. Lieutenant Ransome's confederate in this is none other than our sailing master—a previously reformed gamester. It seems that Ransome goes about lighting the flame of resentment among the Army men, and then Mr Barthe happens along sometime later pretending to be somewhat unworldly, and suggests a friendly wager. I am quite certain they have taken on gambling obligations beyond their ability to discharge, should your enterprise fail."

"Bloody fools!" Hayden spat out. "Clearly they had not been ashore and seen the countryside we struggle with before they began this lunacy. So, now my failure will see the ruin of Mrs Barthe and her lovely daughters? I shall roast Mr Barthe alive."

"Let us hope that none of these Army officers gain an understanding that they have been played for fools, for it will be Mr Barthe forced to walk out, and I do not think he will survive it. I note that Ransome has arranged matters so that it was not he who made the wagers, so Barthe will bear all responsibility for them."

"Perhaps it is Ransome I should roast alive. And this is the lieutenant Hood has sent me? For a brief moment I believed the admiral's acquaintance with my father disposed him to favour me." Hayden shook his head, as though to clear it of illusions. "Of all people, I should have known better."

As he was being rowed ashore, Hayden found his spirits noticeably lowered. He had imagined that, finally, a patron had been found in the service, and one very highly placed. And what had Hood done but saddle him with a scheming lieutenant out to make his fortune at any cost. Hayden himself was not unfamiliar with ambition and with a desire to improve one's material circumstances, but he would not stoop to duping soldiers to do it! If his task was not already difficult enough, now he had two of his senior officers breaking regulations. Ransome he did not care about—the man could pay the price for his folly—but Barthe had supported Hayden from almost the beginning, even under the tyrannical Hart. He did not want to see the man and his family ruined—again—and it frustrated him no end that he should be forced to discipline one of his most loyal supporters. But discipline the pair he must.

Yet in truth, the feeling that he had misunderstood Lord Hood's intentions unsettled him as much as Barthe's gambling. In some strange way he felt humiliated by this, and he could not make the feeling go away.

Seventeen

Four hours' sleep was all the hands were allowed, and Hayden even less. The blocks intended to haul the guns were of such size that a single man could not lift one. The ropes were of compatible diameter. To bear them, a large party of hands carried them over their shoulders, as though they had all been manacled in a line, and held fast to cables fashioned by giants.

The bosun and his crew were kept busy splicing rope and positioning the blocks.

"I'd not bet my pay that she'll pass through the block and make the turn, sir," Germain reported to Hayden. He sat upon a stone, fid in hand, working slack out of the drawing-splice. "I worked she down as much as I could, Captain. But look . . ." He pushed a section up a few inches with both hands, presenting it to Hayden. "She's like a pregnant constrictor snake, sir."

"If it will not pass, we will clap on a stopper, unmake it, pass it through, and make it again."

The bosun nodded, but did not look pleased at this prospect.

Up the slope above them, parties had begun clearing away the bush and moving away any rocks that could be pried up and shifted. That left any number of rocks too great to be moved, many larger than a ship's boat.

By sunrise the rope was ready to be carried up to the high block, which had been rigged to a massive stone by a strap. Men were sent up the slope until a hundred stood evenly spaced, and the rope was started at the bottom by a party that carried the end to the first man, then the second, and so on. When the end had reached the top, the men began to haul in concert, the bosun standing halfway up the slope with a speaking trumpet. "HEAVE!" he hollered. "HEAVE!"

Ten times the men heaved, and then they rested. Then ten more. Any place where the rope passed over a rough corner of stone the bosun's mates rigged a mat to reduce chafe.

The rope had to be fastened by one end at the top, run down the slope and through the block attached to the sledge, then up and through the top block. The fall streamed down the slope, and it was upon this that the men would haul.

The instant it grew light enough to walk without a torch, Hayden left this task to his lieutenant and bosun, and set out for the hillside where Wickham wrestled with his guns. He knew the quickest path now, and even his Corsican bodyguard hurried to keep up. Along the way he saw Moore and several companies of the 51st on a hillside, a scattering of red petals against the dusty green. Having studied the way the Corsicans moved so easily through the countryside, the colonel was accustoming his men to do the same. Hayden was certain he had never met with an officer so diligent and thorough.

As the eastern sky brightened, Hayden emerged at the top of the slope to find Wickham and his fellow lieutenant, not a hundred feet below, deep in conversation. With aching thighs absorbing each long step down, Hayden made his way to them, Wickham calling out and waving as he was perceived.

"It is as we thought, Captain Hayden," Wickham explained as Hayden reached them. "The slope is such that we cannot run the guns up a rope on a block. The rope will stretch too much to allow it." Wickham stared up at the jagged slope above. "The longest sheer legs that we can manage do not extend far enough to raise a gun lying at the cliff's base; it is too distant."

Hayden gazed at the cliff as well. "We will have to raise the guns as we do when unshipping them, Mr Wickham, rigged just so, then we will fasten a tackle to the ring, with the other end made fast to a convenient rock—there are enough about—and we will lift it little by little, taking up on the one and paying out the other." Hayden turned to the lieutenant. "Will that not answer?"

"It might be made to work, sir. I have never seen a gun raised so far in this manner, but I can't think of any reason it should not work, if everyone keeps their wits about them."

"Then let us keep our wits about us. Send the carriages up first. That will accustom everyone to their part without the weight. Do not allow the carriages to be dashed against the stone; we should lose much time bearing others up from the ships."

Hayden left them to carry up spars for sheer legs, and set off back the way he had come.

The rope had not formed its great N upon the slope when Hayden arrived, but had very nearly made a V, leaving only the fall yet to be run.

Hayden observed Lieutenant Colonel John Moore loitering about, speaking with some of the men, but when he saw Hayden he started immediately to intercept him. He seemed always rather sanguine, to Hayden—absorbed by preparations for the coming battle, but never apprehensive. From all that he had said, Hayden suspected his only fear was that he might commit some error of judgement that would cause a British loss or unnecessary deaths. If any man had been born to achieve the status of hero, it was John Moore.

Hayden harboured a similar fear—fear of failure, in Hayden's case—but the idea of his own death always whispered in his mind, and had to be suppressed actively lest it hinder him from performing his duties. At such times, Hayden's faithless stomach would choose to announce itself, sometimes protesting so stridently that others must hear. No small cause of embarrassment, especially upon the quarterdeck.

Moore waved a hand at Hayden as he approached, and the Navy man walked over to meet him, allowing them a degree of privacy.

"Your guns are ready to ascend, I see," Moore called.

"If Corsica will suffer them to do so," was Hayden's response. Until the guns were mounted upon the crest and trained down onto the Convention Redoubt, he would take nothing for granted.

"Corsica is as anxious to be rid of the French as are the Corsicans," Moore assured him. "She will allow it."

"For a country so eager to be rid of the French, she has been uncommonly froward, but perhaps we have had to prove ourselves worthy."

"Let us hope we do not *all* need to prove ourselves worthy," Moore replied. He glanced up at the gathering of Army officers, who appeared to be measuring the progress of the guns with uncommon interest. "I have been informed, Captain Hayden, that one of your officers"—he hesitated—"one of your officers has been speaking to men of the Army and giving you a bad character these last days."

"Ransome."

"You know of it, then? I cannot imagine what the man is thinking. No matter what has transpired between you—"

"Nothing has transpired between us. I only met the man for the first time last evening."

Moore looked confused. "Then this seems very odd. . . ."

"Have you also been informed that after Ransome has spoken to your officers, and created no little resentment toward this arrogant Navy captain who believes he can carry guns to the hilltops where the Army could not, a second man from my ship then happens along and induces your officers into wagering that I will fail—at odds, I am given to understand."

"So that is the explanation." Moore shook his head in near disbelief. "And this man, Ransome, goes about blasting your character for
his own profit!"

"Yes, and he is the lieutenant Lord Hood assigned to my ship after
we had left for Corsica."

Moore kicked a small pebble aside, still shaking his head, clearly
incredulous. "How do you intend dealing with this matter?"

"I have been uncertain, since first learning of it last night, but
now I have fixed upon a plan. Might I ask you the great favour of
attending a brief meeting with Ransome and his confederate in this
scheme?"

"Yes, certainly. And what, precisely, will be my part?"

"If you could stand by and look stern and disapproving, I believe
that will answer nicely."

Moore smiled. "I have understudied officers who mastered every
aspect of stern and disapproving. You may count on me in this
regard."

"Excellent. I shall send one of the hands off with a note asking that
these two gentlemen attend me ashore. Could you meet me in two
hours at the other guns?"

"I shall not be late."

A few moments later Hayden sent a man running off with a note,
then turned his attention to hauling the guns up to the crest. Over the
course of an hour his considerable anger over the gambling scheme
was subsumed in solving the problems that faced him, but once he had
set off to see to Wickham's guns and confront Ransome and Barthe,
he found his choler rising with every step.

He reached the slope where Wickham laboured over his two
eighteen-pounders and solitary mortar and found them preparing to
raise the second gun carriage. Barthe and Ransome were conversing
amiably with Wickham, when they spotted Hayden and Moore converging on them from slightly different angles but apparently about

to reach them simultaneously, or nearly so. Barthe looked a bit sheepish, which actually pleased Hayden a little. Ransome, however, hid all signs that he felt anything but utter ease.

Hayden greeted Wickham perfunctorily, promising to watch the raising of the carriage as soon as he had a word with Barthe and Ransome. Moore followed silently along, playing his part perfectly.

"Mr Ransome," Hayden began as soon as they were out of earshot of any other, "I am very disappointed to learn that you have been maligning my character among the officers of Colonel Moore's companies—"

"Sir—" Ransome immediately protested.

Hayden raised a hand to silence him. "I do not wish to ask Colonel Moore to produce the officers in question, but I have had your words liberally quoted to me and wish to hear them no more." Not allowing Ransome to respond, Hayden turned to Barthe, whose complexion had risen to match the colour of his hair. "And you, Mr Barthe, have been benefiting from the resentment caused by Mr Ransome to induce Colonel Moore's officers into wagering . . . *that I will fail in my attempt to raise guns to the hilltops!*"

"But Captain Hayden—" Ransome began to protest.

"It is true," Barthe interrupted, silencing Ransome, who blinked as though he had been struck and left staggering. "And I am heartily ashamed for my part in it . . . which I entered into of my own choosing. No one else bears any blame."

"I expect all moneys to be returned to Colonel Moore's officers by tomorrow afternoon, at the express orders of Colonel Moore and myself. All wagers are suspended." Hayden looked from one chastened man to the other. Barthe was clearly ashamed, just as he had said. Ransome, however, appeared merely chagrined, perhaps suppressing anger. But contrite he was not.

"After all your years in the service, Mr Barthe, you should certainly have known better. And you, Mr Ransome . . . how do you intend to punish members of the crew for gambling—a vice you are overly familiar with yourself?"

"I am certain the crew know nothing of it, sir," Ransome spoke up.

"And I am equally certain that you are even more naive than you are corrupt. Lord Hood assured me you were a promising young officer. What will he think, now?"

This finally appeared to drive home the seriousness of the offence—Lord Hood would learn of it, the very man upon whom he was dependent for his future in the Navy.

"You may both return to the *Themis* and collect the moneys to be returned. That is all."

Master and lieutenant slunk off down the slope, leaving Hayden and Moore gazing after them.

Moore nodded toward Ransome. "You had best watch that one," he pronounced quietly.

"Indeed. I cannot tell you how often I have seen cunning and foolishness commingled in the same character. The scheme was almost admirably sly, even if the outcome uncertain. But how does he now govern men when he has broken the law he is to enforce?"

"And to go about maligning his own commanding officer in the bargain . . . Such a blockhead should not be able to pass for lieutenant."

"I wonder if Lord Hood has any idea what kind of man he has sent me."

The two remained a moment more, then walked back to the men preparing to raise the gun carriage. The lieutenant in charge had seamen manning the tackle slung from the sheer legs positioned on the ridgetop. A second company manned the tackle fastened to the carriage's stern. The two companies had to both work together and oppose each other, the upper tackle raising the carriage, the lower pulling back enough to keep the carriage clear of the rocky bluff while at the same time paying out to allow the carriage to rise. It was a delicate dance and proceeded in jerky fashion, the lieutenant giving each party orders to haul or belay in turn. It was only by a helping of good fortune that the carriage managed to avoid disaster and alight at the top, where it was rolled clear by a dozen men hauling and pushing.

The young lieutenant did not look pleased by the effort, or was perhaps a little discomfited before Hayden and Moore. Hayden did not want to increase this embarrassment but was truly concerned that a gun raised in such a manner would suffer some damage, so decided he would step in.

"Handsomely done, Lieutenant," he offered. "Let us rest these men and put others in their places." Before the lieutenant could climb down from where he had perched himself, halfway up the rocky spine, Hayden ordered the men to fall out, and began pointing to men to take their places. The lieutenant had used well-formed young men for this task, but Hayden selected a preponderance of older seamen and a smaller number of strong youths. These old hands— man-of-war men—had slung guns aboard ships or lowered them into boats hundreds of times and would know their business.

The first eighteen-pounder had been rigged to raise, trussed up, ready to be slung from a single eye. It took a few moments for the hands to climb up to the base of the sheers, but once they had reached the top, Hayden called out, "Man the falls . . . ! Haul taut . . . ! Hoist away!" The gun shifted in place. "Walk!"

To the men on the tail-tackle Hayden cautioned, "Hold it taut. Now ease away slowly."

The experienced hands gauged just how quickly to ease their fall so that the gun went aloft but remained clear of the rocks. Hayden hardly said a word to them. As the gun rose higher, the pull on the tail-tackle increased, and Hayden ordered more hands to man the fall—an orderly row of strong men, feet planted and leaning back with all their weight. If the rope parted they would all be thrown in a heap, Hayden realised.

The gun went aloft in a slow, smooth arc, the four-sheave block creaking and the line bar-tight. The two spars forming the large inverted V of the sheer legs bent only just perceptibly. The sheer legs were also controlled by a purchase run back at a precise angle to a massive rock behind so that the sheers leaned out from the vertical.

Hayden moved a little up the slope to where he could gauge the gun's height more accurately. "High enough!" he called as the gun passed over the edge of the ridge.

"Ease the tail-tackle . . . More yet . . . Enough!" Hayden crossed a little to his right to be more easily heard. "Roll the carriage under her, if you please, Mr Wickham."

The gun carriage was positioned, shifted a little to one side using bars and brute strength.

"Lower away on the winding tackle!" Hayden ordered. The gun inched down as the men walked slowly forward, Mr Wickham motioning with a hand.

"Mr Wickham, I am going to ease away on the tail-tackle so that you can align the gun and carriage. Be wary, now."

"Aye, sir."

Hayden ordered the tail-tackle eased and the gun was steadied by several experienced hands, all of whom kept themselves out of danger as best they could.

"Mr Wickham, order those others to stand clear. They have no business there." Hayden did not like to see too many men crowded near the gun, which, if the rope parted, would fall and cause grievous injury. Best to give a small number of men involved room to jump clear.

"Avast lowering!" Wickham called suddenly. "My apologies, Captain," he called down to Hayden. "We have to shift the carriage but a little."

"Proceed, Mr Wickham. I shall allow you to give the order to ease away."

The carriage was quickly shifted again, the gun hanging but two feet above. Wickham ordered the fall eased, "Slowly, slowly," until it seated in the carriage. The acting lieutenant took off his hat and waved it as though an enemy ship had struck her colours. The men all cheered.

"Where are the bastards who claimed it could not be managed?" a man called out, to more cheering. Hayden wondered what the French would make of this.

"We've two more guns to raise," the lieutenant called.

"I will leave you to it, Lieutenant," Hayden said. "You seem to have it well in hand."

"Thank you, sir. Shall I rest these men and employ others in their place?"

"Rest them, certainly, but I would employ the same men. They appear to know their business."

"Aye, sir." The young officer took Hayden's point.

Moore intercepted Hayden and shook his hand, a great smile spreading over his handsome face. "Well done, Captain! You have saved uncounted British lives with that act alone."

" 'Alone' is not how it was achieved." Hayden waved his hand to encompass all the sailors. "These men have put both hearts and backs into it, Colonel. No few have sustained hurts, both great and small."

"And my own men owe them a debt of thanks that I shall endeav-our to make clear to them. We shall demonstrate our gratitude by performing our part—driving the French from their batteries and redoubts."

The walk back to his company seemed, somehow, easier, the ex-haustion Hayden suffered, if not lifted, surprisingly diminished. What would Kochler have to say, now? Hayden wondered. His zeal to raise guns to the second battery was renewed.

As he descended to the floor of the narrow valley, Hayden was met by a party of Corsicans, all under arms, of course, and a few mounted on mules. It was among the latter that Hayden found, to his surprise, General Paoli, smiling at him in a manner both charm-ing and amiable.

"Captain Hayden," he called out, "we heard a great British 'Huz-zah!' which I hope indicates you have succeeded in bearing a gun up to the hilltop?"

"It signified that precise event, General," Hayden reported, hap-pily. "We now have an eighteen-pounder staring down at the French in their redoubt, which I believe will give them pause to reflect upon their continued presence on your beautiful island."

Paoli laughed. "Never for a moment did the French think this feat might be accomplished, and I must tell you, Captain, that my own people were of the same opinion. 'Never underestimate the English.' I have said it many times and shall certainly have cause to repeat it again. Nobly done, Captain. Nobly done!"

The old Corsican's bodyguard parted before Hayden, creating a small channel to the general. Paoli beamed down at him.

"Do not let me keep you from your duties, Captain Hayden. But if you have no objections, I shall observe your method of accom-plishing this, for in Corsica we have many hills, and one never can know when a gun might need to be so raised again. Perhaps later we might share a meal, or at least some wine?"

Hayden agreed that this would be most welcome, and carried on his way. Pleasing the old general, he realised, was more gratifying than he had foreseen. There was, about Paoli, some air or presence that made one wish to do this. Captain Bourne, one of Hayden's former commanders, had been the same. Men threw themselves into the most dangerous situations hoping to gain his notice and approba-tion. And yet, how either man accomplished this, Hayden could not say.

When he came within sight of his own party, Hayden observed a large gathering of Army men just below the crest. From this outlook they surveyed the progress of the guns and spoke among themselves.

Immediately Hayden wondered if these were some of the men Barthe and Ransome had beguiled into wagering against them, and among whom Ransome had been attempting to lower his reputation for no reason but personal gain, a thought that vexed Hayden more than a little. He attempted to put this aside to focus his mind on the task required but found his thoughts straying back to Ransome at odd moments, and he would be piqued yet again. The day wore on, unseasonably warm, only a simple breeze from the sou'west—hardly enough to stir a sailor's desire.

Clearing a path up the slope proved a more arduous enterprise than any expected, and devoured all of the forenoon and some hours of the afternoon as well. Hayden spent the time clambering up and down the slope until his legs ached, overseeing the efforts of the men who laboured among the massive blocks.

Although Wickham and the lieutenant had proven that guns could be raised in the manner Hayden intended, the slope here was both notably steeper and more rugged. The height was also greater. Whether it could be managed was unknown, and would remain so for some time.

A more reasonable man might have drawn one of the gun carriages up first, or the howitzer, as a trial, but Hayden reasoned that if they could not carry eighteen-pounders to the crest, there would be no use for carriages or even the howitzer. For this reason, it was his intention to make the experiment with one of the great guns.

"In for a pence, in for a pound," Jinks responded when Hayden explained his reasoning to him, but it was four thousand pounds that concerned Hayden.

On one of his several ascents to the crest that day, Hayden found Moore awaiting him, his entire manner apparently approving of all the sailors' efforts.

"I see a gun lying trussed up and ready to ascend to the heights," Moore observed.

"It is ready, but are we?"

"There is no doubt on that account, Hayden."

The two officers walked the short distance to the place where the engineers prepared the batteries, and stared down at the French below. Hayden was certain that Moore hoped above all things that there would soon be guns upon this very spot, for the effectiveness of the more distant battery was still somewhat in doubt, and it likely would not reach the batteries surrounding the tower above Fornali Bay. Guns upon this spot, however, would be devastating to all of the French positions.

The two frigates lying in the tiny bay between the tower of Fornali and the Convention Redoubt drew Hayden's attention, and not for the first time.

"I have noted, Captain, that the French ships weigh upon your thoughts," Moore observed.

"Yes. I fear they shall be scuttled or burned when the works are carried."

"Better that than they escape," Moore ventured.

"Indeed. But we have need of frigates here in the Mediterranean almost more than anywhere that I can conceive."

"Can they be taken?" Moore asked. He had raised his telescope and directed its glass eye toward the two ships.

"Not easily. They've rigged boarding nets all around, and have no doubt loaded every gun with grape. We would have to cut them out by night. Preferably at the exact moment the works were being carried. I don't think the French will burn such valuable ships until it is apparent they have no choice."

Moore lowered his glass, his countenance pensive. "Has Lord Hood indicated his thoughts on this matter?"

"He has not. I am considering making application to him to allow my crew to attempt to cut them out."

"It seems an excellent enterprise, to my mind."

When Moore and Hayden returned to the place where the blocks were strapped to the rocks, the hands were already bearing the rope

back down to the base. Calling out the names of two of the *Themis'*
men, Hayden sent one down the hill to fetch a glass and then stationed them to watch the French frigates.

"I am most interested to know if either ship has a full muster," he
told the men, "or if they are making preparations to fire the ships.
Keep the closest possible watch—turn about."

As the men were delighted to be spared the brutal toil of raising
guns, Hayden was certain they would not take their eyes from the
enemy ships, lest they be sent back to the ropes.

Hayden then turned to Moore. "The moment of truth," he announced. "Or perhaps I should say 'the several hours of truth.'" He
looked up at the sun. Daylight appeared to be flying with even greater
than usual haste.

"It will be done, Hayden, I have no doubt of it." Moore's face
turned suddenly serious. "I do have one small wager over this matter.
If you bear the eighteen-pounders to the crest, Major Kochler must
seek your forgiveness for his unacceptable treatment of you and
amend his views of the Navy in the future."

"And if I fail in this task?"

"Well, he can hardly treat you worse."

Hayden laughed. "I shall not disagree with you there."

On his way down the slope, Hayden stopped to speak with the
men who manned the great rope, being certain they were able to
continue and seeing to their need for food and water. The day was
warm without being hot, but the task was arduous and lack of water,
even on this mild day, would soon tell.

The sun rode low over the western hills, casting its thin winter
light down upon the blue sea and dusty-green island. An hour would
bring twilight. Hayden had torches and lanterns made ready.

He saw to the eighteen-pounder himself, to be certain it would
not shift on its bed. Satisfied, he turned to Jinks. "You may give the
order to begin."

"Aye, sir. Man the falls!" he called loudly. "Haul taut!" A slight tug on the sledge bearing the gun shifted it into line. "Hoist away! Walk!"

The rope seemed to stretch for an impossible length of time. After several long moments, the rope growing ever tauter, the sledge stirred, scraped forward a little, hesitated, then began the slow, burdensome climb toward the crest. Hayden climbed up beside the sledge, guiding it with a Samson bar. Despite the manifest dangers of this enterprise, hanging back at such a moment would earn him the scorn of the hands. His time with Captain Bourne had taught him that officers need always brave the worst dangers faced by their crews to maintain respect. He did not always do it without trepidation, or even foreboding, but he always forced himself to step forward.

The doubly heavy gun caused the sledge to snag and lodge upon the smallest edge, and the men with the bars were constantly active to keep it from stopping altogether. Knowledge that any stoppage might be the cause of the rope parting galvanised them into prompt action.

The first impediment appeared, and Hayden called out, "Mr Jinks! We shall call a halt in but five yards."

"Aye, sir!"

A long, steep-sided rock greater than a yard in height stood in the way. All progress was brought to a halt while Hayden examined the ground all around.

"Lieutenant!" Hayden called. "I believe we can shift the sledge to larboard and get round."

Two balks of timber were laid athwart the slope, wedged in place by heavy stones.

"They must stand the weight of an eighteen-pounder," Hayden instructed the hands. "They cannot shift."

Pry bars and levers were then employed to shift the gun sideways, an inch at a time, until the sledge rested on the two timbers, which were spaced perhaps six feet apart. These were quickly greased. Taking up his bar, Hayden dug it in beneath the heavy runner. "One and two and three and *heave!* Again!"

The sledge lurched to the side but two inches. And then two more. Hayden was soon dripping with sweat and handed his bar to another while he removed both jacket and waistcoat. Taking back his bar, he drove it into the unforgiving ground just beneath the runner, pressing his shoulder against the top, the sledge relenting and sliding less than an inch.

"That will do," Hayden announced. "Lieutenant! Commence hauling!"

"Aye, sir!" the lieutenant called up. "Man the falls!"

The sledge reverted to scraping and grating up the rocky slope. The heavy runners—two timbers with their bows shaped to an upward angle—left shavings and chips of rust-coloured wood in their wake. The ancient rock was surprisingly sharp, almost serrated, and tore away at feet and hands so that all the men bore small wounds. "Medals," they called them, and went in search of the most decorated man—the least decorated excoriated for not toiling sufficiently and being unwilling to bleed for his country.

A man with a bucket caught them up and Hayden thankfully took the dipper, pouring warmish water down his throat. At that precise instant the sledge slid back and a hissing slash knifed the air. The rope went scything and coiling up the slope, making the most horrifying noise. The men manning the falls threw themselves down, but he heard screams among them. Five feet the sledge grated, then came to an abrupt halt against a stone, the gun straining at its bonds. Hayden dropped the dipper and began clambering up the slope as quickly as his tired legs and arms could bear him.

To his relief he saw Jinks emerging from behind a rock, hatless and dishevelled, but otherwise, apparently, whole.

"Are you injured, Mr Jinks?"

"No, sir, but it near took my head off even as I threw myself down. My hat is gone . . . I know not where." It was then that the moans of the injured men penetrated Jinks' consciousness. He turned quickly up the slope, and then back toward Hayden in distress and alarm. As Hayden reached him the two scrambled up the slope side by side.

He could hear men calling out that they would need a surgeon.

Three men lay in the rubble of the Corsican hillside, one gashed open across his right abdomen. A second bore an ugly purple welt, as wide as a man's arm, across his chest and biceps. Both were in terrible pain and making no secret of it. A third man had been struck on the temple and lay still as stone, though breathing shallowly.

"Mr Jinks," Hayden said, his wits returning. "Climb down and secure the gun. Send a man to the beach to bring a surgeon. We shall make up litters to bear these men away."

"*Captain Hayden!*" came a distant voice.

Hayden turned to find Kochler, and some of the other officers who had been observing the gun's progress, making their way with all speed toward them across the steep slope. "We have sent for our surgeon, who shall hasten to this place with all speed."

Moore was also making his way down the slope toward them.

"Mr Jinks . . ." Hayden prompted softly.

"Aye, sir. Shall I send for the surgeon yet?"

"No. But we will require litters, all the same."

Kochler arrived before Moore, in his wake a few junior officers. For a moment Kochler stood catching his breath, gazing at the fallen men. "Our surgeon shall not take twenty minutes, I am certain." He turned his attention to Hayden. "I am sorry, Hayden. It is the worst luck. But our surgeon is a cunning hand. He shall soon put them to rights. See if he doesn't."

It was the longest quarter of an hour Hayden could recall. The hands tried, with a shirt, to staunch the bleeding of the man who was gashed, but the cotton was soon crimson with blood and the man kept passing from consciousness. Each time his fellows thought he had died, but he would then come around and recommence moaning, faintly.

Finally the surgeon appeared across the slope, leading a small party of men bearing litters. He was soon bending over the wounded, speaking to them in a soft, reassuring voice. Hayden thought him overly young for his position, but he was well made and confident, moving about the rugged slope with a grace that few exhibited. A dressing was soon applied to the bleeding wound, which appeared to be oozing less by the moment, and the three men shifted gently into litters. With difficulty, they were borne across the slope and up. Hayden was not surprised to see Moore lending a hand whenever needed, and taking the greatest care with the wounded, but to see Kochler step in to bear the litters over rough patches was more than unexpected.

Daylight was rapidly slipping away, and Hayden propelled himself down the slope to the waiting bosun. The man was running his fid into one coil of the cable, and muttering a stream of black invective.

"It has a rotten heart, Captain Hayden," Germain stated, prising the stained hemp apart, revealing the black interior. "Just the one strand. How it lasted as it did, I cannot say."

"It is a wonder," Hayden agreed.

"This here's the end of it. Then she's sound as stone, sir." He looked back along the length of the rope to where two seamen stood holding a section up. " 'Bout seven fathoms, Captain Hayden, sir. I've more than half a cable in reserve, so t'would be simple enough to cut this out and splice in a length. Take a little time, I fear."

"It cannot be helped. Let us make up the splices with all speed." Hayden turned around, looking for the lieutenant, and found him down by the gun. "Mr Jinks. We shall splice in some new rope. Find three able seamen and examine this cable from one end to the other. Lay it open, for this was rotten within and showed no signs of it."

"Aye, Captain. There are some cracked planks in the sledge, sir, but I think it will hold until the top."

"I shall climb down and see for myself."

Indeed, there were cracked planks—three of them—but Hayden agreed with Jinks that the sledge would likely hold together until a repair could be effected. Hayden tried not to let his frustration overwhelm him. They had been a few hours from having both eighteen-pounders on the crest! At least the rope had been rotten and had not broken undamaged—that would have been a setback they might never have overcome. There was no question that the cable should have been strong enough to bear the gun's weight, but the extreme slope and the added friction of the coarse stone was greater than forty hundredweight, Hayden believed.

Before the splices were made, the sun settled into the west, leaving an opalescent sky. Jinks picked his way down the slope toward Hayden. "The cable is sound, sir, but for that one section. Here and there, strands have chaffed through, but not so many as to weaken it overly."

"Let us hope that is true. If the rot were greater we should have to send for more cable. I do not like to do this work by dark; it is dangerous for our people, but we have little choice, now."

Twilight waned rapidly, light draining away into the west. All around, the faces of sailors appeared pale, almost haunted, in the failing light. The men were done in.

We are so close, Hayden thought. The work of but a few more hours.

He almost did not want to ask it of them but knew they would jump to the ropes without hesitation when the order was given. They would raise the guns to the hilltop if they had to bear them on their backs, he was sure.

The new section of rope was run through the block on the sledge and then spliced into the existing cable. There was no one more adept at this craft than sailors, but even so, it was not the work of a moment, and the failing light did not help. Torches were lit, but there was that odd, brief period, when the sunlight faded and yet the torchlight appeared utterly inadequate. Somehow, the eye adjusted to it as the night grew darker, and the torchlight seemed almost to grow brighter.

Splices were made, the cable drawn taut.

"Haul away, Mr Jinks!" Hayden called from his place beside the great gun.

The sledge jostled a little as the rope went taut, slid forward an inch, hesitated, then began jarring and jolting up the slope, pitching up or down as it teetered over some rock. Hayden dug his pry bar into the hard ground and diverted the sledge a little to starboard. Two men with torches scrambled along beside, trying to keep light on both sledge and ground, while not setting Corsica afire. The sledge would catch on an edge, and Hayden and the man opposite would pry the bow up, hurrying lest the rope stretch too much. For a foot, the sledge would surge forward, then settle back to grating over stone, as though the gun were some massive black grub inching its way upward.

Halfway up the slope they found a place where the sledge could be wedged in place so that the men hauling might have a short respite. Hands on knees, Hayden bent over to catch his breath, not from the speed of their ascent but from the steepness of the slope. Life aboard ship did not build stamina for such work.

When the men had all drunk their fill from hands bearing buckets and dippers, Hayden called to Jinks to continue. The half-blind sledge went forward—the men with torches appearing to guide it, casting their smudge of light upon the shattered landscape.

The crest appeared, as unexpected as a silent whale rising out of the oily, darkened sea. Hayden called down the slope to Jinks, then collapsed on the gun, drawing in deep drafts of warm Mediterranean air. The smell of the sea reached them, here, and Hayden felt a sudden longing to be on a ship and done with this war on land, for which he had neither training nor inclination.

"I do hope Kochler apologises while I am present," a voice said, and Hayden turned to find a beaming Moore, hands on hips, gazing down at him.

"I find I do not much care about apologies, Colonel. To have managed this thing seems reward enough, at this moment." And indeed it did. Despite his physical exhaustion, Hayden felt a great sense of elation, as though rising to the hilltop had been only the first step and now he was floating higher.

"I offer you my congratulations, Captain!" Jinks said, as he came puffing over the rise.

"And I you, Mr Jinks. It is not every day that one manages the impossible, but so we were informed this task was." Hayden patted the gun with an open hand. "Yet, here is one of Mr Blomefield's eighteen-pounders, upon a mountaintop where it has no business at all." He waved a hand down the slope. "All of these men have much of which to be proud."

"No more than you, sir." Jinks nodded to Moore. "Colonel."

"The men may rest before they carry the rope back down the hill, Mr Jinks, and then we will tackle the second eighteen. All done before midnight, and tomorrow, once the carriages and howitzer have been raised, the men may take their rest or disport themselves as they choose."

"Aye, sir."

A fathom of the rope used to haul the guns, Hayden estimated, weighed five or six stone—dry—and a cable length consisted of one hundred fathoms, more or less. Several cables had been long-spliced together to make the whole, so the weight was very great. Upon this rugged ground a man per fathom of cable was required to move it with any speed, and Hayden hadn't enough, even after he had pressed Corsican militiamen into service; but even so, he was not going to ask aid from the Army. Kochler and many others had been so disdainful of this attempt that Hayden was damned if he would allow the Army to take any part of the credit for the success.

Instead he forced himself up and took hold of a section of cable himself. Every seaman who could walk joined in the work and, though exhausted from their efforts, dragged a fathom of the cable back down to the base of the hill.

The final eighteen-pounder seemed to have doubled its weight. Hayden could hear the men talking as they paused for a break partway to the top.

"I believe someone lied about the tonnage of this gun," one man suggested.

"Falsified the customs certificate, that's sure."

Darkness slowed the ascent and made finding solid footing awkward and difficult. For the men guiding the sledge—and Hayden was one—torchlight did not reveal the sharp edges, the grabbing roots.

Midnight passed before the gun reached the hilltop, and once the halt was called, men collapsed where they stood, too exhausted to even cheer, their faces vacant and shadowed. No one offered congratulations or even muttered thanks; they simply toppled to one side, where they sat and fell into a stupor.

"Sir . . ." Jinks managed after a moment.

Hayden had thumped down on the edge of the wooden sledge, his back against the gun.

"I fear it will soon grow cool, and the men . . . they have no shelter here."

"I will not order them to rise, Mr Jinks; they are fatigued beyond measure. Let them lay out this night. Snow could fall, I think, and they would not be sensible of it. Let us hope they come to no harm."

Hayden felt himself sliding down the rugged slope toward sleep.

"If I may, sir," a voice said quietly, and Hayden opened his eyes to see a figure bent over him. He thought he felt a light weight settle over his body, and realised a rough blanket covered him. He could see torches down the slope where the hands who hauled the guns had fallen upon the unyielding ground. In the faint light, men moved among them, as priests went among the fallen after a battle.

"They've brought us blankets, Captain Hayden," Jinks said, his voice coming from some great distance.

"Who . . . ?"

"The soldiers, sir."

"Wherever did they find them?" Hayden asked, but he fell back into dream before anyone answered.

Eighteen

A league distant, the island appeared verdant, almost lush, but from the deck of the *Themis*, anchored a cable-length from the beach, Corsica appeared a dull grey-green. This was the result of the low branches of the underwood being a woody grey and largely unconcealed by leaves, which, at a distance, had the curious effect of dulling the green, as though the eye mixed the two colours into one.

Upon the nearby hilltops, the batteries kept up an incessant firing upon the French positions below, bombarding them with both shot and exploding shells. Hayden was only a little cheered by the idea that the French were hiding in holes while their earthworks were blasted apart around them. In truth, he was yet too fatigued to take the least pleasure from his accomplishment, as though it had been managed by some others or perhaps completed decades previous.

He gazed, for a moment, down into the perfectly clear waters, which, from any distance, appeared to be the most vibrant azure. He could see the sandy bottom, and here and there misshapen, flattish rocks, like dark shadows on the seafloor. The day, still warm, was very nearly windless, the sea and sky as unblemished as a sudden understanding.

"*On deck!*" came the call from aloft. "*Boat approaching.*"

Many boats came and went, among ships and between the anchored fleet and the shore, but this one appeared to be making its way directly toward the *Themis*—and it was not, Hayden noted, one of their boats. In the stern he could see a midshipman seated by the coxswain, and near to him, some other in a coat of indistinct colour—perhaps green.

Hayden was about to call for his glass when Wickham appeared at his side and, after barely a second's perusal, announced, "Sir Gilbert!"

"Mr Barthe?" Hayden called to the sailing master, who was bent over a small table with his mate.

Barthe straightened, a look of slight confusion on his face. "Sir?"

"Can you make out the occupants of this cutter?"

Barthe crossed the deck to stand at the rail by Hayden, only slightly frustrated to be interrupted during his instruction. "I cannot."

"I am pleased to hear it," Hayden replied.

"Sir?"

"Nor can I make the man out, but Mr Wickham, here, tells me it is Sir Gilbert, a truth I can only discern with a glass. But I'm pleased to hear you cannot make him out, either. My eyes are not failing."

"Pleased to be of service." Barthe hovered, as though about to turn away.

"Carry on, Mr Barthe."

"Thank you, sir."

A few moments later, Sir Gilbert came puffing over the rail, a smile spread over his pleasant face.

"Captain Hayden! I have just been to see the places where you hauled the guns up to the hilltops and had the whole manner of it described to me. Well done, sir! May I offer my congratulations! How General Dundas must grind his teeth to see those guns firing down upon the French—*when he said it could never be done!* But it was done, sir, and not by the Army, neither."

Hayden could not help but be gladdened by the ardour of Sir Gilbert's praise and excitement.

"Colonel Moore tells me that he believes Dundas will give him the order to attack the French positions the day after tomorrow." He began patting his pockets. "Which brings to mind . . . Ah!" He produced three letters, examined the addressees, returned one to his pocket, and handed the others to Hayden.

The hand that addressed the first was known to him. The second, from Admiral Lord Hood.

"Go on! Go on! I am certain you are all in a lather to see what the admiral has written you."

Hayden did not require further encouragement, and broke the seal.

Sir Gilbert watched his face with great attention and anticipation. When Hayden folded the letter without a word, Sir Gilbert laughed pleasantly.

"You needn't be so secretive, Captain; Lord Hood explained his plans to me. You are to go after the French frigates?"

"Indeed. You are singularly well-informed."

Sir Gilbert waved this away with a hand. "I am the representative of His Majesty's government in these waters. Lord Hood confides all to me. And I repay him by repeating nothing, Captain. Can you take a ship into that little bay?"

"No. The batteries would destroy it. We will have to cut the frigates out by night, boarding them from ship's boats. It must be done in concert with the assault on the French positions. If we were to attack before, the French soldiers might come to their aid. If we attack after, the French sailors might fire their ships."

"They would not try to sail them out under cover of darkness?"

"Lord Hood has set a very close watch on them by night, and our frigates would soon have them in a corner in this small bay. The great concern is that the French will either fire or scuttle them before they can be taken. And certainly they must have all their preparations made, given the cannonade raining down on the French batteries."

"The French cannot help but be sensible of their position, here," Sir Gilbert agreed. "Once the batteries were opened on the hilltops, they must have realised the redoubt could not be held." Sir Gilbert looked around the deck of the ship and at the anchored fleet. "A very thankful Madame Bourdage and her lovely daughter took ship for Gibraltar these two days past, where they will go on to England. When you have occasion to return home, I am certain you shall be the beneficiary of such an outpouring of gratitude from these ladies as will make you blush with pleasure. It is only unfortunate that you could not claim all the evacuees as your relations."

"Few families are so large. Would you care for a refreshment, Sir Gilbert? Coffee, perhaps?"

"I should like nothing better."

Hayden was anxious to open his second letter, which was from Henrietta, but schooled his emotions and played a passable host to Sir Gilbert Elliot. Without being indiscreet, Sir Gilbert had a propensity for gossip, and given his circle of acquaintance, this made for fascinating conversation. He not only moved in the highest political circles in England, but was intimate with many of the great thinkers and influential personages. Both the king and the Prince of Wales were known to him, as well as Burke and Fox and a host of others. The First Secretary of the Navy, Philip Stephens, was also a familiar personage.

"You might find yourself addressing him as Sir Philip when next you see home," Sir Gilbert informed him. "I have it on good authority that his knighthood is in the offing. And well deserved it is, too."

The moment Sir Gilbert settled himself in the waiting boat, Hayden hurried back down to his cabin and broke the seal on his letter from Henrietta.

My Dear Captain Hayden:

I began this letter by writing, My Dear Charles, as though we, like Robert and Elizabeth, were cousins, or upon Christian names from childhood. I do not know, quite, what tone in which I am permitted to write, but your last dear letter to me was couched in terms of such unre-

strained affection and warmheartedness that it has emboldened me and made me dare to reply in kind, hoping all the while that I do not presume too much.

I have missed you terribly and you are very often in my thoughts. Women who have sons, husbands, or cousins engaged in this terrible war must always be anxious. How they must all watch the post, fearing that single, fateful letter, yet exalting when that sweetest of missives comes from whatever distant theater, saying that their loved one is well, unharmed, in good health and spirits. You cannot think what this means, and how these poor women then have cause to weep from both worry and relief. And then, but a few hours later, return again to their anxious vigil.

I should not fret so much if you were but a bit more fearful. It was not difficult to read between the lines of your letters telling all that occurred on your convoy, and Elizabeth could not help but confirm my beliefs, as much as she wished not to. It was not quite the routine convoy you described it as.

England remains much as you left it, but for an unseasonably cold winter and very coy spring. Among our little circle, Robert remains perfectly pleased with his new command, and hopes for some action to equal your own. My dear Elizabeth is, as always, busy and content, and would be transported entirely to have her dear husband home. I have but recently returned from Plymouth and can report that Lady Hertle continues to amaze all with her vigor, though I have become aware that the cold winter is hurting her poor joints and she is at great pains to hide this when walking or pursuing needlework, which she has almost abandoned these last weeks.

My own family continue to prosper, and I do hope you shall have occasion to meet them when next you return.

As for myself, I am at my family home along with three of my sisters. The days are much taken up with walking, playing various instruments, reading aloud (my family detests cards), writing almost daily missives to my dearest you, working on the secret novel, and indulging in equally secret pining. Oh, how I hope you will return home before the spring!

I am called away. My father is duplicating the investigations of Mr Newton. I cannot tell you why. It is his latest hobbyhorse and I am his dutiful assistant. Today we have somewhat to do with prisms.

I do pray this finds you in perfect health, content, and anchored safely in some unassailable harbour.

Your captive heart,
Henri

The evacuation from Toulon had few beneficial effects upon the British fleet, but for the number of ship's boats that had been required—confiscated from the French. This surplus of cutters, barges, and gigs allowed Hayden to replace all the boats he had lost in the same harbour.

"Mr Chettle, we will swing the boats aboard and paint them all black—both inside and out."

The angular carpenter might have been trying to hide his disapproval of this order, but he was not entirely successful. "*Black*, sir?"

"Yes. As black as we can make them. Will that be a problem, Mr Chettle?"

"No, sir. I have all the lampblack we should want, sir." He appeared at a loss for words. "It is just . . . uncommon, Captain."

"It will all become clear. Four blackened boats . . . by tomorrow, if you please, Mr Chettle."

"Aye, sir."

"Oh, and the sweeps as well, Mr Chettle."

"Of course, sir."

"Mr Barthe?"

The sailing master came hurrying along the deck with his characteristic waddle.

"Captain?"

"I think it best that our painting not be visible to anyone ashore. Perhaps some drying sails can be arranged to hide Mr Chettle's efforts, if you please?"

The sailing master appeared as confused by the order as Chettle had been, but answered quickly. "Aye, sir. I shall arrange for a few sails to take the air."

"Thank you, Mr Barthe."

Hayden called his officers together, and when they had gathered in his cabin, all silently expectant, Hayden began. "Lord Hood has ordered us to cut out the frigates anchored beneath the batteries in Fornali Bay. I am to get sufficient men from the *Foxhound* to take one ship; our crew will take the other. The attack must be co-ordinated with the Army's assault upon the French fortifications."

"That will explain why poor Chettle is shaking his head as his crew paints the boats black." Wickham was smiling, but whether at Chettle's consternation or at the prospect of action, Hayden could not tell.

Hayden looked at the faces of his officers. "Mr Barthe," he said. "It is apparent by your countenance that you disapprove of this plan, I suspect, heartily."

"Captain, you know as well as I do that the ships will be set afire or scuttled the instant the assault begins upon the redoubt. They'll not let those ships fall into British hands if there is any way at all that it can be prevented."

"I agree entirely, Mr Barthe, but the attempt must be made, and if we can surprise the French crews, I believe we have at least a chance of capturing one, if not both, ships. After all, they will hardly set fire to a ship they are still aboard, will they? If we can engage them and prevent them from abandoning their vessel, we might carry it. We just might."

"I am quite certain we can manage it, sir," Wickham interjected. "If we can come upon them by stealth, sir, so that we are climbing aboard before they are aware of us, it can be managed."

"Are they fully crewed, Captain?" Hawthorne asked.

This was the question Hayden had been asking himself, without a certain answer.

"I set two men to watching them from the hilltop as we raised the guns, and it was their opinion that the ships were not fully crewed. Sailor's uniforms could be seen among the men establishing the works, so I suspect that neither ship possesses a full muster. The captains will not want to find themselves in the situation of having to suddenly disembark two hundred men so that the ship can be fired. No, they will have only a few men aboard. My lookouts thought there might have been as few as sixty souls—no more than eighty.

"Mr Archer, I will leave you in charge of the *Themis*. And before you ask, your request is denied; the senior lieutenant will stay with the ship. Have you been on a cutting-out expedition, Mr Ransome?"

The new lieutenant stirred from thought. "I have not, sir."

"I shall send Mr Hawthorne in your boat; he is a deft hand at such things."

Hawthorne broke into a grin.

"Mr Wickham and Mr Madison will each have command of a cutter. I will command the barge. Mr Wickham, take a seaman with good eyes and station yourself on the hilltop near the number-one battery, if you please. You will observe the French frigates. If their crews suddenly return or their numbers change appreciably, inform me immediately. I will visit the battery tomorrow afternoon to assess the situation for myself.

"I should like to take eighty men in the boats. A cutlass and brace of pistols for each man with shot and powder in proportion. Each boat will carry axes and pikes as well. It is my intention to approach by stealth, cut the boarding nets on the larboard quarter, kill or render senseless the sentry, then board in silence. If we are discovered we shall cut away the boarding nets with axes and get as many men over the side as we can. It will be hot work, I should think.

"Mr Hawthorne, I shall want half your marines with muskets and bayonets, the company divided between the first two boats. There will almost certainly be moonlight, so the hands should wear blue jackets. As my boat shall be the first to approach, I will make a list of the men I want and let you make the arrangements, Mr Archer."

"Aye, sir." Archer attempted to hide his disappointment at being left aboard, and Hayden was pleased to see he was managing nicely.

"Upon concluding here, I will visit General Dundas and learn his intentions. I will speak with Colonel Moore, then pay my respects to Captain Winter of the *Foxhound*." Hayden realised that he felt a great sense of elation at the prospect of action that did not involve dragging heavy guns over hostile countryside. "The armorer should examine the flint of every pistol and replace any that are not perfectly satisfactory. Is there anything that anyone wishes to suggest at this moment?"

The officers all glanced one to the other.

"We might blacken the men's faces, Captain," Wickham offered, "in deference to the moonlight, sir."

"Yes. Mr Ransome, ask Mr Chettle for some cork to burn." Hayden realised Ransome had been very keen to earn prize money. "I might remind everyone that even if we do take a frigate we are under the orders of Lord Hood, who will receive a share, and all the ships present will also receive shares for both officers and crew. I fear no carriages will be purchased with the small moneys we receive."

Smiles and laughter told Hayden that everyone was excited, if not a little anxious, at this enterprise.

"Mr Archer, any man who must go ashore should be strongly cautioned to say nothing of our intentions. Even General Paoli advised me that the French still have their supporters among his people. Best they not learn of our plans." He looked around at the gathered faces, the barely contained eagerness of the middies, Mr Barthe's knowing resolve. The sailing master had served long enough in His

Majesty's Navy to see many a man lost on just such an enterprise. He understood the terrible luck of it all. But he would not shirk or shy— Hayden knew.

"Mr Barthe," Hayden said on impulse, "I will ask you to stay with the ship. Mr Archer will need a sailing master should anything un- toward befall me."

"But, sir . . ."

Hayden raised a hand and Barthe's protest died in his throat, a look of disappointment and frustration overspreading his face.

When the cabin was empty, Hayden found himself taking out Henrietta's letters and reading them all again—an unforgivable use of his time, given the circumstances. He could not forget his prom- ise to return. An idle promise, he knew, even as he spoke it. Nor had Henrietta been so naive—she comprehended the dangers . . . as well as anyone could who had not been in an action at sea. Hayden tied all the letters up in a red ribbon and returned them to a box. He then took quill and ink and wrote her a long letter containing all of his hopes and none of his fears. This he sealed and delivered into the hands of Perseverance Gilhooly with instructions that it be delivered by an officer of the ship into the hands of Miss Henrietta Carthew should he not survive the voyage. The young Irish boy looked ter- ribly alarmed by this, but Hayden felt a great sense of relief. This duty of the heart discharged, he made an effort to focus his mind on preparations for the cutting-out expedition.

The one boat that was not being repainted was quickly manned to carry him ashore, where he went in search of Dundas and Moore. Upon learning that both men were at the nearby battery, Hayden set out to find them. The beaches north of the Mortella tower were crowded with soldiers drilling and sailors bearing ashore all manner of stores. Supplying even a small army required great co-ordination and more men than Hayden had ever understood.

A line of sailors snaked slowly back and forth across the rise to what Hayden thought of as Wickham's battery. Each man carried a hundredweight of either powder or shot upon his shoulders, which was deposited in a cargo net at the trail-head. Using block and tackle, and the sheers, the net was raised up to the level of the battery and quickly emptied by artillery men.

Hayden took the more direct route that the guns had traveled, then clambered up the rocks with the aid of the ropes that had been established for this purpose. The smoke from the battery curled over the edge, carried on a gentle breeze, and stung his eyes. In a moment he was on the crest, enveloped in a caustic, black cloud. He tacked immediately to starboard, holding his breath, and as he came into the clear, found Moore, Dundas, and General Paoli all standing uphill from the battery, field glasses in hand, Moore pointing with one hand and speaking in Paoli's ear.

One of Dundas' aides spotted Hayden and informed the general, who glanced Hayden's way and then raised his glass to quiz the French positions again.

"Captain Hayden!" Moore greeted him. "You have finally come to witness the effect of your guns upon the French. You shall not be disappointed, I will wager."

Moore offered Hayden his glass after the Navy man had greeted Paoli. Even a cursory examination revealed substantial damage to the works of the Convention Redoubt. Not a soul could be seen moving among the earthen walls, and one gun lay on the ground, its carriage smashed. Even as he watched, a ball buried itself in the side of a trench, throwing up a dark blossom of Corsican dirt. Everywhere he looked were small pits, many joined together to form substantial craters.

He could not resist a quick glance to be sure the frigates had not moved, but only their masts could be seen from this vantage.

"Have any of the works been abandoned?" he asked as he returned the glass to Moore.

Moore looked a little troubled by the question. "No. The French have dug themselves in, but we are still managing to kill more than a few, and they must comprehend that we can keep this up indefinitely. It will sap their will to fight, I am certain."

One of the eighteen-pounders fired, the explosion tearing the air.

"The works will still need to be carried," Paoli offered into the silence. "The French cannot, with honour, quit them."

"The general is, no doubt, quite correct," Moore told Hayden. "But you and your men hauled the guns up here at great cost; we shall do our part in driving the French from their positions. Your part is finished, Captain."

"Not entirely," Hayden replied. "Lord Hood has honoured me with the task of cutting out the frigates. This would be best accomplished by night. If our effort can be co-ordinated with the Army's assault on the redoubt, I believe there is an excellent chance of success."

Dundas glanced his way. "I have not yet decided upon the day of the attack, let alone the hour, Captain."

Hayden tried not to show his annoyance at this remark. "I shall patiently await your decision, General Dundas—when you feel the success of an attack is most assured, and not before. I have only come to request that I will be given ample opportunity to arrange my assault on the frigates with your own upon the redoubt."

Dundas did not answer a moment, and then nodded, rather grudgingly, Hayden thought. At no time did he take his eyes from the French positions to acknowledge Hayden.

An awkward moment Hayden stood there, growing more angry and frustrated, when finally Paoli intervened.

"Colonel Moore has kindly offered to escort me down to my mule, Captain Hayden. Perhaps you might walk so far with me?"

"It would be an honour, sir." Hayden nodded to Dundas. "General."

The three men set off up to the crest of the hill, then down the winding path. Hayden could see a band of Corsicans below, perhaps halfway down the slope, two tethered mules browsing halfheartedly among the scrub.

The old general went very slowly along the path, often putting weight on the shoulder of one of his guards. The Corsicans treated Paoli with enormous respect—deference, in truth—which Hayden found touching.

"We did not, Captain Hayden, share the glass of wine that we had intended," Paoli said when they stopped for a moment to allow him to rest. (Moore, seeing the old man's state, had asked if they could take a moment's rest, claiming that he had earlier twisted an ankle.)

"We did not, General, but perhaps we may, yet. After the French have been expelled, then we may all raise a glass."

The old man lowered himself down onto a rock with a sigh. He seemed shrunken and fragile at that moment, his entire manner uncertain—uncharacteristically so.

"Yes," Paoli replied as he caught his breath, "we shall drink a toast to the Corsican and British island, but how long will your people stay, I wonder. Will the British leave and the Austrians come? Or the Spanish?" He shook his head. "Do forgive me. I am easily fatigued, now, and my mood can become very low at such times. I believe the French shall retreat from San Fiorenzo in a few days, and then Bastia and Calvi will fall. Who can see the future? For a time we shall be the subjects of His Britannic Majesty, and I believe Corsicans will experience the greatest freedom they have known since the Bourbons came. I will hope it lasts many years."

He rose then, and kissed both Moore and Hayden on each cheek. "My people owe you a debt. They say that Corsicans never remember a good deed but cannot forget a bad one, but Paoli will not forget what you have done. As long as I am alive, your names will be spoken with great honour here and in the mountains and in the seaside towns. We are a poor people and cannot raise statues, but we can say your names and tell our grandchildren how you raised the great guns to the hilltops when everyone believed it could not be done, and drove the French from our shores to give us our freedom, however long it might last."

With that, Paoli turned and continued his slow descent, stopping at the bottom of the hill to wave once before mounting his mule and riding off, soon lost in a stand of green.

Returning to the beach, Hayden found a good portion of his crew, including midshipmen, practising armed combat, some with wooden cutlasses, others with musket and bayonet, still others with pikes. Hawthorne had, some time before, requested Hayden order the carpenter to make up wooden weapons so that the men might practise their small-arms without risk of injury. He and his officers had drilled the men relentlessly, when weather allowed (quarantine in Gibraltar had seen a flurry of this activity), and Hayden was very gratified with the results. He had always felt that this was one aspect of naval warfare that did not receive the attention it deserved. Losing a man simply because he was uneducated in the use of his weapon was unacceptable to Hayden. In truth, he would feel responsible in such a case, so Hawthorne's dedication to drilling men under arms earned his complete approval.

Among the middies, he found Gould, wooden cutlass in hand. The reefers were still youthful enough that they seemed more like boys at play than men learning to preserve their lives and take the lives of others. Gould, he noticed, was not the least bit cavalier about this exercise and lunged and parried with a ferocity that Hayden found surprising.

Hawthorne noticed his captain and came striding over. He had doffed his scarlet jacket and was, rather jauntily, using a wooden sword as a walking stick. A slick of sweat made his face shine, and his colour was high from exertion. "I hope they are as proficient at killing Frenchmen as they are at murdering each other," the marine officer commented.

"They have shown marked improvement, Mr Hawthorne. My compliments to you."

Hawthorne lowered his voice. "In truth, they were as like to stab themselves, before, but I think they will acquit themselves well enough, now."

The two stood a moment, critically observing the thrust and parry.

"Our Mr Gould appears to be becoming quite a warrior," Hayden observed.

"Indeed. I believe it is born half out of desire to succeed in his profession and half out of desire to preserve his own young life."

"I applaud both," Hayden replied.

"As do I. I fear these blockheads who rush into battle without the least trepidation. Men born without fear often seem bereft of conscience, as well."

Hayden was a bit surprised to hear Hawthorne give voice to this. "I have thought the same. But what does their footfall sound like, I wonder?"

Hawthorne looked at him sideways, a foolish grin upon his face. "Well, I thought it a fruitful line of enquiry at the time."

Hayden laughed. "And so it was. Is there anything you require, here?"

"No, sir. We have come with water and victuals. I wondered when we would get back to fighting the French, Captain Hayden. I always believed hauling guns a waste of your particular talents."

"As did I! But I have just been up to observe the effect of our guns upon the French, and I can report that it is considerably more than satisfactory. The enterprise was very nearly worth the hernias and injured backs."

Hawthorne laughed with pleasure. "I am sure the men in the sick-berths will be much fortified when they hear it."

"Carry on, Mr Hawthorne."

"I will, sir."

In a few moments Hayden's coxswain had delivered him to the frigate *Foxhound*, and into the presence of Captain John Winter. Hayden could not help but take in the austere cabin with its few shabby furnishings. The ancient, little table was such a contrast to the grand affair he had so recently been given.

Winter rose from his chair as Hayden entered, a deluge of paper spread out before him. The man did not smile or look in the least pleased to be receiving Hayden.

"Is it no longer customary to send a note in advance of such a visit, Captain Hayden?" Winter enquired peevishly.

"As I was certain we had both received orders from Lord Hood, I believed that you would anticipate such a visit, Captain."

Winter wore a uniform that was at least a season, if not two, past need of retirement, impeccably clean but visibly mended at the shoulder, at both elbows, and upon the cuffs.

"I am to put a number of my men under your command, I am informed." The man's apparent anger was growing by the moment.

"If you please—"

"I am not pleased! Why a man who has not yet made his post should be given such a command in place of a more experienced officer, I know not." For a second, Winter appeared embarrassed by this outburst, but then a second wave of anger washed over him. "Why is it, Hayden, that you should be shown such favour? Are you a nephew of the admiral's?"

"I am no such thing, sir," Hayden said coolly. "I believe I have been given this command as a reward for my recent efforts—mounting guns upon the hills."

"Rewarded for service rather than parentage? Do such things occur?" The man took a few steps toward the gallery windows, clearly trying to master his emotions. "How many men is it you require?" he snapped at Hayden.

"Eighty men, armed with pistols and cutlasses, with a few axes and pikes as well . . . and the boats to transport them."

"Eighty! I am informed, Captain, that the French frigates do not have their full muster."

"That is correct, sir, or so I believe. We have been observing them and believe they each have sixty to eighty men."

"Well, then sixty Englishmen for each French ship will be more than adequate. I shall allow you sixty . . . and three cutters. And they shall be under command of my own lieutenant or I will not provide them at all."

Hayden was about to protest but realised the futility of such resistance. The man intended to co-operate with him to the least possible degree. This was very common in the service when officers were given orders of which they strongly disapproved. Hayden had likely been guilty of it himself—especially when serving under Captain Josiah Hart.

"Sixty men under your own lieutenant," Hayden repeated. "We have painted our boats black to make them less easily observed by night."

Winter appeared to be freshly offended. "I have never painted my boats black for any reason—not in twenty years of service. I do not intend to begin, now. They will remain white."

"There will almost certainly be moonlight," Hayden informed him.

"White." Winter fixed him with a look of such firmness that Hayden knew he would not alter his decision in the least way.

"I believe the attack will take place the evening next, though it is dependent upon the Army and they will not yet commit themselves to any hour."

"My men could be ready with very little notice."

"I will send word the moment I know more."

Winter merely stared at him; he did not acknowledge that Hayden had even spoken. Making a slight bow, Hayden retreated from the cabin, his considerable temper heating toward white-hot. He was in his boat and being carried across the glassy bay when he realised that he could very easily become Winter in a few years. A man clearly without a patron in the admiralty or among the flag officers. Whether he was competent, Hayden did not know—perhaps not—but surely he was unlucky. Even his post captain's wages should have seen him in better circumstances than he apparently lived in. And to think, he had been resentful of Hayden's connection with Lord Hood, whom he had only just met and was the first man outside of Philip Stephens who had ever shown the least interest in him (and certainly Stephens' patronage had proven more useful in theory than practise). Hayden's anger dissolved away; he almost laughed. Either he was without a patron and struggling to make his way in the service, or his patrons were attaching him to a captain like Faint Hart or having him haul guns up to hilltops for which "less fortunate" captains resented him. It was all rather ironical.

Climbing over the rail of the *Themis*, Hayden discovered Mr Chettle and his mates busily applying a second coat of black to the boats, which already appeared coal-dust dull. Upon stained tarpaulins, imperfect rows of sweeps had been arranged. Thick paint was splashed upon these by hasty ship's boys, who splattered paint upon each other in equal proportion.

"Hey, you lot!" Franks called when he spied Hayden coming over the rail—previously he had been watching with great amusement. "I find a spot of paint on our clean deck and you'll all be hanging from the topsail yard by your ankles until the blood rushes to yer heads and yer eyes pop out."

The boys made a show of applying the paint judiciously, each stroke slowed to a deliberate wobble.

"Mr Archer. It seems you have everything in hand."

Archer touched his hat and smiled. "I hope so, sir. You saw Mr Hawthorne drilling the crew? I gave him permission, Captain. I hope I did not overstep . . ." The lieutenant's sentence drifted and died away.

"I approve of your decision most heartily, Mr Archer," Hayden informed him kindly. Archer was still finding his way as first lieutenant and Hayden tried to support him in every way possible. "Don't forget about blackening the men's faces."

"Aye, sir," Archer said with some relief. "I'll have all the men looking like the ship's boys."

They both laughed. Spotting Mr Barthe on the quarterdeck, Hayden went aft. "Mr Barthe, might I call upon your superior knowledge of the service? Are you familiar with a post captain named Winter?"

"That rum bastard?" Barthe growled. "I had heard he was in command of the *Foxhound*. What have we to do with him?"

"He is supplying the rest of the men for the assault upon the frigates. I have just had a less-than-satisfactory meeting with him."

"There isn't a meaner officer in the service, Mr Hayden. Can't keep a purser because they claim his practises are very sharp and costs them money. Can you imagine? His practises are sharper than a purser's!"

"I was in his cabin and it is . . . shabby, I must tell you. The man was wearing a very ancient coat that had been mended, and in numerous places, too."

"That is him, sir. But it's not due to ill luck with investments, or straitened circumstances, or even economy as we would think of it. No, it is simply meanness. He possesses every farthing he has ever earned, sir. All cunningly invested. Men say he is as rich as a lord. I've heard tell that his wife and children live in penury, Captain Hayden. They even jest that he sends his children out to beg, but I wonder if it is a jest at all. After you have employed his men, he will be sending you a reckoning, I would warrant." Barthe laughed at his own wit.

"Thank you, Mr Barthe. It is always useful to know who we are dealing with. Your knowledge in these matters is invaluable."

"I am most happy to do it, sir." Barthe stepped a little closer, his manner changing. "And as to the moneys, sir. It was all returned, sir, and most ashamed I am for my part in that matter. I do hope you will not hold it against me, sir."

"No, Mr Barthe, but do be wary in the future. We shall need to keep a close eye on Mr Ransome, I fear."

Barthe nodded vigorously. "Aye, sir."

On the gun-deck, Hayden found the armorer, his mate, and several able seamen cleaning pistols and changing flints. Forward, in an area inspected to be clear of all powder, two men had been detailed to sharpening cutlasses on a wheel, one pumping the treadle to make it spin, the other grinding carefully at the cutting edge, a spray of sparks thrown out in a narrow fan.

As the man finished edging his weapon, Hayden caught his attention. "I shall send you my sword, Smithers. It might need to be touched here and there."

Smithers made a knuckle. "It's already sharp as a woman's tongue, Captain Hayden. Perse . . . that is, Mr Gilhooly took the liberty of bringing it to me, sir, and I lavished great care upon it, too, as you will see. It is sharp enough for Frenchmen, I'm quite certain." He smiled. "Mr Longyard has already seen to your pistols, sir."

"Thank you, Smithers."

"Not at all, sir."

Hayden suppressed a smile as he turned away. Harold Smithers— Harry—without ever meaning to, mimicked the airs of his betters, especially in address. He suffered much teasing over it, though very good-natured, for he was, for the most part, well liked and a more than passable seaman. He was every bit as likely to say, "Why, think nothing of it," when the proper response would be "Aye, sir." Hayden indulged it out of simple liking for the man and because everyone aboard was aware that Smithers did not mean the least disrespect.

All about the ship Hayden found his crew in a mood of excitement and expectation. Archer had not made all of the dispositions, yet, so it would be some little time until the uncertain looks would appear among the men—those who had been spared the duty would have neither the stories to tell afterward nor the jealous admiration of their mates. They might, however, live as a result.

A moon, just past full, illuminated plaster-flat clouds pressed hard up against the starry vault. A breeze, frail and irresolute, barely rippled the open bay. In a whisper, Hayden ordered the coxswain to hold his position, muffled oars dipping, silently, dipping.

They were farther off the mouth of the bay than Hayden would have liked, but the white cutters Captain Winter had supplied could be perceived, faint and ghostly, at some distance. Hayden had ordered Winter's lieutenant, a thirty-year-old officer by the name of Barker, to station his boats beyond Hayden's so that they would be partly screened from the shore by the *Themis'* cutters and barge.

Hayden took up his night glass and fixed it on the two ships anchored, bow and stern, in the narrow bay. The bow of the nearest, *Fortunée*, with her beak-head, sprit, and rigging, was just visible against the darker shore, moonlight shining dully off wooden surfaces. With some regularity, a sentry would pass before one of the deck lamps, and Hayden tried to estimate how often this occurred.

The frigate anchored deeper in the cut, the *Minerve*, was obscured by *Fortunée*. Hayden could have ordered the boats to move to the south to open up his view of the bay, but the high tower and batteries on the hill, there, commanded such a view that he feared the boats would be perceived. Hayden swept his glass slowly over these positions, looking for any signs of activity. All remained quiet.

To the right of the bay stood the Convention Redoubt—Moore's first objective—and it, too, was nearly silent. A careful examination of the hillside behind revealed nothing, much to Hayden's relief. Moore would be moving his troops down that slope very soon, if he had not already done so. Even with the redoubt severely battered, the colonel would not want to lose the element of surprise. He and

Hayden had debated this very thing for some time the previous day. Was it better that the frigates were attacked first, or the batteries? Would Hayden's assault on the ships warn the troops in the redoubt, and vice versa? And if so, which would be less to their disadvantage?

A simultaneous attack had been rejected out of hand. Such things were difficult to co-ordinate on land. There were too many unknowns to even begin to hope it could be managed by both land and sea. In the end, they had agreed that overrunning the batteries was essential to driving out the French, whereas taking the frigates would not affect that particular outcome in any appreciable way.

For that reason Hayden and his crews hung off the mouth of the bay, waiting for the first sounds of battle.

"Can you make out anything, Captain?" Hawthorne asked in a whisper.

Hayden shook his head no, then shook it again to discourage further conversation. He saw Hawthorne break into a grin and he did the same, both stifling the urge to laugh. Hayden did not need to ask why—the marine lieutenant looked as absurd, no doubt, as he did, with his face blackened by burned cork, eyes shining out like a drunk's in a mask.

Childers shifted his helm but a little to keep them head-to-wind, and the oarsmen dipped their long, black sweeps into the Mediterranean in a slow rhythm calculated to hold their position. Hayden could hear the men breathing, shifting as they pulled on the sweeps. He could almost sense the apprehension on the smell of their sweat. Waiting to go into battle was never good for morale. It gave the imagination too much time to magnify the strengths of the enemy, and to diminish one's own advantages.

A black cutter moved out of position and drew silently abreast. In the stern, an officer leaned over the rail toward Hayden.

"I just caught sight of Moore's company descending the hill, Captain." It was Wickham speaking. "They are almost at the bottom, sir."

Hayden waved a hand in acknowledgement. Who else but Wickham would be able to see that? Hopefully not the French, who were a damned sight nearer.

After their first, unfortunate, meeting, Winter had sent Barker to treat with Hayden. The man was too old by half to still be a lieutenant, and overly aware of it. In every little thing, he tried to have his way or appear to possess superior knowledge. Over a chart of San Fiorenzo Bay, in Hayden's cabin, the two had argued how best to proceed. Various means of assault were considered, the only point of immediate agreement being that Hayden, with his black boats, should attack the *Minerve*, which lay deeper into the bay. Without admitting it, Barker was clearly concerned that his own boats might be seen and wished Hayden to draw the attention of the French crews.

The plan finally agreed to was, upon hearing the first volley against the redoubt, Hayden would take his boats and slip down the southern shore of the bay, most distant from the redoubt and opposite where the ships anchored. This would allow him to come at the farthest frigate from astern, where the French would least expect an attack. Both officers hoped that the French would be prepared for assault from their starboard sides, and not from larboard, which lay nearest the shore.

It was a simple plan and relied only on Hayden's being able to approach unseen and draw the attention of the French crews, which would allow Barker and his men to approach the *Fortunée*'s bow, where cannon could least effectively be brought to bear. Once this plan had been formed, and Barker had imagined that it was his own, the two had parted almost amiably.

Hayden found himself straining for any sound that would indicate an attack. Moore planned to carry the works at the point of the bayonet, but certainly the French would begin to fire the moment they became aware of the British. Moore, too, was relying on surprise. Most of the guns in the redoubt had been rendered useless— but not all. Grape could still cut down many a British infantryman, and Hayden found himself hoping that Moore would not be among

these. The colonel would certainly be at the front of his company
and most likely to fall—which would be not only the loss of a man
Hayden had come to esteem as a friend, but, Hayden believed, a
great misfortune to the British nation.

He tried to exhale in an even, quiet manner lest his own breathing mask the first noises of conflict ashore. Around him, the small
sounds of the men, the low clearing of a throat, a hand scraping over
an unshaven cheek, seemed impossibly loud. Knowing how the least
sound travelled over water, they all cringed when the slightest noise
escaped.

A dull little explosion, muffled and distant, carried to them over
the rippled sea. A collective in-drawing of air was followed by every
man there holding his breath and remaining unnaturally still. The
sound had been so faint, so indistinct, Hayden began to wonder if he
had imagined it. Just as the men around him began to draw breath,
two more reports carried to them.

"Musket fire!" Hawthorne whispered urgently.

"Mr Wickham . . ." Hayden raised his voice loud enough to be
heard. "Follow us. In line astern."

"Aye, sir," Wickham answered, then whispered to the boat nearest, "In line astern." These three words were repeated, one boat to
the next, until all were informed and in motion.

The men bent to their sweeps, visibly relieved to be moving.

"Softly, now," Childers cautioned. "Softly."

The men eased their cadence and fell into an almost languid rhythm.
Hayden divided his attention between the nearby shore and the frigates on the bay's far side. If they were perceived at a distance, grapeshot
and French musketeers would cut them up horribly.

Aboard the two frigates, a stirring could be heard, men erupting
onto the decks. Hayden listened for the officers' commands, trying
to get some sense of what they might do, but the French kept their
voices so low Hayden could not make out the words. Men did not
appear to be going aloft, which likely meant that they would not try

to sail out in the event of the redoubt's falling to the British. Firing or scuttling the ships must be their intent.

The sound of furious musket fire came from the redoubt, now, and as the British boats entered the small bay, this sound carried to them more readily. Hayden could see the muzzle flash reflecting off the works. To his great relief, no great guns had yet been heard.

The sounds of battle began to increase, with much shouting and firing of muskets and pistols. Even the clash of steel could be heard at this distance, and believing this would cover any small noise made, Hayden ordered the oarsmen to increase their pace.

The bay was very snug, and they had soon travelled to its narrow end.

"Port your helm, Mr Childers," Hayden whispered. "Take us across her stern."

The boat swung to starboard. The moonlight was so bright it cast a broad, unbroken path upon the glassy bay, and Hayden worried that the boats would be seen against this. He found himself ducking down a little, as though to hide, and noticed others doing the same.

Hawthorne grinned at him. The marine was known for his desperate wit as they went into battle—a nervous response that Hayden had seen many times before—and must be finding it difficult to remain silent.

Hayden searched the deck of the French frigate, watching for anyone who might be looking their way. No one. Nor were there any signs of increased alarm aboard the *Fortunée*—though the crew seemed completely engaged in doing something . . . readying the ship for fire, Hayden suspected.

As they neared the stern of the *Minerve*, Hayden found himself holding his breath, waiting for a cry of discovery and a volley of musket fire. A moment he waited, hunching his shoulders and drawing his head down into his collar.

"*Les bateaux! Bateaux! Les Anglais!*"

Hayden all but leapt to his feet, tore a pistol from his belt, and pulled back the cock with two thumbs. With a slightly unsteady hand, he pointed it up at the taffrail, looming above. The call had come from somewhere forward.

A gun fired. A horrible splatter of grape into water and planking. And then a second.

"They have spotted the *Foxhound*," Hawthorne whispered, utterly surprised but also relieved. "Bloody fool captain," he muttered. "Could not spare a bit of paint."

At that moment, none of them had energy to spare in pitying the *Foxhound*. As Childers brought them around the frigate's stern, oars were taken silently aboard, not raised where they might be seen. Balanced with a foot on the rail-cap, men reached for the chains and pulled them forward. Three French boats lay against the hull, only a single boat-keeper present, and he was standing on the thwart, straining to see what went on aboard the *Fortunée*, his back to the approaching British.

Before Hayden could give an order, one of the hands crept forward, bare feet making no sound, and, encircling the man's throat with an arm, drove a blade down into the soft triangle aft of his collarbone. A moment of silent, gagging struggle and the man was gently lowered down into the dark boat.

Hayden went quicky forward between the oarsmen, Hawthorne and Gould behind. Over the bow into the French boat, then up the ladder until his head rose above the deck. Forward he could see a crowd, and then one of the forecastle guns fired. Drawing out his sword, he cut through several ropes of the boarding net.

Hayden turned back to Hawthorne and whispered, "Not a sound."

Up he went onto the deck, conscious that his boots were not nearly so quiet as unshod feet.

A staccato gunfire erupted, now, on both ships, as quickly as cannon could be loaded. Hayden did not like to imagine the effect. Before he had gone a step, he realised he had made a terrible mistake. Half a dozen men were gathered along the quarterdeck rail, leaning out to get a view of what went on forward.

Motioning to Hawthorne to take a group and deal with them, he counted out the first eight, placing a hand on each man's arm and whispering near to his ear: "With Mr Hawthorne."

Hayden had the men step clear of the ladder as they came aboard and crouch down so as to be less visible—given a little cover from the shadow of the bulwark. A moment they waited. Hawthorne and his men did not hesitate but went right at the men, dispatching them in the same manner as the boat-keeper. One Frenchman almost struggled free and managed a half-strangled cry, but no one forward heard over the firing of the guns.

Hayden stood and motioned to Hawthorne, who started down the starboard gangway as Hayden led his own party down the larboard. He hastened forward without raising a weapon or appearing in any way threatening. It was his hope that his blue coat would appear merely dark in the moonlight, and an officer hurrying forward would hardly seem unusual, even if he was followed by a crowd of seamen. But he needn't have worried. So intent was the French crew on driving off the English boats that no one thought to glance behind.

Hayden was twelve paces away before a French sailor looked around. The man watched Hayden approach a moment before realisation struck.

"They are upon us!" he cried in French. *"The English!"*

Hayden rushed forward, but Hawthorne was quicker, running the man through the body with his cutlass. Hayden's first thrust into the uneven wall of men struck bone, the blade deflecting like a bow, but the second, almost instantaneous upon the first, slid terribly into flesh.

And then he was in the centre of a melee, pistols discharging, blades thrusting and parrying. An enormous Frenchman was throwing iron balls with tremendous force, taking down a *Themis* with each one. Hayden pulled out his pistol and shot the man in the chest from

ten paces. The Frenchman, a near giant, lowered the ball he was about
to throw, put a hand to the stain growing on his breast, looked up at
Hayden, raised the ball, and, with a bubbling cry, charged. Hayden
felt himself step back, but then raised his sword, certain nothing
would stop the man.

At that instant, Gould stepped forward and shot the man again,
which did not slow him in the least. Hayden ducked the ball, which
whizzed past his head. A massive fist drove into his shoulder and
he was thrown down, hard, upon the planks, his blade clattering
away. The Frenchman was upon him, fist drawn back, when suddenly he stopped, a look of confusion upon his face. He fell upon one
hip, almost atop Hayden. A blade was thrust through his neck so that
the point appeared out the other side, and another had been run into
his heart. Hayden realised it was Wickham and Gould, who let go of
his cutlass, yanked out his second pistol, aimed it at the man's temple
from six inches distant, and fired. The Frenchman toppled heavily
down and lay utterly limp, his hair in flame. Gould and Wickham
dragged Hayden to his feet and some other pressed a blade into his
hand.

"Are you wounded, Captain?" Gould yelled, his colour high, hat
gone.

"No . . ." Was this true? His left shoulder was all but numb. "No.
I think not."

Wickham and Gould retrieved their blades from the dead Frenchman, and the three were immediately beset on all sides. Hayden
knew not if they lost or prevailed. It was a desperate fight, the deck
slick with blood. Men fell all around, and soon they fought half-
standing upon the bodies.

Out of the corner of his eye, Hayden perceived a substantial battle
going on behind him, and wondered where these Frenchmen had
come from. A man with a pike twice tried to run him through,
which Hayden barely avoided both times. He then tried to strike
Hayden on the skull, which Hayden again avoided, but the point cut

through his coat and right down his front, slicing into skin. This gave Hayden an opening, and with a quick step forward he put his blade into the man's chest.

Hayden stepped back and touched a hand to his belly, half expecting his innards to come spilling out. He was bleeding, certainly, but had not been opened.

"Too bloody near," he muttered.

A body careened into Hayden's shoulder, staggering him to his knees. Leaping up, he saw two men crash to the deck in a tangle, wrestling and grunting, but in the poor light which was English and which French he could not tell. The man beneath was half hidden, his face in shadow—but was it cork-stained? Hayden drew back his sword, but then hesitated.

"Which ship? Which ship?" he shouted at them. Neither man responded or even seemed to notice.

"*Quelle frégate,*" he cried.

"*Minerve . . .*" the man on top gasped, and Hayden ran a cutlass into his heart so that he slumped down onto his adversary. Hayden rolled the dying Frenchman off and found Childers underneath.

"Good Lord, Childers," Hayden said, dragging the coxswain up, "I almost murdered you."

"He . . . choked me . . ." Childers gasped, almost slumping down.

Hayden was near to dropping, himself, when, around him, Frenchmen began throwing down arms and calling for quarter. Quickly, they were herded together, some so badly wounded they could not stand without aid. Hayden bent to catch his breath, but then forced himself upright to assess the situation. Smoke rolled up from the *Fortunée*, and her guns were silent. There was no fighting aboard that ship, nor any sign of men from either nation.

The sounds of firing and battle had also ceased in the redoubt, but had been taken up by the batteries around the tower to the south of Fornali Bay.

"They're firing into the Convention Redoubt, sir." Wickham

stood a few feet away, right hand pressed to his left arm above the elbow.

"Are you injured, Mr Wickham?"

"Not at all, sir. Well, no more than a scratch. I shall hardly need to bother the doctor with it. Mr Ariss can patch me up when he has a moment."

"Where is Mr Gould?" Hayden called out, looking around, fearing he might find the midshipman lying, still, upon the deck.

"Here, sir," some of the crew replied, and Gould emerged from the group, apparently unhurt.

"See to Mr Wickham's arm, if you please, Mr Gould," Hayden instructed. "I have too few lieutenants as it is." Hayden looked about again. "Where is Mr Hawthorne?"

"He led some men below, sir," Wickham informed him, "chasing Frenchmen."

"Ah. Who is hale enough to go to Hawthorne's aid?"

Men, almost unable to stand from exhaustion, stepped forward, and Hayden sent them after Hawthorne, under command of a marine.

"And Mr Ransome, what has become of him?"

"We have him, sir," one of the men replied. "If you please, sir. Over here."

Hayden found Ransome slumped upon a gun carriage, propped up by Freddy Madison and a crewman. A sailor was tying a neckcloth about his thigh.

"Mr Ransome, you appear to be injured."

The young man nodded, looking a little sickly and faint. "Frenchman ran a blade through the meat of my leg, sir. Very little bleeding, though." He pressed his eyes closed and let out a low grunt of pain.

"I am very sorry to see it. Bear him down into the barge. All the most grievously wounded we will send back to the *Themis*. Don't you worry, sir," he said to Ransome, "the doctor will soon see you put to rights." Hayden turned around. "Mr Gould? When you have done with Mr Wickham, see to the wounded, if you please. We shall send them back to the doctor in the barge."

"Aye, sir."

"And you, Mr Madison, take possession of the magazines, if there is powder in them. There might yet be some Frenchmen lurking about."

A crewman emerged from the gun-deck. "Captain Hayden, sir," he called out. "Mr Hawthorne begs that you come at once, sir."

Hayden fell in behind the man and was quickly down the ladder onto the gun-deck. Men with lanterns stood as distant as they could from a barrel, with its ends knocked out, wedged in the centre of the deck. The smell of oil and fat stung his eyes.

"Put those lanterns out!" Hayden ordered. "Station men at the ladder heads. No one is to come below with a light. Do not fire a weapon under any circumstances."

Men ran to obey orders and the lamps were blown out, but before the shadows fell, Hayden had clearly seen a torn and soaked sail and bits of kindling in the barrel.

"There's powder on the deck, sir," one man offered.

"Captain Hayden?" It was the man whom Hawthorne had sent. "Mr Hawthorne is in the hold, sir."

"Lead on." Hayden had thought the barrel, prepared by the French to fire the ship, was why he had been called. "You men, put that barrel over the side. Douse all flame aboard ship until this powder has been cleared away. Wet it down, first."

Hayden descended into utter darkness, suddenly apprehensive that Frenchmen might lurk in the shadows. Down the ladder to the lower deck and then down again onto the forward platform, where there was a blessed bit of lamplight. Hayden found Hawthorne and some hands below, shifting a barrel by brute strength. Another hand was down in the bilge-water on hands and knees, feeling about.

"Mayhap they've opened a seam, Mr Hawthorne," the man said, his voice echoing around the hold.

"A seam!" one of the topmen sneered. "What kind of bloody foolishness is that?" This man, too, plunged down into the water.

"Are we taking on water, Mr Hawthorne?"

Hawthorne looked up as Hayden jumped down onto the barrels. "Aye, sir. It has risen half a foot in but a few minutes, I swear."

Hayden cursed.

One of the hands who was down in the bilge-water banged his fist on a barrel. "We have to move this one."

A large hammer was quickly found and the end of the barrel stove in, brine and chunks of beef sloughing out and bobbing in the bilge-water. Hayden slipped down into the water and helped the men roll the empty barrel out of the way.

The seaman went back to feeling along the hull, water up to his chin. "I can't be certain, Captain. Water's floodin' in. Look at it rise! The ceiling has been chopped away in places. Mayhap they've drilled holes, then rolled barrels back down here to stop us from finding them."

Water poured in so quickly that Hayden could clearly see it rising. Some hands appeared on the platform and stood looking on. "Mr Dryden? Is that you, sir?"

"It is, Captain."

"We shall fother this opening if we can locate it. Have you experience in this?"

"I have, sir." And without waiting for further orders, he set off up the ladder.

Hayden touched one of the men on the arm—with the blackened faces and poor light he did not know whom. "Find men to man the pumps. We are going to lose our prize if we cannot check this water flooding in."

"Aye, sir." The man scrambled up out of the water, and a moment later the hollow rattle of chain in the pump-well echoed around the hold.

Hayden turned to the men who were desperately splashing about in the rising water, hands groping along the submerged planks. "Have you found our leak?"

Even as he said this, Hayden realised that it was almost too deep to do anything about the ingress, even if he were to find its source.

"Keep them at this as long as you can," Hayden said to Hawthorne, then climbed up onto the barrels and leapt to the platform. A river of water trailed behind as he went thumping up the ladder. Upon the gun-deck he found the men at the pumps, frantically turning the cranks and gasping for breath. They did not plan to win one battle only to lose another—and their prize money—but he knew they could not keep this up for long.

Up, into the cool night, Hayden was faced with the terrible sight of the *Fortunée*, burning. Flames climbed the tarred rigging and set aflame the sails furled on the lower yards. From the waist, a column of flame and black smoke erupted up into the night, blotting away stars and flowing out over San Fiorenzo Bay.

"Save us," Hayden muttered. He turned to the nearest man. "Find Madison. I sent him below to take possession of the magazines. I must know this instant if the powder has been carried ashore." He turned back to the burning ship. Every man aboard understood what the consequences would be if the *Fortunée*'s magazines exploded. The men who were not engaged in any activity had moved as far aft as the deck would allow.

Dryden was lowering a sail over the larboard bow, men running ropes, attached to the sail's corners, under the sprit and up to others standing by the starboard barricade.

"Leave this matter to me, Dryden," Hayden informed the master's mate. "Take a lead into a boat and sound astern. We shall warp her astern as far from the *Fortunée* as possible. If we cannot stop the water, I shall attempt to settle her in the shallows."

Dryden made a quick knuckle. "Aye, sir. Depth of hold twelve feet, sir?"

"So I would think. She must settle in fewer than four fathoms—three would be better—if we hope to patch and float her again."

"Aye, Captain." Dryden began calling out names of oarsmen as he hurried aft to the boats.

Madison appeared at that moment.

"Ah, Mr Madison. What of the powder?"

"Gone, sir. But for a small quantity for the muskets and pistols and some cartridges for the great guns."

"Let us pray the same was done aboard the *Fortunée*," Hayden said, feeling a small sense of relief. The powder would have been needed by the batteries and, if it had been left aboard, could have endangered the surrounding French positions when it exploded.

Hayden heard the voice of Mr Wickham, calling instructions. "We shall have to have weights on the ropes to sink them—they will never take up quickly enough."

"Mr Wickham, did I not send you back to the *Themis* with the wounded?"

"No, sir. Excuse me, Captain. I meant, I did not realise that you had. I've only a scratch, sir." His arm was in a sling, but he raised it a little as though to prove it undamaged.

Hawthorne came hurrying onto the deck. "Captain! We've found the leak—or leaks, sir. These cursed Frenchmen drilled holes through the planks and then they must have bunged them up—there must be a hundred of them. They pulled the bungs when we boarded."

"Then we shall have to find them and bung them up again."

Hawthorne stood a moment, chagrined and hesitating.

"Mr Hawthorne?"

"Water's already very deep in the hold. . . ."

"I will see for myself. Mr Wickham? Leave off fothering. I do not think it will answer." Hayden thought a moment. "The men at the pumps must be relieved. Have them stand by the riding bits to cast off. It is my intention to haul her into shallow water, if it is at all possible."

"Aye, sir."

In the hold Hayden found the situation worse than he'd hoped. Men were diving down into the water, searching for holes, but to little avail. The looks on their faces when they broke the surface told all.

He turned to Hawthorne. "Bring these men up to the deck; we might be forced to abandon this ship, yet."

Hayden returned to the deck, where he found the French prisoners sitting in a group, surrounded by Hawthorne's marines, muskets levelled. A shot from the Fornali batteries screamed overhead at that moment and ploughed into the earthworks of the Convention Redoubt. Forward, the *Fortunée* was engulfed in flame; spars began falling to the deck, and the entire bay was illuminated.

Hayden hurried to the taffrail. "Mr Dryden?" he called into the darkness. For a moment he could not find the boat, but then it appeared, a dark apparition in the wash of moonlight.

"Sir," came Dryden's voice, "the stern anchor has been cast in very shallow water. I believe you can warp her directly astern and will find the bottom in sixty yards or fewer."

"We shall go astern immediately," Hayden called.

Hayden hastened to the gun-deck ladder and called down into the darkness. "Mr Wickham. Cast off the bower, but keep the cable taut. We shall warp astern immediately."

"Aye, sir. Messenger almost rigged. I require hands to man the capstan, if you please, Captain."

Hayden found all the healthy men he could and sent them down to the gun-deck.

"You, there!" Hayden called out to one man forward. "You cannot carry that lantern down onto the gun-deck lest you blast us all to hell. Mr Hawthorne, I ordered guards set at the ladder heads. No lanterns below."

"Aye, sir."

Hayden feared that in the confusion he might have ordered the ladder guards below. Everyone was working in near darkness on the gun-deck, for though the fire-barrel had been put over the side, oil and fat and powder had yet to be cleaned away. A light could still set the ship ablaze.

"Mr Madison. Send men aloft with buckets. We will wet the sails and rigging, and then the upper deck. If this breeze were to turn, we would have embers raining down upon the ship."

Hayden stood on the moonlit deck, hands on the cool rail-cap, staring at the darkened shore and then at the cable stretching off astern. He could actually feel heat from the burning ship upon his back.

For a long moment there was no sign of movement. He was about to call for a lead to sound astern, when he realised that the ship was making stern-way; so glassy was the water that the motion was almost undetectable.

Very slowly the frigate went aft, water swirling aside. Hayden could gauge their progress against the firelit shore. And then the frigate came to a gentle stop. Hayden called to the man at the ladder head. "Inform Mr Wickham that we are aground. Thank God."

"Aye, sir."

"Mr Madison. Once the deck has been thoroughly soaked, order all the men down to the lower deck but for a few sentries." If the *Fortunée* exploded, Hayden wanted his men below.

At that instant there was a dull thump aboard *Fortunée* and a section of her quarterdeck buckled upward a few feet, settling in a clatter of burning planks.

One magazine gone, Hayden thought, and not much powder in it. As he watched the ship burn, hardly able to take his eyes away, her main-topmast, yards and all, came tumbling down, tearing away burning rigging. The ship, a virtual inferno, began to drift out toward the larger bay, her anchor cables burned through. The conflagration that had been the frigate *Fortunée* spun slowly to larboard, the flames glittering upon the calm waters. Her mizzen fell aft, crashing into the taffrail. The main tumbled down to larboard. In a few moments she was carried out of the little bay and around the point, where she still illuminated the night.

Hayden turned back to the rail, gazing out over the small V of bay bathed in moonlight. The undulating line of dusky hills blocked out the low stars. Bright flashes of musket fire could be seen as the French retreated toward Fornali, pursued, no doubt, by vengeful Corsicans. Even as grapeshot hissed overhead, Hayden felt a calm come over him. The letter he had written, but not sent, to Henrietta could wait. He would write another, mentioning that they had taken a frigate but without recalling any of the brutal fighting or the men lost—on both sides. He drank in a breath of air, a fragrant zephyr slipping down from the hills, leavened by moisture as it passed over the bay.

A figure appeared beside him at the rail.

"There you are, Mr Gould. Have the hurt been sent off to the *Themis?*"

Hayden could see the boy nod in the moonlight; all his excitement had drained away and he looked about to weep.

"All but a few Frenchmen," he answered thickly, "who are not too badly off, sir. I shall send them along when the boat returns."

"And you? Unhurt, I hope?"

"Scratches and bruises, sir."

"You are one of the lucky ones. I have not thanked you for saving my life—you and Wickham."

Gould looked confused and then surprised. "I suppose we did . . ."

Neither spoke for a moment—a blessed moment.

"We lost a good number of men, Captain Hayden . . . and many of the men I sent back"—his mouth worked, but no words came—"I am not confident they will survive, sir."

"In a few short weeks, Mr Gould, you have seen much of the worst the Royal Navy can offer. If my introduction to the service had been similar, I am not sure how I would have felt."

"I am not at all confident that I am made for this profession, Captain," Gould blurted out. He turned a little away—to hide his face.

Hayden did not quite know what to say to this young man. "The brutality of it all, the killing . . ." But he was not sure what directions his speech would take. "Not everyone can make their peace with it. I am not certain I have, though I have been witness to my share."

"It is difficult . . . sir," the boy replied, struggling to master the emotion in his voice. "That a man I have never met is set on murdering me, and I am equally intent on murdering him, though he has wronged me in no way, nor I him." The boy paused to work some moisture into his mouth. "It seems . . . mad."

Hayden agreed. At times it did seem mad . . . that a stranger might end his life for reasons that sometimes appeared to lose their meaning.

"If you please, Captain . . ." A voice from behind.

Hayden turned to find one of the hands, two yards distant.

"It's one of the Frenchies, sir. His wound has opened and he's gone down in a swoon."

Before Hayden could speak, Gould replied, "I shall see to him." He turned to Hayden. "If you have no other duty for me, sir?"

Even by moonlight, Hayden could see the distress, poorly hidden, upon the boy's face. "By all means, see to the man."

Wickham appeared at the ladder head, looked around the deck quickly, and hurried aft.

"I believe she's settled, Captain Hayden. We're not taking on any more water."

"I believe you're right, Mr Wickham. Do you not feel the difference in her motion—that is to say, there is none."

Wickham fell uncommonly still—for a second he even closed his eyes.

"Well, the bay is very calm, sir."

"Yes, but the deck now slopes forward, as you shall certainly see by daylight. We have some wounded French sailors I should like Dr Griffiths to see. And we should run cables to the main-top. Row a kedge out to starboard and a cable ashore to larboard. I do not think it is likely she will begin to heel, but one can never predict the bottom, and I shall take no chances."

"Aye, sir. May I have Mr Dryden? He is already in a boat."

"Yes, certainly." The next question, Hayden dreaded. "Have we a butcher's bill, Mr Wickham?"

"Fifteen dead, sir," he replied softly. "And many more wounded—twenty-two by my count."

"More than I feared," Hayden replied in a whisper.

"We did not fare so badly as the *Foxhound*, sir. The French fired grape into their boats at very close range." He took a long breath. "I should not want to know how many were lost and maimed."

"Yes, what they were doing so close to *Fortunée* before we had reached *Minerve* I do not know."

Nineteen

Hayden was making a second attempt to tie his neckcloth presentably when there came a knock on his cabin door and Mr Hawthorne was announced.

"Mr Hawthorne. Is there some service you require?"

Hawthorne smiled conspiratorially. He seemed overly pleased with something. "None, Captain. I have only come to wish you luck."

"I was unaware that I should require luck, Mr Hawthorne."

Hawthorne's smile broadened. "You might know there has been some friendly wagering in the gunroom about your audience with Lord Hood. Some think the admiral will grant you your post, Captain."

"I hope I did not hear you say 'wagering,' Mr Hawthorne."

"I used the term only figuratively, sir."

Hayden gazed at the results of his efforts in the mirror. Less than perfect, but it would have to do. In truth, he was rather agitated at that moment, and trying not to rush ahead of himself, for the very reasons that Hawthorne had just explained.

"I fear it will be nothing so propitious, Mr Hawthorne," Hayden replied. "The French have retreated to Bastia, and I believe we shall sail for that same place. There will be more bloody guns to haul, I expect."

"If that is the case, and you are not granted your post, I shall figuratively lose five pounds."

"Well, I should not risk any of my own money on the outcome. I cannot imagine why anyone else would. Even if Lord Hood were to so honour me, I rather doubt the admiralty would confirm it, in my case." Hayden pulled on his best coat, wondering, at that instant, who had bet against him.

Hayden turned away from the small mirror toward his friend. "Presentable, I hope?"

"Perfectly so."

"Then I shall have to excuse myself, Mr Hawthorne. Lord Hood awaits."

Hawthorne opened the cabin door for him and, as Hayden passed through, said, "Luck to you, Captain Hayden."

A preoccupied secretary ushered Hayden into the admiral's day cabin, in which place he found Lord Hood and Captain Winter, the latter clearly rather surprised by his sudden appearance.

Hood looked up, his long face pasty and serious. "Ah, Captain Hayden. Captain Winter and I have just been trying to comprehend what transpired the night the *Minerve* was taken. Captain Winter lost his lieutenant and suffered many killed and wounded in a failed attempt to capture *Fortunée*."

"I am not in the least in doubt of what occurred," Winter said indignantly. He waved a hand sharply in Hayden's direction. "This man was supposed to attack the *Minerve* first, but hung back so that Lieutenant Barker was forced to proceed. Barker was perceived and the French fired numerous rounds of grape into his boats, killing more men than I care to recount."

Hood was not caught up in the indignation of Winter, Hayden

was relieved to see. The admiral turned to Hayden and asked, "Is this your understanding of what occurred, Captain?"

"In truth, sir, I do not know what happened aboard Lieutenant Barker's boats. It had been agreed that my crew would slip down the bay and come upon the *Minerve* from her larboard quarter, sir. We did this as quickly as prudence would allow, for it was our hope to manage this without being perceived, to which end we had painted our boats black and blackened our faces."

A frustrated sigh escaped Winter, which Hayden pretended not to hear.

"Just before we crossed the stern of *Minerve*, we heard musket and then gun fire from *Fortunée* and cries that the English were upon them. Directly we boarded the frigate and took her in a bloody fight, sir. Our own losses were not insubstantial, I can assure you."

"You did not hesitate or delay?" Lord Hood enquired civilly.

"Not for an instant, sir. Lieutenant Barker and I had agreed that he would stand off the mouth of the bay until he heard fighting aboard the *Minerve*." Hayden tried to recall exactly what had gone on that night, but it was all much of a jumble. "There was a great deal of musket fire and fighting quite nearby, in the redoubt. I can only surmise that Lieutenant Barker mistook this for firing aboard the *Minerve* and stood in to the bay too soon."

Lord Hood nodded. "Very well, Captain. Please, take a seat." He turned to Winter. "I am satisfied that Captain Hayden performed his duty in an exemplary fashion, Captain."

"Exemplary fashion!" Winter exploded. "I have near to fifty men dead because of this man shirking. This is not my understanding of 'exemplary.'"

Hood did not speak for a moment, but fixed his gaze upon Winter in a manner that could not be misunderstood. "I comprehend, Captain, that losing so many men is distressing, but I do caution you. Captain Hayden has an unblemished record for coolness under fire. I do not for a moment believe he shied away from a fight."

"Some have given him quite a different character," Winter said, though quietly and without show of emotion.

Hood, who had the reputation of a man with a hot temper, remained remarkably calm. "May I ask, Captain Winter, were your ship's boats painted black?"

Winter drew himself up a little, not hiding his resentment well. "No, sir, nor have they ever been."

"The moon had only just passed full."

"I am aware of it. If Captain Hayden had attacked first, the attention of the French would have been drawn away and Lieutenant Barker would not have been perceived. I am sure of it."

"It is regrettable that he mistook musket fire ashore for fighting aboard *Minerve*. But I must point out that Captain Hayden's boats travelled the length of Fornali Bay without being observed by the French. Indeed, they had crossed the French ship's stern without the French becoming aware of them. Under conditions of bright moonlight, painting the boats appears to have been rather enterprising."

Winter did not answer.

"Have you anything more to say, Captain?" Hood asked of Winter.

"No . . . I have not, sir."

"Then I will not keep you longer from your duties."

Winter rose, made a leg to the admiral, and then strode toward the door without acknowledging Hayden in any way, though Hayden had risen at the same instant.

Hood turned to Hayden. "If you will remain but a few moments, Captain. I have a matter I must discuss with you."

At a motion from the admiral, Hayden took his seat just as the door closed behind Winter. For a moment the admiral said nothing.

"You met Barker, of course," the admiral observed at last.

"Yes, sir."

"A thirty-year-old lieutenant . . . I fear I shall not be able to spare him in my report, though I mislike tarnishing a man's record after he has departed this life."

"I am sure he mistook fighting in the redoubt for gunfire aboard *Minerve*, sir," Hayden replied, not quite sure why he was defending Barker. "Very easily done under the circumstances."

"One mistake of many in the man's career, though this one cost half a hundred lives. Winter must be aware of it. He cannot be so obtuse."

Hayden had not thought that, but was not about to disagree with the admiral on this particular point.

"It seems the *Minerve* will float again. My compliments, Mr Hayden."

"Thank you, sir."

Hood looked up and met Hayden's eye. "You informed Captain Winter that you would paint your boats black?"

Hayden hesitated. "I did, sir."

"I assumed you had. You would not have wanted Winter's boats to be discovered while yours went undetected. Winter still does not understand that this was likely the reason Barker and so many of his crew were killed. That and Barker's incompetence." Hood thought a moment. "I understand Mr Ransome received a wound?"

"Yes, sir, but Dr Griffiths reports that it has shown no inclination to turn septic, so I believe he will recover."

Hood appeared somewhat pleased by this report. "Prize money is not fired out of cannon, is it, Hayden?"

"No, sir, it is not."

"Good that Ransome learns this now. Greed is no substitute for sound judgement."

Hood reached across his table and rustled through a pile of papers. Finding what he sought, he raised a page and shook it gently.

"There is one other matter before us."

Hayden actually held his breath.

"You have been recalled . . . to England."

Hayden was utterly surprised and unable to hide it. "To England . . . When, sir?"

"Immediately."

"I see . . ." But Hayden did not see at all. "Aboard what ship?"

"The *Themis*, Captain. The admiralty, it seems, has need of her."
Lord Hood almost smiled. "You look rather surprised."

"I was sent to deliver the *Themis* to you, Lord Hood. And now the
admiralty want her returned?"

"That is my understanding." Hood seemed amused by Hayden's
confusion. "You will carry the mail, of course, and proceed to England without delay. It is not a cruise, Captain."

"Yes, sir."

"Are you not pleased to be going home, Hayden?"

"I am, sir. Most pleased." Hayden was uncertain of his own reaction, for though he did feel great excitement, he also felt somewhat
distressed. "But I had hoped to see the French driven from Corsica."
Hayden realised that he had wanted to do this for the old general,
Paoli. To help this principled and honourable man fulfil his single
ambition—before it was too late.

"It is commendable of you. I am sorry to see you leave, as your
particular talents will be required. There are batteries to be erected
outside of Bastia, if I can ever convince Dundas to mount an attack."
Hood looked up at Hayden and tried to cover his frustration with a
smile, somewhat bitter. "Nelson will manage it, of course. If not for
officers like Moore, I should rate the Army more of a hindrance than
an aid. That a man like Moore is not a general and Dundas not his
writer tells you everything about the king's army. Our own service
might be less than perfect in our manner of choosing officers, but
we do not let idle boys purchase commissions because their families
have the means!"

Hayden knew many an officer in the Royal Navy who, despite exemplary service of long standing, had not advanced nearly so far or
so rapidly as less capable officers with better connexions. The Navy
was far from perfect in this particular matter.

The admiral stood and smiled. "I wish you the very best, Hayden."

"Thank you, sir."

"You will not forget to remember me to Mrs Hayden—I suppose that is no longer her name?"

"Adams, sir. And I shall not forget."

"I believe you have a very promising career ahead of you, Hayden." The admiral met his eye, a little wash of emotion crossing his face. "I know it is often said as mere matter of form, but I say, with all sincerity, that I believe your father would be very proud of you. I am quite certain of it."

"Thank you, sir." Hayden himself felt a flood of emotion that he struggled to control. "That means a great deal to me."

"Safe return," the admiral said, glancing down and shifting some papers on his desk.

"Thank you, sir. Good luck in your endeavours."

Hood gave a small nod, and Hayden was out and then upon the ladder. A moment later he was in his boat, Childers beaming at him foolishly.

"Shall I return you to your ship, Captain?" the coxswain asked.

"No. Set me ashore. I wish to take my leave of a friend."

"Aye, sir." Perceiving the seriousness of Hayden's manner, Childers stowed his foolish grin and ordered the boat away. All the distance to shore he looked somewhat confused and kept glancing Hayden's way as if trying to read his captain's face.

As Hayden had secretly feared, even if he had hoped otherwise, Hood had not granted him his post. Hayden's disappointment was very great, and he berated himself for getting his hopes up. He, of all people, should know better. But the admiral had treated him with such favour! Had even said what a great future Hayden would have. And yet he would not, despite his friendship with Hayden's father and obvious admiration for his mother, grant him his post, though it was entirely within his power to do so.

Hayden wondered, given the admiral's tirade against the purchasing of commissions in the Army, if he had suddenly felt some reticence over granting rank to the son of a long-dead friend. It seemed a terribly inconvenient time to be growing a conscience over this particular matter!

But Hood had offered something else, and though it was rather expected and somewhat maudlin, Hayden was certain of the admiral's sincerity. The idea that Hayden's father would be proud of him affected him more than he would have guessed. In truth, he was rather moved. And saddened, in the same instant. For the entire journey to shore, Hayden struggled to master his emotions lest he embarrass himself terribly.

Asking after Moore upon the beach, he was directed to the nearby tower, where he found the colonel upon the ramparts. The bay spread out before them, incomparably azure, the distant hills softened by faint haze. Billowing up above the worn hills, foam white clouds, expanding as they rose into the Mediterranean sky.

"Captain Hayden," Moore said, obviously pleased to see him. "We are off to Bastia, I understand."

"Perhaps you are, Colonel, but I am for England."

"England! Have you not just arrived in the Mediterranean?"

"Yes, but the decrees of the admiralty are beyond the comprehension of mere mortals."

Moore looked genuinely disappointed. "It was my hope that we would complete this task together."

"It was mine as well." Hayden shrugged. "But I understand Nelson is quite a hand at establishing batteries."

"No doubt. When not making interest among his superiors, he manages to be an excellent officer."

Both men were silent a moment, Hayden, at least, uncertain of what to say.

"Is General Paoli nearby?" Hayden asked.

"He has retired to Oletta, I believe."

"Ah. Will you take leave of him for me? And repeat my hopes for him and his people."

"It is a service I would perform with the greatest pleasure."

"Well, Moore," Hayden offered, "perhaps what we have accomplished here will never look large in the annals of war, but I am proud of it, nonetheless. It was a great honour to serve with you."

Moore nodded but did not meet Hayden's gaze. "The honour was mine." He paused. "I have not been granted prescience, Hayden, and cannot say we shall ever meet again, but I do wish it."

"Let us agree to introduce our wives, one day, and bore our children with tales of driving the French out of Corsica."

Moore tried to smile. "Yes, let us wish for that. Take my hand, Hayden. I wish you fair winds and a calm sea."

"Success in all your endeavours," Hayden responded.

The two shook hands and then Hayden retreated, down to the rocky bones of the island. For a few moments he toiled along the shore toward the beach where he had left Childers and their cutter. Briefly he stopped and turned round to look back at the tower, the hills of Corsica, in cloud and shards of light, rising up behind. The silhouette of John Moore upon the tower wall, a glass to his eye, gazing off toward the fortress of San Fiorenzo or up into the hills, trying to discern the road he would take to Bastia and beyond.

Twenty

Gould lingered by the taffrail, gazing at the ship's wake curling away into darkness. A scrap of moonlight found its way through shreds of milky cloud and diffused over the racing ship and the nearby seas.

Hayden came to the rail, a yard distant. "It appears, Mr Gould," he observed, "that you manifest more interest in where we have been than in where we are going."

Gould looked up, a little surprised by Hayden's sudden materialization. "I was merely contemplating all that has occurred since first I came aboard. A great deal, sir."

"And what do you make of it all?"

"I do not know if I can say, Captain." Gould fell silent a second and Hayden thought that was likely all the answer he would get, young men not being terribly adroit at explaining such things. "I spent much of my childhood puttering about Plymouth Sound, sir, and though it changed every day, it was always much the same, if you take my meaning. I set foot aboard the *Themis* and all at once there were gales and ships exploding, battles and pestilence, war upon land, and great port cities being taken and then falling again. I've been in fights for my very life, sir, and taken the lives of others." He paused a moment. "It is as though I spent all of my life in a curtained room, and then one day was thrust out into bright, blinding sunlight. All those years I spent dreaming of adventure, and now it is my life before that seems like a perfect idyll." A moment he considered. "Yet, how does one go back into the darkened room?"

"Some do, Mr Gould."

"I have no doubt of it, sir, but I am not sure I am one of them. I think all of my senses would feel as though they were being starved, Captain Hayden. It is not that I do not long to see England, sir, and my mother and father and brothers and sisters. I do, with all my heart. But now that I have seen this war close to, and comprehend that I am fully able to play my part in it . . . well, I should feel like a shirker, Captain, if I gave it all up, now. There is duty, after all, and I cannot ask all of you to fight this war for me while I sit peacefully at home in my little room."

"You comprehend, Mr Gould, that you might be called upon to kill again?"

Even in the faint light Hayden could see the boy's face change.

"I do, sir, and I don't believe I shall ever make my peace with it." He shrugged, almost embarrassed. "That is the nature of war, and I shall have to do my part, though I detest the killing of others with all of my heart and soul."

"As do I, Mr Gould. Even so, I try never to hesitate, for that moment of indecision might bring about the death of one of my crew mates, and I am more able to live with the death of a stranger, who wants me dead, than with the loss of one of my own people."

"I agree, sir, wholeheartedly."

"Then you mean to continue with the service?"

"I do, sir."

Hayden was very surprised, but gratified. "I am glad to hear it, Mr Gould."

For a moment they stood gazing at the ship's wake etched on the black ocean. Hayden had a brief feeling that perhaps he had done well by this young man.

"May I ask you a question, Captain Hayden?"

"Yes. Certainly."

"Do you think I might make a passable officer, one day?"

"Far more than passable, Mr Gould. I think you shall make an excellent officer, if you continue to apply yourself as you have these past months."

"That is my intention, Captain. I want to stand my lieutenant's examination upon the moment I am nineteen years."

"I am confident you will acquit yourself with honour, Mr Gould."

A throat was cleared behind, and Hayden turned to find Freddy Madison standing two yards distant.

"Begging your pardon, Captain, I have been sent to invite you to table, sir."

"Is it that hour, already?" But apparently it was. "Go along, Mr Gould," Hayden said. "I wish to have a word with the officer of the watch."

When Gould and Madison disappeared below, Hayden turned back to the rail, gazing out into the liquid night. There was no pressing need to speak with the officer of the watch; Hayden had only wanted a moment alone. England on the morrow—if the wind held. For all the weeks of their return, Hayden had been wondering at this sudden recall. With all that he had learned from Barthe, he thought it likely that he was being brought home to do nothing but linger upon the land, without a commission of any sort. He rather doubted that Stephens, his one ally in the admiralty building, had arranged his return. When first Cotton had saddled him with the *Themis*, Hayden had been so resentful—a job-captain yet again—but now the thought of having her taken away was more than distressing. He knew the ship, officers, and crew. All were more than he could hope for. He worried, too, about what would happen to the good men who had served so loyally through all that had occurred over the last few months. Would they suffer the same fate as he? Was it guilt by association?

This return to England was so fraught with hopes and fears. There had been times on this voyage when he could not bear to be parted from Henrietta for another minute, let alone several more weeks. He yearned for her. Dreamed of her, and thought of her constantly. How he hoped she might be in Plymouth visiting her aunt. If only.

The ship's bell rang, jarring Hayden from his thoughts. His shipmates awaited. Their last meal together before they were all cast to the wind.

Despite their return to late winter, and the coolness of the night, the gunroom was a place both light and warm. When all were seated, and an unusually large body it was, Mr Smosh raised a glass.

"To our successful voyage," he said.

Barthe, who had begun to lift his glass—water, only—returned it to the table with such rapidity that it slopped over. Others followed, though with a little more decorum, leaving only the clergyman with a raised glass.

"Oh, my," the clergyman muttered.

"Mr Smosh," Barthe admonished him, "it is the worst luck to toast a successful voyage before the ship is safely in port."

Hawthorne laughed. "See what a collection of superstitious heathens you have fallen in among, Mr Smosh?" The marine raised his glass. "I shall take a little wine with you, sir, for I believe we shall arrive just as safely whether we toast or not."

Uncertain quite what to do, but not wishing to offend the smiling marine, Smosh completed his toast with a sip of wine. He then retreated into an embarrassed silence.

Hayden could not allow this. "You see, Mr Smosh, like General Paoli, Mr Hawthorne is a man of the Enlightenment. Not only does he know everything worth knowing about the latest advances in scientific agriculture, he has shed superstition altogether."

"And religion, too, I dare say," Wickham interjected.

"Not in the least true," argued the sailing master. "Mr Hawthorne worships Venus."

Which statement was met with much laughter. A toast was drunk, first to the goddess, and then to all the fair Venuses any of them had ever known or even seen, which was regarded as a suitable replacement for "wives and sweethearts."

The first course was served, and there was a brief moment of relative quiet.

"Dr Griffiths," Hawthorne observed. "Are you well, sir? I have never seen you looking so melancholy, and as you are of a decidedly morose character, that is saying a great deal."

The doctor paused with a soup spoon hovering. "I was thinking that it is very likely that this will prove the last time we shall ever sail together, and though I mislike almost every man aboard more than words can express, I felt a strange sadness settle over me."

"It is the soup," someone offered.

But the laughter was brief and forced.

Hawthorne saved the silence. "I am quite sure you are not shut of us yet, Doctor. Captain Hayden shall be granted his post by the lords of the admiralty, the *Themis* shall be his, and off we shall all set on a cruise that will make us rich beyond the dreams of avarice." He smiled at the surgeon. "Is that the phrase, Doctor? 'Beyond the dreams of avarice'?"

"I believe it is, and I do hope you are correct."

"I still do not understand why Lord Hood did not grant you your post, Captain," Gould wondered innocently. For this he received a glare from Barthe.

"Is this another superstition?" Smosh asked, glancing from Barthe to Gould and then back. "One does not speculate about officers making their post?"

"In truth, officers do little else," Archer informed him.

When the small laughter this occasioned had died away, Hayden, in an odd mood, turned his attention to Mr Smosh. "And what of you, Mr Smosh? Will you continue in the service or have you seen enough of this life?"

"Indeed, Captain, I have no other wish but to continue. I am rather embarrassed to admit so romantical a notion, but I have felt a growing attachment to the sea." Smosh's smile made it difficult to know if he was being ironical. "I find seamen refreshingly candid, and if you add to that an opportunity to see the larger world . . ."

"And get yourself blown to hell in the bargain," Hawthorne interjected, and then hastily added, "or heaven, in your particular case."

The clergyman's smile disappeared. "I am in God's hands, Mr Hawthorne. I accept whatever fate He decrees." The smile returned. "Like so many of my fellows in the church, I have decided to take up the study of natural philosophy. It is my intention to learn the names of all the birds and shrubs, the purpose of every creature in the sea, and the species of every cloud. After I have made numerous important contributions, the opportunity for which shall be afforded by our travels, my name will, I am confident, be put forward for membership in the Royal Society. At which point you shall all have no choice but to treat me with the respect I am due."

"Mr Smosh," Griffiths declared, "you are held in the highest regard among the men of this ship. If not for Mr Ariss"—he nodded to the surgeon's mate—"Mr Gould, and yourself, the influenza would certainly have claimed more souls than it did. Many of us, I believe, were brought back from the precipice by your diligent ministrations."

There were nods and words of concurrence all around the table.

Spoons descended and were raised in a strangely syncopated dance. A full topsail breeze heeled the ship, strained the shrouds—a banshee muttering—and a quartering sea rolled the ship slowly forth and back.

The mood around the table that night was one Hayden had remarked many times before, as voyages drew to a close. All of the men present anticipated a return to England and loved ones with the

greatest possible joy, yet the feeling in the gunroom was underlaid
by sadness or perhaps regret. An end to the familiar. The beginning
of the uncertain—England and the ambiguous relations and commerce of the land faring.

Landsmen were often heard to say "out of my depth." Seamen,
Hayden had often thought, were like boats hauled up onto the land,
removed from their element. "On the hard," the seamen said of such
vessels. And that was the seafarer, too. And yet they longed for it . . .
until they were about to raise the shores of fair England, when a
cool, little breeze of distress touched them.

As bowls and dishes from the first course were cleared, Hayden
took the opportunity to raise his glass.

"I should like to make a toast, though highly unpalatable to present company: I give you the finest group of officers I hope ever to
serve with. Gentlemen." Hayden raised his glass to the men seated
around the table.

"It *is* a highly unpalatable toast," Hawthorne agreed, "for we cannot raise glasses to ourselves. So I must reply—to Captain Hayden,
post or no, he brought the convoy through after Pool was shut of
us, sank a frigate and a seventy-four, brought us out of Toulon when
we were certain to be made prisoners, hauled guns to the mountain-
tops, and cut out as sharp a French frigate as you are likely to find."

"To Captain Hayden."

This small ceremony had the effect of rendering Hayden unable
to speak for a moment, such was the upwelling of feeling.

A song was then sung, as melancholy as the mood.

The meal came to an eventual, though regretful, conclusion, and
as the officers streamed out, Hayden asked the sailing master to meet
him in the great cabin.

When Barthe arrived, but a moment later, Hayden rose from his
perch upon the gallery bench, and took two paces, gathering his
thoughts.

"Mr Barthe," Hayden began, turning toward the sailing master, seated by the table, his colour high, despite refraining from all spirits that evening, "may I ask you a question?"

This request appeared to surprise the sailing master, who drew back with a look of some confusion. "Certainly, sir."

"Are you in possession of some knowledge regarding Lord Hood's apparent decision not to grant me my post?"

Barthe shifted uncomfortably in his chair and placed a hand on the edge of the table. "You know the service, Captain: there are always rumours, most unsubstantiated if not outright fabrication . . ." His sentence trailed off.

"I am certainly not asking you to break a confidence," Hayden stated quickly. "If you feel you cannot, in good faith, speak . . ."

"It isn't so much that, Captain—certainly I could never reveal how I came by this knowledge . . ." Again the sailing master's voice trailed away, and he sat for a moment, staring down at his knees. A slight nod of the head, and he looked up. "I cannot tell you if this is true, sir, but I was informed that Lord Hood would never grant you your post because he was aware that the admiralty would not confirm it. He comprehended that this would occasion great embarrassment, from which he hoped to preserve you."

"Ah," Hayden breathed. "And why is it that the admiralty would not confirm my appointment, I wonder. Other than the First Secretary, I have laboured under the belief that no one within the confines of that building was aware of my existence."

"It would seem, sir," Barthe replied very quietly, "that it is not the case. I do not know who, sir, but there is someone who is very familiar with the name Hayden. The rumour I heard, Captain, was that more than one man had his hopes pinned upon your dear mother, in her youth, but these hopes were dashed when your mother became attached to your father."

Hayden stopped, utterly still. "Mr Barthe . . . if such an event did transpire, it would have occurred over a quarter of a century ago. Disappointed hopes, and any resentment they might have engendered, could not persist for so long, nor can I believe that anyone would seek their revenge upon the child of this union; we are not Corsicans."

Barthe shrugged. "It would seem impossibly petty, and perhaps it is not true, but I was told that some gentleman within the admiralty is determined to block your advancement. Lord Hood did all that he could for you, leaving you in command of the *Themis*. It is as though you are caught in the middle of a pushing match—one gentleman driving you down while another forces you up. The sum of all this is that you cannot move either way. One blocks you from gaining your post; one will not allow the *Themis* to be given to another. It is not the strangest story I have heard in my career."

For all of him, Hayden wanted to ask Barthe for a name, but knew that he could not. The sailing master had revealed more than he had wanted to as it was.

"Thank you, Mr Barthe."

"I am terribly sorry, Captain," the sailing master replied, "to be the bearer of this news. And as I have said, I cannot vouch for the truth of it."

"Do not apologise. If it proves true, certainly it would explain many things that have occurred."

"I can tell you this, sir: The captains of the fleet—those who could see beyond their own noses—thought you a most enterprising officer. Our escape from Toulon was much discussed, and raising guns to the hilltops, in defiance of the Army's predictions, met with great approval."

"It would certainly please me to learn that I was finally overcoming the character that has been attached to me since I served under Hart."

"Oh, I think you have an excellent character among the captains of Lord Hood's fleet, sir. Very good, indeed."

Unfortunately, Hayden could not forget Winter's unkind words aboard the *Victory*. Certainly that man was not singing his praises—

nor would be Pool. "Thank you, Mr Barthe. I do hope that proves true."

Barthe was about to rise, but stopped. "You are a very decisive officer, sir, if I may say so. It is a quality that could benefit us all, both ashore and afloat."

Hayden tried not to smile. "If you are referring to my reticence regarding certain affairs ashore, I can assure you that my mind is completely made up on that matter."

"I am very happy to hear it, sir. May I offer my congratulations?"

"Not quite yet, Mr Barthe, and I would prefer you not mention this to any other."

"Certainly not, sir."

"Good evening, then, Mr Barthe. We shall likely be in Plymouth on the morrow, and very happy Mrs Barthe and all of your daughters will be to see you home, I am sure."

"Not as happy as I shall be to see them, sir. Good night, Captain."

Hayden crossed to the gallery bench and sat down, gently, elbows on knees, fingertips of either hand touching. There it was. Someone within the admiralty was blocking his rise in the service . . . due to disappointed hopes! But could such a thing be true? Could there be any man embittered and vindictive enough to punish the child of a woman who had injured him? The answer was, Hayden well knew, certainly there was. And perhaps it was not Hayden's mother the man reserved his resentment for—but Hayden's dead father. Was he not told, repeatedly, that he reminded people of his father?

Hayden shook his head and laughed. It seemed utterly mad. Certainly, he would rather believe that someone blocked his way for private reasons than that he could not progress in the service because he was thought a blunderer. Many a man of limited ability told stories of lack of connexions or of enemies within the service who blocked his advancement. Did Hayden really want to join that pitiful company?

Best to say nothing, but keep his ears open. He never paid much attention to rumours within the service. Gossip had always seemed to him to be the preoccupation of lesser minds. A terrible snobbery. It was time to begin listening a little more carefully. After all, he would have the well-being of a family to guard in the future. A little wave of anxiety washed through him at this thought. What if Henrietta had suffered a change of heart?

He took out all of her letters and spent the next hour reading them through from first to most recent, and when he was done, he felt utterly convinced that her heart was more constant than sunrise. Every day her feelings would be renewed as bright as the day before. He hoped only that his would always shine as strongly.

It was as though he had never left. Plymouth, dripping under a sheen of English rain, a low ground-swell unsettling the harbour. The blue Mediterranean sky and warm, windless afternoons seemed impossibly remote—memories of a summer long past when he had been young and in the admiral's favour.

Hayden was anxious to get ashore, now that all his doubt had been swept away. To this end, he had sent a note to Lady Hertle at the earliest permissible hour. It was his secret hope that Henrietta visited her aunt and that he could see her that very day and ask the question to which he was determined to have an answer. That he had hesitated at all now seemed impossibly foolish, and he hoped that Henrietta had not been injured by his reluctance or experienced a change of heart.

Paperwork fanned across Hayden's beautiful table, the quantity being far too great for his small writing-desk. Both Mr Barthe's log and his own journal lay open as he composed his account to the admiralty and letter to the port admiral. There were moneys to be accounted for, stores to be tallied, requests to the Ordnance Board and the Victualling Board. The Hurt and Sick Board must be alerted to the injuries among Hayden's crew, and the Navy Board could not be ignored. The Hurt and Sick Board had requested a detailed account of the influenza, which fortunately Griffiths would write; Hayden only need add a few observations and a signature. Then, of course, there was the First Secretary of the Navy, Mr Stephens, to be sent a missive. Hayden still did not know why he had been so quickly recalled to England and hoped that Philip Stephens might be inclined to intercede on his behalf. Mr Barthe's news of the previous night seemed somewhat unlikely in the light of day, but Hayden could not discount it, either.

All his officers hoped for leave to visit loved ones and friends, and no one wanted to be left aboard to oversee the thousand details required to make the ship ready for sea again. Hayden counted himself among the latter. Hood might have left him in command of the *Themis*, but he was not so certain that his friends in the admiralty, whoever they might be, would keep him in that position. Add to his uncertainties want of a ship, and it appeared quite a list.

Thus it was later in the afternoon that Hayden found an excuse to venture ashore, ostensibly to deliver some papers personally. No reply had been forthcoming from Lady Hertle, which made him think that his note had gone astray or that Lady Hertle was not at home that day. Once his errand had been dispatched, Hayden resolved to make the short walk up to Lady Hertle's residence, all the while preserving hopes that the good widow was out visiting with her niece, Henrietta, and that upon their return they would be overcome with delight to discover he had returned, months in advance of his most optimistic predictions.

The door was answered by Lady Hertle's footman—the same old seaman Hayden remembered from his earliest visit. The man, who in the past had always appeared pleased to see him, maintained, this morning, a stony dignity.

"My note of this morning to Lady Hertle has gone unanswered," Hayden explained, "which led me to believe it had gone astray or that Lady Hertle was not at home. I have taken the great liberty of presenting myself at her door, in hopes that I might send up my card."

"I shall inform Lady Hertle of your request, sir, if you will wait." Instead of granting Hayden entrance, he then closed the door and left a surprised Hayden standing upon the step.

A few moments he waited thus, both embarrassed and confused by this unusual treatment, before the servant returned.

"Lady Hertle is indisposed," the man informed him, his face betraying not the least emotion.

"I am sorry to hear it," Hayden answered. "May I leave a note for her?"

"She has your note of this morning, Captain. I hardly think you need disturb her with another."

Hayden was so surprised by this he hardly knew what to say. Before he could form a reply, the servant spoke again.

"Good day, sir," he said, and shut the door.

For a moment Hayden stood there, injured and confused, and then terribly, terribly alarmed. Lady Hertle had ever been pleased to see him, and his great ally in his courtship of her niece. To be treated thus . . . it bespoke the most awful possibilities.

Hayden returned to his ship, unable to focus his mind or energies on the thousand tasks that required his attention. Finally, upon a very insistent enquiry by a concerned Mr Hawthorne, he admitted what had occurred.

"You must speak to Miss Henrietta, immediately," Hawthorne said, "and put to rest your fears."

"I cannot leave my ship—not for several days."

The two sat in the great cabin, Hayden so anxious and distressed he could hardly keep to his chair.

"If I am to believe you, Captain," Hawthorne observed, "it is not your ship. Archer is more than capable of doing all that is required, in any event."

"I have given Mr Archer leave to visit his family."

Hawthorne bounced up. "Let me have a word with our young lieutenant."

Ten minutes later the marine was back.

"All is arranged. Mr Archer has agreed to delay visiting his family. There is a late coach that shall see you in London Wednesday morning before first light. That affords you full two hours to prepare. In what manner might I assist?"

In short order, Hayden took leave of his remaining officers, all attempting to hide their own anxieties about the future, which occasioned a great sense of guilt within Hayden, who felt ashamed that he had been so preoccupied with his own matters he had forgotten his shipmates. Not a single officer aboard was the least certain of returning to the *Themis*, or any other ship for that matter.

Feeling like a truant, Hayden boarded the coach for London, taking a seat outside in less-than-promising weather. The physical discomfort of the journey was nothing to the mental anguish he experienced. Why would Lady Hertle, who had treated him as a nephew, snub him so cruelly? Certainly he had been irresolute in his courtship of her niece, but not unforgivably so, or so he had thought. In truth, he often believed that Lady Hertle comprehended the reasons for this better than others—approved it, even. And Henrietta had said on more than one occasion that she did not believe in precipitate courtships or impulsive offers of marriage. As this was the one sin that could be laid at his door in regards to Henrietta, he was utterly unable to explain Lady Hertle's treatment of him.

A gale forced him into oilskins, and chilled him through, until he shivered uncontrollably, more susceptible to the cold, somehow, since his near drowning in the winter Atlantic. By the time the coach reached the outskirts of London, Hayden, who had hardly slept the entire thirty-six hours, was utterly spent, both physically and emotionally, and his nerves in such a state that he could hardly think what to do.

Alighting from the coach, it was too early to present himself at the home of Robert and Elizabeth, who he hoped might shed some light on what had occurred with Lady Hertle but, more importantly, would know the whereabouts of Henrietta. As he hoped to press his suit at the first possible opportunity, he had resolved to speak with his prize agents that morning so that he might have a better idea of how his finances sat, before embarking on married life.

Sending his baggage on to the inn where he customarily resided when in the city, he broke his fast at the coaching inn, then walked the half-mile to his prize agent's, arriving before their hours of business. A bleak half hour was consumed wandering the nearby streets until the prize agent's office opened.

A young clerk went off to announce him to his employer, who Hayden was certain would be pleased to see him, given his recent good fortune. He was, immediately, ushered into the office of Mr Reginald Harris, who rose, a broad smile overspreading his thin face.

"May I offer my most heartfelt congratulations, Captain Hayden. I must declare you one of the most fortunate men in all of England."

Hayden felt at least some release of anxiety. "Thank you, sir. Have we received so much for the sale of the *Dragoon*?"

The look on the prize agent's face changed, becoming a bit amused and wary, as though he thought Hayden practised upon him. "I am referring to your marriage, of course."

It was Hayden's turn to be confused. "My marriage? I believe these congratulations are premature, Mr Harris, as I have only recently determined to ask for the hand of a certain lady."

Bemusement changed to confusion. "Do you jest, sir?"

"In no way."

The man seemed unwilling to accept Hayden's meaning. "You have not recently married in Gibraltar?"

"I have not. Whatever are you talking about?"

Harris slumped down in a chair, an air of utter misery overcoming him. "This is the worst possible news." He tried to speak a moment but could not find words. Finally he said very softly, "I have advanced moneys to a woman—to a woman and her mother—who claimed to be your wife, recently married. She produced a certificate to that effect, from Gibraltar, and a letter from yourself, requesting that I advance her funds against your prizes."

If the man had produced a pocket pistol and shot him, Hayden could not have been more staggered. "But . . . you do not advance funds against prize money. That is your policy—'strict and invariable,' as I have been informed on numerous occasions."

The man nodded agreement, a hand rising to his forehead. "We do not, but in this case, Madame Bourdage and her daughter were in such unmistakable distress . . . and we so certain of receiving a handsome sum for the *Dragoon*. . . ."

Hayden closed his eyes, the extent of his folly suddenly overtaking him. "And Madame and Héloïse Bourdage were so very beautiful and apparently guileless. . . ."

The man looked up. "You know them, then?"

"Yes, I aided them after they had been evacuated from Toulon. It was through my agency they were carried safely to England." Hayden so wanted to sit but did not. "And *thus* I have been repaid."

The agent almost brightened a little, a predatory look in his eye. "Well, Captain Hayden, if you aided them in coming to England, then you must bear some of the responsibility—"

"I bear none of it!" Hayden interrupted, his considerable temper unchecked by lack of rest. "I made no request that you advance funds to Madame Bourdage, nor for a moment did it ever occur to me that you would do such a thing, as it is against your express policy."

"Did you or did you not provide them with a letter of introduction?"

"Indeed I did, as I have done for many another. The letter said nothing of Héloïse Bourdage being my wife, but was only a general letter of introduction—the sort gentlemen write every day."

The man waved a hand, as though sweeping this statement away. "There it is, then, by your own admission."

"Whatever can you mean, sir? I played no part in this deception that has been perpetrated against your company. It is entirely your own error."

"I will consult our barrister, but I am quite certain that we shall not pay you this six hundred pounds twice."

"Six hundred pounds!" Hayden put a hand to a chair back. "I will consult my barrister, for I do not require you to advance me the moneys twice. Once will be more than adequate. It is entirely upon your head if you have given money to impostors. Certainly every officer whom you represent trusts that you will not give their prize money away to anyone coming through the door and laying claim to it. Admit it, sir, you were taken in by their beauty and their very accomplished acting."

"As were you, sir."

"Yes, much to my regret, but as I was no part of their scheme, and only an innocent victim, you cannot attach any of the blame to me."

"We shall see, Captain Hayden."

"Indeed we shall."

Hayden exited the prize agent's and hurried north toward the home of Robert and Elizabeth Hertle. His fears grew with each step, until he was almost running along the paving stones. Oh, how he regretted helping these women! And listening to Sir Gilbert Elliot, who had requested this favour. Now he would be embroiled in a suit in the courts—all because he had attempted to rescue two women who appeared to be in the greatest possible distress. If only he could discover them before they spent the whole of the six hundred pounds, then he could bring the law down upon them.

The distance to Robert's home was covered in record time, and Hayden found himself tugging on the bellpull at a very early hour. A moment later, Anne answered the door, and Hayden felt so relieved to see this servant, who had known him many years.

"Anne, I cannot tell you how relieved I am to see you. Please tell me that Captain or Mrs Hertle is within, or that Miss Henrietta is visiting."

Anne appeared more than surprised to see him; she almost swayed back a little on her feet. Immediately she recovered but offered no smile or greeting, which only added to Hayden's distress.

"Captain Hertle is upon his ship, sir," she informed him. "Mrs Hertle is at home, though it is very early, sir, if I may say so."

"Indeed, and I am sorry for it. Will you inform Mrs Hertle that I am here and request the honour of speaking with her immediately upon a matter of the utmost importance?"

"I shall, sir."

For the second time in three days, a door, which had always been opened to him, was shut in his face and he was left outside, rocking from one foot to the other.

Anne was absent for so long, he began to think that he was to be left there with no response or explanation, which he knew would cause more injury than he might bear. Finally, after more than a quarter of an hour, Anne appeared again—not Elizabeth, as he'd hoped—and thrust a note into his hand. She made no other explanation but retreated immediately, closing the door behind her.

With a growing sense of dread, Hayden broke the seal and unfolded the stiff paper and read.

How could you ever have been so pitiless and cruel? I do not wish to receive you, Captain Hayden, not today nor at any other time, nor do I wish any communication from you.

There was no signature, but Hayden knew Elizabeth's hand. He pressed three fingers gently to his brow and closed his eyes a moment. Clearly news of his alleged marriage to Héloïse Bourdage had reached all of the people it should not. He thought of pulling the bell again, but decided instead to retire to his inn, where he might collect his thoughts, and write a letter to Elizabeth that he dearly hoped she would read.

Poor Henrietta, he thought. Certainly she must not have wanted to believe that he had married on some impulse, but then, no doubt, reports of the striking beauty of Héloïse Bourdage would have reached her. . . . Many a man would have been swayed by such beauty, despite any other attachments or commitments. Had Henrietta, by some stroke of ill luck, set eyes upon Héloïse?

He was, in short order, at his inn, where he was met by the owner. "May I offer my congratulations, Captain Hayden," the man said.

Hayden was forced to lean against the wall, so exhausted was he. "How do you know of this?"

"Why, Mrs Hayden and her mother stayed here a fortnight. I have never met more gracious or lovely women, if I may say so."

"And they paid for none of it, I assume?"

The man looked somewhat taken aback by this. "Your own wife, sir? Of course not. They have received quite a lot of post, sir. Shall I fetch it?"

"Yes, why not."

Hayden was not the least surprised to find a sheaf of bills from creditors—milliners, clothiers. Madame Bourdage and her daughter had bought shoes and trunks and all manner of apparel. Clearly they dined in great style, dressed in the height of fashion, and spared no expense when it came to entertainment. And they were gone. Had been so for some time. Hayden expected that they had quit not only London but England as well.

All told, their bills amounted to something over three hundred pounds—almost three years of his income! A visit to Mr Archer's brother, the barrister, would be the next order of business.

Before he had the heart to inform his innkeeper that he had not, in fact, married while away, he was told that a gentleman enquired after him. Expecting yet another creditor with some claim on his limited funds, he descended the stairs and was let into a small sitting room where a man perched on a chair, a hat on his knee.

"Captain Charles Hayden?"

"I am," Hayden admitted, though at that moment he wished he could say otherwise.

"Henry Morton. My services have been engaged by the prize agent, Mr Reginald Harris. I am a thief-taker."

Hayden sat, and the man followed suit.

"I am to search for two women who apparently have perpetrated a fraud upon Mr Harris, stealing from him a substantial sum. May I ask, Captain, how you came to know these women?"

"I am not sure, Mr Morton, that I am inclined to answer your question, as my prize agent, this very morning, informed me that I would be liable for the moneys these women have taken from him— fraudulently taken from him—though it was done without my knowledge, my permission, and while I was absent from England."

The man leaned a little closer. "You do comprehend, Captain Hayden, that were your name to be attached to this crime in any way, it would go very seriously against you? The punishment for theft of such magnitude is hanging, sir."

"I cannot be implicated, Mr Morton, as I have just learned of it this morning. But it does not seem to matter to Mr Harris, who informed me that the full six hundred pounds would come out of my prize money, whether I was aware of the crime or not."

"The affairs of Mr Harris and yourself are no concern of mine, Captain. I have been engaged only to discover Madame Bourdage and her daughter. Perhaps, if I can find them and prove that they alone perpetrated this fraud, then you will be cleared and this will aid you in the matter of Mr Harris and the six hundred pounds. How did you first meet Madame Bourdage and her daughter?"

There seemed to be, in this interview, a certain inevitability, and Hayden was encouraged to learn that Harris was making a serious

attempt to recover the moneys, which would appear to indicate he
had little faith in winning a lawsuit against Hayden. Taking a deep
breath, Hayden let it out in an embarrassingly theatrical sigh, and
answered, "I had just come from speaking with Admiral Lord Hood
upon the *Victory*, and had made the acquaintance of Princess Marie,
who was fleeing the Jacobins."

"Who?"

"It is of no import. Madame Bourdage and her daughter were on
the upper deck among the refugees who had evacuated Toulon. They
overheard me speak French, promising to rescue Princess Marie."
His voice thickened. "Immediately, they knew me for what I was."

Twenty-one

Percival Archer, KC—the very brother of Lieutenant Archer, who had advised so many of the *Themis'* officers throughout the recent court-martial—listened to the final words of Hayden's account with all of the disinterest of a judge trying a man for murder. Not once during Hayden's narrative did this neutrality of countenance show the least sign of transforming. And now he regarded Hayden with a distressing, reproachful silence, which had the effect of making Hayden feel even more a fool.

"You do realize, Captain Hayden, that I am not a solicitor and my opinion might be less than authoritative?"

"I trust your judgement completely."

A quick gulp of air. "Your prize agent, Mr Reginald Harris, fell victim to a deception," Archer began, "and violated his own stated principles by advancing funds not yet received from the Prize Court. I do not believe a court of law will hold you in any way responsible for his folly. Immediately—this very morning—you should notify both your prize agent and the Prize Court that this gentleman no longer represents your interests and has no legal right to collect moneys on your behalf. This should be done in writing. Such a step is justified by Mr Harris' foolishly paying out money on your account, without your permission, to complete strangers. As to the debts of Madame . . . what was her name?"

"Bourdage."

"The debts of Madame Bourdage and her daughter . . . we do not yet know their full extent. It appears they are many and various and might not all come to light for some time. You must place notices in the *Times* and the *Chronicle* warning merchants and shopkeepers that Mademoiselle Bourdage is not your wife and stating that you will not honour any debts accrued by her or her mother. I will instruct you in the precise wording. I fear, however, that you shall be forced into court more times than you would like by diverse merchants and innkeepers who have been victimised by the charms of these women, which are, apparently, considerable."

"Certainly I was deceived."

"As was as formidable a gentleman as Sir Gilbert Elliot, if that draws a little of the sting from it." The barrister made a sour face. "I think you will win all of these various actions, but I fear your legal fees might be considerable if numerous merchants come forward with claims."

"I should rather give the money to you than pay the debts of those two women—though I do feel compassion for their victims, among whom I count myself."

"They have certainly placed you in a most difficult situation, but we will take on these creditors one at a time, and I dare say, we will rebuff most if not all of their claims. I will not lie and tell you this will be easy or pleasant, but I believe, in the end, we will prevail. Set your mind at ease on that score." He tried to smile. "May I ask you a question, Captain, on another matter entirely?" An upward gesture with a hand. "That is, if we have concluded this business."

"Yes, certainly."

"How progresses my younger brother's career? I ask this out of the most profound concern for his future and well-being."

Hayden was a bit surprised that his legal situation, which seemed utterly impossible and complex to him, had been so summarily dispatched. The barrister's assurances, though welcome, had done very little to relieve the dismay he felt, but he hoped the much-looked-for relief of this anxiety would arrive shortly. "I believe Mr Archer's career progresses apace. I have noted a marked increase in zeal in your brother since Captain Hart quit our ship. Indeed, he has proven something of a revelation, these last months. I have come to believe he will make an exemplary officer."

"I suspect you did not hold this opinion formerly. . . ."

"Situations alter, as do men. I am very pleased with his progress."

"I am happy to hear it. In truth, I am relieved. He has long been a worry to me. Perhaps Ben has told you that I am his legal guardian—or was?"

"I did not know."

"Since the death of his mother. We are but stepbrothers, Ben and I. Our father passed on some years ago and then his mother followed—far too young. As I am his elder by just shy of fifteen years, I became his guardian. He seemed inclined to do little, lest the reading of rather tawdry adventure novels is now counted a vocation, so I pressed him to choose a more pragmatic path. To my great astonishment, he chose the Navy. This was, to my way of thinking, a rather misguided decision, as it seemed to me nothing could be further from his nature than such regimentation, but he had some romantical idea of going to sea, and I eventually gave my consent. It has always been my belief that young men should be allowed to make their own mistakes"—a quick smile—"and then employ lawyers to extricate them. I found him a position with Captain Hart through the agency of friends. It was, I now realise, a grave error. My brother, who has always been rather . . . contained within himself, became even more so. I thought him deeply unhappy and expected him to give up this foolish idea at any moment. I still marvel that he did not. And now you tell me he might become an officer. I rather expected his fate was to be an author of tawdry adventure novels—a good-natured ne'er-do-well. After but a few years in my profession, you come to believe that human beings can no longer surprise you—but my own brother has done just that."

"He has not lost his taste for reading, I will tell you, but he was not alone in that pursuit aboard our ship. Our midshipmen formed a debating society and read all manner of books and pamphlets so that they might argue their merits and demerits. Your brother joined in with great enthusiasm. But I do not think that reading is harmful, unless one is inclined to believe everything cast into print."

For a moment the barrister's mask of neutrality seemed about to be pressed aside, as a little tide of emotion swept over him. Instead he produced a sheet of paper and a pen.

"Let us make certain of the wording of the notice that should be placed in the papers, and write the letters to your agent and to the Prize Court. Tell me again the names of these women?"

Before he could speak, Hayden's stomach growled loudly in response.

"Do excuse me," Hayden said.

Archer did not raise his head. "Bourdon?" he asked.

"Bourdage."

Twenty-two

Hayden could not remember feeling so ineffectual. Above all things, he must speak with Henrietta, and that was the one thing he was utterly unable to do. Where she was, he did not know, and there appeared to be no way of discovering her present location. It was like being becalmed on a glassy sea when one desperately needed to reach a nearby harbour. One spent every second watching the horizon, the sky, praying for any sign of a breeze, even a zephyr. A man in such a situation could be reduced to willing the wind to appear—and there was hardly any endeavour more futile.

If only Elizabeth Hertle would consent to see him . . . but she would not. He was not certain she remained in London: Was she with Henrietta? Hayden could not believe that Robert would not grant him a hearing—their lifelong friendship would entitle him to that—but Robert was at sea and beyond reach or recall.

It had occurred to Hayden that the agency of a mutual friend was required, but the two people with whom Hayden was acquainted well enough to ask such a favour could not be found. His frustration was all but unbearable.

As a result, he was reduced to writing letters of the rather pathetic pleading variety. Mrs Robert Hertle he did not think would read any letter originating with him, but Hayden was too aware that a letter sent to Robert might not find his ship for weeks, perhaps months—

far more time than he could possibly wait. Certainly he could write to Henrietta at her family home, but there was hardly any guarantee that she would be in residence there, or that she would open such a letter if she were. Her well-meaning family might even withhold it, for all Hayden knew.

If only Robert were in London! The worst of all this was that all misunderstandings could, he believed, be easily swept aside by a simple explanation. He had not married Mademoiselle Bourdage— he was merely the victim of a deception.

Perhaps Mrs Hertle or some friend might find his notice in the papers and inform Henrietta. The frustration of it was that the notice would not appear for a full three days.

Again, he took a seat at his small writing-table and dipped his quill in ink.

Dear Robert:

I trust, you, in the name or our long friendship, will do me the honour of hearing me out. I have been the victim of the most scandalous fraud. Two French émigrées—a Madame Bourdage and her daughter Héloïse Bourdage—have been claiming that I married this young woman in Gibraltar. They have even produced some falsified licence to verify their claim. Nothing could be further from the truth. The worst of this is, at the request of a man of some consequence, I claimed these women were relations of my mother's so that they might then travel to England. In other words, I perjured myself, after their escape from Toulon, so that they might find a place of safety. And for this they have rewarded me by running up tremendous debts in my name, convincing my prize agent to advance them moneys not yet paid out by the Prize Court (from Harris, if you can believe it!), and generally ruining my good name. I have engaged the services of a barrister to deal with all the creditors and Mr Harris, who is attempting to hold me responsible for his act of folly.

All of this, however, is of small matter. What pains me above all things is that Miss Henrietta somehow learned of these women and their claims and believes that I did marry this young émigrée. At least, so I imagine. I cannot discover the whereabouts of Miss Henrietta to have an explanation with her, nor will Mrs Hertle or Lady Hertle receive me or read my correspondence. Had I been guilty of this heartless act, I could not blame them, but my actions have been blameless, if a little naive.

Please, Robert, I beg you write to Mrs Hertle and Miss Henrietta at first opportunity and inform them of my situation. I can hardly bear to be treated like some callous rogue for much longer. I cannot explain it, but accused of some terrible act long enough, even an innocent man begins to feel guilt.

Your servant,

After a careful reading, Hayden deemed the letter acceptable, folded it, sealed it with wax, and addressed it, taking time to read the address twice lest he made some error that would send it astray.

For a moment he leaned his weight against the chair back and stared out the window. Clocks began to chime at that very moment. Three of a morning. Sleep, never a commodity easily procured, had become even more rare. He was, at once, unable to sleep, and almost overwhelmed by fatigue.

"Always torn in two," he whispered to the room.

He reached out and slid before him an undefiled sheet of paper. For a long moment he stared at its pristine surface, wondering what words he might place there to somehow, magically, make Henrietta open the letter. Would she open it out of curiosity? Out of regard for him? Or would she simply toss it in the fire?

"She will give me a chance," he said aloud. "In her heart she must know that I could not so betray her."

But barely a moment later he was not so certain.

A half-hour of pacing over the creaking floor was required, but then he took his seat again before the empty page.

My Dear Henrietta:

Before anything else is said, I must inform you, all rumours that I married while parted from you are utterly untrue. No such thing occurred. Two women, French émigrées, mother and daughter, have been making this false claim and using my name to amass a vast quantity of debt, and to acquire substantial sums from my prize agent. Neither Lady Hertle nor Mrs Hertle will speak with me or read any correspondence I write, so I have been at my wits' end to find some way to send you word of what has occurred. I am also very dismayed to think that the claims of these two women have caused you distress. The worst of all this is that, at the request of Sir Gilbert Elliot, I aided these two women in coming to England and they have repaid my kindness by using my name to defraud any number of merchants and my prize agent, and to cause you pain. Seldom has a good deed been so unjustly repaid.

I do hope you will read this and understand that I did not betray your trust in any measure and that my heart has not changed in the least these past months except that it is even more your own.

This letter was not so easily dispatched and was written twice more, though it actually varied little, before Hayden was prepared to commit it to the post. London had begun to shift restively by this time, waking slowly, the grinding wheels of tradesmen's carts and delivery drays echoing along the still-darkened streets.

Hayden lay down again in his narrow bed, and for a time hoped that either the notice in the papers or the letters he had written would bear fruit. A brief, troubled sleep crept over him and he tossed and rolled like a ship on the sea.

London had not long risen when Hayden sent his letter off to Mrs Hertle by a servant of his landlord's and entrusted his other letters to the post. All through the morning he waited, hoping that Elizabeth would relent and read his letter. That was all he asked—that someone would give him a fair hearing.

Twice, letters were delivered to the inn, and the post came as well, but no one brought word to him, nor did his enquiries produce the desired results. He paced. He ate little. Gazed hopefully out the window. Then paced again.

About two of the afternoon, when he sat trying to fix his mind upon a book, he heard a footfall upon the stair and then a knock at his door. Having decided that it was better not to live in expectation every moment, Hayden was quite surprised. Springing to the door, he found the landlord's daughter bearing a letter.

"The letter you have been awaiting," the girl said with a curtsy.

Very deliberately Hayden did not snatch it up, but retrieved it with an air of equanimity he did not feel. He thanked the girl, gently pushed his door to, and tore the letter open with his fingers.

It was from Philip Stephens, First Secretary of the Navy. Hayden's presence was requested at the admiralty—at his earliest convenience.

The dun brick structure that housed the admiralty was, by day, ever a scene of blue-coated bustle. The carriage gate and gates that allowed the entrance of men on foot were almost never passed without a polite moment of allowing others to exit or enter before. Beyond, in the courtyard, irregular circles of officers formed here and there, largely by rank, though not exclusively so. Sailors went to and fro bearing messages, and names were called out across the yard as sea officers greeted their fellows, some of whom had not been seen in months or years.

Hayden's name, however, was not called, and he crossed the court-yard apparently without anyone being aware that he existed. The First Secretary, he was informed, would see him at first opportunity, and Hayden found a convenient column to lean against while he awaited Mr Stephen's favour.

Many another's name was announced while Hayden loitered, be-coming more embarrassed by the moment . . . as though he were of so little consequence he had been forgotten. Just when he became convinced that indeed that was the case and he would have to submit his name once again, it was, miraculously, declared.

He was quickly upon the stair among the throng of officers coming and going. Here, someone did call his name, and though Hayden raised a hand in response, he was never certain who it had been. With his heart pounding from more than the exertion, Hayden was ushered into the room of Philip Stephens, First Secretary of the Admiralty.

Since their last meeting, a few days before the now infamous court-martial of the *Themis'* officers, Stephens appeared little changed. The same inflamed arteries afflicted a bulbous nose. The same spectacles sat, slightly askew, upon his narrow face. Immediately the First Sec-retary rose to greet him, emerging briefly from behind his desk, then retreating there again. Both lowered themselves into chairs, and Ste-phens, who had removed his spectacles, gazed at him a moment with the same emotionless stare that Hayden well remembered. Men would commonly size up a cut of beef with more feeling.

"Are you well, Captain Hayden?"

"Very well, sir. I hope you are the same."

The First Secretary made a noncommittal little shrug. "I under-stand you are embroiled in some legal troubles?"

How Stephens knew of this, Hayden could not say. Had the story been so quickly circulated?

"It appears I am, though a very reputable barrister assures me that I will not be held responsible for any of it."

"Well, it is nothing to the service, thankfully. I do hope it turns out well. Such matters are invariably unpleasant and rob us of much-needed sleep." Stephens produced a square of linen and began the familiar ritual of cleaning his spectacles. "I do hope your barrister can take the matter entirely in hand. I have arranged to send you back to sea"—the hands stopped working the linen—*"immediately."*

"But I cannot possibly leave England!" Hayden blurted out. "There are matters that require my entire attention."

"And why is that, pray?" Stephens asked, his mouth turning down but a little.

"It is this legal matter you have mentioned. Well, not precisely that, but it has unfortunately spilled over into my private life. There are matters I must attend to—matters of the greatest urgency."

Stephens sat back a little in his chair, steepled his fingers just as Hayden remembered, and regarded him coolly. "I will tell you in all honesty, Captain, there is but one route that will carry you to the destination you desire—making your post. That route involves proving to the lord commissioners that you are thrice worthy of this rank. You must prove yourself and then prove yourself again, and yet once more until the powers that be can have no choice but to grant you your post. My position will not allow me to explain further, but if you do not accept this commission, Captain Hayden, it may never be within my power to offer you anything like it again. I will own that I have secured you this position at no small . . . sacrifice to my-self." The steepled fingers flexed once. The gaze did not falter.

Hayden had so few supporters in the service, he could not afford to alienate the most powerful and steadfast, even if the First Secretary's efforts often seemed to produce mixed results. It was very clear that Stephens' continued support depended on Hayden's full co-operation.

In a voice both small and dry, Hayden replied, "Of course. I accept it most gratefully. Excuse my . . . my hesitation."

For a moment the First Secretary said nothing. "There is a French frigate inflicting substantial losses among the ships of our merchant fleet. For some time now we have been endeavouring to discover from where it sails, with little result. Most recently, however, it has come to light that it is almost certainly sailing from Le Havre. Are you familiar with this port?"

"I am," Hayden answered, his mouth going unaccountably dry.

"So I hoped. It will be upon you to take this frigate a prize or destroy it. The sooner this is managed, the better."

"What ship shall I be given?"

Stephens looked mildly surprised by this question. "The *Themis*, of course. It is to your great good fortune that no other will have her. I should never have been able to secure you such a vessel without your post."

Hayden's mind was racing. "I will need to gather my crew."

"They are all speeding toward Plymouth as we speak," the First Secretary informed him, "and your lieutenants have been busily watering and taking aboard stores. I believe you shall find your ship ready to sail, or very nearly so. I suggest you secure a place upon the mail coach this evening. I want you at sea—and beyond recall—as soon as can be arranged. Is that understood?"

"Completely."

"Luck to you, Captain."

"Thank you, sir. Apparently, I have need of it."

Twenty-three

L uck appeared in the form of Midshipman Lord Arthur Wickham. He was standing in the coaching inn courtyard, one foot set upon his sea-trunk as though he were afraid it might slink off into the gathering dusk. The young man almost gave a little jump of joy, so pleased was he by the appearance of his commanding officer and friend.

"Captain Hayden!" The boy broke into a grin. "Are we aboard the same coach?"

"If you are travelling to Plymouth, I would wager we are." Hayden, who had been dreading the thirty-six-hour journey, was equally happy to find the midshipman.

"Why, sir, it is a great stroke of good fortune. And the weather looks very promising, barely a rain cloud in sight."

"Very promising indeed. Are there any other of our shipmates aboard?"

"I don't believe so, sir."

"No matter, we shall certainly make do with each other's company. I am very pleased not to be travelling alone, I will tell you."

"As am I, sir. The novelty of it wore away some time ago."

The mail coach was soon drawn into the yard and the team exchanged by the ostlers, the tired horses led away by diminutive stable boys, who clicked and muttered to them in a private language known only to boy and horse.

"Wotcher, Bill, 'e's a biter, that one," one of the boys warned, just as the horse referred to took a halfhearted lunge at the boy's shoulder and received a smack across the nose with a leather rein for his offence.

Hayden and Wickham watched their trunks being loaded and then mounted to the outer seats, taking their places among diverse travelers, a woman and her grown daughter among them. Almost immediately the coach lurched off into the night, beginning its journey across the greater part of the breadth of England.

Wickham was very circumspect, and had been raised in the best possible circumstances, so would never enquire into Hayden's private life. He did, however, direct the conversation near enough to similar matters—twice bringing up "marriage" in a different context—to allow Hayden the opportunity to announce his news, if he so desired.

For his part, Hayden desperately wanted to speak of all that had happened with someone—even someone as young as Wickham—but the utter lack of privacy in their present circumstances simply would not allow it.

Not long after they had passed the outskirts of London City, however, their fellow travellers all settled into silent states, and if they did not sleep soundly, they at least dozed.

Hayden then chose to relate to the midshipman a truncated version of the story, being careful not to reveal the distress he felt about all that had happened. Wickham's response was to assure Hayden that all would be well, and in short order, too, which had some small effect on Hayden's mood.

The young gentleman was soon asleep himself, leaving Hayden alone with the English countryside and a moon that floated among clouds, casting its pale light down upon the land like a sorrowful, fading sun.

The second morning of their journey brought them to the towns of Dock and Plymouth, where a herd of bullocks blocked up the streets and drovers cursed at all and sundry. Ordering his trunk delivered to the *Themis*, an impatient Hayden, followed by Wickham, finally hopped down from the carriage, determined to continue on foot. Soon they were striding through side streets and alleys, making their way around the great, lowing pox of bullocks that spread along the high street.

In but a few moments, they were descending the steep hill where the quay hove into view with its fishermen and costermongers. Hayden soon found them a boat to bear them to the *Themis*, but Wickham was suddenly overwhelmed by a need to write to his father.

"I'm very sorry, sir," the boy apologised, "but it is on a matter of some importance. I will follow along directly, by your leave, sir."

Hayden did not hide his annoyance well. "Will you be very long?"

"Not at all, Captain Hayden. Nary a moment."

"Well, quickly, then."

Wickham rushed off and in less than a quarter of an hour returned, jumping down into the boat beside Hayden, full of apologies and "if you pleases." Immediately they set off into the bay, the waterman bending to his sweeps. With each plunge of the oars Hayden felt his ability to resolve matters slipping away in his wake. Life ashore was not suspended while he was at sea—this fact had somewhat surprised him when he was a young midshipman. Parents aged, siblings grew taller, the sick passed away, and young girls married. And all of these things happened without reference to him, as though no one were the least concerned what he might think or feel about any of it. When last he had been at sea, his life ashore—his other life—had been thrown into turmoil. He wondered what would happen, now. Would the Prize Court finally award him his money, or would the law courts hold him responsible for the veritable mountain of debt

those French women had built up? He might return to find himself
in possession of a handsome sum, or he could be ruined.

Would Henrietta learn the truth of what had happened, or would
she meet some other and forget him?

"There is our ship, sir," Wickham informed him.

Hayden looked up and saw the *Themis* lying to her anchor a short
distance off. The ship that no captain would have. "The mutineers'
ship," she was called. The only post ship in the Royal Navy lacking
a post captain. A kind of limbo where one could not ascend to para-
dise but neither could one fall further. Hayden's home, between na-
tions, between ranks, between money and poverty, love and loss. A
place he seemed destined never to escape.

"She looks very fine, does she not, Captain?" Wickham said.

"Dante would be pleased."

Wickham was not sure if he made some jest. "Pardon me, sir?"

But they came within hailing distance of the ship at that moment,
and Mr Barthe discovered them and hurried to the rail.

"There you are, Captain," he called from the quarterdeck. "We
are waiting upon the pleasure of the powder hoy, our victualling is
not complete. We've not enough shot to fight an oyster smack, and
the bosun has no cordage." The sailing master appeared to lose track
of his catalogue of complaints, then gazed unhappily off toward the
distant dockyards and slammed a pudgy fist on the rail. "Fucking
Navy!" he declared, causing both Hayden and Wickham to erupt
into laughter. Neither could tell why.

AFTERWORD

Many of the events depicted in this book occurred, and several of the characters existed. I have been as true to these people and events as the demands of writing a novel would allow. There often comes a point, however, in the writing of this type of book where one must decide if one is a novelist first or an historian. The answer, and not without some regret, is that I am a novelist.

Many readers will recognise Hayden's escape from Toulon as a real event involving the frigate *Juno*. I have depicted this as accurately as I was able, inventing only the dialogue among the characters (although the words of the boarding Frenchmen were recorded, after the fact, and I have not changed those). This escape, a magnificent example of seamanship and sheer nerve, lent itself perfectly to fiction and could be managed by changing only the name of the ship and exchanging the real officers for our fictional ones. History is seldom so co-operative.

The story of what occurred, only weeks later, on the island of Corsica was not so easily dealt with. The main events described in the book are true: raising the guns to the hilltops, taking the tower on Mortella Point, and the Convention Redoubt. Even the animosity between the two services—and Dundas and Hood, in particular—is accurate. The officer actually responsible for hauling the guns was a Captain Cooke (I have also found his name spelled Cook, and I believe his first name was George). I apologise to all his descendants for stealing away his role and giving it to Charles Hayden. Although Hood and Dundas could not bear each other, Lieutenant Major Kochler (whose name I have also found spelled Koehler) was, as far as I can discern, perfectly co-operative with the Navy, as was Sir John Moore. As Hood and Dundas seldom appeared, I needed some officer to exemplify the animosity between the services and Kochler was, regretfully, given this assignment. The sailors actually hauled two sets of guns to the hilltops—smaller guns to begin, and then, when it was realised these would not answer, the larger guns. I originally described both of these operations, then realised it was simply repetitive and cut out the section where the first guns were moved.

In describing the hauling of the eighteen-pounders, and throughout all of the Corsican section, I relied heavily on the diaries of Sir John Moore and Sir Gilbert Elliot. What neither of these wonderful journals described adequately was the ruggedness of the terrain. I was fortunate to visit the site of these actions on the island of Corsica, and can assure you bearing a small desk over that ground and up those hills would be more than most of us could manage. Imagine pulling the wheels off a North American minivan and dragging it up a steep slope littered with rocks the size of cars and you will gain some appreciation of what the sailors accomplished. I will post some photos of the area on my Web site (sthomasrussell.com), so readers who are interested may see for themselves. Bear in mind that the actual hills are much steeper than they appear in the photos.

Paoli, who I will admit is one of my heroes, I have tried to render as honestly as I could. He was, I believe, a tragic figure who devoted his life to seeing his people free, only to be driven into a final exile, his dream in ruins. There is a wonderful statue of him in a square in the old capital of Corte.

Some historical figures are readily rendered into fiction, but Sir John Moore was not one of them. The problem was that the man appeared to have been near to perfect. He was well-read, spoke several languages fluently, was tremendously brave, was a brilliant officer, was well liked and respected—the man was even noted for being handsome. In his diary he foresaw many of the problems the British were creating for themselves on Corsica, and he seems to have understood the people and the situation far better than Sir Gilbert Elliot, with whom he eventually clashed. Depicting this warrior-saint in a novel was extremely difficult, because the truth is, flawed heroes are more interesting. I did the best I could to render him human.

The cutting out of the *Fortunée* and the *Minerve* did not actually occur, and I apologise for taking such licence. The two frigates existed and were anchored in Fornali Bay, but they were scuttled, and only the *Minerve* was refloated by the British. I did not want to attach Hayden to Moore's company for the taking of the Convention Redoubt, as this battle was mercifully short and carried out by the Army (although there were sailors present—in support; I don't believe they took part in the fighting). I did want Hayden involved in some way and decided to alter the scuttling of the *Minerve* somewhat.

Corsica became almost a character in this book. We enjoyed our visit there. The island is very beautiful and varied, the people were gracious and welcoming, and the food was often fantastic. I hope to return someday.

"Romeo" Moat is based on a real character named Coates, who was so inconsiderate as to not quite coincide with the dates of the book, so I had to reinvent him—though only a little. Although descriptions of Coates' performances exist, no one ever recorded, as far as I know, his reworking of Shakespeare's plays, so I was forced to take this on myself.

Another section, the intent of which was almost entirely comic, was the golf match. I did take some licence here, for the sake of humour, and I hope the golf historians do not send me too many letters of protest.

As I have noted before, I am not a trained historian and, no doubt, there will be some errors in this book. I have done everything to depict the period—and life aboard ship, in particular—as accurately as possible. Here and there, events and characters have been altered slightly to make what I believe is a better book. And it is always to be remembered that historians often disagree. Who can be sure what is fact and what is true?

ACKNOWLEDGMENTS

I have so many people to thank for their assistance and support that I hesitate to begin lest I forget someone. John Harland answered all my queries with his usual grace, clarity, and speed; I cannot thank him enough. Liza Verity of the National Maritime Museum in Greenwich did the same, suggesting reading when I was stymied. Tito Benady kindly answered all my questions about historical Gibraltar, and Lyman Coleman, retired senior padre of the Canadian Armed Forces, was my resource for things doctrinal and suggested a number of books that helped enormously. As always, I have to thank my amazing agents, Howard Morhaim in New York and Caspian Denis in London, as well as the tireless Katie Menick; my editors, Alex Clarke and Rachel Kahan, for all their support; and Professor John McErlean, whose writings on the Corsican campaign led me to the diaries of Sir John Moore. I would like to express my appreciation to the librarians at the British Library and the National Maritime Museum. They put their encyclopaedic knowledge at the service of scholars every day and occasionally assist a floundering novelist. Caspian Denis lent me his name for a character who did not turn out at all as expected. Lieutenant Caspian Saint-Denis bears no resemblance to my British agent other than the similarity of name. Thanks go to all the staff at the Grind for supplying liquid inspiration every morning.

Owing to the production sequence, John McKay's wonderful illustration of the *Themis* appeared in *Under Enemy Colors*, but my thanks did not appear in the acknowledgments. My apologies to John. I have a large version of the illustration over my desk, and it gives me pleasure every day.

Finally, I must thank my wife, Karen, and my son, Brendan, for all their understanding and support throughout the process of writing this and several other books. Their encouragement and optimism are unwavering, as is my love for them.